TREASON'S RIVER

Also by Edwin Thomas

The Blighted Cliffs
The Chains of Albion

TREASON'S RIVER

Edwin Thomas

Thomas Dunne Books
St. Martin's Press ♠ New York

THOMAS DUNNE BOOKS.
An imprint of St. Martin's Press.

www.thomasdunnebooks.com
www.stmartins.com

ISBN-13: 978-0-312-32516-9
ISBN-10: 0-312-32516-9

First published in Great Britain by Bantam Press,
a division of Transworld Publishers

First U.S. Edition: January 2007

10 9 8 7 6 5 4 3 2 1

For Iona
Dux femina facti

The Fates never decreed that I should go anywhere, but someone should be the worse for it.

Aaron Burr

There is, on the other hand, no enterprise in which individuals can engage, more dangerous or more rash than a conspiracy, for it is both difficult and extremely dangerous in all its stages. Whence it comes about that, though many conspiracies have been attempted, very few have attained the desired end.

Machiavelli, *Discourses*

1

IF YOU HAVE JUST OFFENDED THE MOST POWERFUL MEN IN ENGLAND, you have two choices. You could, no doubt, buckle on the breast-plate of faith, raise the sword of truth and the shield of what-not, and stoutly face your foes. But if, like me, you took a more sensitive view, you'd see that all the regalia of righteousness would only weigh you down while you got on with the business of running away as far and as fast as possible. Which is why, on a warm day at the beginning of September, I found myself sitting in a tavern on the Falmouth quayside, with a glass of hock in one hand and a ticket for the New York packet in the other. I had cast off every encumbrance which might draw me home, and if the price of my safety was listening to pious Yankees drone on about liberty for a few months then I was happy to pay it.

Perhaps, had I been more sensible of my prospects, I would have paid for the voyage myself, and not accepted it on charity so will-ingly as I did. But I was fleeing in haste, and did not think to check the teeth of the mount that Mr Nevell – who worked for the Post Office – offered me. So much did I know.

I had been expecting him since I arrived there, and especially since that morning, when I had seen the packet leave her mooring in the harbour and warp her way out to the Carrick Roads. I could see her there now, straining on her anchor and ready to sail the moment the mails arrived. I drained the last remnant of my wine, and promptly poured a fresh glass. After three days sitting at the same table in that tavern, one wary eye on the door and another on the traffic outside the window, I welcomed any relief.

A motion by the door caught my eye, and my hand dropped to the pistol at my belt. A man stood in the threshold, blocking out the bustle of the taproom behind. Though not as tall as I, he had stooped to clear the lintel, and his face was temporarily hidden. He must have ridden hard to get there, for his wrinkled boots and breeches were plastered with dust and his brown hair was blown askew. Only the immaculate cloth of his claret-coloured coat remained untouched, though I do not know how he had preserved it.

His head came up, and I let go my pistol as a familiar pair of cool blue eyes met my own. His features were handsome, if slightly crooked, as though he were forever remembering some private amusement. It was a friendly face, though I knew it masked a hard and intricate mind, a precise mechanism which kept secrets as a clock keeps time. Springs would uncoil and gears revolve invisibly; only rarely, at the hours he chose, would the case crack open to reveal glimpses of its workings.

He slid onto the stool opposite me and stretched his arms, tipping back his head in a yawn. 'Jerrold. I thought I should find you here.'

'I've expected you these last three days.'

Nevell's gaze rested a moment on the empty bottle beside me. 'I trust you found sufficient entertainment.'

'Precious little, when every minute I was glancing over my shoulder in the fear that some ruffian from London might be taking aim for me.' Barely three weeks earlier I had turned up a man whom the government had hoped would disappear. For my pains, they had tried to kill me. Though the affair was concluded, I feared my role was not yet universally forgiven. Hence my haste to be away.

Nevell waved one of the servants to bring him a fresh glass. 'Soon, Jerrold, you will have your escape. As I mentioned in London before you left, I have a slight errand that will take you safely away from your enemies for a time.'

'Excellent. I trust you are not going to send me crawling down the cannon's mouth?'

'Quite the contrary,' said he, with what seems in retrospect a scandalous dishonesty. 'I have spoken with the Admiralty, and arranged that you will be seconded to the Post Office these next few months.'

'What did my uncle say to that?' My eminent uncle occupied a lofty seat on the Admiralty board, which he clung to despite the antagonism of the new ministry. It was he who had first dragged me into the navy, though I had since given him ample cause to regret it.

'Your uncle did not discourage it.'

The thought of my uncle brought a sour taste to my mouth, and I hurried to quench it with wine. 'If I am to be employed by the Post Office, what is the errand?'

'You are to deliver a letter.'

I sat back, unamused. 'It was an honest question.'

'And an honest answer. It is a small note, a trifle, but too sensitive for the regular mails. You are to deliver it to a gentleman in America.'

Squinting, I lifted my glass and watched Nevell's face distort and bend through its lens. 'That is all? Deliver a letter?' I was instantly suspicious.

Nevell gave a most charming smile. 'The simplest of errands.'

I had never yet known Nevell to offer a simple errand, but I could hardly give him the lie directly. I opened my hand and laid it on the table. 'I suppose you had best give me this letter.'

'I regret I cannot. It is not yet in my possession.' He pulled a watch from his pocket and snapped open the casing. 'Listen, Jerrold. In two minutes you will leave this house and turn left along the quay. You will turn left again, into a steep alley which leads up the hill. You will see a naval officer walking towards you – his name is Beauchamp. Hail him with the greatest familiarity; insist that you and he were shipmates aboard the *Bellona*.'

'But I've never sailed on the *Bellona*,' I objected.

'Lieutenant Beauchamp has. Engage him in conversation – tell any lie you like, but by all means keep him talking. And make sure that he does not look behind him.'

I realized that my mouth had slacked open, and took the opportunity to fill it with wine. Even when I had swallowed, all I could think to ask was, 'How do you know this?'

Nevell stood and beckoned me to follow. 'The fruits of a curious disposition. We must hurry, or we will miss our man.'

I had spent three days eager to be away from the tavern, but it was with the greatest reluctance that I left it now. Nevell's impermeable good humour, I found, generally effervesced in inverted proportion to the depths of his dark schemes.

Outside the tavern, the quay thrived with activity. Bare-headed porters manhandled great piles of crates and boxes, while sailors rolled huge casks over the paving stones to thunderous effect. Brigs and sloops and small craft of every description jostled to reach the wharf, their yard-arms almost touching, so that a topman could have walked the entire length of the harbour without ever setting foot on deck. Further out in the broad bay, larger vessels lay at anchor where the white sails of attendant gigs and hoys flocked about them. Puffs of cloud mirrored their movement in the sky above, and a snapping breeze pressed me with the smells of salt and fish.

I turned left, and immediately jumped back. Amid all the bustle and noise of the dock, I had not heard the approaching rumble of wheels: now I saw a heavy wagon, with eight shire horses in harness, toiling its way past. A thickset driver rode alongside, flicking at the beasts' backs with the tip of his long whip, while a quartet of militia men, muskets on their shoulders and eyes straight ahead, guarded the flanks and rear. Beneath a flap in the wagon's canvas covering I saw the snub-nosed muzzle of another weapon lurking. Any brigand who accosted this wagon hoping for easy pickings would I suspected, be lethally disappointed.

4

'Hurry,' hissed Nevell in my ear. 'Lieutenant Beauchamp will be here presently. Remember: the *Bellona*.'

I squeezed through the narrow gap between the wagon and the houses, trying to ignore the high wheels rolling past my ear and the hostile glances the guards shot at me. It was with some relief that I gained the opening of the alley which Nevell had described – though when I glanced around he had vanished.

I did not like this ridiculous scheme, and I liked it even less now that I was alone. For a moment I considered abandoning it outright, returning to the tavern and another bottle of hock. But there was something about Nevell, for all his bonhomie, which discouraged any thought of retreat. Besides, I could already see a figure in a blue coat hurrying down the stairs ahead. With the utmost reluctance, I climbed towards him.

I did not dare look at him until I heard him almost upon me. Then I raised my eyes, and even before I had had time to register his face I was babbling.

'Beauchamp? Beauchamp! Is it you? The *Bellona*. Surely you cannot have forgotten me?'

My prattle served its purpose. He halted, and stared at me with undisguised suspicion. If he was a lieutenant, he must have come to the navy late, or found few friends in the Admiralty, or proved an even worse officer than I: his face was creased into middle age, and a grey streak ran through his dark hair. There was no welcome in his eyes, and my gaze hastily shuffled down. A brown leather satchel was clenched in his fist, so tight that the knuckles bulged through his sallow skin.

'Who are you?' he demanded.

'Martin Jerrold,' I stammered. His direct hostility unnerved me, and I struggled to follow Nevell's instructions to keep him in conversation. 'The *Bellona*. You were on the *Bellona*. I was on the *Bellona*. Beauchamp,' I added, as though the name were a charm.

'I served on the *Bellona*.' The fingers around his satchel squeezed still tighter, so that the leather bulged between them. 'But I confess, sir, I do not recall that you were there. What name did you give?'

'Jerrold. Lieutenant Jerrold. Surely you remember. The *Bellona*.'

This was madness: I had nothing to say, nothing to support this lie save the two names, and if I repeated them again he would doubtless knock me down for a lunatic. How had Nevell expected me to hold him in conversation?

'Thrilling times we had, were they not?' I gabbled. 'Giving the Froggies a taste of our iron, showing old Boney he'd never get his way while old England was afloat.'

'I do not recollect I ever fired a shot in anger aboard the *Bellona*.'

Over Beauchamp's shoulder, in the steep alley beyond, I thought I glimpsed a movement. I remembered Nevell's injunction – *make sure that he does not look behind him* – and tried desperately to keep my eyes from drifting and betraying the approach. Yet I could not hold Beauchamp's gaze with my own, for fear my face would reveal the lie.

Though he did not understand the charade, Lieutenant Beauchamp had evidently tired of it. 'I do not know who you are, sir, or what you intend, but I cannot think we were ever acquainted. You are in error, I fear. Now, if you will let me pass, I shall bid you good day.'

'Enough of this poltroonery,' I cried with desperate humour. 'Of course you remember me. We—'

What lie I might have concocted next I do not know, for I was at my wits' end. But at that moment the claret-coated figure I had so studiously tried to ignore rose up behind Beauchamp, one arm raised above his head. I broke off my gibbering, and must have shown some sign of shock, for Beauchamp began to turn.

'What the devil . . . ?'

With a deft flick of his arm, the claret-coated figure brought down something hard and blunt on Beauchamp's neck. All colour drained from the officer's cheeks; his eyes widened, then sagged shut, and he dropped to his knees. Only a firm hand on his collar kept him from toppling forward on his face.

'You . . . You hit him,' I stammered. I've never had any manly qualms about charging my enemy from behind, or planting a knife in his back, but even so this seemed a brute piece of infamy.

'Of course,' said Nevell. He squatted beside Beauchamp's prostrate body, rifling through the fallen satchel with the practised manner of an expert. 'How else could we have come by this?'

He pulled out a dark package, wrapped in oilskin and bound with thick twine. Three seals pursed the fabric together.

'What's in there?'

Nevell pointed to the knots. 'How should I know? Somebody has evidently taken great precautions to ensure its privacy.'

'I thought you were in the business of reading other people's correspondence.'

'And so I am.' Nevell glanced up and down the alley. 'But not, I think, in public.'

I looked back down to the body at my feet. The eyes were still closed, but the gentle swell of his chest proved he still breathed. 'And the unfortunate Lieutenant Beauchamp? What will become of him? Surely you will not leave him here?'

'Of course not,' said Nevell, indignant. 'That would lay him vulnerable to all manner of injuries.'

'He might even be robbed.'

I had meant it as a joke, but no sooner had I spoken than I saw two men appear from a doorway a little way up the hill. Their broad shoulders barely fitted between the alley walls, and there was menace in their gait as they descended the stairs. Their eyes were shaded under the brims of their squat hats, and their rough-hewn cheeks were dark with grime and stubble.

Nevell showed no concern, but hailed them amiably. 'Lieutenant Beauchamp has suffered an unfortunate accident. You had best rescue him and keep him safe until he revives.'

'Best to bind 'im, sir?' asked one of the ruffians.

'A sound lock on the door will suffice. Keep him quiet until I return.'

The man touched the edge of his hat, then crouched down and lifted Beauchamp over his shoulder like a sack of peas. The officer moaned, but did not wake.

'What now?' I asked. I had an uncomfortable feeling that I could guess what Nevell purposed with the package, and whom he expected to deliver it in Beauchamp's absence. For now, though, he kept hold of it, and briskly started down the stairs to the quay.

'We must hurry. The mail coach will be here soon, and then the *Adventure* will be away. Time, tide and the mails wait for no man.'

As we emerged from the alley I saw that a small crowd had gathered on the quayside. Instinctively, I hung back, fearing that perhaps our violence on Beauchamp had been observed and reported. But they all had their backs to us, and were instead watching the wagon I had passed earlier, now unloading its cargo. The half-dozen soldiers who had escorted it stood vigilant, holding back the onlookers, while a sweating crew of stevedores hove away a great collection of strongboxes. They must have been well filled, for even the stout Cornishmen struggled to carry them down the stairs to the waiting boats.

'He'll be praying for a swift and peaceful voyage,' said Nevell, indicating a gentleman standing beside the wagon.

Whatever his business, he must have made a fine profit from it, for his entire body was swollen like a pigskin to an enormous girth, which the broad topcoat he wore did little to hide. One might almost have expected him to topple over from the sheer weight he carried were it not for the stout legs, thick as gammons, which supported his frame. His head seemed to tumesce from his shoulders rather than sit on them, twisting slowly back and forth as he watched the strong-boxes with a prowling, proprietorial air.

For all that, I did not afford him a second glance. Instead, my attention lingered on the creature at his side: a young woman, probably not yet twenty, her form fine and dainty. Though her companion loomed over her like an ogre, she stood close beside him, a gloved hand resting on his arm in perfect intimacy. Her head was turned away from me so I could not see her face, but the ripe swellings of her feather-white dress, the elegant profile, and the golden hair which escaped her bonnet and danced in the breeze, proffered a tantalizing beauty.

8

'If she's his wife, he must be a good deal richer than he seems,' I said.

'If she's his daughter, her mother must be a veritable angel,' Nevell answered.

'Or he's been cuckolded.'

Utterly under her spell, I had stopped still to gaze. Now Nevell tugged me on. 'You will presently have all the time you desire to admire her at close quarters. For now, every minute is precious.'

I dragged my eyes unwillingly away and followed him along the quay. I do not know where I had expected him to take me with the stolen package under his coat, but I had not thought it would be back to the bustling tavern where we had met.

'A glass of wine to toast me on my way?' I asked. 'A stirrup cup?'

But Nevell shunned the taproom and instead climbed a flight of stairs to a thin corridor, lit at either end by grimy windows. Without hesitation, he strode up to a door and rapped a quick double knock, which after a short interval he repeated twice more.

The door swung in, opening on to a bedroom. It was humbly furnished – a bed, a wardrobe, a night-stand and a table under the broad window opposite – and there was a strange, singed smell in the air. Before us, holding open the door, stood a nervous-looking man with a stooped back and round spectacles. He wore no coat or hat, only a brown apron over his shirt; given a boot and a hammer, he might have been taken for a cobbler. Though he had a naturally retiring manner, ever shying away, he did not seem the least surprised to see us.

'Mr Dawes, Lieutenant Jerrold,' said Nevell.

'How do you do?'

'Mr Dawes is from the Secret Office.'

It seemed one could not turn a corner or enter a room in Falmouth without finding Nevell's accomplices lurking there. Perhaps I should have wondered that so many of the Post Office's secret agents were engaged on this business, and wondered more urgently how I could excuse myself from it, but there was little time for contemplation. Already, Nevell and Dawes were standing by the window, examining the package closely.

'Sealed three times,' said Mr Dawes, twisting it so that the sunlight picked out the crusted wax. 'Three different waxes, three different seals, and more inside, I'll warrant.'

'Can you duplicate them?' Nevell's humour was gone now, driven out by cold imperative.

'Then there's the twine.' Dawes gave no sign of having heard Nevell. 'You couldn't cut those knots – have to pick them apart. And perhaps . . .' He fumbled in the pocket of his apron, extracting a bronze jeweller's glass which he clamped to the lens of his spectacles and pointed at the cords.

'What is it?' I asked, craning my neck to see.

'Look for yourself.'

I took the glass and pressed it to my eye. The world fell away, leaving only a writhing tangle of hairy ropes bulging before me.

'What am I looking for?'

'The heart of the knot, where the cords are pulled tightest. In between the strands.'

I peered closely, but could see nothing out of the ordinary. Frustration warmed within me as I felt Nevell's and Dawes' expectant gazes; I heard the clink of a chain, and the snap of Nevell opening his watch case. Still nothing.

'There appears to be a small piece of wool caught in the knot,' I said doubtfully.

Unseen hands snatched the parcel away, and I looked up in surprise.

'Exactly.' Dawes seemed unaccountably pleased with me. 'A strand of blue wool tied into the knot. Undo the rope and the wool falls out, and the recipient will know of it.'

'Ingenious,' said Nevell. His open watch was still in his hand. 'But as you have noticed it, you need only replace the wool when you retie the knot.'

'Assuredly. But men who would employ such devices may have other tricks to play. It will take time to unravel them – and longer still to repair them.'

'You have a quarter of an hour.'

'Quite impossible,' insisted Dawes, with implacable authority. 'Even mixing the waxes and engraving duplicate seals would take half a day. And that would be at best a clumsy substitute.'

I failed to understand Nevell's haste, and said so. 'You have both message and messenger in your care. Why not just cut it open?' Among the tools laid out on the table was a silver scalpel, and I reached to pick it up. Before I could touch it Nevell had seized my wrist and dragged it away.

'It is imperative that the letter arrive untouched, in appearance at least.' If he noticed my resentment at his brusque treatment, he ignored it. 'Otherwise they will know they are observed and they will change their plans to thwart us.'

'What plans?' I asked.

'I don't know.'

'Whose plans, then? Who are "they"? Lieutenant Beauchamp?'

'I do not know that either.'

'Then what . . . ?'

Nevell glanced out of the window, then took me by the arm. 'You may wonder that I am so abrupt, but every minute is essential.'

'Then be candid with me. Do not drag me around like some blind dog on a leash. What do you know?'

'Enough to make me anxious. You are aware, I presume, of the government's unpopularity: they court prejudice by busying themselves too much emancipating negroes and Catholics, and show little stomach for waging war with the French.'

I nodded. 'But I could read this in the newspapers, and a great deal more besides. I do not need secret letters to reveal it.'

Nevell continued undaunted. 'When governments prove feeble, others step in. Power abhors a vacuum, Jerrold, and even more than that it abhors losing money. While this government dallies, merchants lose trade and markets. Meanwhile, the government antagonizes our military by threatening reform, and prosecuting generals for factional gain. I do not need to tell you that an illegitimate alliance between war and commerce would command a formidable power to advance its interests.'

'How?'

'In all sorts of ways,' said Nevell inscrutably. 'Precisely how, I cannot say. But there are disquieting facts. An entire fleet and a thousand soldiers have vanished from the Cape of Good Hope, contrary to all orders from London. Two more frigates are reported absent from their station in the West Indies, again without sanction. Meanwhile vast sums of money depart these shores in disguise: drafts from banks which do not exist, payments for cargoes which were never sent. And in the coffee houses of the Strand and Threadneedle Street, all manner of unlikely intercourse is observed.'

'What do you imply? That a conspiracy is afoot? That thieves and mutineers lurk in dark corners, waiting to overthrow good King George and plunge England into desperate ruin?'

'Not necessarily,' said Nevell coolly. 'But some facts are unanswerable. Most pertinently: that the men we are watching have written a letter too sensitive to be trusted to the mails.'

'Perhaps they wish their business to remain private.'

'Indeed, but why go to such trouble? They know that the Post Office will read their post, but they know equally that we would never abuse the confidences of commerce. Unless it concerns the nation's enemies, our discretion is absolute. Legitimate military dispatches should be entrusted to the navy. So why bind this package up with snares, and send it by the hand of an anonymous officer, unless its contents are truly extraordinary?'

Whatever mechanism regulated Nevell's passions, it had clearly been wound to a great tension: his usually composed face was flushed and wild. I could not match his enthusiasm, but I could at least suggest an answer to his question. 'Why not ask Lieutenant Beauchamp?'

'I will, when he recovers his wits. But I fear he will know no more of his errand than a dispatch horse knows what its rider carries. These men I have spoken of, they will have recruited a willing dupe, sympathetic to their cause and content to remain ignorant.'

'They'll be upset to learn he's been robbed and locked away in Falmouth.'

Nevell leaned forward. 'They would be – if they learned of it. But—'

He broke off. From under the window I heard the clatter of hooves and coach-wheels, then the squawk of a post-horn blaring its punctuality.

Nevell swore. 'The New York mails. Our time is up. Where is your sea-chest?'

'Downstairs, in the parlour.'

Nevell thrust the package into my hands.

'What am I to do with this?' I feared I could guess the answer all too well, but still I prevaricated.

'You are to deliver it to a Mr Tyler, in Pennsylvania.'

It might have been Mesopotamia for all I knew. 'Who is he?'

Nevell shrugged. 'I have not the least idea.' He twisted the package in my hands, so that the underside was turned up. Printed on the oilskin in bold, black letters I read: *Mr Tyler, M'Culloch's Inn, Pittsburgh, Pennsylvania.*

'You want me to deliver this to some far-flung corner of America?'

'Of course – you work for the Post Office now.'

'And then what?'

'You must learn what you can of Mr Tyler and his scheme, then stop it.'

I felt familiar pangs of panic roiling in my stomach. 'But if you do not know what he intends, why—'

'Whatever Mr Tyler and his English correspondents purpose, it is evident that they are trying to stir up some mischief in America.'

'Which is surely better than stirring up mischief in England?'

'No.' Nevell was leaning in close to me, hissing in my ear. 'Britain depends on America like no other nation. We rely on her to supply the raw ingredients for our industry, and to buy back the goods we manufacture. Most of all, we rely on her merchant shipping to carry our trade, and to bring home the produce of our colonies. Without the income from that trade we would be unable to maintain our power, and the war would be lost. Our relations with America are already fraught with ill feeling; anything which might tip us into outright war would be ruinous to British interests and *must be stopped.*'

Nevell looked more agitated than I could ever recall having seen him. That alone should have been reason enough to refuse his errand, but he had turned away and was hurrying down the stairs.

'How am I to stop it?' I asked.

'Act as the situation demands. Gain Mr Tyler's confidence, learn the nature of his scheme and his English allies. You,' he added, beckoning a servant loitering in the passage, 'fetch Lieutenant Jerrold's trunk from the parlour and bring it outside.'

He pushed through the door onto the quay, which now seemed more alive than ever. The mail coach had drawn up directly outside the tavern, its horses sweating in their traces, while long leather portmanteaus were carried to the waiting boats. Each required two seamen to lift it.

I caught up with Nevell on the edge of the quay.

'This is madness,' I pleaded. 'They will find me out at once – I can hardly pretend to be Beauchamp.'

'Better to be yourself,' Nevell advised. 'If they ask for Beauchamp, tell them he was unavoidably detained.'

'But I know nothing of their business.'

'No less, I suspect, than did Lieutenant Beauchamp. Do not be afraid to reveal your ignorance.'

That would certainly be the easiest part of my task. I was about to remonstrate further when I heard a voice beside me. 'Take your boxes, shall I, sir?' One of the sailors had sidled up to me and was waiting expectantly. He nodded at the two sea-chests stacked next to him. 'Your boxes, sir? For the *Adventure?*'

I glanced at the chests in surprise. One was certainly mine, brought there by the porter from the tavern. The other, though almost identical, I did not recognize.

'You may take mine,' I said, feeling the fist of inevitability closing around me. 'The lower one,' I added, kicking it with my toe. 'The other is not mine.'

He touched a knuckle to his forehead and hoisted the chest onto his shoulder. Looking down over the quay, I could see a jollyboat waiting for me at the foot of the stairs, the sailors already on their oars.

Nevell was still beside me, and I attempted one last bid for mercy. 'This is bound to end in disaster,' I pleaded. 'I have not even the first idea what it is about.' I pushed the package towards him. 'You should take it.'

He shook his head, though he had the grace to don an air of regret. 'I am needed here – and England will be no safer for you, with the enemies you have made. You are not in good odour with the government, but carry out this mission and they will forgive you a great many things.'

He put his hand on my shoulder and fixed me with his grey, impenetrable eyes. 'I am relying on you absolutely. In America you will be beyond all reach of advice or assistance. Use your initiative, find out what scheme this Mr Tyler has concocted, and stop it dead.

'All depends on you.'

2

WE ROWED OUT TOWARDS THE *ADVENTURE*. SHE WAS A HANDSOME enough ship, I suppose, every part of her built for speed: the hungry bowsprit reaching forward over the water; the single line of her low deck, unbroken by any forecastle or poop; the high masts and the long, lean hull. Even the windows of the stern cabin raked aftwards, as though blown back by her momentum. Yet her pace was not without its costs. In a fight, the hull would prove little better than blotting paper, and her dainty spars would snap like twigs.

The jollyboat knocked against *Adventure*'s side and I stood up. I could almost look straight on to her deck, so low did she sit, and it took only a few steps to climb the ladder. It was strange to come aboard with so little ceremony, no bosun's call or mustered hands; the busy work on deck continued oblivious to my arrival.

At last, a stolid man in a blue coat crossed to greet me. By his dress, and the confidence of command he exuded, I guessed him to be the captain.

'Captain Trevelyan,' he said curtly. 'You are one of the passengers?'

I nodded.

'Well, which are you? Jerrold or Beauchamp?'

The sound of Beauchamp's name unnerved me a moment, and I was slow to respond. 'Jer . . . Jerrold.' Then, as an afterthought: 'I

16

saw Lieutenant Beauchamp before I departed, and he informed me he would not be making the voyage.'

The captain shrugged. 'In any event, he has missed his opportunity.'

Even as he spoke, I heard the anchor chain rattling through the hawseholes. The jaunty notes of the capstan fiddler died away, and the hands ran aft to the halyards. To my eye, she seemed woefully undermanned: she was twice the size of the cutter I had served on in Dover, and supported three masts in place of the cutter's one, but carried only half the crew. If it came to a fight they would be hard pressed to man both guns and sails – though looking at her armament, a meagre five six-pounders prettily arrayed along each side, they would have little hope anyway.

Perhaps aware of her precarious defence, and no doubt inspired by the Post Office's punctual zeal, her crew were at least prompt. The anchor was not yet on the cathead, and the baggage from the jollyboat had barely touched the deck, but already the ship hummed to the sounds of yards rumbling up the mast, of canvas snapping in the wind as the men sheeted it home. At the foot of the mainmast, the black portmanteaus were lined up like fat-bellied sows, bulging against one another. The bag which had accompanied me in the jollyboat had been opened, and I saw a sailor place what appeared to be two iron ingots inside before fastening it shut again.

'In case we're taken,' said the captain, following my puzzled gaze. 'Better to sink the mails than see them fall into French hands.'

I hoped the same practice did not apply to the passengers. But I had no time to enquire, for Captain Trevelyan was immediately summoned by the business of putting to sea, and our conversation ended. It was a queer feeling to be aboard a ship getting under way and yet have no part in it: despite all the hours in my life spent on deck wishing myself in my cot, there was something disquieting in the indolence now I had achieved it. Doubtless a few storms and midnight calls for all hands would cure me of that.

With nothing to keep me on deck, I resolved to examine my new quarters and meet my travelling companions – the golden-haired girl from the quay among them, I hoped. I was sure I had seen her being rowed out to the ship, but thus far there was no sign of her.

Wherever she might be, there was little hope of finding her in the murk below decks. Beyond the companionway, a thin door led aft to a narrow mess room, perhaps twenty feet long and half as wide, most of it occupied by a table and two benches. It was hard to see more, for the only light came from a feeble, grimy skylight, but there seemed to be half a dozen doors leading off the central saloon. The cabins, I presumed, wondering which was to be mine.

Even with feet thudding above, and the hull straining all about, the squawk of hinges was loud in those confines. I jerked up, and promptly bent over in pain as I crowned myself on the damnably low ceiling. Straightening, I saw that a gloomy figure dressed in black had stepped from an adjacent door in the bulwark, one I had not seen from the other side. His skin must have been pale indeed, for it seemed to trap whatever light was in the room and reflect it back. I could not see his eyes, which were sunk like two craters, but there was a stoop in his back which betold long ages below deck.

'Welcome aboard, sir.' His voice was faint; unaccountably, it filled my head with thoughts of scuttling spiders.

'Who are you?' I demanded.

'Fothergill, sir. Servant to the mess room.'

He did not strike me as a servant, for all that he seemed to be perpetually shying away. If anything, he seemed more like a clergyman fallen below his station, but I did not enquire.

'You are Lieutenant Beauchamp, sir?'

'Jerrold,' I said, more shortly than was polite.

'We were expecting Lieutenant Beauchamp.'

'Lieutenant Beauchamp was detained ashore.'

He tipped his head back a little, as if watching me through narrowed eyes, though of course I could not see them. 'Indeed, sir?'

Barely an hour earlier I had helped Nevell bludgeon and rob the unsuspecting lieutenant; my conscience was not yet steeled to discuss his whereabouts, least of all with this funereal steward. At least, I suppose, the darkness masked the guilt on my face.

'I should be grateful if you would show me to my berth.'

Fothergill bowed, and shuffled forward to the second door on my left. 'Middle starboard cabin, sir.'

I followed him and peered in. All the walls were painted white, but the effect was more sepulchral than comforting, for the gloom within was even more pronounced than in the mess room. There was no window or scuttle, but perhaps that was as well, for I could hear the sea sluicing and gurgling against the hull a few inches away. On an even keel the deck would barely protrude above the water; heeling over in a larboard wind, with the seas up, we would be quite submerged.

As my eyes comprehended the darkness, I took in the hutch that was to be my living for the next six weeks or more. Instantly, the prospects for the voyage diminished. A single bed spanned the compartment's entire width, though even that was too short for me to lie straight – as many restless nights subsequently attested. Otherwise, there was barely space to stand, and that small area was cluttered with a washstand and my chest, which one of the crew must have brought down. Even the prisoners on a Medway hulk hardly endured such wretched confinement.

'Shall I leave you to make yourself comfortable, sir?' enquired Fothergill, hovering like a moth at my elbow.

'Thank you.'

I sank onto the bed, leaving the door open so that I would not be in complete darkness. After three days sitting in the tavern, more had happened in the past three hours than I could rightly take in. Beyond the wooden walls of my solitude, the *Adventure* would be gathering speed, her canvas gilded by the late-afternoon light; she would slip between the twin fortresses of St Mawes and Pendennis and come about, tacking hard as she escaped the lee of the land and felt the brunt of the west wind. And I would accompany her, loaded in her hold like so much cargo, because of Nevell's infernal package.

I patted my coat, and felt the bulk still there where I had concealed it. That was reassuring – though also disquieting. I would have to find some place to secrete it, for it was too big to keep about my person through the whole voyage. Unhopefully, I looked about my cabin. There was the mattress, but having seen all the devices which sealed the package, I feared to lie on it lest I crack the wax or injure the contents. My trunk was hardly inconspicuous, and the matchwood partition-walls were barely thicker than my finger. I did not care to start prying open the hull. I slid off the bed and knelt down, working at the decking to see if any planks could be prised loose.

'Hah.' I had not seen it before, but now, kneeling beside it, I noticed a small drawer set into the panel of the bedstead. Shuffling back, I tugged it forward until it came free of the bed. As I had hoped, it was shorter than the width of the bed, yet the housing reached all the way to the hull. With a furtive glance into the mess room lest anyone witness me, I took the package and slid it to the back of the hole. It fitted perfectly, and when I replaced the drawer and pushed it in, it closed as snug as before.

I stood up, much relieved, and looked in admiration on my invisible handiwork. The package could stay there all the way to New York, and I need not be forever peering over my shoulder in fear for my burden. All it needed was a few stockings in the drawer to complete the façade of innocence.

I bent down to my trunk, unlatched it, and lifted the lid. There were no stockings, nor any of the clothes I had packed in it that morning; instead, to my amazement, all had been replaced by a squat cask whose dimensions fitted the trunk's interior perfectly. I leaned over, and through the seams in the staves sniffed the familiar siren-scent of brandy.

For a moment I was still, quite bewildered; then I strode to the door and craned my head into the mess room.

'Fothergill,' I bellowed. 'Fothergill!'

A dark figure rose from my left, a cloud of white ash billowing around him. He must have been cleaning the stove.

'Yes, sir?'

'A damnable thing has happened. All my effects have been removed from my chest, and replaced with a cask of brandy. Can you explain it?'

Fothergill nodded gravely. 'It sometimes happens, sir.'

'That is not an explanation. Where – where are my clothes?' Thank God, I thought, that I had not entrusted Nevell's package to the trunk.

'They'll turn up shortly, sir, I shouldn't wonder.'

And without so much as a word of apology, Fothergill retreated back to the stove. I had half a mind to take him by the ear and thrash him, though of course I was too craven to attempt it. Instead, I resolved to bring the matter before Captain Trevelyan. I pushed past Fothergill through the aft door, and immediately found myself in a narrow passage with a twisting stair rising to my left. Ahead of me was another door, doubtless to the captain's day cabin. I gave it an angry rap, and was sufficiently vexed that I did not notice the voice which summoned me but charged in like a hussar. And stopped short.

In a ship-of-the-line, it would have been termed the great cabin; on this slip of a ship, they called it the saloon, though even that exaggerated it. Only a dwarf, or possibly a man who had endured too many hours in the passengers' quarters, could have deemed it spacious. Nonetheless, it was by some distance the most comfortable berth on the vessel, and it enjoyed the inestimable virtue of a broad row of windows across the stern. After fumbling in the dark so long, my eyes struggled with so much light, but I could make out a plush banquette running the breadth of the ship under the windows, and an elegant occasional table with two high-backed chairs. Two cots were stacked like coffins against the starboard side, doubtless ready to be hung from the hooks in the ceiling at night. And in the middle of the cabin, her white dress almost gossamer with the light behind it, stood a figure who was most assuredly not Captain Trevelyan.

Fortunately, shock forestalled any lascivious thoughts. True, I did gape, but I flatter myself it appeared more natural surprise than lechery.

'I beg your pardon, madam,' I mumbled at last.

I had not seen her face on the quay, save in profile; now, my wits returning, I could admire it directly. Her startled cheeks were flushed like berries against the cream of her skin, and there was a girlish pertness in the poise of her nose and chin. My eyes followed her figure down, taking in the slender neck until it vanished into the carelessly disordered bodice of her dress. She had removed her bonnet, and with her golden hair hanging loose to her shoulders she was a study of innocence. Only her eyes seemed misplaced, slightly too narrow when they should have been wide and willing.

'I was seeking Captain Trevelyan,' I explained.

'This is his cabin.' Like her eyes, her voice did not quite fit the angelic picture: it was sweet and clear, certainly, but flecked with notes of knowledge, of amusement and pleasure. A voice which invited collusion, and offered it.

'Are you Captain Trevelyan's . . . ?' I faltered, unsure what I should suggest.

'His wife?' She laughed, and immediately I wanted to hear it again. 'I am not his wife.'

She let the sentence hang, just long enough for my mind to conjure all manner of disreputable explanations.

'My father and I are taking passage to America.' Was it my fancy, or was there a sly rebuke in her tone? 'Papa is quite married to his comforts. He has hired this cabin from the captain to alleviate the ills of the journey. He says it will be a great deal more convenient than the regular cabins.'

He was right, though he must have paid Trevelyan a handsome price for the privilege. I remembered the great pile of strongboxes I had seen being transferred from the guarded wagon on the quay, and decided he could probably afford it.

Rather later than was polite, I remembered my manners. 'I beg your pardon,' I said, affecting humility. 'I had thought to find Captain Trevelyan in here. You must excuse me. It has been a pleasure to make your acquaintance, Miss . . . ?'

'Lyell.' The name slid off her tongue like honey.

'Lieutenant Martin Jerrold.'

She gave a mock curtsey. 'Captain Trevelyan gave me to believe he was the only officer aboard the *Adventure*.'

'At present, Miss Lyell, I am on leave. From the navy.'

Her eyes widened and she clapped her hands together. 'The navy? How *gallant!*' A frown creased her immaculate brow. 'Then why...?'

Too late, I realized Nevell had despatched me without any plausible excuse for my errand. Before I could betray myself, however, I was saved by a thumping footfall in the passageway. The door slammed against the bulkhead, and the enormous man I had seen on the quay lumbered into the room. He was speaking to someone behind him, but at the sight of Miss Lyell and me alone in the cabin, he broke his sentence and bellowed, 'Who the devil are you?'

I have learned from experience that in such situations there is the fact of innocence, and then there is the appearance of innocence. The former was undeniable; the latter, I fear, I rather diminished by my leaping back in fright, knocking into the occasional table and toppling it onto the floor with a crash. The new arrival's eyes bulged out like sails in a storm – fortunately for me, his corpulence did not permit any hastier movement – while behind him I saw Captain Trevelyan enter.

Mercifully, Miss Lyell kept her senses. 'This is Lieutenant Jerrold, Papa. He was seeking Captain Trevelyan.'

The fat eyes swivelled towards me. 'Have you no manners, sir? How dare you presume to thrust yourself uninvited into my daughter's acquaintance? I had understood from Captain Trevelyan that our fellow passengers were to be gentlemen.'

As he spoke, he had been edging ominously towards me; now Miss Lyell headed him off, sweeping across the cabin and taking his arm. 'Oh, Papa! Do not be so cruel. We are not in town, here. We are at sea, and we must not be too proud or disdain these men their nautical ways. Why, this dear little boat is so small I collect we shall all be on terms of the greatest intimacy before the voyage is done.'

In all her prattle there had been not a hint of the slyness I had glimpsed earlier, merely simpering innocence. Only in her last words did I sense a subtle thread of suggestion, though perhaps I imagined it. With her monstrous father bearing down on me, I was certainly in no position to consider it.

'At any rate, what was it you wanted with me?' Seeing his opportunity, Captain Trevelyan steered the conversation to less contentious grounds.

After so much confusion, I needed a moment to remember. Doubtless that fed Lyell's suspicion, but at last I recalled: 'My chest. Some villain has stolen all my effects, and replaced them with a cask of brandy.'

If I had hoped for sympathy in my plight, it was in vain. Miss Lyell giggled, then touched a demure hand to her lips, while her father puffed out a vast sigh of contempt. Trevelyan was more restrained, though there was an open incredulity in the look he gave me. 'Let us see,' was all he said.

He followed me back through the narrow passage, leaving Lyell to upbraid his daughter's immodesty and repair the occasional table. I squeezed into my cabin and dragged the chest to the doorway so it would be in the light.

'You see,' I said, flinging open the lid.

Trevelyan peered over my shoulder. Under his gaze, three pairs of stockings, a razor and soap, a flattened hat and a bottle of wine lay innocently on the shirts and breeches folded beneath.

My shoulders, formerly stiff with self-righteous indignation, slumped forward. 'I . . . They were not there ten minutes ago,' I mumbled.

'It would seem they have returned from their turn about the ship.' Trevelyan's voice was cold and derisive. 'Now, if you have finished wasting my time and bothering my passengers, I will attend to matters of seamanship. Good day.'

As soon as he was gone, I pulled the cork from the bottle and took a consoling draught. I had done it again. There was not a ship I could board, it seemed, as officer or passenger, but that within a few hours her captain would think me an absolute idiot.

3

WHATEVER MISS LYELL HAD INSINUATED WITH HER PREDICTIONS OF
intimacy, the simple face of her words was no more than truth. Even
having removed themselves from the mess room, she and her papa
could not distance themselves from their fellow passengers. We
were eight in total: myself and the Lyells; a jovial Bristol merchant
named Kittering, forever trying to engage us in amusements; a
sallow cleric bound for a parish in Boston, travelling with his wife;
and a pair of majors destined for the Bermuda garrison. Among
these, Miss Lyell was quickly adopted as the favourite. Each morning, one of the sailors would bring her chair to the foredeck, and
thereafter she would sit like Cleopatra on her barge, rapt in
fascination as one admirer or another pressed her with his wit and
gaiety. Only the cleric's wife proved immune, standing by the
weather rail and pursing her lips at the wind while her husband
leafed through theological treatises.

On the second night from Falmouth, Captain Trevelyan borrowed
his cabin back from the Lyells and entertained the passengers to
dinner. It was not a comfortable occasion: we had known one
another just long enough to have exhausted the obvious conversations, but not so long as to have discovered any acquaintance
worth extending. At least, I suppose, we had not yet had a chance to

become enemies. And in the *Adventure*, we had one common thread to cling to.

'What I do not understand,' said Lyell, waving his fork and splashing Trevelyan with gravy, 'is why you keep the mails on deck. I cannot think that England's correspondents would be comfortable knowing that their letters are left in the open air, exposed to every depredation of storm and sea. Why not lock them in the lazaret, or at least shelter them in the hold?'

It was a fair question. Ever since leaving Falmouth the black portmanteaus had sat by the mainmast with only a tarpaulin to cover them. It did not seem a satisfactory arrangement.

Now Kittering, the merchant, joined in. 'And the crew – what of them? You trust them, do you, that they will not reach in during the night watches and pilfer the posts?'

'Or turn them into casks of brandy?' suggested Lyell. Polite laughter rose around the table. It had not taken long for word of my idiocy to spread through the company.

Trevelyan smiled. 'There is no chance of that, you may be assured. My crew are honest enough. As for the hazards of the sea, the portmanteaus are sewn tight. The paramount concern is that if danger were to threaten, we would lose no time hoisting the mails over the side and depriving our enemies of their intelligence.'

'Enemies?' gasped Miss Lyell. 'Do you really think we are at risk, Captain Trevelyan?' She was seated to his right, at the far end of the table from me, but it seemed she was suddenly unduly flushed about her collar.

Trevelyan leaned comfortingly towards her. 'I doubt it, Miss Lyell; I do not wish to alarm you. But it would be overly sanguine to think that the oceans are entirely England's own. There are enough ships out there, Spanish and French and their privateers, that we should be on our guard.'

'And what if one of them finds us, eh?' asked one of the majors. 'She's hardly the *Victory*, your command. Not much bite in your broadside, I fancy.'

26

Miss Lyell tittered; Trevelyan scowled, and waved to his steward. 'The logbook, if you please.'

The steward disappeared into the adjoining room and returned with a leatherbound book. Trevelyan took it and opened the cover. 'The instructions laid down by my lords the Postmaster General are these. "You must run where you can. You must fight when you can no longer run, and when you can fight no more you must sink the mails before you strike."'

'Run where you can?' echoed the major. 'That does not sound so heroic, so *Nelsonian*, do you think, Miss Lyell?'

It sounded like perfect sense to me; I wished I had discovered the merits of postal service far earlier in my career. But while Trevelyan muttered something about discretion and valour, and the major congratulated himself on his wit, Miss Lyell had fixed her gaze on me.

'Lieutenant Jerrold is a naval man, is he not? Have you ever fought a sea battle, Lieutenant?'

Of course, I should have heeded the Post Office's excellent advice and fled away from her dangerous questions. But when you have enjoyed a few glasses of claret, and a fair-haired angel is quivering her bosom at you from the far end of the table, temptation is hard to resist. Particularly when you have a trump to play.

'I was at Trafalgar.'

That impressed them. All around the table I saw their faces register respect, excitement and jealousy – that a hero of the greatest battle of the age should be seated in their midst.

'But Lieutenant, that is thrilling,' breathed Miss Lyell. Her voice almost trembled with awe. 'Did you see Lord Nelson himself? Did you witness his tragic, noble sacrifice?'

I did not, for the simple reason that I had spent the entire battle locked in the hold, barely conscious from all the brandy I'd drunk. I omitted that fact.

'There was so much smoke I could hardly see the sword in my hands. I just kept hacking away until the Frenchies stopped coming . . . *England expects*, Nelson said, and – well, I fancy I did my duty well enough.'

27

Despite the adoring looks that Miss Lyell was beaming at me, and the impotent envy on Trevelyan's face, I was keen to leave the topic before they guessed that the ace in my hand was actually a knave. But now Kittering was speaking.

'Were you actually aboard the *Victory*?'

'The *Temeraire*,' I said warily. I did not wish to discover that he had some brother or cousin who had been there with me.

'You wouldn't have seen much action there, I suppose,' said Lyell. He was closer to the truth than he guessed, but his comment drew his daughter's indignation.

'On the contrary, Papa. The *Temeraire* was at the very heart of the battle – I recall it from the newspapers. A French ship came along one side and a Spanish on the other, and the poor ship might have been quite crushed between them, yet eventually Lieutenant Jerrold and his crew prevailed and forced *both* enemies into surrender. Was it not so, Lieutenant?'

I raised my hands in modesty. 'Naturally, it was not so simple.'

Naturally, it was all a lie – and not of my own devising. Admiral Collingwood had reported it, from where I cannot guess, and *The Times* had obliged by reprinting his fiction on the front page. None of my brother officers, so far as I knew, had troubled to correct the matter.

'Well, well. A hero of Trafalgar in our very midst. We must have a toast.' Kittering raised his glass.

I tried to look humble. 'And to Nelson, of course.'

'To Nelson,' they chorused.

'Tell me, sir,' said Kittering, when the glasses were emptied. 'How is it that a man of your undoubted abilities should be sailing to America? Surely the command of some dashing frigate would be more apt, a chance to sail into the teeth of the enemy and bloody his nose a little?'

'Perhaps Lieutenant Jerrold lacks influence at the Admiralty,' Miss Lyell suggested. 'Are you the unfortunate victim of faction, Lieutenant?'

Once again, I could not resist the opportunity her question presented. What better way to insinuate myself into her father's good offices, to convince him of my reputation, than to demonstrate the patronage I enjoyed? 'I have no lack of favour at the Admiralty, thankfully. In fact, my uncle sits on the board.' I named him, and enjoyed the nods of recognition which passed around the cabin. They were not to know that my uncle tolerated me only insomuch as my disgrace would redound to his own discredit. Lyell must have known the name as well: across the table I could see him watching me with greater interest and, I fancied, a new regard.

But my answer had not satisfied Kittering. 'If you do not want for influence, then why are you bound for America?'

I hesitated. In my cabin the night before I had devised some story of a suffering aunt in need of her devoted nephew. But now, with the eyes of the company upon me – Miss Lyell's chief among them – that seemed a feeble pretext for abandoning my heroic career.

'Sometimes, I fear we must forgo the glories of the cannon's mouth for a higher cause. There are ways of attacking our enemies which are not always reported in the newspapers.' I winked. 'I dare say no more. Duty stays my lips.'

That roused them. Miss Lyell squealed with delight; Captain Trevelyan looked grudgingly impressed, while the others marvelled that they should have a secret agent in their midst. I could not see Mr Lyell's reaction, but as I beamed back the collective admiration, I felt he was giving me a very curious look indeed.

I wondered afterwards how wise it was to have alluded to my mission, but the immediate benefits were apparent the following morning. I had finished breakfast, and was standing at the taffrail watching the receding wake, when I noticed I was not alone. Miss Lyell had sidled up beside me and was leaning out, her gloved hands clasped over the water.

'I feel so isolated here,' she said, presumably excepting the two-dozen men at work behind her. 'To be beyond all sight of land, like Noah in his ark – and to know it will be full forty days and forty nights before we reach shore.'

'At least, I fancy, we can hope for finer weather than Noah.' Since leaving Falmouth we had enjoyed blue skies and brisk winds. Captain Trevelyan had been able to set stuns'ls and royals, and the *Adventure* bulged like a cloud as she hurried across the ocean.

'I suppose we shall have to turn the tedium to our advantage and spend the voyage improving ourselves.'

'I'm sure you could not be improved upon at all, Miss Lyell.'

She laughed prettily, and squeezed closer to me. 'Then we shall have to start on you, Lieutenant. Do you paint?'

'All I could paint on this ship is the gunports,' I demurred.

'Then how do you fare with the modern languages? Do you speak French?'

I coughed. 'In the navy, such accomplishment is considered tantamount to treason.'

'Oh come, Lieutenant. Surely you should know your enemy. Surely that is what *Nelson* would have expected. It is decided: I shall be your tutor, and you will be my obedient pupil. The journey will pass so much more quickly that way. Though you must be accustomed to such voyages, I suppose?'

With the constant mill of blockade duty, I had barely left sight of land in all my service. I did not think this the moment to confess it. 'There is always a part of me which yearns to be home.'

'I am pleased to hear you say so. One reads of the intrepid adventures of our noble sailors, and wonders what sentiments can beat beneath those firm and steady breasts.'

Well, I could have opened her eyes on that account, but prudently chose otherwise. Besides, I was distracted. She was standing rather closer to me than propriety allowed, and the roll of the ship's deck kept pressing her against me in a most unseemly and delightful way. Despite the steady breeze, she wore neither cloak nor spencer, and I could feel the curve of her body through the thin cloth of her dress.

'I suppose it must be cruel for you to be parted from your dear ones so long,' she said lightly.

I slid a glance sideways, trying to guess the intent behind her words, but her eyes were fixed on a piece of flotsam which had drifted across our wake.

'A man of action is rarely afforded the succour of affection.' I tried to affect a tragic air, and imagine myself as such a man. 'There are no cords of love to bind me to England.'

An unusually large wave must have struck *Adventure*'s side, for Miss Lyell was impelled against me quite forcefully. It was a moment before she regained her balance and was able to right herself. Even then, our arms remained touching.

'My poor lieutenant,' she whispered, so heartfelt that I had to believe her sincerity. 'Forsaking love like a modern Galahad. Is there none of the gentle sex who has touched your heart?'

'No longer.'

I suppose I should have been gratified by her attentions, her solicitous sympathy, but I was not. There was no longer so much artifice in my tragic demeanour, for her words had touched a wound which, though I insisted it was past, still troubled me.

'If I had a father—'

A candlestick shied through the air, narrowly missing my left ear.

'If you had a father, he'd have married you off to some fisherman when you were fourteen, and we'd never have met.' I stepped smartly sideways as the candlestick's pair flew past me and crashed into the corner.

'I wish we *had* never met!' Isobel shouted.

As the fond parting of two lovers, this was not precisely what I had hoped for.

Nor had I foreseen its coming, though that was doubtless part of the quarrel. For the past three weeks I had been charging around the country as if my very life had depended on it – which, in fairness, it had – and each time that Isobel had managed to catch me up, circumstance had driven me away in pursuit of my quarry. I knew it had troubled her, that it had sparked suspicion and temper, but I had assumed she would appreciate the forces which compelled me on – the same forces which now sent me to America. I had not expected the news to provoke this bizarre confrontation.

'How can you say you wish we'd never met?' I asked, baffled. 'A moment ago, you wanted me to marry you.'

It was the last thing I had expected to hear when I returned to our room at the boarding house, after a day in town cajoling my prize agent to advance me the monies to equip myself for the voyage. I had hoped to find Isobel awaiting me in her patent invisible petticoat, ready to offer the pleasures of the marriage bed – not the shackles of the institution itself.

'Marry you?' I'd echoed, half thinking she teased me. 'Don't be absurd.'

It was an honest answer, no different to what any man in my position would have given. But perhaps I should have guarded myself better.

'Absurd?' spat Isobel. She swung her legs off the bed and stood, then advanced towards me. 'You didn't think I was so absurd all those days and nights I was in your bed. Or when you asked me to follow you out of Dover.'

'I didn't say that *you* were absurd, merely that the idea of us marrying – now, of all times – is . . . impossible.' I was retreating towards the door. 'In less than a week I shall be aboard ship for America, and I cannot say how long it will be before Nevell's damned errand allows me to return. Think of it: a girl in your position, a man in mine . . .'

'What position is that, Martin? An officer who couldn't find the enemy at Trafalgar, who couldn't keep command of a ship that was chained to the riverbed? I might not have a father in a vicarage or an uncle at the Admiralty, but at least I've got some pride. And if I did have a father, he'd have made certain sure you didn't treat me like this. What about my reputation?'

'Reputation? You were a washerwoman – among your more reputable professions.'

It was at that moment that the first candlestick had come flying at me.

Though almost a foot shorter than I, Isobel's fury seemed to have made good the deficit of inches. 'I've trusted you, Martin. I trusted you when you took me out of Dover, and I've trusted you even when it seemed that every time I found you you were running away again.'

'Because some particularly vicious lunatics compelled me,' I protested.

Isobel took no notice. 'But if you're leaving me again, going off to America for months or even years, then I'll need something more to trust in. I'm eighteen; I can't be keeping all spoony for you if you're not coming back for me.'

'I am coming back,' I insisted.

'For me?'

'Yes.'

'Then prove it. Say you'll marry me.'

Of course, I should have told her 'yes' right there, and perjured myself later when she wasn't raving like an Irishman. If she'd been my uncle, I'd have whimpered my complaisance quick enough. But I'd already had to duck two candlesticks, and I'd be damned if some eighteen-year-old imp could browbeat herself onto the Jerrold escutcheon. How would I have explained it to my parents?

I folded my arms, feeding on my own righteousness. 'I won't have it. If you will not trust me now after all I've done for you . . . Indeed, if you cannot trust me, why on earth should you want to marry me?'

Isobel's face was flushed and trembling; she seemed to need all her strength to hold herself together, to keep from melting into a pool of tears. The mere sight of her effort lanced my composure like a boil, but there were no words I could say.

'Goodbye, Martin.'

She looked down. Perhaps she was seeking some other object to hurl at me, but there was nothing left. She ran out of the door and vanished.

On the deck of the *Adventure*, I had lapsed into silence while I remembered the scene. Now I felt a warm touch against my side, and realized that Miss Lyell had cosseted her slight frame under my shoulder, close beside me.

'My poor lieutenant,' she cooed. 'Can there be anything more desolate than a hero, a lion of Trafalgar, suffering the pangs of unrequited love?'

Well, perhaps I did suffer from unrequited love, though on the opposite end of it, I suspect, to what Miss Lyell presumed. I did not trouble to correct her, for it seemed to me that she might offer a welcome remedy for a weary heart. If, of course, there was anywhere on this floating snuffbox where we might enjoy an intimacy.

'Lieutenant Jerrold!'

I spun about like a servant caught in his mistress's bedchamber. Miss Lyell was more discreet. Though she barely seemed to move, she was immediately at a demure distance from me and exclaiming, 'Oh Papa! You have quite startled Lieutenant Jerrold. He was explaining to me the workings of the rudder.'

Lyell's thick eyebrows seemed to bristle out at me like pikes. 'Lieutenant Jerrold would do well to keep his wisdom to himself. If I may enjoy a word alone . . .'

Miss Lyell seemed to melt away. Before she had reached the mainmast, Captain Trevelyan was deep in conversation with her.

Lyell gripped my arm, as different a touch from his daughter's as could be imagined, and I steeled myself for a lecture on the inviolability of his progeny's virtue. You may gather it would not have been the first time I had heard such sentiments from an angry father.

'I have come to warn you, Lieutenant.' As I had feared. 'I do not know what your other merits may be, but your indiscretions are a menace to all around you. If you had nothing else to say at dinner last night you should have held your damn tongue and left the conversation to prating merchants.'

So surprised was I by this unexpected rebuke, and so vigorously did he shake my arm, I could find no words to defend myself. I could barely remember what I might have said to provoke him so. I did not think I had been overly forward with his daughter – though a father's suspicions are easily roused.

'How dare you speak so brazenly, so casually, about your mission? With so many enemies ranged against us, a little discretion is the very least the situation demands.' He leaned his face in towards me, his fat lips mashing and writhing together. 'You would do well to hold your tongue until we reach harbour in New York. You may be assured that I shall be watching you closely.'

He snapped his hand away from my arm, almost ripping a hole in my sleeve, and strode away towards the fo'c'sle. Clearly my dark hints towards secret missions had angered him, but why? Was he a zealous patriot, alert to anything which might betray his country? Or did he know more of my errand than I would wish?

I sighed. It would be just like Nevell to bind me to such an ally and then refrain from warning me. And even though Lyell had not expressly mentioned my attentions towards his daughter, it would be hard to press my suit with those fat eyes boring into me the entire voyage.

I looked down the deck. Miss Lyell had regained her canvas chair and was holding court to Kittering and the clergyman.

It would be a long six weeks.

4

CONTRARY TO THE PROMISE OF HER NAME, THE *ADVENTURE* OFFERED an uneventful passage. For a time we amused ourselves with conversation; when we tired of that, with whist; and when that too paled, with backgammon. I did not much mind that, since Miss Lyell persisted with her scheme for improving me. Each afternoon we sat together while she drilled my vocabulary and deplored my pronunciation. I made a poor student, for I concentrated rather more on the allures of her figure than the intricacies of the French language. But something must have seeped through, for eventually my brief words became stammered sentences, and at length even halting conversations. For the rest of the time, I retreated often into the darkness of my cabin. There I would extract my precious package from its concealment and hold it, turning it in my hands and staring at the impenetrable knots and seals which bound it.

There were three seals, as Mr Dawes had observed, and within a week their forms were stamped in my mind. One was a single letter, a solitary, rampant 'A' with flowering serifs and curlicues. The second took the image of a bird, a dove or a pigeon it seemed to me, surrounded by a motto too small and indistinct to read. As for the final seal, that needed no effort to remember it, for it was as familiar to me as my own signature: the wound rope and anchor of the

36

Admiralty. To have that emblem stamped on so wicked and malignant an object disquieted me even more than the thing itself. I stared at it for hours, wondering who Mr Tyler of M'Culloch's Inn, Pittsburgh, might be and what mischief my message for him might portend. Though even if I learned that, I thought dismally, how could I ever hope to defeat it as Nevell had ordered?

Of course, I found no answers.

One Thursday afternoon, during the dog watch, I was in the mess room playing cards with Kittering when the jug of water we were using to let down our brandy ran dry.

'Not to worry,' I said, upending it over my glass and watching the last drops trickle out. 'Better the water runs out than the spirits.'

Kittering groaned. We were near the tropics now, both sweating freely from the heat, but he felt it worse than I. 'Dammit, Jerrold, you cannot expect me to drink this neat. Not in this infernal climate.' He mopped his brow. 'My head, you know.'

I called for Fothergill, but there was no answer. It was actually something of a relief, for whenever we were together his gaze seemed to fix on me with the most severe attention.

'You will have to refill it yourself from the cask in the foc's'le,' I told Kittering. I picked up the cards and started dealing them out again.

'You go,' he retorted. 'You lost the last hand. And the heat in the bow will be unbearable.'

It was too hot to argue. I squeezed out of the door and past the main ladder, ducking beneath the beams as I walked through the crew's quarters. They were all on deck, and their chests and hammocks were stowed neatly against the sides so that the room seemed empty. An amber light and the smell of wood shavings filled the air; it reminded me of exploring some long-forgotten attic on a summer's day.

I passed the forward ladder and stepped into the galley. The fire was doused and the cook absent, but I knew what I needed. I pulled open the hatch set into the floor in the far corner, and dropped down the narrow ladder to the forepeak stores. There was hardly any light in these depths, and though I could hear the ocean rushing past the hull all about me, the air was stifling. As my eyes adjusted to the light, I saw chests and barrels piled high about me, a veritable warehouse of provisions. One, in particular, caught my eye.

'What . . .'

It looked to be my own sea-chest, though I could not imagine how it should have come to be down here. I had seen it in my cabin a mere half hour earlier. Too befuddled to be angry, I tipped it open.

One small mystery was solved as a squat cask of brandy, nestled tight inside the chest, met my gaze. Sniffing it, I smelled the brandy within. Why someone should have wanted to store it in a sea-chest identical to my own, rather than simply in the barrel, I did not know, but obviously the similarity had confused others besides me. They must have put it in my cabin when they were loading the ship, and only realized their mistake when I complained. It would have been gracious of them, I thought, to explain the matter, rather than allow me to make a fool of myself before Trevelyan and Lyell.

I looked around at the rest of the stores. Half of them were entirely as I would have expected, sacks of flour and barrels of pork and peas, the same as you would have found on any vessel. But interspersed among them was a considerable amount of luggage – trunks and chests, and even a canvas valise – which, when I delved into them, yielded a sizeable supply of cheese, potatoes, pairs of shoes, glassware, and several more casks of brandy.

I shook my head to clear the drowsiness which had seeped in. I had spent enough time battling smugglers in Dover to guess what this little store signified. If Trevelyan winked at it, and so long as we were not all thrown in gaol by the customs officer when we reached port, I would not complain that the men of the Post Office delivered more than mail. I found a water butt and filled the jug, then climbed back to the main deck. Though before I returned to my cards, I did make sure to check my chest and its contents.

Thirty-eight days after leaving Falmouth, we reached Bermuda. From first light we could see the lush bulge on the horizon, little more than a hummock swelling out of the ocean five hundred miles from anywhere. From our low vantage, it appeared as a single, long island, though the master's chart showed it to be a veritable archipelago of tiny islets, narrow channels and treacherous reefs, curved around like a skeletal hand beckoning westwards.

'How enchanting,' said Miss Lyell, standing beside me at the weather rail. 'Have you been to the West Indies before, Lieutenant?'

I cleared my throat, gratified for the opportunity to demonstrate my knowledge. 'Actually, Miss Lyell, we do not call Bermuda the West Indies. We are a thousand miles from Jamaica here.'

She stuck her tongue out at me. 'They seem much the same to me. All these little islands with their blackies and their horrid climates.'

I did not risk her displeasure by pointing out that the temperature was pleasantly warm, much like an English summer's day, though we were in the second week of October.

'At any rate, it will be nice to stretch our legs on land.'

It seemed I was not the only one who thought so. No sooner had we passed into the opaline waters inside the reef and dropped anchor in the bay than the crew were lowering boats and making ready to go ashore. At first I thought it a commendable zeal to deliver the mails, but they paid the black portmanteaus by the main-mast no heed, instead forming a human chain down into the forepeak and bringing forth a vast pile of boxes and chests. One looked suspiciously similar to my own, though out in the sunlight I could see telltale dents and scratches which belied that fear. It was loaded into the jollyboat, stacked perilously high with the rest of the cargo, and long before the native hawkers had paddled out to meet us the crew were rowing away into the harbour.

'They seem keen to be ashore,' I said to Captain Trevelyan.

He looked peculiarly nonchalant, given that the greater part of his men had just absented themselves so peremptorily. 'They'll be back soon enough, certainly before we sail. We must allow them their little adventures, you know.'

'What was in those boxes?' I pressed, feigning ignorance. I wanted to know what Trevelyan made of it.

'Provisions,' he said shortly.

I did not pursue the matter. By his tone, I guessed he knew exactly what contraband cargoes his men delivered.

Presently, a small boat proceeded out among the vibrant flotilla which surrounded us, bringing the customs inspector and the postal agent to perform their duties. On their return ashore, Trevelyan, the Lyells and I chose to accompany them, for there were hardly men enough left aboard the *Adventure* to row the gig.

'We cannot delay here long,' said Trevelyan.

We stood clustered on the jetty, alone in the stillness of the early afternoon. The air was not infernally hot, but so heavy with moisture that it seemed to seal the heat into my body.

Trevelyan pulled out his pocket watch. 'We will sail this evening on the ebb tide. I will have the boat take us back at four o'clock.'

Miss Lyell took a fan from her reticule and flapped it at her throat. 'Must we leave so soon, Captain? This little island seems so picturesque. It would be such an enchanting place to explore.'

'I regret we cannot delay.'

'Then I shall see as much as I may in the few hours you permit us. Lieutenant Jerrold has promised to introduce me to the delights of the island.'

That was the first I had heard of such a plan, and I looked uncertainly at Lyell to see what he would make of having his daughter squired around a tropical port by a lieutenant of dubious character. To my relief, he seemed utterly uninterested.

'You do as you like,' he said curtly. 'I have business I must attend.' Without admonition or a word of goodbye, he turned and walked away. After a brief reminder not to be late returning, Trevelyan ambled off to pay his respects to the port admiral.

'Now we are quite alone,' said Miss Lyell. Her eyes glinted with mischief. 'I trust you will show me all the pleasures of the island.'

It was all I could manage to resist a lecherous smirk. 'I thought you disliked the island, its darkies and its horrid climate.'

'That was the West Indies I spoke of. This is Bermuda.' She hooked her arm around my own and pulled me towards the nearest street. 'Or do you have a *chère amie* to see here? I know the reputation of sailors.'

'Not in this harbour, Miss Lyell. Not yet.'

I grinned – then, remembering that her father was not far away, craned my neck about in fear he had seen our intimacy. Miss Lyell must have noticed the awkward movement, for she giggled.

'We are quite safe. If Papa has business here you may be assured that nothing will distract him from it.'

Perhaps I should have thought to wonder what business might blind him so thoroughly to his daughter's improprieties, but in truth it suited me too well to quibble. We wandered along the waterfront arm in arm, admiring the new Customs House, the pink sand beaches across the bay and the ships at anchor in the harbour. There were three men-of-war among them: an old seventy-four with an admiral's blue flag drooping from her mainmast; a frigate, and a sloop, both doubtless returned from patrolling the American coast. Behind them, on the shore, I could see vast piles of cedar trunks, and the skeletons of half-completed sloops sitting in their slips.

'What will you do when we reach New York?' I asked, trying to fill an ungainly silence which had fallen between us.

Miss Lyell shrugged delicately. 'I will go with Papa, of course. He has his affairs to manage – investments or consols or speculations, or whatever they may be. I confess I do not trouble to understand it.'

'And when you return to England? Do you have a prospective husband awaiting you?'

She scowled. 'Saving my father's business, I cannot think of anything more tedious.'

'But surely Mr Lyell is keen—'

'Keen to marry me off?' She wrinkled her nose in distaste. 'Why should he be? He does not need the money that a rich connection would bring, and he fears that any lesser suitor would merely be bent on avarice.'

I tried to look suitably shocked at the thought of such unscrupulous rogues. To be alone with a beautiful and apparently willing girl was good fortune enough; that she should also be wealthy beyond the need for marriage was particularly fascinating.

'I had not realized your father to be so . . .'

'Rich?' She laughed, mocking me. 'He believes that ostentation simply serves to dissipate his wealth.'

'But he does not even travel with servants.'

'Why should he? I can answer his needs well enough, and save him ten shillings a week. As for servants, he does not trust them, certainly not with the cargo he has aboard the *Adventure*.'

In all the voyage, nobody had managed to establish precisely what brought Lyell to America – and, in turn, what he brought with him. I had not dared ask; when Kittering had attempted it once, a harsh stare and a haughty silence had been his only answer.

'What cargo is that?' I said, all innocence.

Throughout our conversation we had strolled through the dusty streets of the town's hushed afternoon. Now, Miss Lyell suddenly stepped in front of me and spun about so that I collided front on with her. Instinctively, she reached her arms around my waist to keep balanced, and I found my own arms grasping her to me. I looked down: her flawless eyes were staring straight up at me, half closed against the sun, and her chin rested on my chest.

'All this talk of my father's business, Lieutenant.' Her voice was fine, barely a whisper. 'I begin to wonder what truly interests you.'

'This.'

I leaned over and touched my lips to hers. At the back of my neck, I felt her hand pulling me down, forcing me into her. Our mouths opened and met; I could feel her whole body pressing against me through the damp muslin of her dress. My senses succumbed to the overwhelming sweetness of her scent.

I stroked one hand up the slope of her back, over the summit of her shoulder, and down her collar to the glistening skin at her bodice. And then, just as my fingers sank into the valley between her breasts, she stepped smartly away, smoothed down her dress, and was immediately a model of propriety. In the doorway to my left, deep in shadow, I saw the saucer-white eyes of a slave woman watching us without expression.

Miss Lyell reached into my waistcoat pocket and, with a demure smile, pulled out my watch.

'Why, Lieutenant,' she exclaimed. 'It is four o'clock. Captain Trevelyan will be expecting us back at the ship.'

Captain Trevelyan could have been awaiting us at the last judgement for all I cared. I reached out to pull Miss Lyell back, but she was too quick: she spun away, and began walking gaily down the road. Flustered and frustrated, I could only follow.

We sailed on the tide that evening, watching the low archipelago sink into the haze behind our stern. All of the crew had returned from their excursions on shore, and whatever they had accomplished there it put them in a fine humour. The same could not be said for me, for after the fleeting bliss of our liaison on the island Miss Lyell's affections seemed as cool as ever. And then there was the intelligence Trevelyan had had on the island: the port admiral had warned him, he said, that privateers had been sighted cruising off the American coast.

'But I thought our mastery of the seas was absolute,' said Lyell, when he heard the news. He looked pale, doubtless thinking of his precious cargo in the lazaret below.

Trevelyan shrugged. 'Mostly it is. But they still sting us where they have the chance, and disrupting the mails is a favourite game of theirs.'

Each morning after that, when I took my stroll on deck, I would gaze on our meagre armament and imagine the broadside bouncing off the hull of some hulking privateer. Which is why I would have felt a particular terror when the shout came from the mainmast look-out, if only I had been able to hear it.

5

WE WERE EIGHT DAYS OUT OF BERMUDA, AND MAKING GOOD progress with a stiff westerly on our beam, when it happened. I had gone below to find Kittering, who had made some advance towards Miss Lyell the previous evening and was now licking his wounds in his cabin. Naturally, I had no sympathy for him – indeed, I welcomed his misfortune – but he owed me some money in respect of a game of backgammon, and I was keen to have it off him.

'Is she not the most sublime creature,' he mooned. 'Yet cruel, Jerrold – cruel as the Medusa.'

'She rebuffed you, I take it.' I was curious to hear his story, not least from the jealous fear that she may have offered him her favours before casting him off.

Kittering propped himself up on his bed. 'She laughed at me. She said her father would never hear of it, that he would think I aimed beyond my reach.' He paused, nursing the memory. 'He is very rich, you know.'

'Is he?' I spoke carelessly, for if I were to press my suit any further with Miss Lyell I did not want it reported that I thought of gain.

'Oh yes. The rumour in London is that he is worth seventy-five thousand a year. He has made one fortune from the sinking fund, and a second investing the proceeds in industry. I am told he owns half of Birmingham.'

Well, he was welcome to that – though I did begin to understand why Miss Lyell's rejection had left Kittering so heartsick.

He pointed aft. 'What do you suppose he carries in all those strongboxes stored in the lazaret?'

'If it's more than the two guineas you owe me, I don't care.' I tried to steer the conversation to more profitable grounds. 'If I am to—'

I broke off. As I turned to follow Kittering's gesture aft I saw a dark figure on the far side of the mess room, edging open the door to my own cabin. He glanced about furtively, then scuttled inside.

'Do you have a gun, Kittering?' I whispered.

He looked at me as though I were mad. 'A gun? Of course not. Why—'

'No matter.'

I crept out of his room towards the dining table, skirting around the well of light which the skylight cast. As quietly as I could I took a stool and raised it over my head, then tiptoed to my cabin door.

The dark figure was kneeling beside the bed, almost indistinguishable against the gloom which surrounded him. As I watched in mounting fury, I heard the rasp of the drawer being pulled from its housing, and the scrabbling of a hand reaching into the space.

I peered closer, trying to make out more of his villainy. That was a mistake: the stool I held knocked into the doorframe, and in my surprise at the sudden noise I dropped it to the floor. It thumped into the deck like a cannonball, and even as it rolled away from me the figure by the bed leaped to his feet and spun around. Mercifully, he did not appear to be armed. Instead, he was holding a small basket of linen.

'Mr Fothergill!' I said hotly. 'What in all damnation do you mean by this? Captain Trevelyan will hear of it, you may be sure; I will see you flogged from one end of the ship to the other. What in hell's name did you think you would find, prying about under my bed?'

Fothergill's impassive face soaked up my anger unflinchingly. 'A stocking, sir.'

'*What?*' I picked up the stool from where it had fallen. 'Do not sport with me, Fothergill.'

'I was preparing the laundry, sir.' He shook his little basket at me.

'Under my bed?'

'Sometimes stockings fall behind the drawer and get lost.'

I shook my head in disbelief. 'I keep my stockings in my sea-chest.'

Fothergill stepped towards it. 'Shall I take them for you, sir?'

I could have thrown the stool at him for his impertinence. 'No! You can explain to me why—'

Fothergill never did explain himself, for at that moment I heard a great drumming of feet over my head, and felt the ship heel hard to starboard. I thrust out an arm against the bulkhead to steady myself, and as I regained my balance I heard someone pounding down the main ladder for'ard.

The door to the mess room burst open and Lyell stepped in.

'Lieutenant Jerrold!' he cried. 'We rely on your courage.' He paused, perhaps wondering why I was standing outside my cabin with a stool in my hand. 'The lookout has sighted an enemy.'

At first, there were grounds to hope that Lyell had exaggerated. Snatching a telescope as I gained the deck, I trained it in the direction the lookout had indicated. Even through the glass, the ship which had occasioned the disturbance barely broke the horizon – far too far to tell whether she was friendly or otherwise.

'What do you make of her?' I asked Trevelyan, having nothing to offer myself.

He lowered his glass. 'Big enough to give us trouble if she wants to.'

'But too big to catch us, surely.' I glanced aloft at the fields of taut canvas stretched above us. 'If the wind holds, we can outrun her with ease. And she may not be an enemy at all.'

'We'll take no chances. I want as much sail as she'll bear. We'll lay off to leeward and see if she follows, then tack to windward after dark.'

For the rest of the afternoon, and well into the evening, we stood by the stern and watched the distant ship's pursuit. Gauging her progress became an itch, a craving: without a glass she was all but invisible, especially as night drew on and the horizon dimmed, yet we were forever finding excuses to take a telescope from the rack and assure ourselves that she still followed. At times I even caught myself hoping that she would catch us, simply to answer the mystery of her identity, though I was quick to dismiss such nonsense. But though she looked to be under full canvas, the distance between us never closed.

Dusk came early that day. Throughout the afternoon the wind had been rising, and the blue sky had firmed into cloud: first white, then ever darker shades of grey. Eventually, Trevelyan had to order us to shorten sail. All night I lay in my cabin and listened uneasily to the footsteps above me, the ropes creaking and the hull groaning. Every so often I dismounted my bed and pulled out the drawer, to feel the package hidden behind it and be sure it was still there. I was not at all happy about Fothergill's intrusion, though I had not reported it to the captain. In the current commotion he would not have thanked me for complaining that I had caught the steward fetching my laundry. And still I wondered, as I lay there in the dark, whether it might be the package which drew our pursuer after us.

At dawn, I stumbled out of my bed and went on deck. Expecting the worst, I had dressed in my blue uniform coat. Though I've done as much as any man to disgrace that uniform, it was a curious comfort to me, a mantle against the impending dangers. I suppose it also made me a more obvious target.

'Is she still there?' I asked, sweeping the glass across our stern.

Grim-faced, Trevelyan pointed to larboard. Although the wind was sharp and blustery, and the clouds still hung low, I did not need a telescope. All our manoeuvring through the night, the changes of sail and tack, had availed us nothing: she had come level with us, and now followed a parallel course a few miles off our beam. I trained the telescope to see her better, bracing it against the heaving deck.

'A brig. No colours – only a red pennant at the mainmast.' I waited for the swell to lift her side into view, then counted quickly. 'Eighteen or twenty guns.' Twice as many as we had – and probably twice the size as well.

'By her build, I'd guess she's Spanish,' said Trevelyan from behind his own glass.

'Or a prize,' I countered.

'But whose?'

Trevelyan beckoned to the master. 'Run up the private signal, if you please.'

A black and yellow flag raced up the foremast, snapped tight by the gusting wind. We stared across the heaving waves and their whitecaps, every one of us praying that the signal would be recognized and answered. There was no response.

'She's easing her helm,' called one of the seamen. 'She means to catch us.'

True enough, the ship's bow had come down a couple of points, so that our courses converged. If the wind kept up, it would not be long before she crossed our path, broadside on and with the weather gage.

'All hands aloft!' shouted Trevelyan. 'All hands aloft, and make all the sail she'll bear. Topgallants and topsails both. Bear up the helm five points to starboard, if you please – we'll outrun this pirate yet, I fancy.'

To my astonishment, not one of the seamen moved. None of them ran up the rigging or hauled on the halyards, and the only movement of the wheel came as the helmsman nudged it this way and that to keep us on an even course.

Trevelyan's face bulged so crimson I thought he might have suffered a seizure. 'Have you all gone deaf? In a few minutes we will be under the guns of a superior enemy who will either pound us to matchwood or send us home in chains. Have you forgotten our orders? We must run where we can.'

One of the seamen – the bosun, I gathered, from the brass whistle chained around his neck – shuffled forward. 'Beggin' your pardon, sir, but there's no purpose runnin'. She's too close, I reckon.'

He spoke cautiously, almost gingerly, but it did nothing to placate Trevelyan. 'The devil you say! With this breeze at our backs and a full spread of canvas, we can run them all the way back to Bermuda.'

The bosun made a show of looking at the sails, and at the wind which still kept our signal flag fully extended. 'I reckon not, sir. No purpose in a chase.'

His words were so impudent, and so bare-facedly contrary to fact, that I wondered if he had lost his mind. I could think of no other explanation; it seemed a queer time for a mutiny. Off the larboard bow, the unknown ship was drawing steadily nearer.

'What would *you* have me do, then?' Trevelyan asked bitterly. 'Turn and fight, broadside to broadside? We might as well turn the guns inboard and shoot ourselves, save them the powder and shot.'

All the seamen, who had gathered in a circle on the afterdeck, nodded. 'No gain in fightin',' I heard one say.

'Then what – strike our colours and let them take us?'

'Only thing for it,' said the bosun blithely.

I could not believe what I was hearing. I've little taste for battle myself, but this was beyond cowardice. Trevelyan thought so too.

'This is madness. If you will not think of your honour as men, at least think of your own interests. Do you want to see yourselves made captive?'

'Not much chance of that, sir. A privateer won't want a flock of prisoners ballasting her down. She'll drop us in the Carolinas, or Virginia, and we'll work a passage home. An' all with a few bob in our pockets, on account of the insurance from the cargo what we lost.'

'What cargo?'

The bosun shifted uneasily on his feet. 'Our little adventures, sir. The spirits and that.'

'But you unloaded all that in Bermuda – and sold it at a handsome, free-trading profit, I'll wager.'

49

The bosun grinned. 'Insurers didn't see that, did they, sir? There's an extra six months' wages to be had in what they don't know.'

At last, I began to understand why he and his men were so unwilling to obey Captain Trevelyan, so insistent on surrendering the *Adventure* at the first opportunity. It was a brute piece of infamy, though obviously beneficial to them. For my part, as a serving officer of His Majesty, I did not think my captors would give me up so lightly.

Lyell, who had lumbered out of his cabin to witness this exchange, now spoke up. 'Do you mean to say that you would allow this ship to be captured merely to line your pockets with the proceeds of the insurance on items you have already sold?' He sounded incredulous, though whether from outrage at their duplicity or admiration for their commercial nous I could not tell.

'That's puttin' it harsh, sir. I'd say we'd no choice but to strike, and we made the best of a bad lot. You'd understand that, bein' a businessman and all.'

'Nonetheless, I cannot allow it to happen.'

'And what will you do?' Faced with the betrayal of his crew, Trevelyan had slumped into despondency. 'Will you fire the guns and steer the ship and unfurl the sails all by yourself?'

''E'd snap the mast off if 'e went up there,' sniggered one of the men.

Lyell ignored the gibe, and turned to address the crew. 'Gentlemen, you are evidently sensible to your profit. Men of business.'

There were murmurs of agreement.

'In that case, I propose a bargain of my own. I have, sitting in innocence below this very deck, a cargo of immense value to me, one I would despair to see in the hands of the enemy. I think you can guess what I speak of.' His voice faltered a little, and I saw the sailors leaning closer. 'I know it is of little import to you, but to me . . .' He straightened. 'Yet if you insist that your hearts will be ruled by commercial necessity, I have a proposal for you. How much will your insurers pay you for the cargo?'

'Ten pounds, give or take.'

'Ten pounds, eh? And that is if you do go free, and your insurers do not learn that you had already sold the cargo, or that you willingly engaged in the morally hazardous act of surrendering yourselves for profit. An uncertain proposition. What can I offer you in its stead?' He was in his stride now, animated by the energy of the Exchange or the coffee house. 'How does this strike you? Fifty guineas a man, in gold, if we reach New York safely. What do you say to that?'

Whether at the thought of rescuing a fair-haired maiden in peril, or of the five-fold return they would make from Lyell's investment, the crew were united in their agreement. The bosun knuckled his forehead and ran to the mainmast, while the topmen swarmed up the ratlines. The wheel went over, and I saw the bow turning away from our pursuer.

Trevelyan alone seemed unmoved by the new spirit. 'That was a fine speech, Mr Lyell, but I fear you are too late. We have lost what little advantage we had.'

As if to prove his argument, a flat bang echoed across the ocean. Away to starboard, a plume of white smoke rose from our enemy's forecastle, and seconds later it was repeated in the cloud of spray which erupted from the water ahead of us. There was no advantage in dissembling now: at our enemy's stern, I could see a flag unfurling in the breeze. The red and gold stripes, and royal crest, of Spain.

All action halted on the *Adventure*'s deck, and the men stared uncertainly at Lyell. This was something none of them had accounted for.

Lyell looked to Trevelyan. 'Well, Captain? "You must run where you can. You must fight when you can no longer run." It seems that the luxury of running is denied us.'

' "And when you can fight no more you must sink the mails before you strike." Look at her, Lyell: she outmans us, and will outgun us faster than we can outsail her. It would be doom to oppose her.'

Lyell rolled his eyes. 'Possibly, but we've more chance of seeing safe harbour if we fight than if we strike. I do not wish to spend the next five years rotting in a Spanish gaol on some fever-infested island in the Indies.'

'What would Lieutenant Jerrold do, I wonder?'

Startled by this latest question, not from Lyell but in his daughter's clear, ringing voice, I looked around. She was standing at the top of the main ladder, her hair blowing loose in the wind and her legs spread apart to brace herself against the swell. I had never seen her more beautiful.

'Well . . .' I floundered to conjure an acceptable answer, when the paramount thought in my mind was safe surrender. 'Our enemy certainly has an overwhelming force. There would be no shame on Captain Trevelyan if he deemed it prudent . . . ah . . .'

To my dismay, Miss Lyell mistook my equivocation. 'You see, Captain? Even though Lieutenant Jerrold understands your fears, he cannot bring himself to allow them. Yours is the course of prudence, but there are surely times when prudence must submit to higher virtues – gallantry and fortitude. Surely you are not deaf to their entreaties.'

'I dare say that if you lack the stomach for a fight, Trevelyan, another can be found to take command. A hero of Trafalgar, no less,' Lyell suggested slyly.

Whatever the deficit in Trevelyan's courage – not that I judged him, mind – there was no faulting his pride. He visibly flinched at Lyell's comment, so hard that for a moment I feared an enemy marksman might have struck him with a musket ball.

'You will not see me relinquishing my command in the face of danger, Miss Lyell,' he promised. 'Bosun, reef all but the tops'ls, then clear for action.'

I was appalled. I could not fathom why the Lyells should goad him into battle, for it seemed suicidal madness to me. Yet there was nothing I could do; certainly not when Miss Lyell ran over to me, squeezed my arm, and whispered, 'I know you will prevail, my Truest Hope.'

I was not at all sure. We had squandered vital moments with our arguments and the Spaniard had closed fast. She was now not above a mile away, broad of the larboard quarter. As I stood by the fore-mast, supervising the gun crews, I saw her gunports lifted and the snouts of her cannon poking out.

'She'll aim to dismast us,' Trevelyan called. 'We're no use to her if we sink. Rig those nets smartly and get the mails brought aft.'

A detachment of seamen stripped away the tarpaulin which covered the heavy portmanteaus and dragged them to the stern. With some effort, they hoisted the bags onto the rail and made them fast to the davits, so that they dangled freely over the water like a bunch of grapes.

'In case we gets taken,' the gunner beside me explained. 'One chop and down they goes. Saves us the trouble of throwin' 'em overboard.'

A noise like a thunderclap filled the air. Instinctively, I dropped to my knees behind the gunwale, though the shots fell well astern of us.

'Best get below, Miss Lyell,' said Trevelyan. 'The next one will come a good deal closer. Down with the helm,' he added to the steersman. 'See that the guns are double-shotted, if you please, Mr Jerrold.'

I gave him a queer look. 'But that won't serve unless we come to close quarters.' At which distance all the shot in the world would not undo the Spaniard's stouter hull.

'God damn you, Mr Jerrold, you will kindly take my orders or remove yourself to the passengers' quarters. You may have the experience of Trafalgar, but I fancy I know how to handle my own ship.'

He strode back to the helm, and I was left to echo his orders to the men. 'Ram home shot and wad.'

'Hard-a-lee,' ordered Trevelyan. 'Run out your guns.'

'Run out your guns,' I repeated.

I did not dare contradict him in front of the men, but my mind was in turmoil. What was his plan? Our advantages, if any we had, were speed and agility, yet Trevelyan seemed to be closing with the enemy. Did he hope to cross her bows and rake her stem to stern? If so, he had precious little time. She was coming up fast on our larboard side, with barely five hundred yards of clear water between us. I could see her gun crews hauling on the tackles, heaving out the guns for another broadside.

I saw Kittering standing by his cannon, lanyard gripped tight in his fist. 'Get down!' I called, though I doubt he heard me.

Trevelyan's ploy had failed. The Spaniard was to windward, and as she came past our beam she choked the air from our sails. The *Adventure* slowed; her canvas began to twitch and shiver, and there was little we could do save watch as our enemy's full armament, nine fat guns with the tapered muzzles of carronades, drew level.

'Fire!' shouted Trevelyan.

It was as though the entire, murderous cycle of carnage had been compressed into a single second. Feeble though they were when set against our enemy's armament, or the great guns I had commanded aboard the *Temeraire*, our cannon thundered out their broadside in a torrent of flame and smoke. They hurled themselves inboard, tearing so hard on their tackles it seemed they must rip the gunwale to pieces; and in that same moment the answering blizzard of iron hit home in the spars and rigging above. A block fell and landed in the netting over our heads; I could see the end of the mizzen gaff dangling precariously where a shot had almost sheared it in two. Splinters rained down on us, and I dropped my gaze to the deck, shielding my eyes.

As we had expected, the Spaniard had aimed most of her broadside high, hoping to disable us and leave us open for the taking. But whether by design or otherwise, some of her broadside had gone lower: near the bow, a jagged hole had been gouged out of the bulwark, while one of the stern davits looked to have been shot away completely so that the mailbags dangled by a single rope. A couple of the seamen were streaked with blood where splinters had caught them, but otherwise we seemed to have been fortunate with casualties.

I ran across the deck to where Trevelyan stood by the helm. His face was pale, and his knuckles white around the hilt of the sabre he carried.

'For pity's sake, turn and run before we are dismasted,' I begged him.

'That is no longer possible. If we show her our stern she'll rip the guts out of us.'

'She'll rip the guts out of us anyway.'

Behind me, I could hear the crews working frantically to reload the guns. On the *Temeraire* we would have had a second broadside well away by now, but these men were too few and too unused to battle for that. One of them had dropped his worm-iron in his haste; another was running out a gun with the rammer still protruding.

Trevelyan sliced down his sword. 'Fire! Fire!'

Only one of our guns was ready, and it made little more than a lonely pop after the blast of the last broadside. Our enemy was not so tardy: across the water, I saw her full length erupt in flame as she delivered a second dose of iron. This time she aimed lower, to clear our decks and break our will. The larboard gunwale exploded in splinters, hurling back the men who stood beside it. Blood was sprayed across the deck but I had no time to gape at it, for one of the guns had torn loose from its mooring; I had to leap aside to be out of its way before it smashed into the starboard bulwark. The helm remained mercifully untouched, but the rest of the deck was a shambles of debris and broken men. The *Adventure* was disintegrating under the onslaught.

'Strike,' I implored Trevelyan. 'Strike and save what you can. There is no dishonour in surrendering an unfair fight.'

He seemed not to hear me. He gripped his sword and stared across the water, through the weaving tendrils of smoke to where our enemy bore remorselessly on. Our own efforts barely seemed to have scratched her.

Once again, her guns rumbled out of their ports. I fancied I could hear the squeak of the trucks as they rolled into position.

'Sweet Jesus have mercy.'

Another broadside, and the ship convulsed down the length of her keel with the impact. All around me men were thrown to the ground, either by the shuddering deck or by the fragments which scythed through the air in a slaughtering storm. Screams rose in their wake, yet above all else came the twisting, agonized protest of fractured timbers. I looked up. The mizzen topmast had been struck square on; it tottered against its hounds, twisting and writhing in its rigging, then broke free. With an excruciating crescendo it toppled over, bucking like a leaf in a breeze as it tore away the stays and braces. I ran forward out of its path and dropped to the deck beside one of the cannon, hoping it would shield me from any falling spar. A loose rope cracked over my back like a whip and I squealed, convinced my spine would be snapped in two, but it was a glancing blow barely worth a bruise. Then the noise subsided, the air cleared, and a relative hush fell over the ship.

I stood. The entire aft quarter of the *Adventure* was covered with the ruins of the mizzen. A portion of the topgallant mast had smashed open the mess-room skylight, and a topsail had covered the helm. Everywhere, the ship was snared in tangles of rigging. Almost the only mercy was that the topmast had fallen clear of the deck, into the water to starboard. It had not come free, though: remnants of its rigging still held it against our side like a giant steering oar, its fractured stump thrust high over our heads.

Men were running aft now with axes, hacking at the wreckage, though there seemed little order to their efforts. I tried to find Trevelyan, who must have been standing perilously near where the mast had fallen, but I could not see him. I felt a tug on my arm.

'Yes?'

It was the bosun, blood streaming from his cheek where a six-inch splinter had pierced it. He had to repeat himself twice before I could understand him.

'What now, sir?'

'What do you mean?' I looked around in desperation. 'I am not in command here. Where is Captain Trevelyan?'

He pointed to the fallen sail. 'Under there.'

'The mate?'

'Dead, sir.'

I grabbed him by the arm and shook him. A fresh trail of blood oozed from his cheek. 'Then you are in command, Bosun.'

He shrank away. 'Not me, sir. I'm not an officer. I ain't never been in a sea fight before – I'd not know where to start with somethin' like this.' He nodded towards the enemy, whose guns had fallen ominously quiet. 'You was at Trafalgar.'

How he expected that to help I cannot guess: even if I had been at my station at Trafalgar, commanding a battery on the lower gun-deck of a ninety-eight was nothing comparable to this mismatched duel. But there was no gain in indecision. If nothing else, we would need someone in command to surrender the ship.

'Very well. Get your men working to clear the mizzen. We can achieve nothing until the helm is clear. You two' – I pointed to Fothergill and Kittering who were standing by the main hatch – 'take Trevelyan below to the surgeon and see what may be done for him.'

Though I held no commission, and though I doubted my command of the *Adventure* would last above quarter of an hour, the eagerness with which the men jumped to obey was astonishing. Even the bosun, who had quailed at the thought of captaining the ship, was all brisk efficiency as he marshalled the men on the stern. Not that I expected it to avail us much.

I crossed to the larboard side and looked out. I could see immediately why we had gained respite from the Spaniard's guns: our courses had diverged so that we were almost at right angles to each other, like two arms of a compass. It was the mizzen, I realized. Hanging off our hull on the leeward quarter, it was dragging in the water, acting as a pivot and turning our bow downwind, away from the enemy. So abrupt had been its effect that the Spaniard had not had time to alter course, but had been carried some distance beyond us. Now, though, she was moving, and what little relief I had felt vanished in an instant. She was not following our course to stay broadside on, but instead turning upwind, tacking about. In a few minutes she would cross our unprotected stern and rake us to pieces, while with the mizzen still bound to our hull we would be anchored in place.

'Here, sir.' It was Fothergill. His shirt was covered in blood, but it must have been Trevelyan's blood, for he was unharmed. He was pressing something into my hand. 'I thought you could use it, sir.'

It was Trevelyan's sword, the handle still wet with his blood. I took it with a nod of thanks, though I doubted what I would use it for. Perhaps to cut down the colours and offer the enemy captain my surrender.

I looked back across to the Spaniard. For the moment, she was pointing away from us, a quarter-mile off our larboard quarter, but as soon as her bow came through the wind we would be lost.

'Stand clear!'

The crew at the stern ran forward as, with a heavy grumbling, the mizzen topmast came free of the ship. It slid over the side, dragging a tangle of fractured spars and tackle after it, and splashed down into the water. The effect was immediate: freed of the encumbrance, the *Adventure* began to press forward under the following wind.

'Good work, Bosun,' I said. *Probably futile*, I did not add. The Spaniard was still coming about behind us, though she had slowed somewhat. Her main course was flapping about uncertainly, and one of her topsails seemed to be braced backwards. I doubted it would offer much relief.

'What now, sir?'

I looked blankly at the bosun. The only answer in my mind was that we should strike, save ourselves while we could before the Spaniard tore us apart. I had no business commanding the *Adventure*, and there would be no dishonour in surrender. And yet . . . Surrounded by her expectant crew I could not bring myself to give the order. Ten minutes earlier, with the last broadside ringing in their ears and their captain felled, they would gladly have embraced defeat. Now, I sensed, they wanted one last effort to prove they had given their all. It would be a long spell in the Spanish gaol if they did not believe that.

If I could not surrender, I would do the next best thing. 'Get the men aloft,' I told the bosun. In his delusion that we were a ship-of-the-line, Trevelyan had taken us into battle with all but the topsails reefed. 'I want every scrap of sail she'll carry, as fast as you can.'

'Who'll tend the guns?'

I looked at our larboard battery. The gun which had broken free was now lashed impotent against the far side; another's carriage sagged against the deck where its axle had broken. Only three remained intact.

'Those guns won't save us now.' Not that they ever would have. 'Get aloft, while we still have masts to climb.'

They might not have distinguished themselves as gunners, but Captain Trevelyan's crew were deft seamen. The topmen had the gaskets off the mainsail in moments, while the men on deck hauled on the clewlines. The canvas bucked and billowed in the wind, then swelled out as the *Adventure* began to gain momentum. Even so, I could not believe it would save us. If we escaped the range of the Spaniard's raking broadside we would still be downwind of her, and without our mizzen we would never outrun her. At best, we were only delaying our doom.

'Captain! Captain Jerrold, sir!'

Surprised by the unfamiliar title, I turned around. The gunner was standing at the larboard rail, pointing back to the Spaniard with a disbelieving grin spreading over his face. She was not moving. Her bow pointed clean into the eye of the wind, and her sails were blowing angrily into the masts. It almost looked as though she was moving backwards.

'She's in irons.'

There was a look of wonder in the gunner's eyes. With the wind dead ahead, the Spanish ship had lost all steerage way and could not move.

A surge of excitement gripped me – excitement, spurred by a clutching fear that the moment would pass and that we would fail to grasp the opportunity. If we could not take advantage of her distress to cripple her now she would quickly come around and pound us into pieces.

'Down with the helm,' I called. 'Keep her on the beam, not too close to the wind. Bosun, get the yards braced round. You' – I pointed to the gunner, aware that I did not know a single man's name – 'load the larboard battery. If you can borrow a couple of the starboard cannon, so much the better.'

The *Adventure* came around. With her mizzen reduced to a stump she had become more unstable, her movements sharp and ungainly, yet she seemed to come up to the wind more quickly than before. Even so, it felt an eternity that I watched her bow swinging about, the bosun bracing the yards to our new tack and the gun crew man-handling the cannon into position. I kept darting glances towards our enemy, convinced I would see her freed from her straits and ready to pour a broadside into us. But though she had men frantically working the sails, she did not move. Inch by inch, we edged across her stern.

'Aim low, and plumb down the middle,' I reminded the gunner. 'Make every shot count.'

'Aye, sir.' He knuckled his forehead, and squatted by the first cannon, pushing the quoin in almost as far as it would go to depress the barrel, and muttering instructions to the men with handspikes beside him. 'There she goes, nice an' steady. Right a touch. There.'

'You may fire at will,' I told him, superfluously.

The *Adventure* was moving steadily now, her sails full and her pitch even. The clouds had scattered, punching ragged blue holes in the sky, and the pale sun gave an almost spring-like touch to the ship. It felt most incongruous to be standing there with the smell of powder still in my nose, and blood splashed across the deck. At long last, the Spaniard had begun to make some headway out of the wind, but it was too late. Our bow went past her stern – I could see her name now, the *Bernal Diaz* – then our foremast, and then our first gun.

'Fire!'

For the last time that day, the sea echoed to the roar of gunfire. It rippled slowly along our deck like a sombre drumbeat as, each in turn, the four cannon we could bring to bear came even with her stern post. The gunner ran from gun to gun, pausing only to check the sighting and jerk the lanyard, and a quarter of a mile away the Spaniard's stern was pulverized.

'Look at her wheel,' I ordered the bosun, who stood beside me with a telescope trained on the enemy. 'Are they turning it?'

He chuckled. 'Aye.'

'And the rudder – is it moving?'

He paused, long enough that I almost snatched the glass from his eye to see for myself. If we had missed her steerage fittings she might yet get under way and catch us.

'Dead in her gudgeons, sir.'

Whatever vital force had sustained me to that point drained away in an instant, and I felt only an overwhelming need to lie down. My legs sagged under me, and I became aware that my throat was achingly dry. Even my eyes no longer seemed so steady.

'Well done,' I said. It was the most I could manage without giving my stomach the opportunity to empty itself.

There was one more surprise that day. As I went below to see how Captain Trevelyan fared, I heard the men on the foredeck cheering. I paused on the ladder while I struggled to make out the words.

'Huzzah! Huzzah for Captain Jerrold!'

6

WITH THE DAMAGE WE HAD SUFFERED, OUR PASSAGE NORTH WAS
slow, but we did not meet the Spaniard again. Aboard the *Adventure*
I basked in my newly won reputation. My health was toasted from
the fo'c'sle to the captain's cabin; we held a service of thanksgiving
on the maindeck, and Miss Lyell pronounced it a triumph to
rank with Trafalgar. Even Trevelyan, who had lost the lower half
of his right leg crushed under the mizzen, shook my hand from
his bed and admitted he'd misjudged me. Amid all the euphoria, it
would have been churlish to remind them that my principal
contribution to the battle had been the leaving of it as sharp as
possible.

Lyell seemed particularly pleased. I had not seen him on deck
during the fight, but afterwards he congratulated me warmly for my
resolve. 'I confess, Lieutenant, I had wondered whether you were
the man for our task, but I see now that you possess all the virtues
we require.'

There was something curious in his use of the present tense – I
hoped he did not anticipate my virtues would be required again –
but I did not dwell on it. 'Our victory owes as much to you,' I said
graciously. 'If you had not persuaded the men to fight, all our efforts
would have availed nothing.'

'They jumped soon enough when they saw the colour of my gold,' he agreed.

'But not just the gold, surely? Your appeal to their honour, to defend your daughter, swayed them just as much. When they saw how you valued her I doubt there was a man among them who did not feel himself shamed.' Actually, I suspected the gold had played the greater part, but I was in a mood to flatter Lyell – and assure him of my regard for his daughter.

Unfortunately it did not have the effect I intended. 'What are you talking about? I made no mention of my daughter.'

'The cargo of immense value you spoke of. Surely you meant . . . ?'

Lyell gave a cruel smirk. 'If they chose to believe that I would offer almost two thousand pounds because I worried for my daughter, then so be it. Evidently the credulity of our simple sailors is not exaggerated. But you and I both know, Lieutenant, that there is only one reward worth the hazards of war. Gold.'

He chuckled to himself, shivering the rolls of fat around his neck, and ambled away.

We sailed into New York under blue skies. It was early November, and the air was cold. As the pilot took us past the curve of Sandy Hook and up through the narrows, the shores were emblazoned with a forest of colours, every hue of the autumnal palette. In between the trees I saw houses, elegant two-storeyed mansions whose gardens ran down to the water. It was my first glimpse of the New World, but my curiosity was tempered by considerable anxiety. In the two weeks since the battle I had been able to forget the errand which had brought me aboard the *Adventure*, and given no thought to how it would unfold once I reached America. I had enjoyed my heroic reputation, and even forgotten to worry about the package under my bed. Now I was confronted with inescapable reality. I did not know how I would get to Pittsburgh, nor even where I might find it – somewhere west, I thought vaguely.

Fortunately, there were others who took an interest in my accommodation.

'Where will you be staying, Lieutenant?' Miss Lyell asked me. We were standing near the *Adventure*'s bow, watching the rocky banks of the waterway glide past.

'I have not settled on anywhere.'

'Then you must come with us.'

'Oh.' Her direct invitation took me aback, though I could not deny I would enjoy continuing her acquaintance. 'How about your father?'

'But he will be delighted, and very much relieved that you are to accompany us. The streets of New York are not so safe, you know, for innocents abroad.'

I doubted any of us could lay much claim to innocence, and doubly doubted that my presence would do anything to protect it. Quite the reverse, I hoped, where Miss Lyell was concerned.

'It would be my pleasure.'

Though a relative infant among cities, New York had already enjoyed a prodigious growth, and exhibited a maturity which many more venerable cousins would have envied. A handsome aspect presented itself as we crawled up the East River: stout, redbrick warehouses lined the foreshore, with a host of ships in the slips before them, while the roofs which crowded behind seemed to stretch back for miles, to a thickly wooded escarpment filling the horizon. A pleasant array of cupolas and spires rose above, investing the whole with a sober dignity.

That good impression did not last long. As we approached our slip the babble of the city began to drift out across the water, and by the time we had edged our hull against the wharf it was an all-consuming cacophony. Stevedores and wharfingers thronged the dockside bellowing offers of work, though I was surprised they wanted for labour: every available scrap of ground was crammed with bales of cotton and wool, hogsheads of sugar, barrels of salt provisions, casks of rum, and a hundred other wares in their various crates and cases. It might have been the East India docks in

London, or the Isfahan bazaar, rather than the provincial harbour of an erstwhile colony.

I confess I found the scene, with its frantic hubbub and bustle, a touch overwhelming. Lyell, by contrast, seemed to drink it in like *eau de vie*.

'Look at it,' he exclaimed, sweeping his arm across the vista. 'Tell me what you see, Lieutenant.'

At that moment, my eye was actually resting on the powdered bosoms of a pair of prostitutes. I tried to elevate my gaze and respond positively. 'Trade?'

A ham-like fist thumped onto the larboard rail. 'Precisely. Trade and commerce – the fruits of our colonies married to the product of our industry. That is not America's wealth before you but Britain's: rum and sugar from our West Indian islands, yarns for the looms of our great mills, food for the ships which master the oceans. And in return, as much steel, cloth and glass as Birmingham and Manchester can manufacture.'

The sight of a man in a blue coat climbing over the side stemmed his discourse. He scowled. 'A shame that we must suffer governments to diminish the business of profit.' He turned to greet the new arrival, lifting his hat in an unconvincing attempt at civility. 'Good day, sir. You are come from the Customs House, I take it.'

The visitor gave a brisk nod. 'Captain Trevelyan tells me you have some cargo aboard.'

'A few boxes in the lazaret.'

The customs agent opened the ledger he had tucked under his arm, and pulled a pencil from his pocket. 'How many boxes?'

'Eight.'

'And what are the goods?'

'Tea.'

The agent stopped writing, and looked up in surprise. 'Tea? In the lazaret? That must be an uncommon valuable blend.'

'Not terribly valuable,' said Lyell, all nonchalance. 'Though I dare say that an enterprising man might turn it to profit if he had a mind. Perhaps you would like to come and inspect it.'

He led the agent below, while I went to my cabin and ensured that I had packed all my effects into my chest. When I had locked it, I snaked my arm under the bed and pulled out my packet. The brown oilcloth and the knotted twine were all as I had left them, though the writing had faded during the weeks at sea. The wax seals glinted in the light, flashing up at me like eyes, and I hurriedly thrust it in my pocket. Then I stole upstairs before Fothergill could find me. I did not know whom he served, and I had no proof that he was anything more than a steward. But I had not forgotten him rummaging in my drawer just before we encountered the Spanish privateer, and he seemed to have an uncomfortable knack for appearing whenever the packet was in my hands.

Lyell and the customs agent had emerged from the lazaret when I regained the deck. Whatever the agent had found must have satisfied him, for his manner had softened and he was all smiles and handshakes. Only his blue coat seemed to have come off the worse, hanging askew where a bulging burden in the right pocket dragged it down. Beneath his contented gaze, a chain of sailors were hauling Lyell's strongboxes up through the hatch and onto the pier.

'A pleasure to do business with you, sir,' the agent was saying. 'If you ever have more goods you need to bring in, just send word to me at the Customs House and I'll see to it myself.'

'Excellent.' Lyell pumped the agent's hand, then bid him good-bye and ambled across the deck to me. 'Whenever you are ready, Lieutenant. I have given instructions for our baggage to be taken direct to our lodgings. They are not far.'

Over his shoulder, I could see a train of porters carrying the strongboxes across the bustling street and through the front door of one of the lofty warehouses. A wooden sign proclaimed it as the premises of the Phoenix Company of London, and was decorated with the image of a bird soaring upwards, and the Latin motto *Ex Flammis Fructus* – 'Bounty from the Flames'. But I was not interested in the warehouse; I was staring at the strongboxes. Their sides were painted with the word TEA in fresh black letters, and below the label each bore the large stamp of a flowering, curlicued letter 'A'.

I knew the design. It was the same as I had gazed on any number of times, pressed into the wax which sealed my package. And now that I looked closer, the emblem of the Phoenix Company of London seemed remarkably like the package's second seal, the bird I had taken for a dove.

I felt a hand on my shoulder.

'Come,' said Lyell. 'We had best be about our business.'

I climbed down the *Adventure*'s ladder and stepped into the New World.

7

A SHORT WALK ALONG THE WATERFRONT AND A BRIEF TURN INLAND brought us to our hotel almost immediately. I could see why Lyell had chosen it: if his avaricious soul could conceive of a New World paradise, this one street, Wall Street, must be it. Banks and insurers jostled with one another in their broad-shouldered buildings, while merchants and factors and exchanges squeezed between them. Nor was commerce confined to the privacy of the great houses: even outdoors, auctioneers who could afford no better raised themselves on puncheons of rum or bales of cotton and conducted their business with the crowds who flocked around them. Cries of 'Another cent' and 'Once, twice' filled the air, until I began to wonder whether the whole city itself would not change hands if a man tipped his hat at the right moment.

Having pushed through the tumult in a fever of confusion, I was eager to gain the sanctuary of our lodgings, but in this I was disappointed. From the outside, the Tontine Tavern looked more like a bank than a hotel: a fine brick building with narrow windows, fronted with a portico and surmounted by an imposing pediment. Steps led up from the road to its elevated front door, but as we stepped inside, far from escaping the noise, we actually increased it. The front room was packed with sober-suited gentlemen all talking and clamouring and waving papers in the air in a host of conversations and transactions. At first they were too rapt in their business to notice our arrival, but as first one and then others caught sight of Lyell they swarmed to speak with him. His daughter and I were pushed aside as a circle formed, and a hundred questions assailed him.

'Have they reversed the *Essex* judgement?'

'What news of Madison and Pinkney?'

'Does Fox still live?'

'Is there to be an embargo?'

Doubtless a thousand fortunes rested on the answers to those questions, but they might as well have enquired after the state of the moon for all I knew. I drifted away, wondering what strange manner of hotel Lyell had brought me to, and whether the roar of commerce would subside or continue unabated through the night.

As I edged through the crowd, a small man in round glasses snatched at my arm. Without introduction he asked, 'Are you arrived from London?'

I nodded dumbly.

'Tell me, how is the price of tobacco there? Up or down?'

'Up?' It was as much a question as a statement – I neither knew nor cared – but it seemed to please him enormously. He gave my hand a vigorous shake; then, as abruptly as he had approached, he scurried away shouting he would have a hundred shares of Virginia at eight and two bits.

Miss Lyell had vanished somewhere in the mêlée. Left alone, I found a servant hovering by the wall and established, counter to my every impression, that there was indeed lodging to be had, on the upper floors. I mentioned Lyell's name, and was immediately led up three flights of stairs to a comfortable, well-proportioned room with a bed in the corner and a sash window looking out over the rooftops of New York. I threw my coat over a chair and sat back on the bed.

I was in a new city, a new country – a new side of the world, even – but those cares were nothing against the designs I had seen on

Lyell's chests. Two men on the same boat bound for the same port bearing cargoes under the same seal did not admit to happenstance. So far as I could see, that allowed only one explanation: Lyell was in league with whoever had sent Lieutenant Beauchamp's letter, the very conspirators whom Nevell – and, apparently, I myself – were supposed to thwart. That made him liable to know a great deal more about the scheme than I did; the longer I spent in his company, the more likely I was to betray my ignorance. I did not like to think what would befall me if he discovered my deception.

I was sorely tempted to abandon my mission altogether, to jump back on board the *Adventure* and sail home. But I doubted Nevell would forgive such a craven abdication, and he was one of the few friends I could trust in England.

No. I would take the first coach to Pittsburgh next morning and hope that Lyell's part in the business took him no further than New York. If he remarked at my undue haste, he could always ascribe it to enthusiasm.

A knock at the door rapped into my thoughts and I almost leaped off the bed. In the midst of such gloomy and fearful contemplation I could not bring myself to answer it. I sat still, straining my ears against the silence, and wished I had locked the door.

The knock came again and still I waited, unmoving. I thought I saw the handle begin to turn and cursed myself for not locking it, but almost as quickly it eased back into position and I heard footsteps padding away down the corridor. It might easily have been a porter with my chest, or Miss Lyell establishing my whereabouts, but I could not stop myself from trembling long after the sounds had died away.

I did not leave my room again that day. I dined in solitude, and when Miss Lyell called to ask if I would join them in the coffee house I pleaded illness. The commercial noises from below subsided at two o'clock, so suddenly that it must have been a customary arrangement. The sounds from the street, by contrast, did not die down until very much later; even after nightfall I could hear the clatter of carriages and the shouts of hawkers, the general hubbub which seemed to attend the city's inhabitants wherever they gathered. It was not one tenth the size of London, yet already its boisterous spirits were her equal.

The next morning, I slipped out of the coffee house before the Lyells were about and, upon enquiry at a reading room, learned that the most direct road to Pittsburgh would begin with a journey to Philadelphia; furthermore, that the stage coach would leave from Fraunces' Tavern at the junction of Pearl and Broad Streets. Unfortunately, by the time I had walked the half-mile to reach it through streets crowded with dray-carts, barrows and carriages, the coach had departed.

'She'll leave again tomorrow,' the ostler told me. 'Seven in the morning.'

That left me another day to lie idle in the city – another day in which I risked betraying myself to Lyell should I meet him. I could not sit in the hotel all day for he would surely find me there. I would have to stay abroad on the streets, and steal back late at night. It was not a happy prospect.

At least, though, there was plenty to see. From the tavern, I walked past the bridewell and an almshouse and turned onto an elegant thoroughfare which they called the Broadway. The houses here were tall and gracious, not unlike the fashionable terraces of London, though of red brick rather than yellow. The footways were paved with a similar brick, and planted with lofty poplars which doubtless gave a welcome shade in the summer. The sun was out and the sky an impeccable blue, though the November air was crisp on my cheeks. For a time I was able to forget my cares as I admired the trades on display – jewellers, hatters, milliners, drapers, pastry-cooks – and the finely dressed women who patronized them.

Unaccountably, I found my thoughts turning to Isobel. Perhaps it was the memories of walking down the Strand with her in London and seeing her delight; perhaps it was the stirrings I felt seeing so many *embonpoints* precariously covered by light French silks and crêpes. Whatever the cause, it was a welcome distraction from my

71

more immediate concerns. What was Isobel doing now, I wondered? Would she have stayed in London? I doubt she would have returned to her native Dover, for she had no home there save the poorhouse, and enemies who would not welcome her back. Had she found another man? Though I no longer had any claim on her affections, the prospect troubled me. She had wanted me to marry her, after all – it would be a rank betrayal to forget me so quickly.

For a moment, I had almost found myself wishing her present with me there, soothing my fears and offering her commonsense advice, but the thought of her dancing around London with some upstart dandy on her arm quelled that desire instantly. Still, I could show her my generosity of spirit, demonstrate that I harboured no grudge. The gleam of a jeweller's window caught my eye as I walked past, and on impulse I broke my stride and stepped in. A pair of golden earrings seemed a suitable present: a souvenir of my visit to America and a signifier of my enduring fondness for her. The jeweller wrapped them in paper for me, and took my guineas without any quibble.

As I continued down the Broadway the shops began to give way to houses. The buildings were older in this part of the city, some of them still bearing the steep, step-gabled roofs of the Dutchmen who had first settled Manhattan. Off the main thoroughfare, the streets were pinched closer together, and the houses built of timber. It seemed a strange contrast, a remnant of a pioneering settlement in the midst of the otherwise modern city.

Beyond the end of the Broadway, the island tapered to the point past which we had sailed the previous morning. There was a battery here to guard the approach, but the greater part of the ground had been laid out as a park. Long avenues of elms and oaks led on to fine views over the harbour, while children played cricket on the lawns.

'Lieutenant Jerrold!'

The voice surprised me, though I knew it even before I had turned to see her. Miss Lyell was standing on the gravel walk in a close-fitting green dress, with a spencer over her shoulders and a smart beaver hat cocked atop her golden curls. She did not appear to be chaperoned.

'How do you do?' If my manner was a touch stiff after two months' close companionship at sea, it was because I had hoped to avoid her and her father entirely. Though now that we had met, I could not deny a certain uncomfortable pleasure at her presence.

'How do you find the city?' I asked.

She slid her arm into mine and started forward, drawing me after her. We were almost at the end of the path, where the gentle park ended in a rocky embankment and the confluence of the two rivers with the sea.

'It is a little dull, don't you think?'

'You prefer London?'

'London is very fine, I grant you, but it wears on me. The society there can be so . . . inflexible. Papa spends all his time at the bank, or in his clubs and coffee houses; we do not entertain very much. I am glad to see more of the world.' She squeezed my arm.

'And how long will you stay in New York?' The question was of more than casual interest to me.

'Another day or two, I collect. Papa insists that he must make some journey to the interior of the continent soon, though I fear it will be a great hardship if winter approaches.'

I felt my spirits circling ever lower. 'Whereabouts into the interior?'

'A settlement called Pittsburgh,' she said with disdain. 'No doubt it will consist of a log hut and three wigwams, and be populated with the most tedious savages.'

It was the answer I had feared. For a moment, I did not know what to say, whether to admit it as my own destination or feign ignorance. Miss Lyell removed the matter from my hands. 'But of course you will see it for yourself. Papa tells me that you are bound there also – is it not a curious coincidence? – and you will accompany us on the journey. I think he is much relieved that he will have a stalwart hero to defend him – as I am.'

She stopped and gazed up at me. She had reached back a hand to keep the hat from sliding off, so that her spencer fell open and her breasts pressed forward towards me. With the sun gilding her ivory complexion and the emerald pendant gleaming at her throat, her beauty was irresistible.

The breeze filled my senses with the sticky salt air of the harbour and I leaned forward to kiss her. My lips touched hers, then glided over her cheek as she ducked gracefully aside and pressed a quick kiss behind my ear. She stepped back.

'You presume too much, Lieutenant,' she rebuked me. A strand of hair had fallen down over her face, and her breathing was agitated. 'I am not some French ship that you can seize for your prize as the fancy takes you.'

She was playing with me; I could see the mischief in her eyes. 'You must forgive me, Miss Lyell, if I gave offence. *Je ne peux pas résister ton beauté.*'

She teased a finger against my chest. '*Ta beauté.* But I forgive you, Lieutenant. A man should not fear to pursue his desires, though a less *sociable* place might be better suited to it. We must not take our pleasures at the expense of reputation.'

I believed I understood her perfectly. Suddenly, the long journey to the depths of the continent seemed an entirely more agreeable prospect – if we could avoid her father.

On impulse, I reached into my pocket. 'If I cannot give you a kiss, perhaps, for now, I may give you these.' I handed over the jeweller's packet, and she beamed with excitement as she pulled away the paper. 'No doubt they seem a meagre trinket to you. But I hope you will take them as a token of my admiration.'

With an expert hand, she plucked the earrings she wore from her lobes and dropped them into a velvet bag in her reticule. Then, equally deftly, she fastened my gifts in their place.

'They are perfect,' she declared, though of course she could not see them. 'But I hope you do not think this to be sufficient gift.'

She laughed at the confusion evident in my eyes, and lowered her voice to a suggestive whisper. 'I will want more than *token* evidence of your affections presently.'

74

There was a wicked promise in her words, and my face must have betrayed my lascivious thoughts for she laughed at me and spun away. 'For now, we had best return to Papa. He will be expecting us for dinner.'

The streets were busy and hectic as ever as we approached the Tontine Tavern. An auctioneer was knocking down hogsheads of sugar at a furious rate, while opposite a cleric in black was nailing up a broadside denouncing some vice or other. I took Miss Lyell's arm and steered her between the rush of carriages and wagons, taking care to avoid the mounds of dung which steamed in the road. As I looked up, a figure loitering by the tavern steps caught my eye.

'You!' I hailed him, letting go Miss Lyell and stepping towards him. 'A word, if you please.'

He did not please. As soon as he heard my shout he jerked up his head from his hunched shoulders, then turned and hurried away around the corner of the building. Before I could follow, a curricle had blocked my path, and by the time it was past he had vanished.

'Whatever are you doing, Lieutenant?' asked Miss Lyell.

'I thought I saw Fothergill waiting at the tavern.' In fact, I was sure of it. I had had a good glimpse of his face, and he was not a man easily mistaken.

'The steward? But why should he not be there? He will not be required aboard the *Adventure* now, and we are not so far from the docks here.'

All she said was perfectly true, but it did not convince me. I was suddenly anxious to return to my room.

'I will join you in the dining room,' I told Miss Lyell.

Even before I reached the room I could see that something was wrong. Light was shining into the corridor from my doorway, though I was certain I had left it locked. I ran the last few yards and saw the splintered timber around the lock where the door had been prised open.

The room was in chaos. The bed had been overturned and the

75

mattress hacked apart with a knife, so that its horsehair intestines bulged out of the wounds. A similar fate had befallen the seat of the chair, while the contents of my chest were strewn across the floor. They had even taken an axe to the chest itself: a fractured hole gaped where they had chopped through the bottom.

As I gazed on the ruin with disbelieving horror, I heard heavy footsteps in the hall behind. I turned and saw Lyell in the door. His face was flushed, and his breathing laboured.

'What the devil has happened here?' he bellowed. And then, more quietly, glancing over his shoulder, 'What has become of your package?'

8

I STARED AT HIM. MR LYELL SEEMED TO KNOW A GREAT MANY THINGS
that I had thought secret: the sensitivity of my mission, my
destination at Pittsburgh, and now the very existence of the package
itself. How he came by his knowledge I could not guess – nor
whether it marked him as friend or foe. That mattered nothing.
Lowering in my doorway, his fat eyes trained on me like carronades,
he was irrefusable.

I crossed the room, knelt by the fireplace, and prised up the
hearthstone. The package lay in the hollow beneath, untouched and
undisturbed where I had left it that morning. Reluctantly, I lifted it
out.

'If this was what they wanted, they'll have left empty-handed.'

I sat down on the mutilated bedstead – what would they have
done to me had they found me there, I wondered? – and wrapped
my arms about myself to keep from shivering. Nevell's blithe
assurances that this would be a harmless errand were coming to seem
ever more indefensible. And I feared Mr Lyell now assumed me his
accomplice. How could I escape him without stirring his suspicions?

'I cannot stay in New York a moment longer,' I declared. 'The
threat to my mission is too great.' To say nothing of the threat to my
person.

Lyell stared at me darkly, perhaps weighing my true motives. I blanched under his gaze. 'Naturally this is a dramatic turn of events, but you must have expected it. Our enemies will not sit idly by. You must refrain from hasty judgements, and you will not find a coach to Pittsburgh at this hour. We will leave in the morning.'

I strove to think of some gambit to dissuade him. For once, inspiration came promptly. 'Surely it would be unwise for us to travel together? We should not risk all our eggs in the same basket.'

'Once I would have agreed with you. We should not even have come this far in the same vessel. But now that our enemies have shown their determination, consolidarity is our truest hope. I am a man of commerce, not war – I rely on you, Lieutenant, to guard me.'

If that was his hope, then I might yet be rid of him all too easily. I was about to attempt one last protest but he spoke over me.

'Anyway, you cannot leave this evening. There is a meeting I must attend tonight and I will need your protection.'

At least that might take me away from the hotel, perhaps to the safe surrounds of a bank or a room in a gentleman's club.

'Where is the meeting?'

'In a graveyard.'

We stole out of the hotel like thieves, swathed in our dark greatcoats. It was a cold night, and our breath puffed out in clouds before us, but we did not have far to go. At the far end of Wall Street, past the silent eminences of the great banks and government buildings, we found a towering church spire and an iron gate beside it.

Lyell turned to me. 'Are you armed, Lieutenant?'

My low spirits managed to plumb a still greater depth. 'Should I be?'

Lyell rolled his eyes, not deigning to answer my question.

'The men who ransacked my room took my pistol.'

Lyell reached into the pocket of his greatcoat, withdrew a pistol and handed it to me. Its rare quality was immediately evident. The octagonal barrel seemed almost to aim itself, steady even in my nervous hand, and the trigger felt feather-light under my finger. Moonlight picked out the name etched on the lock. MANTON.

'They tell me nothing kills a man more reliably,' Lyell gloated. 'Not, of course, that I hope to need it.'

He squeezed through the gate, and I followed him into the mournful surrounds of the cemetery. I might almost have imagined myself on some wild moor or desolate heath, for the path wound between humped tussocks and mounds, and high trees grew wild. The gravestones stood like slabs of silver in the moonlight, some remarkably weathered for so young a city.

With mounting terror I followed Lyell. His black vastness was like a cloud before me, a malevolent presence which damped out the moonlight wherever he trod. He led me quickly to a remote corner, and a monument which looked more a mausoleum than a grave: an elevated sarcophagus topped with a stone pyramid, with urns and fluted columns at each corner. It was ominously fresh: no moss discoloured the white marble, and the inscription was sharp from the mason's chisel. I leaned close to read it.

To the memory of Alexander Hamilton

The PATRIOT of incorruptible INTEGRITY
The SOLDIER of approved VALOR
The STATESMAN of consummate WISDOM

I had never heard of this moral prodigy. 'Who was he?'

'The Secretary of the Treasury. He was shot in a duel.'

That did not sound like consummate wisdom to me. 'By whom?'

'The Vice-President of the United States.'

Clearly I had much to learn about the political life of our former colony. Before I could wonder at it, though, I heard the crunch of footsteps on the path behind. I spun about. A man was walking towards us, a black cloak wrapped around his shoulders and a hat shielding his face. I glanced at Lyell. He did not seem alarmed –

indeed, was stepping forward to greet the man – but I put a hand on my pistol just in case.

'Mr Lyell,' said the new arrival. He was an American. 'Welcome to New York.'

'A fine welcome it's been so far. Our enemies have already torn Lieutenant Jerrold's room to pieces trying to find the message he carries.'

The hat turned towards me. 'I guess you weren't in the room at the time?'

'Fortunately not.'

He proffered a hand. 'Sam Ogden.'

'Martin Jerrold.'

'Lieutenant Jerrold represents the naval aspect of our designs,' Lyell explained.

Mr Ogden nodded. 'I was expecting they'd send Beauchamp.'

'Our plans changed at the last minute. Beauchamp was to have sailed on a navy vessel, but our adversaries got wind of it. Then he was to go on a packet, the same as mine. At the last minute Lieutenant Jerrold took his place.' Lyell looked at me keenly. 'We have not had much opportunity to discuss it thus far – I felt it best to mask our connection until we had arrived.'

'Less said, least heard,' Ogden agreed. 'I've heard you had a touch of trouble on your voyage.'

'A Spanish privateer.'

'Do you think she knew your business?'

Lyell shrugged. 'Thankfully, Lieutenant Jerrold crippled her and made good our escape before we could find out.'

'That won't be the last trouble you'll meet, I'd wager. The Spanish already have their agents sniffing about, and the British won't be far behind. You'll likely need that pistol in your pocket before you get to Pittsburgh.'

It is hard to exaggerate the pure misery I felt at that moment. To be in a graveyard in the dark, desperately ignorant of the scheme that had snared me, with two men who would kill me if they learned of my duplicity, was not how I had hoped to spend my time in

America. I leaned against the late Mr Hamilton's tomb, though the knowledge of his fate made it little comfort to me. For a moment I genuinely considered pulling out my pistol and shooting Lyell dead, but I had only one shot and I doubted I would escape Mr Ogden and his associates for long in that unfamiliar city.

Meanwhile, he and Lyell were still talking.

'Have you managed to dispose of my bullion?' Lyell asked.

'The tea you brought from England? That's been up and down Manhattan today more times than a South Street whore. A deposit here, collateral there; finance to underwrite a speculation in the Gennessee somewhere else. I've turned it into more bills, bonds, certificates and stocks than you could imagine. We even turned sixty dollars' profit on a trade in government paper.'

'Mr Hamilton would be delighted,' said Lyell, rapping a fist on the sarcophagus beside him.

Ogden laughed. 'Don't tell the colonel.' Reaching under his cloak, he opened a leather bag and pulled out a sheaf of papers. 'It's all in the bank now, and I'll be hanged if anyone can figure out how it got there, let alone how it got in the country. Here are some cheques and drafts for you to take to the colonel.'

Lyell stuffed them in his pocket. 'Much obliged. You've performed an invaluable service.'

'I'm like you, Mr Lyell – an investor in search of returns.'

'You will find them,' Lyell promised.

'I hope so. Give my regards to the colonel.'

And with that cryptic remark, Mr Ogden vanished into the autumn night. After a discreet interval, Lyell and I followed.

'We should rise early tomorrow,' he told me as we reached the hotel. 'We must be away before our enemies can find us.'

But no matter how early we left, it seemed there was no hope of that for me while I travelled with Mr Lyell.

9

A RAP ON MY DOOR SUMMONED ME BEFORE DAWN. A MIST HAD come down in the night, filling the streets with a dank, sour-smelling fog; it wrapped us so tight we could imagine we were the only ones abroad at that hour. Occasionally we heard shouts, or the rumbling of some distant cart, but otherwise we proceeded through the fog alone: Lyell a dark, mountainous blur before me; his daughter and I behind; and a negro servant wheeling our luggage in a squeaking barrow at the rear. I still had Lyell's pistol in my pocket and I kept a tight grip on it, though the fog had probably damped the priming. If a Spanish assassin came upon us here he would have little difficulty disposing of us unseen.

I had thought we would make for Fraunces' Tavern, but instead Lyell led us directly to the western waterfront, and after brief negotiation engaged a wherry to take us across the river. The city receded into the mist almost as soon as we had pushed off, and we were alone on the water. Miss Lyell, seated on the bench beside me, clutched my arm and huddled close.

I did not wish to impress Lyell with my ignorance, but nor could I enjoy any comfort if I did not know his intentions.

'Where are we going?' I asked. 'The coach leaves from the corner of Broad Street.'

'Which they will almost certainly be watching. We will join it at Paulus Hook, on the New Jersey shore, and pray we have eluded them.'

I did not ask who *they* might be. After that, the only sound was the splash of the oars in the glassy water.

On the far bank of the Hudson, at a mean little town called Paulus Hook, we found an inn where we could breakfast. The hot food warmed my spirits, and the fog began to lift. At last the *Industry* stage rattled into the yard, and soon we were snug in her cabin. Lyell dozed in his corner while Miss Lyell sat opposite me under a morass of shawls and blankets, her head peeking from a vast fur capelet. She affected to read a novel, though she cannot have been very comfortable in it for every five minutes she seemed to be rearranging her posture, which occasioned much brushing together of our legs. Sometimes I would catch her eyes peeking over the cover of her book, and she would hold my gaze with delicious amusement before returning to her reading. For the rest of the time, I stared out of the window, counting the carts we passed and examining the new country.

It was a strange land, neither so pleasantly civilized as England nor so savage as I had expected of this untamed continent. We were never isolated – you could always see the next farm or inn or church spire – but the settlements did not seem deeply rooted in their environs. Beyond the farmlands which had been cleared around each house, thickly grown pine forests swallowed up the landscape, so that the settlements seemed perpetually besieged by nature.

Nor had they achieved much with the establishment of roads. A dreary ceiling of cloud had descended, and the showers which whipped over us every quarter of an hour turned the track to mud. High, unbridged rivers frequently broke our progress, and we would have to huddle in a rotting skiff while the coach was poled across on a scow. The rain seeped into my shirt and down the back of my neck, while black scum from the seats smeared itself over my breeches. It was no small mercy when we pulled into the town of New

Brunswick for lunch, though even that relief was tempered by the discovery that our carriage would go no further. Instead, we were transferred into a cart little more than a hay-wagon, its only condescension to our comfort a flat roof on wooden pillars, and leather curtains which could be rolled down the unboarded sides. We soon discovered that they could not be left up, on account of the prodigious quantity of mud which was admitted, but once they were down we were left to endure almost complete darkness.

Other passengers joined us at New Brunswick: a pair of young men making for their college; a minister returning to his parish; a Philadelphia merchant and a colleague from Connecticut; and a well-dressed, dark-skinned gentleman who said nothing, but kept his own counsel on the end of the bench. I could see little of him save his eyes, which gleamed even in the gloom, but as the miles shook and rattled under our wheels I became convinced he was watching me. I put my hand to my pocket, reassuring myself that the package and the pistol were still safe, and when I risked a sideways glance at him again his gaze had moved on.

It was late afternoon, our last stage of the day, when he sought my conversation. I was staring into space, drained by the exertions of fighting the bucking coach and hungry from the early hour at which the Americans dined, when I saw him gazing at me, clearly expecting an answer to a question I had not heard.

'I beg your pardon. My thoughts were elsewhere.'

'I have asked: are you an Englishman?'

'Yes.' I spoke guardedly, for there was an accent to him which was neither English nor American, but seemed to hail from the Continent.

'Then we are at war.' He smiled as he said it, baring a row of white teeth in the darkness. It was not what I anticipated, nor what I wished to hear from my travelling companions. It must have shown in my face, for he laughed softly. 'I am from Spain. José Vidal, at your service.'

I did not give him my own name; he did not seem to need it. But we had been overheard. One of the students sitting beside us, a broad-shouldered fellow with a cocksure bearing far in advance of his years, took it upon himself to intervene.

'I overheard your remarks just now, and I'll warn you straight: we don't hold with all your old world quarrelling over here. Amity to all and entangling alliances with no-one, that's our way. You could learn from us.'

I was tempted to cuff the boy for his earnest priggery – without England's might protecting their precious trade, the Americans would have found it a deal more trouble building their self-righteous paradise of wealth and liberty. But the silver-tongued Mr Vidal was all mollification.

'We can learn much. Here in America, English and Spanish are peaceful together, yes, Mr Jerrold?'

'Say, that's more like it,' beamed the American. 'Why don't you shake hands on it?'

Mr Vidal's hand was already hovering in the gulf between us. With the utmost reluctance, I reached across and met it. I barely intended to touch, but he gripped me like a vice, far harder than was courteous, and did not release me for some moments. As he did, his nails scraped across my wrist like claws.

For all that, I had a greater concern. 'How did you know my name? Are we already acquainted?'

'Perhaps. I have spent some time in London recently. But I think not.' Again that smile. 'I heard your wife call it to you.'

Miss Lyell, seated beside me, burst into laughter. 'You see how attentive you have been to me, Mr Jerrold? You have quite convinced this poor little Spanish gentleman that we are married. Is that not charming?' She pinched my arm. 'You must be more measured in your affections, or we will scandalize our companions.'

'We are merely travelling together,' I explained.

'Though we really might as well be married. Travelling in these extremities must be a far greater intimacy than marriage, I always think.' Miss Lyell's leg squeezed against my own.

Vidal raised a pencil-thin eyebrow. 'You travel alone together. Is that permitted in England?' He was suddenly leaning forward, staring at Miss Lyell with such candid appetite that it seemed his eyes alone might unlace her stays. She wriggled a little in her seat, and though she affected to speak lightly I could sense Vidal had agitated her.

'There is no impropriety. My father is with us.' She indicated him, sitting stony-faced at the end of the coach. 'He will see that I am not seduced by foreign desperadoes on our travels.'

'And where do you travel?'

'Philadelphia,' I said quickly. I knew nothing about this Mr Vidal, but he inspired deep anxiety, and it seemed prudent to hide our ultimate destination from him.

'Do you have business there?'

'Our business is our own.'

I had spoken so brusquely that I half expected the fraternally minded American to protest. But before he could rebuke me, our conversation broke off as my side of the cart bounced into the air. I was flung from my seat and found myself lying on the mud-streaked floorboards, with the ground rushing past between the cracks below and an overbearing weight pressing on my back. The driver naturally saw nothing of this and did not flag his jolting pace one whit, so it was some time before we had extricated ourselves from our tangle. As I regained the bench, I patted my pocket to ensure that the package was safe.

The pocket was empty.

I fell back to the floor, scrabbling about in the darkness amid the mud and the boots. There were murmurs of astonishment above my head, and several hands reached in to haul me back, perhaps thinking I had again been pitched off my seat. I shrugged them away. There was no thought to my actions, no reason – only a desperate compulsion to find what had been lost. Once, in battle, I had seen a sailor's arm carried clean away by a cannonball, and watched in horror as he ploughed through the carnage on deck seeking the missing limb. In my frenzy to find the package I was hardly more moderate. And the consequences if it were gone would be almost as ruinous. Could it have fallen through the cracks in the floor and even now lie disintegrating in some muddy puddle a quarter of a mile back?

As my eyes began to master the darkness I became aware of a pair of gleaming riding boots before my face. I looked up, beyond the crimson velvet breeches and coat, and saw Vidal's moustachioed face peering down on me like a master at a disorderly hound. About him, the other passengers looked curiously at my antics.

'There was a package in my pocket. It must have fallen out when we hit that rut. Has anybody seen it?'

Half a dozen heads shook helplessly in the gloom. At the far end, where Lyell sat, I heard a hiss of breath. I did not dare turn to meet his anger. Vidal's face lowered over me in triumph.

'But this is absurd,' said Miss Lyell. 'Mr Vidal picked up your package – I saw him myself.'

I got to my feet and sat down on the bench, leaning forward to look Vidal close in the eye. 'Is that true, Mr Vidal?'

For a moment we were locked in silent contest. The fingers of his right hand twitched towards his belt, where something bulged from his hip, while his eyes darted left and right. I could almost see his mind calculating the odds; had he been nearer the rear of the cart, I think he would have leaped down and run. As it was, hemmed in by the other passengers, he could not move, while I kept my own hand thrust prominently inside my coat pocket.

'I pick it up to keep safe. You take.'

He reached inside his coat. My hand twitched and he shot me a disdainful look, then pulled out the familiar package. The seals were unbroken and the cords still tied. The relief flooding through me was so great that I almost dropped it as I took it.

With the little charade past, the other passengers turned back to their own affairs. Vidal, though, still leaned across the cart, staring at me.

'I hope you will deliver it safe to M'Culloch's inn at Pittsburgh,' he said softly. 'There are many dangers on the way. Anything can happen.'

*

We halted for the night at Princeton, a mean little town chiefly noted for having hosted a battle during the war of the rebellion. It possessed little more than an inn and a seminary, though that at least was an improvement on its namesake in Devon, which possessed only an inn and a prison. Fortunately the staging-house was more comfortable than I had expected, and I was able to procure myself a private room with a proper bed and sheets. The thought of sharing quarters with Vidal, or, almost worse, having to bundle in a communal bed with Lyell, was too terrible for my battered constitution.

Exhausted from the ceaseless travelling, I fell into bed early. But by some perversity of my nature, or perhaps the frailty of my nerves, I could not sleep. I lay there for what seemed hours, rolling over in my bed, pulling on extra blankets and discarding them, trying to conjure innocent, soporific thoughts when my mind insisted on ceaseless activity. Lyell and Vidal, Nevell and his damned secrets, the Spanish broadside opening up on us, and a New York graveyard in the dead of night combined with the endless miles of rutted turnpike and weatherboard houses. Above all there was the package preying on my cares: unknowable, yet all-consuming.

Eventually, I must have fallen into a half sleep. Unreined, my thoughts took on new and improbable life: I found myself running down a muddy track pursuing Miss Lyell as she waved the package in the air, taunting me with it. Her dress billowed behind her, always just beyond my reach.

The road turned into a corridor, and Miss Lyell slowed. She had come up against a door in the far end, and was frantically trying to open it. I could hear the clatter as she fought with the latch, and the rasp as it lifted.

I sat up in bed. The rasping was not confined to my dream – it was sounding from the bedroom door. In the moonlight which streamed through the gauze curtains I could see the latch come free and the door edge ajar. An orange arc of candlelight opened into the room – a crack at first, then ever wider. I reached down to the floor beside my bed and grabbed the Manton pistol, training it on the door with trembling hands.

'Mr Jerrold?'

Miss Lyell's voice was urgent, yet such was my confusion that I did not answer immediately. Still uncertain that it was not part of my dream, I laid aside the pistol, and as she stepped through the door I crossed to meet her. Almost before she could put down the candle I had pulled her close to me; I forced her mouth open with my own, thrilling at her moan of pleasure, while my fingers dug into the soft flesh of her breasts. Spinning her round, I guided her back towards the bed, and as I did so our lips pulled apart.

'*Martin*,' she hissed, and I was so surprised by the use of my Christian name that my hands dropped away. 'You are mistaken.'

A crushing wave of mortification broke over me, chased quickly back by angry disappointment. Though now that I looked at her closely, I could see that she had not dressed for seduction: instead of a chemise or petticoat she wore a dark riding dress with a fur-trimmed cloak over her shoulders. Standing there in my nightshirt, my intentions all too evident, I felt not a little ridiculous.

I heard an unmistakable heavy tread in the corridor and flopped onto the bed. Lyell's silhouette filled the door like some spectre of the Apocalypse.

'Catherine has roused you, has she? Then dress yourself and join us in the stable yard. Leave your chest – I have arranged for a wagon to bring it to Pittsburgh – and take only what you may fit in a saddlebag. And your package, of course. You have that gun I gave you?'

I nodded dumbly. Miss Lyell followed her father downstairs and I pulled on my clothes as fast as I could. As to what was happening, I did not even attempt to comprehend it. I felt as though I were standing on a ship in a storm, with all the cannon cut loose and careering about the deck; simply to avoid mortal harm sufficed me for the moment.

The Lyells were waiting in the stable yard with one of the ostlers. He looked as befuddled as I did, but had managed to saddle a trio of horses and lead them into the yard. There was a black gelding for me, a mare for Miss Lyell, and an enormous carthorse for Lyell. He took even longer than I to mount, kicking at the stirrups and almost strangling the poor beast with the reins. His daughter was more accomplished: she slipped onto her mare with practised ease and was immediately stroking its mane and whispering in its ear. I was startled to see that she did not ride side-saddle, but swung her legs astride the horse like a man. Her skirts rode up, exposing slim, silken calves very white against the mare's dark flanks.

I had little time to admire them. Lyell threw the ostler a coin, growling at him that he should forget all he had seen, and then we were trotting out of the yard and away from the inn. On the outskirts of the town we met a drunken pair of students from the college, singing lewdly as they staggered out of a ditch, but after that we were alone. Even without the encumbrance of Lyell's weight we could not have travelled quickly. Although the rain had stopped, ragged scraps of cloud still blew across the sky tearing rents in the moonlight. Sometimes they hid it altogether, and then we would have to rein in our horses and wait, for we were so far from civilization that the darkness was complete.

'Where are we heading?' I asked Lyell during one of these interludes. We were still on the turnpike, though its autumnal condition left it too treacherous to attempt blind.

'A village called Attleborough.' Lyell had craned his head to look back, though I cannot imagine what he expected to see in the darkness.

'Where is that?'

'Off the main road, which is all that matters. When Mr Vidal finds we are gone in the morning, he will not think to seek us there. I wager he'll make all speed to Philadelphia, which will only waste more of his time.'

I had thought that Philadelphia was our destination, a staging post to Pittsburgh, but clearly Lyell had decided otherwise.

'You fear Mr Vidal so much?'

'He is an agent of Spain – he as near as told it to our faces. I need not remind you what we must fear of the Dons.'

In fact he could not remind me, for I had never known it. Again, my perilous ignorance began to panic me, and I must have conveyed it to my horse for he began to huff and twitch under me.

'You have already allowed him within a hair's breadth of stealing your package,' Lyell continued, 'and he knows we are travelling together. If we tolerate his presence on our journey, he will surely strike again at a time when there are no witnesses in crowded carriages to see him.'

I would rather have trusted my luck to the carriage and the company of our fellow passengers: gallivanting off alone in the dark seemed a sure way to invite disaster, whether at Vidal's hands or from the cutthroats who surely frequented the roads. Besides, Vidal had seen the address on my package. He knew our destination, and could follow us there at speed. But Lyell was not a man to be contradicted, certainly not on a moonless road in the dead of nowhere.

'We could denounce Vidal to the American authorities,' I suggested. 'They would doubtless be sensitive to a Spanish agent in their midst.'

Fortunately, the night kept me from observing Lyell's reaction. The scorn in his voice was sharp enough. 'That is a poor jest indeed, Lieutenant. Denounce Vidal to the Americans? He would denounce us in turn, and we would be ruined. Hah!'

This last interjection was not directed to me, but to his mount, whom he seemed to imagine as some fleet champion rather than a lumbering shire horse. The moon had reappeared, and we were able to continue our journey between the sleeping towns and fields. Perhaps a poet could have hymned their serene beauty, but to me they seemed menacing, a besieging wild where Spanish spies, American bandits, savage Indians, bears, wolves and panthers might lurk in malevolent concert. I hunched low on my horse, gripping the reins as though they suspended me from a precipice, and succumbed to a fog of despair.

Miss Lyell, by contrast, appeared to be in her element. Her golden hair was tied back with a scarf, blowing behind her, but otherwise she wore no cap or bonnet. She sat straight-backed in the saddle, rising and sinking with the rhythms of her mount in a way that was sensuous to behold. With Lyell sitting squat on his plodding beast, we must have made a strange sight to any farmer looking out of his window that night.

After some hours' riding, we crossed a river and passed out of New Jersey into Pennsylvania. Immediately, my spirits lifted. My knowledge of the American geography was meagre at best, an almost completely blank chart, but I knew the name of Pennsylvania. How could I forget it, when it was inscribed like some archaic rune on my package. In Pennsylvania, I would find Pittsburgh; at Pittsburgh, M'Culloch's Inn and its enigmatic occupant, Mr Tyler.

In my former dejection, I had allowed myself to lag behind the others. Now I kicked after them. 'How far to Pittsburgh?' I called to Lyell.

'Three hundred miles.'

We could make that in a week – less, if the roads improved. I trotted up beside Miss Lyell and for the last few miles we amused ourselves staging mock races with each other.

Just before sunrise, we left the southerly road and turned west. The sky was lightening behind us, and the clouds which had obscured our progress in the night now became a canvas on which the sun's pink and orange hues could shine. Before us, though, the land stayed wrapped in darkness as we rode ever deeper into the continent.

10

IF OUR MIDNIGHT RIDE HAD SERVED TO ESCAPE VIDAL, OUR subsequent route gave him little chance to find us. Sometimes it seemed we must have lost even ourselves. Eschewing all but the rudest civilization, and going by roads which could rarely have seen a hoof, let alone a wheel, Lyell led us through the rough farmlands of eastern Pennsylvania. It is as well I never saw a map, or I would doubtless have despaired of our meandering course. Once, when I could see by the sun that we had spent almost a whole afternoon reversing the morning's progress, I complained to Lyell, but he merely muttered something about tacking when the wind was against us. So it was with no small surprise that on the fifth day we came over a hill to see a well-built, elegant town on the slope of the valley opposite. It was by far the most substantial place I had seen since New York: its houses were for the most part of brick and stone, and its streets well paved. Several grand buildings hinted at some civic pre-eminence, while no fewer than seven spires bore witness to the inhabitants' devotion. To me, after days of lone cabins and hamlets, it might almost have been London.

'Lancaster,' said Lyell, when I asked its name. 'We will spend the night here.'

'Surely we would do better to avoid it. So large a town on the westward road must be somewhere our enemies might watch.' I did not like the discomfort and monotony of the country, but I liked the prospect of meeting with Vidal rather less.

'There are reasons.'

Lyell spurred – or rather, prodded – his horse, and we continued into Lancaster. I had expected that the myriad churches might forebode a censorious town, but that was not the case: there must have been a dozen taverns for each church, every one of them thriving. To my surprise, Lyell ignored the more fashionable hostelries near the centre and instead brought us to a mean, crooked building near the outskirts of the town. The company within seemed to consist principally of labourers recently returned from the fields; though five days' riding had left our clothes stained and worn, we were still the most agreeably dressed by some measure. Miss Lyell drew frank stares from all quarters as she entered, and I pressed closer to protect her.

Like most American taverns, privacy was not much on offer, but Lyell managed to find a corner where we could sit away from the common table. There was no wine, so we drank beer, and the landlord's daughter brought a plate of bread and cheese which was wholly inadequate to my appetite. I gobbled down the supper, and was moving to seek an early bed when Lyell laid a hand on my arm.

'Wait.'

He had taken a seat facing the door, and all through the meal his eyes had been darting over my shoulder towards it. I had thought he merely feared thieves, but it now struck me that he had an air of anticipation, waiting.

'Are we expecting company?'

Lyell grunted, and pulled a box of cards from his coat. We played a few hands, though neither of us was concentrating: he watched the door, and I kept wishing we were not there. Miss Lyell won most often, blithely declaring herself blessed by fortune.

In fact, Lyell need not have troubled with such vigilance. When our visitor arrived he might as well have brought a butler to announce him, so plainly did he stand out in the rude company. Our attire had at least been coarsened by our travels; his was fit for a turn on Pall Mall. From the shining buckles on his shoes to the curls of his powdered wig, not one thread, stitch or button was out of place.

The room fell silent.

'I guess he turned the wrong way for the palace,' some wit in the crowd called out. There was widespread laughter, and a group near the stove broke into a chorus of 'The Bonny Beau'.

The visitor straightened his posture and tipped back his head, though he could not keep his cheeks from flushing. Looking neither left nor right he progressed across to our table, and I slumped lower in my chair as I felt the collective gaze of the room turning on us. If Lyell had chosen this hole of a tavern to be inconspicuous, he had sadly misjudged it.

The new arrival took a chair and seated himself, wincing as he did so. All his refinements of manner could not mask the curse of piles. Close to, his features were as precisely measured as his suit; his bearing was stiff, though more from anxiety than pride, and his manner indefatigably correct. His tight-set mouth seemed capable of moving only at the corners. He gave the impression that the least demonstration of feeling would be a grievous personal betrayal.

'This is Mr Merry,' said Lyell, without apparent irony. 'Britain's ambassador to the United States.'

The sombre head seemed to incline a fraction, though it may have been the effect of a swinging lamp. 'Minister plenipotentiary,' Merry sniffed. 'The King does not send ambassadors to *lesser* nations.'

The disdain in his voice was evident. If he was responsible for our diplomacy with America, it was no wonder our relations were in such parlous condition.

'You choose an unusual place to meet, Mr Lyell,' said Merry, his tone inflected with the merest hint of disapproval.

'Unusual circumstances demand it. You are doubtless known to the better parts of society here; it would be better if they did not see us together. Besides, we have already survived two encounters with the damned Spaniards and I am keen to avoid their attentions.'

Merry permitted himself the merest hint of a smile. 'The Spanish have not had all the run of the table. I have had word from General Beresford.'

'Well?'

'He and Commodore Popham have taken Buenos Aires. The Spanish are routed, and South America is open.'

Lyell thumped his fists on the table. 'Thank God for that! And London? What do the fools in the Admiralty and Parliament make of this impromptu victory?'

'I do not know. They would have received the news only weeks ago. Their views have not yet reached Washington.'

I could not contain my confusion. 'What? Have we invaded South America?'

It was a rash question. Merry's eyes immediately turned on me in suspicion, while Lyell fixed me with a quizzical gaze. Wilting under their stares, it was all I could do to remember Nevell's advice. *Do not be afraid to reveal your ignorance.*

'I – I came to this project late,' I stammered. 'There is a great deal I have not learned.'

'So it would appear,' Merry sniffed.

It was Lyell who unexpectedly aided me. 'Sir Home Popham, acting under our direction but without orders from the weak-kneed fools in London, has taken his fleet and the Cape garrison and seized Buenos Aires.' He turned back to Merry, his face bright with triumph. 'Now it is out of the government's hands. Our papers will declare for Popham, lionize him as the new Nelson; perhaps our friends at Lloyd's will make a presentation from the Patriotic Fund. Grenville and Fox will have no choice but to allow it, and to reinforce our position. They cannot stop now until all of South America is freed from Spain, and opened to our commerce.'

I tried to keep from gaping. 'You have used British troops to launch a private war for trade?' It seemed more akin to piracy.

Thankfully, Lyell mistook my shock for admiration. 'Our project is bigger than you suppose. Popham and his army have struck in the south; now it is left to us to deliver our part of the bargain in the north.'

I noticed Merry's discomfiting eyes still watching me. 'And what is your role in this?'

'Lieutenant Jerrold is here to ensure that the navy play their part,' said Lyell.

'At your service,' I mumbled, shrinking still further into my chair.

'He carries dispatches for the colonel.' Lyell turned to me. 'It was Mr Merry who first brought this scheme to our attention, you know.'

'I was not aware of that.'

'Colonel Burr approached me in Washington. When he advised me of his plan I had no hesitation in recommending it to Whitehall. And when our ministers dismissed it, Mr Lyell and his confederates were prompt in seeing the possibilities.' Merry had clasped his fingers together so tight that the knuckles were white as bone. 'We will break this impertinent country, Mr Jerrold, we will break it.'

'And make a handsome return on my investment, I hope,' added Lyell.

'Tell me, Lieutenant, how many ships have you brought?'

That halted me sharpish. I had been so busy trying to understand their talk of wild schemes to overthrow nations that I had not expected this direct, disastrous question. All I could think was to take a leaf from Nevell's book.

'That is confidential.'

Merry frowned. 'Not to those who are party to the scheme, surely?'

I tapped my coat. 'I have in this pocket secret dispatches which contain all the particulars. I will surrender it to the named addressee, and to no other man.' I leaned forward earnestly, warming to my theme. 'Why do you think I was recruited to this business so late? The government's spies had collared Lieutenant Beauchamp, who was to have come in my place. I will not risk a similar fate by idle gossiping.'

It was a dangerous improvisation, but it seemed to suffice for Merry. He turned to Lyell. 'I was not aware that our plans were so close to discovery in London.'

'Grand schemes are never far from disaster – that is why Lieutenant Jerrold rightly insists on such secrecy. The present ministry are adept at reading private correspondence. They almost discovered the Buenos Aires expedition too soon, but Popham and Beresford outwitted them.'

Merry shifted on his seat in some discomfort. 'I do not have your fortune, Lyell: if this goes ill for us and redounds on my career I will be ruined.'

'Or hanged for treason.' Lyell did not seem concerned by the prospect, though it left me quailing even more. 'Nonetheless, we must confide in our precautions and put our faith in Colonel Burr.'

It seemed this was the dozenth time I had heard mention of this colonel – first by Mr Ogden in the New York churchyard, and now by Mr Merry and Lyell. Evidently, he was of some significance to their plans. I was not sure I wished to meet him, but if I was to uncover the secrets of this conspiracy I would have to learn something of him. As nonchalant as I could manage, I said, 'I thought that Mr Tyler was arranging the American end of the business.' Merry's irritable gaze turned on me, and I held up my hands in innocence. 'I left in haste, and received only the briefest instructions.' So much was true – damn Nevell.

'Mr Tyler has been our correspondent, so that no connection with Colonel Burr can be proved. But Tyler is merely Burr's lieutenant. Burr is the true genius behind this scheme.' Merry looked to Lyell. 'Have you met him? He is a remarkable man, and animated by such a spirit of revenge against President Jefferson that he will never surrender his cause. I confess it is the attentions of our own government which concern me more.'

'Put them out of your mind,' said Lyell. 'Even if they do guess our intentions, it is too late. And what could they do? Send some sapskull from the Secret Office to spy on us. By the time he had written his report to London the business would have been concluded.'

He reached under his coat and pulled out the pistol he had kept there since Princeton, just far enough that its blued barrel could be seen poking from the fabric.

'And if we do come upon some agent of the government, we will certainly know how to dispose of him.'

I wondered if it was my addled imagination, or whether his gaze had rested on me a moment longer than was comfortable.

11

WE LEFT LANCASTER NEXT MORNING, THOUGH LYELL INSISTED WE first procure some of the local produce. I assumed he meant beer, for the smell of the maltings was everywhere, but instead he led us to a small gunsmith's shop on the main street where the aroma was more in the way of scorched metal and oil. The proprietor seemed to have stepped directly from the farthest reaches of the American wilderness: his shirt was fringed with leather tassels, and his cap sewn from the fur of some hapless animal he had killed. Stuffed trophies were mounted on the wall, doubtless in testament to his guns' prowess, though to me they only served as a catalogue of the perils we had to face. A giant bear, his face still contorted in his death snarl, proved particularly unsettling.

Lyell spent some time in conversation with the gunsmith, hefting one gun after another with an expert enthusiasm, and eventually settled on a pair of long rifles.

'Do you think we will need those?' I asked nervously.

Lyell ignored me.

'Is good choice,' declared the gunsmith. His words were almost unfathomable for the thick German veneer which overlaid them. 'American guns are best in world. Lancaster guns are best in America. And my guns' – he winked – 'best in Lancaster.'

'Not quite your thirty-two-pound cannon, Lieutenant, but enough to teach our enemies a lesson if they come.' It was extraordinary how having a gun in his hand could improve the humour of a man like Lyell. To my dismay, he handed one to me. It was surprisingly light for its size.

Lyell took boxes of ammunition and grease patches, and two flasks of powder, and then went to the saddler next door to obtain holsters and gun belts. The purchase of two low-crowned, broadbrimmed hats completed our *tout ensemble*, and a curious pair of ruffians we must have looked as we rode out of the town with our London suits and our Lancaster hats, the rifles slung over our backs and our spare clothes rolled up in blankets behind our saddles. The presence of Miss Lyell, whose finely tailored habit and upright bearing bespoke her breeding all too clearly, could only have added to the incongruity.

'Are you sure this is the least conspicuous mode of travel?' I asked Lyell. We were some three miles out of the town, riding through a rich, cultivated country studded everywhere with brick farmhouses and immense barns. 'If we were in a coach, we would surely be less obvious.'

'Our enemies will count on that fact.' Lyell swayed atop his carthorse. 'All they would need do is watch the coaching inns. This way, we may travel at our own pace and rest where we choose.'

He did not convince me. Nor, as the days wore on, did my spirits rise. We were in the middle of November now: the last leaves were falling, and the forests which surrounded us became grey and spiny places. The farms we passed grew ever smaller, their dwellings diminishing from proud brick houses to weatherboarded cottages, and then single-roomed cabins whose log timbers still bore the marks of the axes which had hewn them. The fractured, untamed countryside gave us only one road to follow, the government road from Philadelphia to Pittsburgh which Lyell had previously been so eager to avoid. It did us little good. Twelve miles from Lancaster it deteriorated into a rutted track which the vast burden of traffic only served to worsen.

It astonished me: in this remote place, with winter closing its fist and the roads so precarious, I should have thought the population would stay safe at home. Instead, not half an hour went by that we did not meet some fellow travellers: wagonners from Baltimore and Philadelphia carrying English manufactures into the interior, which interested Lyell mightily; packers and packhorses; local countrymen hurrying to the towns to buy curing salt or, more commonly, whiskey; and even whole families who, undeterred by the season, were removing themselves still deeper into the continent with their children and livestock in tow. Their motives were evident, for riding in the opposite direction we often encountered prosperous settlers moving back to the civilization of the coast. In contrast to the thread-bare possessions of those going west, the eastbound travellers dressed fashionably, rode handsome mounts and were succeeded by great trains of baggage in carts. Doubtless the hopeful watched these prodigies and dreamed of equal increase to their fortunes, though I fear they deluded themselves, for the former greatly outnumbered the latter.

It was a sociable road, but the combined effect of so many wheels, hooves, paws and feet, to say nothing of the rain, was to churn the path to a mire. The streams and creeks which flowed across our way remained unbridged save by single tree-trunks stripped of their branches, which the locals called Indian bridges; horses and carts had to splash through the water and often sank deep into the muddy, trampled banks. So it was no surprise to me when, on the fourth day from Lancaster, Miss Lyell's horse went lame. We left it to mend at the next farm we passed and, as gallantry demanded I offer Miss Lyell my own mount, I was left to walk on foot. By the end of the day my legs were frail as straws, and my feet swollen with blisters.

'How much further to Pittsburgh?' I asked. I was sitting in the parlour of the inn, my boots and stockings removed as I applied a concoction of bran and vinegar to my feet. Miss Lyell had retired, while her father sat in the chair opposite with a bowl of egg punch.

'Ten days, perhaps.'

I groaned – audibly, for I had just prodded a blister. 'I will need another mount, then. I cannot walk all that way.'

'Of course you can walk. You are a young man in his prime. It cannot be above one hundred and fifty miles.'

'Look at my feet,' I implored him. 'They will be bloody stumps before we have gone half so far.'

Lyell did not appear to have heard me. 'It will not slow us down much. My horse manages little more than a walking pace.'

'It will slow you down a great deal when you have to carry me to Pittsburgh.'

'Pardon me.'

We both looked up. As ever, we had secluded ourselves in a dark corner of the room, but the inn was busy that night and offered little privacy. Now one of the company had approached and stood over us with a glass of whiskey in his hand.

'I'm sorry for the eavesdropping – I was passing by and couldn't help but hear it. You were saying you needed a horse?'

'No,' said Lyell.

'Yes,' I countered.

Of course I did not trust the man – ever since our encounter with Mr Vidal, I had scanned every face I saw for signs of malice – but I refused to countenance walking a hundred and fifty miles over mud and mountain simply to save a few dollars from Lyell's purse. Besides, this man did not look dangerous. He was clean-shaven and dressed better than most of the customers at the inn: his brown coat was not lavish, but sturdy, and the few repairs in the fabric were neatly sewn. With his greying hair and his lined, weatherbeaten face, he looked no different to the dozens of gentlemen farmers we had met that week.

'I regret I do not have the funds to purchase your horse,' said Lyell. 'Though no doubt he is an admirable beast.'

The man smiled. 'That'll be fine, cos I'm not much interested in selling him. I need him to get me home. But I'd be happy to share him with you, walking and riding in turns, if that'd help. All I'd ask is some coin for the feed.'

'Thank you for your offer, but we do not desire travelling companions. Even Mr Jerrold here would concur in that.'

He looked to me for acquiescence, but I withheld it. 'How far are you going?'

'Over the mountains. I've a farm at Greensburg. Yourselves?'

'Our destination is our own affair,' Lyell muttered.

'Pittsburgh.' Lyell's insensitivity to my plight had angered me, and I relished the chance to contradict him. I was also keen to gain even the partial use of a horse. 'We would welcome your company, sir.'

He offered me his hand. 'Zadok Harris.'

'Martin Jerrold. My disagreeable companion is Mr Lyell.'

Lyell's eyes burned like coals, but he did not argue the matter further.

I confess I did awake to doubt my wisdom the next morning, but all reservation vanished at the agony I felt just hobbling to breakfast, and the relief when I climbed into Harris's saddle. Besides, he proved a generous companion. He allowed me to ride far more often than was my due, frequently on the steeper or stonier parts of our path, and his familiarity with the road improved our lot considerably. He quickly saw that we preferred to avoid the more populous inns and taverns, though he was too polite to enquire why, but nonetheless managed to find houses whose unpopularity owed nothing to deficiencies of comfort. These tended for the most part to be owned by Germans, who provided clean beds and good drink and otherwise left us in peace.

Our way now led us into the Blue Mountains. From the time Harris joined us they had been visible, a vast rampart across our path stretching north and south as far as the eye could reach. They rose so steeply from the plain that we needed several hours to climb the few miles to the summit ridge. The air was dank, the slopes covered with gloomy pine forests, and as we crested the top we had to pass through a notch between lowering peaks.

'This would make a fine spot for an ambush,' I grumbled.

Harris, walking along the road beside me, looked up. 'Are you expecting to meet with danger?'

'Lieutenant Jerrold does not fear danger.' Miss Lyell was as quick as she was misguided to defend my honour. 'He was at Trafalgar, you know, and I myself have seen him withstand a far superior foe almost single-handed.'

'You're far from the sea here, Lieutenant.'

'With further to go.' Looking ahead, I could see a deep valley chequered with small squares of farmland, and another ridge of mountains beyond. They did not look far away, barely half a mile, but I guessed the distance was deceptive. My heart sank.

'*Mr Jerrold.*' The sudden urgency in Harris's voice spun me about. He was staring into the forest, still as stone. 'Do you keep a running ball in your rifle?'

I nodded, craning forward on the horse to try and see what had so alarmed Harris. 'What is it?'

'Something moving in the woods.'

'A fox?'

'Bigger than a fox. A bear, or maybe a man.'

In that lonely place, neither was welcome. 'What is he doing?'

'Hard to see. Give me your gun.'

In the panic of the moment I did not think to question him. Fumbling with the strap, I pulled the rifle over my head and passed it down to him. He thumbed back the lock with expert hands, and raised it to his shoulder.

'What is he doing?' hissed Lyell. I could not tell whether he referred to Harris or the creature in the woods, but the American answered for both.

'I can't see for sure – he's hidden in the trees. Maybe . . .'

The blast of a shot echoed like cannon-fire in the stony notch, rolling away down the mountain. In the aftermath, I thought I heard a scuffling in the trees, though it might equally have been the wind blowing the leaves.

'Did you hit him?' Lyell had dismounted from his horse and was cowering in its shadow, the rifle in his hand.

Harris shook his head. My rifle had pitted his cheek with black powder grains, and must have given him a fair kick in the shoulder, but he remained entirely composed. 'Whatever it was, it's gone now. Do you want to try finding it?'

'No.' For once, Lyell and I spoke as one. Running around lonely woods in pursuit of an enemy who might or might not exist did not seem a sensible course.

With many glances over our shoulders, and taut fingers on our rifle triggers, we descended from that place as quickly as we could.

We were almost a week in the mountains, a seemingly endless round of hauling ourselves up steep slopes only to trip down the reverse; of roads forever doubling over themselves; of a cheerless, broken country which left me utterly dispirited. Even Miss Lyell was no comfort: the inns offered little more than mattresses on attic floors by way of bedrooms, and there was never an opportunity for a private moment together. Worse, she seemed to be forming an attachment to Mr Harris. When he rode, she sidled her horse close to his and affected great delight in his conversation – tales of Indian raids and battles in the revolution and wild animals which all passed three feet over my head. But when I rode I could not catch her gaze, for her attention was forever directed downwards. She even begged Harris to school her in her riding, which service he performed with much arranging of her knees just so, and a firm hand on her back to perfect her posture. He did not effect any change at all that I could notice, but she seemed well pleased by it.

On the fifth day, at the top of another interminable ridge, Harris called a halt. 'This is it,' he announced.

I looked around. I could see nothing of consequence, not even a tumbledown shack for travellers to recover from the ascent, as was sometimes offered. Surely this could not be Pittsburgh.

'This is where the east ends and the west starts.' Harris swept an arm backwards. 'Behind us, the rivers run down to the Atlantic. Ahead, they all flow west to the Mississippi.'

'Is that an ocean, Mr Harris?' Miss Lyell asked.

He chuckled. 'No, ma'am. She's a river, biggest in the world, I guess. All you can see, and as far as you can go beyond that – no-one knows for certain how far – is her basin, all draining south towards Mexico. There's no turnpikes or highways to speak of in that country, for you don't need them with the river. She carries it all: settlers and travellers, trade and war, the full length of the land.'

'It sounds magnificent,' breathed his eager pupil. 'Far grander than the mean little rivers we have in England. Will we see it on our journey?'

'I'd hope not, not if you're stopping at Pittsburgh. That's but the head of the Ohio, and there's a thousand miles of that before you meet the Mississippi.'

'Some day you must take me,' said Miss Lyell. 'It sounds most romantic; I should so love to see it.'

'It would be my pleasure.'

Unlike Miss Lyell, I had no desire to tour the geological marvels of the western states. The closer we came to Pittsburgh, the more keenly I felt the obligation of my mission weighing on me. *Learn what you can of Mr Tyler and his scheme, then stop it*, Nevell had told me. I had done little enough towards the first part of that instruction; as to the second, it seemed hopeless. Lyell's conversation with Mr Merry had demonstrated the scale of their ambitions. If they had stolen fleets and armies to overthrow South America, what enormities might they purpose here – and how could I hope to stop them?

And then there was the letter. At the very least, I had to deliver that. I had thought that with the end of the journey in sight my apprehensions would lift, but in fact the opposite was true. I became obsessed by the fear that having travelled so far, through such dangers, the package would be snatched from my hands at the last; that a cruel fate was toying with me. Each rustling leaf or snapping branch had me whipping around in panic, while every time I saw a traveller approaching along our road, however distant, I was at once convinced he must be some agent of the enemy, and did not relax until he was well past. No wonder Miss Lyell spurned my company for Harris's.

The penultimate day of our journey was to be our last with Harris. We were approaching Greensburg, where he kept his farm; he had invited us to stay the night, and assured us that we could make Pittsburgh in an easy day's walk or ride. He had even offered me the use of his horse, which I could return on my way back.

'Perhaps you and your father'll be able to stay for longer, when you've finished your business in Pittsburgh,' he pressed Miss Lyell. 'Maybe even for Christmas. December's no time for a young lady to be battling those mountains.' We were in the last days of November, the nights already marked by a stiff frost that began to thaw only in the mid-morning.

'The water on the road freezes, and it's like climbing sheets of glass,' Harris was saying. 'You could break all four of your horse's legs, to say nothing of your own, and be trapped up there for days. Sometimes it's weeks before the mails can get through. Greensburg may not be London, but I figure we could keep the fires going and find some way to amuse you over Christmas.'

'I should like that very much, if Papa will allow it.'

'You'd be most welcome too, of course, Lieutenant.'

I tried to summon a smile. 'I fear I must decline. My duties command haste.'

Lyell grunted some approving comment – presumably he wanted me well away from his daughter – but she, to my surprise, would have none of it. 'But you must join us. It will be so gay if you are there, and we would tremble to think of you crossing those horrid mountains all alone. Do you not think so, Mr Harris?'

Her words inspired pathetic gratitude in me, though I doubted they pleased Mr Harris. True, he had never shown me anything but kindness and civility, but I suspected he would far rather have Miss Lyell to himself. Before he could demur, something in the road caught his eye.

'A turkey,' he said, pointing to the plump shape pecking at the road ahead of us. 'How far off do you reckon it is?'

'Two hundred yards?'

'My dollar says you can't hit it with your rifle from here.'

I suspected his dollar spoke truly, but I could not show unwilling. I unslung the rifle from my back, trained it on the gobbling bird and discharged it. A sore shoulder, an agitated turkey, and a dollar less in my purse were my only rewards.

Harris turned to Lyell. 'If I may?'

He took Lyell's rifle and squinted down the barrel, swaying it left and right, for my initial shot had sent the bird scurrying away. With my ears still ringing, his shot sounded curiously flat. Nor did he seem to have fared any better than I, for the turkey continued to run about in the road, flapping its wings as it darted this way and that.

'Your American woodsman's skills are not all you have led us to believe,' I teased him. 'At least my dollar is safe.'

Two hundred yards away, the bird suddenly toppled over to the ground.

Harris cocked an eyebrow at me. 'It may be your dollar's not so safe as you suppose.'

As we walked up to the dead bird I saw the full genius of Harris's marksmanship. He had not just hit the turkey, he had shot its head clean off at the neck. The red pouch on its throat still heaved as blood flooded into the road. Miss Lyell looked at Harris in awe, while even her father was impressed.

'I'd venture there is not a man in England who could match that trick,' he said.

'At least we'll sup well this evening.' Harris squatted by the carcass. With an expert hand, he tied off the bleeding neck, then bound the feet. 'Obliged if you could help me get him on my saddle,' he said to Lyell.

Lyell slid off his horse and lifted the trussed bird, while Harris tried to make it fast to his pommel. It took some time, for the rope was too short.

'I think I've another length somewhere here.'

Harris unbuckled his saddlebag and delved inside, leaving Lyell holding up the bird like a butcher. Miss Lyell watched from her mount, while I kept care of the rifles.

'I believe you've some papers in your bag, Mr Lyell,' said Harris conversationally, still rummaging for the rope.

Lyell stiffened, though the upside-down turkey carcass in his hands did little to bolster his dignity. 'What the devil do you know about them?'

'Not so much. But I know I'd like to take them from you.'

At first I thought I had misheard. Lyell was still standing there with the dripping turkey, and Harris had barely raised his voice. Then Miss Lyell uttered a small gasp, touching her hand to her mouth as Harris turned back to face us. There was no rope in his hands, but instead a bristling pair of pistols. One was trained on Lyell, the other, almost absent-mindedly, towards me.

'You'll keep hold of that bird if you don't mind,' said Harris. 'Stays your hands from mischief. And you, Mr Jerrold, you'll hold onto the rifles. You could pull the trigger if you liked, but I've a notion you'd find you'd forgotten to reload.'

'Damn you, Harris!' Lyell's face was as red as the turkey's gullet. 'You cannot do this to us.'

'Well now, the way I see it, it's me who's got the guns – the loaded ones, anyhow. I guess I can do pretty much as I like.'

He looked about. None of us contradicted him.

'Good. Now, Miss Lyell, if you'll get down off your horse and look in your father's saddlebag, I've a notion you'll find a packet of papers.'

Miss Lyell's face was pale as ice as she dismounted and walked stiffly to her father's horse. She still had her reticule on her arm, I noticed: it seemed an incongruous frippery in our desperate plight.

'Are these the papers?'

'Bank drafts? Cheques?'

She scanned them quickly, then nodded.

Lyell's face was contorted in anguish, and his arms trembled from the weight of the turkey, but he made a stoic attempt at negotiation. 'Those drafts are worth one hundred thousand dollars, Mr Harris. You could take half for yourself, and leave without violence.'

Harris chuckled. 'I could take it all for myself, with or without the violence. But I figure my superiors wouldn't care for that, so I'll just hold on to them for safe keeping. And your papers too, Mr Jerrold.'

What little composure I had retained drained away. I slumped forward, leaning on the rifle for support. The turkey's blood suddenly seemed thick in my nose, and the urge to wretch almost overwhelmed me. It was as I had feared: I had come so far, so close, only to fail. Again.

'I'd prefer that you didn't reach out the package yourself, Lieutenant. Who knows what else you might find in there. If you'll oblige me again, Miss Lyell, I expect you'll find it inside his coat on the right. It doesn't do to clap your hand on your valuables each time you pass a stranger,' Harris told me. 'Sends something of a signal, if someone's watching.'

Miss Lyell stepped towards me so that we stood facing each other awkwardly, like lovers. She slipped her hand into my coat, and I felt it brush over the butt of the pistol in my belt. As our eyes met, I shook my head the merest fraction. Harris still had his gun trained on us.

She found the package and pulled it free. Without realizing, I had been holding my breath; now, as the package slipped from my pocket, I exhaled, as though she drew my very life from me.

She turned back to Harris. 'You are a perfect villain,' she informed him, holding out the bundled papers.

He ignored the insult. 'As you'll see, my hands are a bit full just now. You keep those for the moment, and get back on your horse.'

A spur of hope rose in me: once mounted, she could yet be away with the precious papers. Harris must have seen it in my face, for he laughed.

'She'll be coming with me. Being a man of finance, Mr Lyell, you'll appreciate it's always wise to take insurance. I'm

111

thinking you'll be less likely to come charging after me if you know your bullet's liable to hit your beautiful daughter here.'

Miss Lyell gasped, and staggered backwards. The papers fell from her arms into the muddy road. For a second, Harris's gaze dropped towards them in irritation, but even as I considered whether I could draw my pistol he had snapped his attention back to us. Besides, it had been two days since I checked the priming, and there was every chance it would not discharge. Mr Harris, I felt, was not the sort of man to allow misfires.

'Pick those up,' Harris told Miss Lyell. And then, more concerned: 'What are you doing?'

Ignoring the papers, Miss Lyell had opened her reticule and was fumbling inside it. With three of us to cover now and only two guns, Harris's pistols swayed uncertainly between us.

'I feel faint,' Miss Lyell announced. Indeed, her cheeks, pale at the best of times, were now marble-white, and it was with obvious difficulty that she kept from fainting. 'I must have my vinaigrette.'

She pulled a small silver box from her reticule. Snapping open the lid, she held it beneath her nose and breathed deeply. A little vigour returned to her face.

'You'd best make sure you've enough of that,' Harris cautioned her. 'I won't care to see you falling from your horse every mile and slowing me up.'

'You are a vile thief, Mr Harris,' said Lyell. 'If you were in England, you would indubitably be hanged for your temerity. Even in America, I am quite certain that justice will overtake you. I will personally ensure it.'

'Justice? Mr Lyell, it's justice I'm after; and it's you it's overtaken.'

The gun in Harris's right hand jerked at Lyell. Miss Lyell, who had returned the vinaigrette to her reticule, now fumbled for it again, though she would need more than vinegar to compose herself if Harris made good his threat.

'What? Will you murder me on the road like a common highwayman?'

'It's lucky for you I haven't already done just that. If I didn't think my boss would rather have you alive to confess to your treason, I—'

As suddenly as if he had been felled by the gods, Harris broke off, took one step backwards, and collapsed onto the ground. His arms flopped out, still grasping their pistols, though he would never fire them again. A small round hole had been punched plumb through the centre of his forehead.

Such was the confusion of my senses it was only then that I became aware of the bang, the loud explosion which had punctuated the argument. The acrid smell of powder reached my nostrils and I turned. Miss Lyell was standing quite still, her legs apart, her chest heaving under the bosom of her dress which had an unsightly black stain splashed across it. In one hand she held her reticule, and in the other, still raised, a tiny pistol barely five inches long. A curl of smoke rose from the muzzle.

'You ... you shot him,' I stammered. Relief and shock and disbelief mingled in my voice, in marked contrast to Miss Lyell, whose face remained composed, her eyes very bright.

Her father crouched by Harris's body. 'Dead.' With little reverence for the departed, he frisked Harris's coat. A flask, a knife, a pouch of tobacco and a few dollars in change were all he found. 'Take this,' he ordered, thrusting the money into my hands. 'If the corpse is found, they may believe he was murdered by thieves. And pick up your package.'

Dumbly, I did as he instructed. We dragged the body into the woods by the roadside and covered it with fallen branches and leaves. It would do little to deter the scavengers, but even Lyell could not bring himself to leave Harris entirely exposed in death. Then we hurried back to the horses.

'Leave that,' said Lyell as I struggled to move the turkey's carcass. 'It will explain the blood on the road. Now, let us be on our way. Mr Harris was no ordinary brigand: he knew precisely what we carried, and he scrupled at nothing to seize it. It defies imagination that he did not have accomplices.'

That got me back on my horse quick enough. I could only wonder in misery at the attention my package had attracted since leaving

England: first Fothergill rummaging for it under my bed, then Mr Vidal trying to snatch it on the Princeton coach, and now Harris's effort at highway robbery. If they represented their respective nations, then it seemed I had Britain, Spain, and now America ranged against me. Nor had it escaped my notice that each encounter brought ever greater dangers. Perhaps next time they would simply put a bullet in my skull and take the package from my dead hands.

It was not a consoling thought to carry with us as we carried on down the road.

12

WE RODE INTO PITTSBURGH THE NEXT EVENING. DESPITE LYELL'S forebodings we had not met any dangers since leaving Mr Harris to rot in the woods, though that had not prevented fear from consuming my thoughts. I ate little, and drank too much of the local apple whiskey – first to numb my fears, then to numb the effects of the earlier draughts. By the time we arrived my head felt as though it had been jammed in the chamber of a cannon, and my limbs were stiff as teak. It was not just the riding: the weather had turned bitterly cold, offering up winds which tore through my greatcoat and rains which sleeted all heat from our bodies. When we reached Pittsburgh it seemed there was nothing in my veins save ice and liquor.

After so many travails, we had little difficulty finding our destination. Pittsburgh was a small town set on a promontory at the junction of two rivers, and it was not hard to obtain directions to the inn. I felt no relief at having arrived, for the town exuded an ominous welcome. High, wooded hills rose around it on all sides, and the houses were blackened by the heavy coal which smoked from every chimney. The unpaved streets were ankle deep in mud, and though the hills gave some protection from the wind they did not keep the rain from falling in sheer, oppressive columns.

115

At a crooked street corner, near the western end of the town, we found what we sought. After so many weeks I had difficulty believing that I stood in Pittsburgh, Pennsylvania, staring at a white-bricked building whose handsome sign proclaimed it to be M'Culloch's Inn. Perhaps I should have paused to reflect on the moment, to savour the fact that I had come so many thousands of miles through such hazards to deliver my package safely, but with the rain drizzling down the back of my neck and my feet sinking ever deeper into the roadstead, I did not. Handing my bridle to the groom I hurried inside, not even troubling to wipe the mud from my boots. My hand groped in my pocket, felt the packet and pulled it forth. It was sprayed with weeks of mud, and a small splash of blood which may well have been Harris's, but the seals were intact and the knots secure. I held it before me like a votive offering. For all Nevell's instructions to learn its contents and thwart the conspirators, at that moment I simply ached to be rid of it.

A girl, a pretty young thing in a blue smock, appeared in the hallway before me. She looked disapprovingly at my haggard attire, and the dirt I had dragged across her threshold.

'I require a room and a bath,' I told her, though so much was evident. 'Then you may fetch me Mr Tyler, and inform him that Martin Jerrold has arrived with a package for him.'

She nodded, and ran into an adjacent room. When the door reopened, a stout, red-headed man with a full beard and whiskers appeared.

'Mr Tyler?' I said.

'William M'Culloch.'

'Ah. I wonder, might you introduce me to Mr Tyler? I understand he is lodging here.'

Mr M'Culloch ruminated on this. 'Mr Tyler,' he repeated at length.

'Yes.'

'Mr Comfort Tyler?'

'I believe so.'

'You've missed him.'

116

I almost dropped the package into the pool of mud and water at my feet. 'What?'

'Left yesterday.' And then, thinking I still did not understand: 'He's gone.'

A darkness overwhelmed my soul, and it was all I could do to keep from falling to the floor and sobbing under my coat. Lyell faced the reverse with sterner resolve. 'Did Mr Tyler leave any indication where he might be found?'

The innkeeper gave him a cool stare, bridling at his brusque tone. 'Not for any Mr Jerrold.'

'For a Mr Lyell, perhaps? Or a Mr Beauchamp?'

'My, but you've a few names between you.'

He paused, pondering the three bedraggled travellers making a mire of his hallway. I half expected him to send for his horsewhip and drive us back out into the storm, but, like his fellow Pittsburghers, he had not come to this remote settlement in the farthest reach of civilization to turn away custom.

'Will you be taking a bed for the night?' he asked.

'That depends as to whether I have business to keep me in Pittsburgh,' answered Lyell. 'At present I see little to delay me here.'

M'Culloch crossed to a dark-stained sideboard by the wall, picked up a pewter tankard, and fished inside it with his fingers. He withdrew a creased piece of paper which he held just beyond our reach.

'We may require a room after all,' said Lyell.

M'Culloch handed him the paper. Lyell unfolded it, scanned it then passed it to me.

If any man comes asking for Comfort Tyler, send him to call on Mr McMeekin at the West Street jetty. He will know where to find me.

It was written in a neat hand, and dated the previous day. I looked to M'Culloch, who evidently knew its contents.

'There's no gain going to the jetty tonight. McMeekin won't have the boat loaded until tomorrow afternoon. You'll find him in the morning, sure enough, and he'll take you to Mr Tyler.'

I did not like this talk of boats – the thought of having to endure still more travels to seek out the elusive Mr Tyler was almost too much to stomach. But Lyell was satisfied.

'We will take two rooms, and find Mr Tyler in the morning.'

Though I heaped coals on the fire before going to bed, it was a cold night I spent at M'Culloch's Inn, and little better in the morning. We could walk the streets without fear of losing our shoes, but only because the frost had frozen the mud solid, and at the riverbank a veneer of ice was creeping out into the fast-flowing stream. This late in the season there were few boatmen who would brave the river, and we had little trouble finding McMeekin's boat. It was a strange craft, though, as I was to learn, typical of the American interior. At first sight, it did not look much like a boat at all, for drawn up on the shore it resembled nothing so much as a long, low hut whose far end had subsided into the river. It must have measured about sixty feet, with a rudimentary cabin running most of its length which allowed only short decks at front and stern, loaded with casks and long, steel-banded chests. No concession had been made to grace or manoeuvrability, for her bows were as straight and square as her sides. There did not appear to be any means of propulsion.

A short, thin man was standing on the muddy shore, hammering at a portion of the hull and smoking a clay pipe.

'Are you Mr McMeekin?' I hailed him.

My words interrupted him in mid-swing. His hammer caught the trenail sideways and catapulted it from its hole.

He swore. 'Who are you?'

'We are looking for Mr Tyler.'

He tapped the bowl of his pipe on the hull. 'Lots of folks looking for Mr Tyler – and some he'd be particular fond of not seeing. Besides, he's gone. Left two days back.'

'I know. I was told you might direct us to him.'

'Might do, if I knew your business. Then again, if I knew your business I might not.'

'You would certainly take us to him if you knew our business,' said Lyell.

'What'd that be then?'

'We have papers for him. From overseas. And money,' I added. 'We could pay you well to take us to him.'

'I don't need your cash,' said McMeekin. 'If Mr Tyler don't want to see you, then no money's going to get you there on my boat. And if he do, well, then I'm going that way anyhow.'

'He will want to meet us,' I insisted. 'We have come all the way from England to see him.'

That drew the boatman's attention. 'From England? And you said you'd some papers for Mr Tyler?'

'A package.' I began to reach into my coat, but the boatman waved me to stop.

'No need to go wavin' it all about. How many seals it got on it?'

'Three.'

'And what're they of?'

I could have drawn those seals in my sleep. 'A letter "A", an anchor, and a bird.'

McMeekin nodded. 'Good enough for me. But I can't take you to Mr Tyler.'

'What?' Having shown so much of our hand, Lyell was in a dangerous humour. 'We will not suffer you to sport with us, Mr McMeekin. We have proved our good faith; if you do not reciprocate you will find us dangerous enemies.'

Even the laconic McMeekin was taken aback by Lyell's ferocity. 'I wasn't fixing to be no wiseacre.' He knocked against the hull. 'My boat's not ready. I need some trenails to fix her, and they ain't coming 'til this afternoon. If you can wait for tomorrow, I'll gladly give you a passage to the island.'

Whether from a desire to please or some unforeseen difficulty, McMeekin had been overly optimistic. When we sent a boy from the inn to enquire after his progress next morning we were told it would need a further day at least before his repairs were accomplished.

It necessitated another day in Pittsburgh, and that tried my nerves still further. We none of us dared leave the inn for fear of being recognized by our enemies; we moved between our rooms and the parlour, always wrapped in warm cloaks and keeping close to the fire. A miserable bunch of puritans we must have seemed to Mr M'Culloch. Months of forced intimacy had exhausted our conversation, and after the scourges of the road we no longer felt the strength or need for idle pleasantries. Lyell stayed in a high-backed chair reading a series of some local newspaper, while I sat opposite sipping whiskey and staring into the fire, wondering why neither seemed to warm me. Behind us, Miss Lyell played her solitaire incessantly at the table. Ever since the business with Harris she had become quite antisocial, her eyes dull and her face still. I did not blame her: it was a horrible thing for any man to kill another, even in extremity, and a hundredfold worse for a lady. I tried to convey my sympathy, to tease out her melancholy, but my every enquiry met a curt response.

At last, on the third morning, word came from McMeekin that he had procured all the trenails he needed, hammered them into his boat and made her ready. Even Miss Lyell was encouraged by the news. We packed our chests, which had arrived by wagon from Princeton, and hurried down over the frozen streets to the water-front. The ice seemed to have encroached another foot into the stream, but the boat had been launched into the water and now bobbed beside the jetty. Four boatmen were about her sides wielding wooden poles, while McMeekin himself stood on the roof holding the end of a long steering oar which sloped over the rear deck into the river. He waved as he saw us.

'It's as well you come when you did. River's freezing fast – might not've been able to go if we'd left it longer.'

'Then there is no time to lose.' Lyell swung his leg over the side and stepped onto the boat, causing it to rock alarmingly. His daughter hitched up her dress to follow, and in an instant two of the crew had abandoned their poles and rushed to assist her.

McMeekin tipped his hat. 'Welcome aboard, miss. We'll have you down to Mr Tyler in no time.'

I was standing on the jetty about to board when suddenly I felt as though I had been punched in the face by one of those long poles. *Tyler*. I patted my hands over my coat, then tore it open and reached inside, feeling frantically in the pockets. As I had feared, the bulge which had sat against my chest for the past month was gone.

'What are you doing?' snapped Lyell, poking his head from the cabin doorway. 'Will you keep us waiting until we are embedded in three feet of ice?'

'I must go back to the inn,' I mumbled. 'I have left something in my bedroom.'

'Dammit, Jerrold, this is no time for delay. If you have forgotten your razor or your boot polish you may doubtless procure a replacement down river. You—'

Ignoring him, I turned and ran back into town, slipping and skidding on the icy streets. When I reached the inn I did not ring the bell but raced straight up the stairs to my room. The door was open, and I could hear a tapping within. It was the girl, one of M'Culloch's daughters, on her knees by the fireplace sweeping out the grate. She looked up at me in surprise as I burst in.

'Did you lose something?' she asked. Ignoring her, I crouched beside the bed and ran my hands under the mattress. Internally, I cursed myself with a thousand condemnations, and some of the anguish must have shown on my face for she added, with concern, 'Do you want me to fetch the doctor?'

My fingers touched a lump between the bedstead and the mattress, fastened round it, and withdrew it. There it was, the faded address still legible on the oilcloth. *Mr Tyler, M'Culloch's Inn, Pittsburgh, Pennsylvania.* How could I have forgotten it at this ultimate stage, having brought it so far? At that moment every shred of scorn and obloquy my uncle had ever hurled at me seemed entirely justified.

'That is all,' I explained to the girl.

I backed out of the room and hurried down the corridor, eager not to antagonize Lyell with further delay. I met M'Culloch on the stairs.

'Mr Jerrold.' His eyes narrowed, and there was a hostility in his tone which I had not noticed before. 'I thought you had gone.'

'I had. I forgot something in my room and returned to retrieve it.'

'There were some men called for you just after you left.'

In my haste I had begun to edge past him; now I stopped still. 'Which men?'

'A sheriff and two magistrates from Greensburg. Said the corpse of a man'd been found in the woods thereabouts – shot through the head. Said they'd made enquiries, and he'd been seen in company with two Englishmen and a woman on the road to Pittsburgh. Wanted to know if I'd seen them about my inn.'

I gripped the banister tight. 'What did you tell them?'

M'Culloch's face stiffened and he stared me hard in the eye. 'I'm a lawful citizen, Mr Jerrold, and I don't hold with murder. I told them I had a party of Englishmen and a woman under my roof, but that they'd gone this morning. They wanted to know where you went, and I said I didn't know but I thought you might be making down river.'

'Thank you, Mr M'Culloch.' Touching my hat, I tried to squeeze by, but in an instant M'Culloch's arm had shot out and blocked my way.

'I wouldn't want it said I harboured a murderer, nor let him escape.'

I drew myself up as stiff as I could muster. 'Mr M'Culloch, I can assure you that I am no murderer. As for the body, perhaps it belongs to some brigand. Perhaps he fell in with these innocent Englishmen, befriended them and then, in a lonely place, attempted to rob them and defile their fair companion. If, to defend her honour, they confronted the villain, and if, in the scuffle, a shot was fired, might they not pause before consulting the authorities? Far from home and ignorant of local custom, fearful lest the dead man's friends pursue them, might they not hide the corpse and allow that natural justice had been served?'

M'Culloch's arm still blocked my way, but his gaze was less certain. 'Was that how it happened?'

I chose not to answer. 'You have daughters, Mr M'Culloch. Imagine one of them on her knees in the forest, begging the cold-hearted villain to spare her virtue, her shame, and him laughing in the face of all entreaty. What would you do?'

M'Culloch considered this so long I could have kicked him down the stairs. A clock in the hallway below ticked out the seconds, and I wondered how long Lyell would wait for me, or whether he would abandon me in Pittsburgh. And what if the sheriff returned to this house?

'Did anyone see you enter just now?' M'Culloch asked.

I shook my head.

'Then let no-one see you go. If I were you, I'd be gone from the state of Pennsylvania by nightfall.'

He lifted his arm. Nodding my thanks, I ran down the stairs and out of the front door, pulling my hat low over my face as I reached the street. Fortunately the cold had made high collars and tightly wrapped scarves the fashion of necessity, so I did not stand out as I hurried back to the boat. Lyell was standing on the foredeck to greet me.

'I trust your *ensemble* is now completed? Perhaps you would like to acquire some fine Pittsburgh ironware, or a lump of coal to take home to your sweetheart, before we go.'

I vaulted onto the deck. 'We must leave now,' I gasped.

'I am glad you have discovered urgency.'

'They found Harris's body. There are men in town seeking us.'

That stopped his sarcasm. Turning to McMeekin, who was smoking his pipe on the roof of the cabin, he began clamouring that we must be away this instant or there would be the devil to pay. McMeekin rose and took his steering oar, the crewmen cast off the mooring lines and poled us out, and presently we were in the current and gathering speed.

I looked back. With few boats on the river the dockside was almost deserted, but a few stevedores and porters were out plying their trade. None of them seemed to pay us the least attention: if we were braver than most travelling at this time of year, there was nothing otherwise remarkable about our boat, and it was too cold to stand around gawping.

I was just ready to seek the warmth of the cabin when a movement on the receding shore caught my eye. Three men had run out onto the jetty and were standing at its end, their black cloaks billowing in the breeze. They were too far distant for me to see clearly, but as they waved their arms and gesticulated I fancied they were pointing at us. Even as we rounded the first bend in the river and drew out of sight, they were still there, watching.

I went below.

Whatever other lies he had told us, Mr Harris had given a faithful description of the river: it was like a turnpike through the countryside, with farms and settlements in abundance on the flat land either side. Each had its own landing stage from where the inhabitants could hail the passing river traffic, but we steered clear of them, for both shores still lay within the state of Pennsylvania. The innkeeper's warning was hot in my ears. For the most part I kept inside, huddling by the brick fireplace in the middle of the rudimentary cabin. Even so, I could see our course through the open door, and it baffled me. At first we seemed to be going west, then north, then west again, and then almost due south, until I worried that presently we would come clean about and see the smoky air of Pittsburgh rising before us once more.

On the second afternoon, one of the crew thrust his head into the cabin and announced that we had passed beyond the borders of Pennsylvania. With some relief – the chimney smoked terribly, and I had borne a cruel headache for the past few hours – I ventured on deck. The river was high, and the boat scudded along at a pace I would not have expected from her squat frame, though it seemed to owe little to the crew. They stood at her corners with their poles, occasionally planting them in the river

124

to fend off floating debris or sandbars, but otherwise untroubled. Atop the roof, McMeekin still stood by his steering oar.

'Where are we now?'

The boatman pointed to larboard. 'That's Virginia. Opposite's Ohio.'

The names meant little to me. 'And this river?' I was struggling to remember Harris's geography lesson.

'This here's the Ohio River.'

'That's a pretty name.' Miss Lyell had followed me out of the cabin and stood by the bow with her shawl pulled tight around her shoulders. 'Does it mean anything?'

'It's an Injun name, miss. Means the River of Blood.'

If I had doubted the wisdom of fleeing headlong into the American wilderness with little notion of my destination and a horde of enemies in pursuit, this latest information made it a still more dismal prospect. It was no great feat to imagine my own blood feeding the river's hungry current – indeed, the image was rarely far from my thoughts. I looked around with renewed apprehension. Beyond the ribbon of civilization which clung to the banks, steep hills rose above the valley, their slopes covered in a skeletal forest unbroken by any road or pasture.

'We seem to be moving with some haste,' Miss Lyell observed. 'Yet I see no sail or oars. Is it really just the flow of the river which drives us?'

The boatman nodded, his jaw chewing up and down on a wad of tobacco. 'Can't outrun the river, I guess – leastways not at this time of year. She'll get us where we're goin' quick enough.'

I noticed a certain deficiency to his method. 'But how do you return up river?'

There was a brief delay as the boatman dug in his pole and pushed us clear of some eddy in the water, though I could see nothing on the surface. 'You could cordelle her.'

'How's that?'

'Well, it's a durn sight easier explainin' it than doin' it. You take thirty men and a rope, fix it to the boat, and pull for your life.'

'All the way up the river? But Mr Harris said it was a thousand miles long.'

'The Ohio's a thousand – the Mississippi adds another thousand or so if you're comin' up from N'Awlins.'

'Where?'

'N'Awlins. Noo Or-Lee-Ans,' he enunciated, thrusting out his lips like a cow. 'End of the river, but for the delta.'

'And you haul these boats back two thousand miles against the current?' A life in the sultan's galleys hardly seemed more arduous.

'Naw – ain't no point. Too much hard work.' The boatman gave a sly grin at my evident confusion, and spat his tobacco into the river. 'Boat ain't worth above sixty dollars – you'd spend more'n that paying your crew to come back.'

'Then how . . . ?' For a moment, I imagined an endless fleet of these flatboats flowing out of the river to drift forever around the oceans.

'We sell the boats in N'Awlins and break 'em up for the lumber. Then we walk back.' He looked around with an exaggerated smile, taking in the scenery like a witless tourist. 'Yes, sir: a ride down this river's a one-way trip.'

After that I did not speak much to the boatmen, save to establish that we were not ourselves bound two thousand miles to New Orleans. Mr McMeekin laughed: no, he said, we were merely going three or four days down river to the island where Mr Tyler could be found. I was not so certain: it seemed equally probable that we would reach this island only to find Mr Tyler recently departed, that we would continue down this river forever one stage behind him until eventually we dropped off the edge of the continent.

Each day, the farms on the riverbank grew more infrequent, and the occasional towns smaller. The river grew wider, and the current stronger. Our only diversion was choosing whether to stay in the dark, smoky cabin or to go out into the freezing air where our cloaks were soon coated in ice. Nor was my humour improved when, one afternoon while McMeekin was napping in the cabin, I snuck out onto the rear deck and examined his cargo. The casks were mostly filled with provisions – salt pork and flour and beer – but the long, steelbound boxes I had observed on our first meeting were another matter. Darting glances all about to see that I was not observed, I lifted the lid and stared down. Eight muskets sat in the casket, neatly interleaved. The gleaming oil on their barrels looked untouched.

I stepped back and stared around. I counted twelve of the boxes – almost a hundred guns. Even by the standards of America, where men carried rifles as their counterparts in London might carry handkerchiefs, that seemed excessive. And though I was no marksman, I knew enough to recognize the difference between a rifle and a musket. The farmers and backwoodsmen of this country needed guns which could fell foxes and pheasants and the occasional Indian with a single shot. Rifles, with their superior range and accuracy, were perfect. Muskets, with their poor range and rapid fire, were weapons for an army.

'I thought you'd be interested in these, Lieutenant. Do you approve?'

I spun about. McMeekin had emerged from the back door of the cabin and was holding a taper to his pipe, trying to light it. He grinned at me.

I tried to hide my terror. 'They are . . . very fine.'

'That's not but the last batch, mind. There's plenty more already on the island.'

'Really?' I let the lid drop shut, flinching at the bang.

McMeekin was still staring at me expectantly. 'Do you think they'll do?'

'Oh yes,' I assured him. If you wanted to equip an army they would do very nicely indeed.

'The colonel said we could always get more down river.'

'He's probably right.'

McMeekin smiled. 'He usually is.'

It was dusk on the fourth day of our journey when we reached the island. We had been bearing south, but a bend in the river brought us round due west. The winter sun was sinking directly before us, its last rays painting the sky a delicate confection of pinks and violets. Standing at the front of the boat wrapped in my greatcoat, I had to lower my eyes for fear of being blinded; all I could see was a few dozen yards of water shimmering ahead of us.

'Will we make a halt for the night?' I asked McMeekin.

He did not answer. He had given his steering oar to one of the crew and was perched on a barrel staring intently into the distance.

'There she is.'

Shading my eyes with my hand, I followed his gaze. A little way down the river, about a mile distant, the waters parted around a narrow island in mid stream. It was hard to see with the sun, but I thought I could discern a broad, white building against the dark curtain of trees beyond.

'Blennerhassett Island,' said McMeekin.

'Who lives there?'

'Mr Blennerhassett.'

As we drew nearer, and the sun dipped lower, I began to make out more of the house. I could scarcely credit my eyes. For the past few days we had seen only timber barns and farmhouses; now, perched on an island at the very edge of civilization, we were confronted with a fantastical construction, a two-storey mansion in the Palladian style which could have graced any estate in Surrey or Hampshire. A wide pediment capped its frontage, and at the sides two graceful colonnades led out to the wings. There was even a gravel walk leading up to its front door. With the last flashes of sunlight probing through the trees behind, and the windows beginning to glow yellow with lamplight, it was like some homely vision of paradise. I hardly dared blink for fear it would vanish; I barely even noticed when Miss Lyell sidled up next to me and put her arm through my own.

'What is this place?' she breathed. Her cheeks were red as cherries in the winter chill, and her hand cold to my touch. Absent-mindedly, I began stroking it to warm her.

We were evidently not the only ones to have discovered it. Half a dozen boats were moored by the shore, and I could see campfires burning on the open ground behind. The smell of roasting meat drifted across the grey water, and with it the sounds of voices and laughter and singing. Suddenly, I was very hungry.

We drifted nearer, until we were level with the end of the island. Then, with much heaving on the poles and shouting from McMeekin, we brought our bow around and turned across the current. Two of the crew leaped into the water and splashed ashore with ropes, winding them around posts and hauling furiously to bring us in. There was the merest ripple of a shudder as we touched the bottom, and a soft grating as our bow slid onto sandy soil and came to rest.

Forgetting all decorum, I jumped over the prow and ran up the beach. Three figures were standing there, watching us: a man and a woman with hands clasped before them, and a negro butler in a frock coat and breeches, carrying a tray of steaming glasses of wine. He stepped smartly forward, proffering them to me, and I took one unthinkingly.

'Welcome,' said the woman. She was tall and slender, little older than I, with wild dark hair and luminous eyes. Her black cloak was buttoned up to her chin against the cold, yet if anything it only served to accentuate her beauty. 'We hoped you would come tonight.'

'Did you have a good journey of it?' the gentleman beside her asked. He had a hooked nose and a fragile face, his hair falling in tumbling curls about it. He leaned forward to peer at me as he spoke, and though a pair of round-rimmed spectacles was perched on his nose he still gave the impression of not seeing me clearly.

'Are you Mr Tyler?' I asked.

'No.'

My face fell.

'I am Harman Blennerhassett,' he said. 'Welcome to my island. 'Mr Tyler is awaiting you inside the house.'

13

THE BLENNERHASSETTS LED US ACROSS THE LAWN TOWARDS THE house. It was as though we walked through a military camp: fires were lit all around us, and beyond them muskets stood in neat tripods before rows of tents. There were men everywhere, sitting by the fires with fiddles and songs, stamping their feet against the cold as they stood sentry duty, or hurrying to and from the great house. I rubbed my eyes, wondering if they would disappear like pixies on a summer night, but they did not.

We crossed a carriage drive – was there room on this island for a carriage? – and climbed the few steps to the mansion. The front door was thrown open, and from within came warm firelight, and the hesitant tinkling of a pianoforte. As I passed the threshold I noticed the doorplate, and blinked in renewed astonishment as I saw a lion and a unicorn holding a quartered shield, the arms of Great Britain. Was this a palace?

'We heard you were coming, of course, and delayed our dinner,' the dark-haired woman was saying. 'Micajah will show you to your rooms if you're wishing to dress.'

The negro butler led us up a curving stair, to what seemed a miniature ballroom. Golden braids and curlicues gleamed in the plaster ceiling, while the floorboards shone with a high polish. I could almost imagine a prince and a princess dancing on its surface beneath the flickering chandelier.

The butler escorted the Lyells through a door on the far side of the room, then returned and brought me to my own bedchamber on the opposite side of the house. It was by some distance the most comfortable, generous accommodation I had encountered since . . . I could not remember when. A carved mahogany bedstead laden with snow-white sheets stood in the corner, damask curtains were drawn across the windows, and my feet seemed to hover on a thick carpet. Suddenly I felt very drab, as though every speck of mud and dirt had come alive and was crawling across my skin.

'They'll be 'semblin' for dinner in fifteen min'ts,' the butler whispered, backing out through the door and pulling it shut behind him.

I threw myself down on the bed, breathing in the crisp scent of the linen. It was almost as broad as I was tall, wide enough for three men at least, yet it seemed I would enjoy it all to myself. For three months I had crossed oceans and continents; braved treacherous friends and desperate battles; sailed, ridden, driven, walked and floated some four thousand miles – all to deliver Nevell's infernal package. Now I was in a house filled with the conspirators I was meant to overthrow, with Mr Tyler himself awaiting me downstairs, and half an army camped on the front lawn. It was not a happy predicament. Yet at that moment, all I wanted to do was close my eyes and wrap myself in the bed's embrace.

In deference to my hosts, of course, I could not. Someone had laid out a cleanly pressed shirt and a new coat by the dressing table; they were a little small, but more respectable than the clothes I had not changed since Pittsburgh. I splashed some water over my face to wash away the worst residue of the journey, buttoned my coat, and went downstairs to meet the long-sought Mr Tyler.

There had been days and nights – many of them – when I had dreamed of this moment: that I would step forward, give my burden into Mr Tyler's hands and be rid of it. I had not imagined that it would take place in an elegant drawing room, its walls panelled from floor to ceiling with burnished walnut and hung with venerable portraits. Three people were gathered around an octagonal side-table: Mr and Mrs Blennerhassett, and a man I did not recognize. Whereas our hosts could have passed at any assembly or ball in London, with only their slightly antiquated fashions to betray them, this guest had a coarser, less refined air about him. His much-darned coat suggested more familiarity with horse than carriage, and there was a wildness in his eyes, a hunger, which did not bespeak a gentleman. With his grey hair and his creased, hardened face, I guessed him to be about forty. He looked up sharply as I entered the room.

'Mr Tyler, allow me to introduce Lieutenant Jerrold,' said Mrs Blennerhassett. I did not think to ask how she had learned my name, for all my thoughts were overwhelmed by the other name she had spoken: Mr Tyler.

He offered a brief nod. 'Welcome.'

I reached a trembling hand into my pocket. 'I have a package for you.'

'Good.' He was not unfriendly, but there was a certain martial economy to his words. 'From London?'

'Yes.'

I handed him the package, and suddenly felt a little giddy. There were settees on both sides of the room, but as none of the company was sitting I was obliged to remain upright.

'Good news?'

'I believe so.' It ought to be, after all I had suffered to deliver it. 'As you will observe, I have not read it myself.'

Tyler held the package below the chandelier, examining it closely. It had not come through its travel without incident – stained with mud and blood, and with a few creases in the oilcloth which had not been there in Falmouth – but the seals were intact and the knots tight.

'Are we late? Do forgive us – it is so long since I saw a bath that I confess I indulged myself quite freely.'

132

We all turned to see the two Lyells standing in the doorway. Mr Lyell had done little save brush the mud from his black suit, but his sobriety served only to illuminate the brilliance of his daughter. Her travelling clothes were gone, and in their place she had donned a silken wisp of a dress. The fabric glistened in the candlelight, barely rising to her breasts, though so smooth and pale were they that they almost appeared of a piece with it. Below her bosom the dress plunged sheer to her ankles, while above, her neck and shoulders stood entirely exposed. Two small loops about her arms were the only condescension to sleeves; they twitched as she moved, and it seemed that a single false step might slip the entire garment from her body. With her golden hair swept up behind her, and a diamond collar about her throat, she was a vision of beauty fantastical to behold. Even the myopic Blennerhassett looked amazed.

A bell sounded from the next room. Mrs Blennerhassett clapped her hands. 'That will be Micajah with dinner.'

Harman Blennerhassett took Miss Lyell's arm – gingerly, lest he work some disaster on her dress – and we followed them through the folding doors.

I could no longer be surprised by anything in this house, this out-post of gentle comfort so deep in the American wilderness, yet there was still a feeling of unreality as we processed into the spacious dining room. The table was laid for six, though it could have enter-tained twice that number, and a quartet of black and white footmen stood attentive against the ruby walls. The sideboards at each end of the room sagged under the weight of silver plate, while the table was hardly less heavily laden with pies, fish, fowl, vegetables and a haunch of venison.

Mr Blennerhassett went to the foot of the table while his wife took the head, indicating that Lyell should sit on her right. The place on her left she offered to me, but I demurred in favour of Mr Tyler. I wished to be opposite Miss Lyell, to feast my sight on her.

The servants served out the soups while Blennerhassett carved the joint. When all our plates were filled he raised his glass.

'Your healths, Miss Lyell, Mr Lyell, Mr Jerrold.'

'And yours.'

The wine was French, and sublime. I drained my glass to my hosts' health, and immediately summoned the servant to recharge it. After so much apple whiskey it was like nectar.

Across the table, Miss Lyell had engaged Blennerhassett in conversation. He leaned in to hear her with his head bent in concentration, so close that he must have been able to stare straight down onto the busk of her stays.

'We started the house eight years ago,' he was saying. 'Though of course it did not come on quickly. This was all forest, you know; we had to fell the trees and dig up all the stumps before we could even put down the foundation stones. Margaret and I were our own architects. Everything you see is precisely as we made it.'

'But you are not Americans. However did you come to choose this wild and desolate place?'

'We came over from Ireland ten years back.' Unconsciously, he removed his spectacles and rubbed them on his lapel. 'We were . . . Well, I had a disagreement with King George about who should rule Ireland, and I didn't think I'd win it, d'you see? So we sold everything at home and made our way here.'

'But do you not find it most dreadfully lonely here?'

Did I imagine it, or did Miss Lyell lean a touch closer? Vexed, and entirely superfluous to their conversation, I turned away. To my left, Tyler and Lyell were deep in some tedious discussion of politics, with Mrs Blennerhassett occasionally interjecting some opinion. I had little to offer on that subject, and they showed no interest in hearing it. I returned my attention to Miss Lyell.

'Everything you could desire floats down this river,' Blennerhassett was enthusing. 'Wines, silver, clothing, furniture, gossip – and of course the most delightful company. We could hardly be better placed if we lived on Pall Mall, and London is such a slum, you know.'

'You seem to have a great deal of company camped outside at present,' I observed.

Blennerhassett tutted, as though I had committed some distasteful solecism. 'If you do not object, we will talk of business after the ladies have retired. Even if we are at the edge of the world here, we are not entirely beyond civilization.'

Chastened, I looked back at my plate. To my surprise, Miss Lyell now intervened on my behalf.

'You must forgive Lieutenant Jerrold his impatience, Mr Blennerhassett. He is a man of action and decision. Why, have you heard the adventure of our voyage to America? Mr Jerrold single-handedly saved us from certain death.'

She smiled at me, and again I felt the fortifying power of her gaze. A silver candelabra sat on the table between us; its flames, the diamonds at her throat, her flashing eyes and the shimmer of her dress all seemed to fuse into a sparkling constellation of delight. I called for another glass, and listened to her begin to relate the story of our battle with the Spanish privateer. My initial embarrassment quickly faded as the wine began to unknit my nerves, and she proved an engaging storyteller. Several times, confessing her help-less ignorance of matters nautical, she turned to me for the correct term or phrase, and I became ever more forward in volunteering facts or amending her recollections. Gradually the whole table was drawn into the tale, listening with rapt attention as she described the mutinous crew, the overwhelming odds, the terrible punishment we had taken and our last, desperate broadside. Somewhere about the moment where our mast was shot away I felt a soft slipper crook itself around my ankle and tug it forward under the table. She never broke her tale, but I fancied I saw inviting glances flashing across the table at me.

'It seems Lieutenant Jerrold is a useful man in a sea fight,' said Tyler, when Miss Lyell had exhausted her account. 'Although I trust you'll have a bigger deck to stand on next time you engage the enemy.'

'I do hope so.'

From there, the dinner progressed in an agreeable blur of conver-sation, laughter, food and drink – and the warm pressure of the slipper against my stockings. I felt a brief alarm when Mr Tyler excused himself from the table, the package obvious in his hand, but when he returned twenty minutes later it was with a look of approval on his face. The second course was brought out, and then the desserts, which included a great amount of fruit both fresh and preserved. Miss Lyell expressed astonishment at the presence of a pineapple.

'The soil in these parts is wondrous fertile,' Blennerhassett explained, with the enthusiasm of a horticultural zealot. 'It seems there is nothing that cannot come out of it. Why, I sometimes say to Margaret that you could sow a stone and in six months you would have a cliff.'

'But in December? Surely the frost would ravage it awfully?'

'I have a glasshouse which gives me a perpetual summer, even in the depths of this dismal season. Perhaps tomorrow I may show it to you?'

'That would be very kind.'

Mrs Blennerhassett stood. 'I think, my dear Miss Lyell, that you and I should retire to the drawing room and permit these men their business.'

To my lingering regret, the slipper uncoiled itself from my leg. When the ladies had gone, Blennerhassett rose.

'We will take port in my study if you're agreeable, gentlemen?'

We rose, and followed Blennerhassett through the entrance hall and a parlour, out into the chill night. The campfires on the lawn were damped down now, the men doubtless shivering in their tents, but I could still see shadowy figures processing up and down near the landing, muskets on their shoulders. Were they expecting an attack?

A short, curving colonnade brought us to one of the outbuildings. Blennerhassett unlocked the door with a key from his waistcoat and admitted us to a warm, cosy study where a large log fire burned high in the grate. Once again the contents of the room were entirely at odds with my expectations. Scientific devices of every description were jumbled on shelves and tables: scales, measures, flasks, glasses and telescopes, together with an ocean of books and papers strewn between them. His affection for science was obviously promiscuous, for I could see volumes of horticulture, of astronomy and taxonomy, botany and natural philosophy all sprawled open.

Only one island of order stood free of the chaos, a square card table entirely covered by an outspread map. Even here, the man's eclectic tastes were evident, for its four corners were weighted down variously by a volume of poetry, a sextant, a cigar box and a teacup so long disused it had gathered a scum of dust. In the centre of the map, as casually discarded as the teacup, lay the unfolded oilskin of my packet. It almost felt blasphemous to see the cords cut and the seals snapped open, with crumbs of the wax still scattered over the map, but my attention was fixed entirely on the two pieces of paper lying amid the packaging. The compulsion to know what secret message I had carried so long and through such dangers consumed me, yet all I could make out were strange lines of indecipherable symbols.

Tyler reached over the table and picked up the papers, setting them aside on a workbench behind him. When the decanter had gone around and the butler left, he leaned forward and tapped his finger on a spot near the centre of the map.

'Well – Mr Lyell, Mr Jerrold – here we are. I guess now you've come so far, you'll want to see we've justified your faith.'

I looked down on the map. 'A New Map of the United States of America' its legend proclaimed, though at first it looked as though the cartographer had overestimated his task and abandoned it halfway through. The eastern portion of the country was completely filled in, a tapestry of roads, towns, rivers and mountains which bespoke a tamed and obedient land. But from the centre of the map westwards it was an unsettled and unnamed emptiness, a white expanse broken only by a few small rivers, mere cracks around the edges. Like a gulf between these two worlds, splitting the continent almost in two, ran the Mississippi River.

'As you'll have seen, we've assembled the army here on the island,' Tyler was saying. 'But we can't stay long. The word's gotten out, and Jefferson's men'll be closing in on us fast.'

I did not like the sound of that, though it was hardly surprising. It seemed our enemies had been closing in ever since we stepped foot in America.

'We've got six boats here and another twelve just up the river at Marietta. There'll be more to meet us coming down the Cumberland. All told, I figure we've enough craft for fifteen hundred men, along with their arms and provisions.'

'Do you have any artillery yet?' Blennerhassett enquired.

'We'll find that in New Orleans, before we strike west.'

'How many men have enlisted thus far?' said Lyell.

Tyler ignored him. 'For now, our prime need is money. It's not a cheap business equipping an invasion, you'll appreciate. The funds you've brought from England, Mr Lyell, will be a great help.'

'You anticipate yourself, Mr Tyler. Where is Colonel Burr? The arrangement was that I would meet him here to discuss his scheme before any monies changed hands.'

Even a man like Tyler, well versed in abrupt frontier manners, recoiled under Lyell's bite. 'The colonel was called away down river on business. He'll be in Kentucky or Tennessee, seeing to something or other.'

'When will he return?'

'He won't. His orders were that if he hadn't returned by the twenty-eighth of November we should set out. It's the eighth of December now, and we cannot delay. The river's already beginning to freeze about us, and it's said the county militia may be called out. The longer we stay here, the greater our danger.'

That did for me. Perhaps it was the port which sapped my reticence, sitting on top of the claret and Madeira I'd had at dinner; perhaps it was the sheer unreality of sitting in those learned surrounds with a gang of conspirators speaking of armies and artillery; perhaps it was simply the frustration of my ignorance, or the dregs of Nevell's instructions stirring within me. I banged my glass on the table and stood.

'I beg your pardon, sirs, but you have me at a disadvantage. At the shortest possible notice I was given a package to bring to Mr Tyler, which duty I have discharged faithfully and at no little hazard to myself.' So much, at least, was true. 'I do not ask much in return, but having proved my good offices, I beg you enlighten my ignorance as to your intentions. Or, if you would rather, leave me to my bed.'

I sat down again, trembling. Lyell and Tyler had fixed me with probing looks, while Blennerhassett polished his glasses on his neckcloth. Had I grievously misjudged the matter?

'Of course,' said Tyler. 'I had forgotten.'

I slumped back, unable to keep from smiling with relief.

'How much do you know?'

The crackling fire still burned hot against my back, but the smile on my face was frozen as stiff as the trees outside the window. All three of my companions were watching me intently. I reached for the decanter to steady my nerve, then purposely passed it to Lyell on my left. It moved around the table, the liquid tumbling into the glasses and splashing blood-red droplets over the pristine wilderness on the map. All too soon, the decanter was back where it had started.

'They told me to bring you the package,' I began. 'They said it contained something of the utmost delicacy. They said . . .'

I paused, trying to cut a path through the thicket of confusion in my mind. I was a naval officer, carrying a packet with an Admiralty seal on it. Nevell had warned me of an illegitimate alliance between war and commerce: if Lyell spoke for the commerce, then perhaps I was to represent war. At any rate, I could guess that had Lieutenant Beauchamp been in my place, he would have known enough not to blanch at talk of treason. I leaned in closer, resting my arms on the table.

'They confided in me that there are certain endeavours of which our government might not approve, but which are nonetheless vital to the interests of our nation. They suggested that although this could not be done in any *recognized* capacity, a young officer might yet win the approval of his superiors by participating.' Each word I spoke was like a footstep on thin ice, and each time that I did not shatter my precarious ground my confidence grew. I decided to stop before I overstepped myself. 'They told me to put myself at your disposal, and to trust that whatever you asked of me would be coincident with my duty. Here I am.'

I picked up the decanter and started it around again, though my glass was drained almost before Lyell had filled his.

'And you are satisfied that you will not compromise your honour with us?' Tyler pressed me.

I shrugged. 'I cannot know unless I know what you intend. But I will believe what my superiors have told me.' I tried to remember my uncle's periodic effusions against the current ministry. 'Lord Grenville and his friends seem more interested in negroes and papists than in prosecuting the war against Buonaparte. If you aim to hurt France or Spain, and serve England – then, sir, I am with you.'

'Well spoken. Your superiors were right to trust in you, and you in them.'

It seemed an eternity since I had last drawn breath. Now, at last, I began to breathe easier. I could consider what dangerous folly I had embarked upon later.

'Look at this map,' Tyler began, 'and imagine that the continent is divided lengthways in four. East of the Appalachians you have the old colonies, the original thirteen. Between the mountains and the Mississippi, the new states and territories, where we are now. West of the Mississippi you see the other half of her great basin, Louisiana, that President Jefferson purchased off Mr Buonaparte a few years back. Finally, beyond that, Spanish territory, Northern Mexico.'

I peered at the map. The first two divisions were clear enough, but I could see no line demarcating the boundary between the latter two. 'Where does Louisiana end and Mexico begin?'

'Somewhere in the Rocky Mountains. No-one's precisely sure,' Tyler admitted. 'Leastways, not for the moment.'

'That seems careless.'

'Mr Buonaparte didn't give many particulars at the time. Told us to fight out the details with the Spanish, as I heard, and was happy enough to take our money.'

'Not your money,' Lyell corrected him, 'our money. Mr Jefferson could not have purchased one acre of Louisiana without the bonds we converted for him in London. Eleven million dollars all told.'

I stared at him in disbelief. 'You gave eleven million dollars to President Jefferson, and he then made about and paid it to Buonaparte?'

'Not gave, Mr Jerrold; floated. At a twenty-five per cent profit. You cannot afford to be squeamish about such things in our business.'

'Anyhow, that's by the way,' said Tyler. 'It's here that concerns us.' He tapped his finger on the westernmost part of the map, the Spanish territory. 'Mexico. You're a naval man, Mr Jerrold – have you ever taken a Mexican treasure ship?'

I had not, but I knew of those who had and had earned enough from the prize money to leave the sea for ever.

'Each year, Mexico sends a treasure fleet home to Spain loaded with all the gold and silver they've prised out of her mines. The whole value of the colony sailing out of Vera Cruz, and it comes to something above four million dollars.'

'Which Spain then passes on to her French allies,' said Blennerhassett. 'Which Buonaparte uses to buy ships and guns and men to fight his wars.'

At last the mystery began to lift. 'So you plan to reach Vera Cruz and cut out the treasure fleet?' It was not a new idea: similar schemes had been rumoured around the navy for years. I did not know that I wanted any part of it, but if I could stay alive, I could foresee a sudden upturn in my fortunes.

Tyler was shaking his head. 'You've misunderstood me. We don't want the treasure ships.'

'Don't we?'

'Why take the egg when you can have the goose?'

I struggled to follow. 'But that would mean . . .'

Tyler nodded. 'We're going to invade Mexico.'

At first I thought I had misheard; then that it might be some strange manifestation of American humour which I did not recognize. But all three of my companions were nodding seriously, and the smirk on Lyell's face bore no trace of mirth. I stared at the map, at the vast extent of the Mexican territory which stretched clear through fifteen degrees of latitude, over three thousand miles long. How could the men gathered on this island hope to overcome it?

Another thought struck me. 'But is America at war with Spain?'

'That's being arranged,' said Tyler. 'If we aren't already, we surely will be by the time we reach New Orleans.'

'We have a confidante on the Mexican border,' explained Blennerhassett. 'General Wilkinson, who commands the American army there, is our man.'

'Spain and America have been quarrelling over the boundary line for months,' said Tyler. 'The country's ready for war. All we need now is for the general to provoke it at an opportune time, and our army will sweep into Mexico.'

'How many men do you have?' I asked. Beside me, I noticed Lyell lean closer in interest.

'By tomorrow night, we will have enough boats and arms for an army of one and a half thousand.' There was something evasive in Tyler's answer which belied his confident tone, but he hurried on before I could consider it. 'General Wilkinson and his men will join us at New Orleans, together with the artillery. And then there are Lieutenant Jerrold's ships.'

All eyes turned to me for confirmation of this last fact, and once again I felt the drop of fear in my stomach.

'Yes, absolutely,' was all I could think to say. I glanced over Tyler's shoulder at the letter discarded behind him, the letter I had brought; I wished to all heaven I could read it. Before anyone could question me further, I hurriedly asked, 'But why so much secrecy? If war with Spain is inevitable, and you will invade Mexico on behalf of America, surely all our skulking about has been needless.'

There was a silence, and again I wondered if I had overstepped some invisible mark of ignorance. Tyler cleared his throat.

'We're not exactly acting on behalf of the United States,' he said. 'More in what you might call a personal capacity.'

I gaped. 'You will invade Mexico with your army, and turn it into your own private empire?'

Blennerhassett nodded.

'An empire which at a single stroke will cut off France and Spain's supply of bullion, and open new markets to British trade,' said Lyell. 'Britain will gain from the debilitation of her enemies and the increase of her commerce, and we will profit handsomely from the investment. We already have Spain on the run in South America, at Buenos Aires; now we will strike in the north and deliver the *coup de grâce*.'

There were open smiles all around the table. The decanter went around again and Blennerhassett raised his glass. 'To the riches of Mexico.'

'To Mexico,' we chorused.

The fortified wine and the hot fire breathing on my back warmed my soul. On the map spread out before us Mexico seemed mere inches away. With the army camped on our doorstep, the stands of arms we had brought in the flatboat and the laughter in the room, all these dreams of conquest almost seemed tangible.

Half an hour later, in the solitude of my room, it seemed a thoroughly less appetizing proposition. I sat on the edge of my bed and pulled off my shoes, flinging them carelessly in the corner. The fire in the grate was burning lower, and as it ebbed so too did all the promise of Tyler's scheme. It was lunacy. Even if he had his fifteen hundred men on the island, could he really transport them two thousand miles down the river in the grip of winter? And even that would take them only to New Orleans; from there, there would be hundreds more miles overland into Mexico. From what I had seen thus far of the American interior, and the ominous white spaces on Tyler's map, I doubted it would be an easy march – even without a Spanish army opposing us. As for the idea that two battalions of mercenaries could topple an empire, that seemed the height of optimism. Yet Lyell and his allies had already achieved it in Buenos Aires.

And then there are Lieutenant Jerrold's ships. I remembered Tyler's words, and shivered. The knowledge of how false, how precarious, was my membership of this expedition chilled me. I had already come close to tripping over the precipice of my ignorance; could I truly sustain the pretence all the way to New Orleans, and beyond into Mexico? At some point I would be discovered, and I did not care to contemplate what fate would befall me then.

Yet, of course, if I went even half so far I would have failed. *Learn what you can of Mr Tyler and his scheme*, Nevell had instructed me, and much against my expectations, I had succeeded. *Then stop it.* How could I? Alone against an army, removed from all hope of support, I could do nothing. England was too far away, while even if I had known how to betray the conspiracy to the American authorities I would not have dared. Nevell had impressed upon me the paramountcy of avoiding conflict with America: if they learned that a confederacy of Englishmen were plotting to establish a private empire on their western border, in the heart of their continent, there would surely be war.

Through all these discomforting thoughts I always returned to a single point: the package, the letter I had brought from England for Tyler. If it came from Tyler's accomplices in London, it must give some hint of their strategy. It might also shed light on how I might proceed.

A memory rose in my mind, of Mr Harris lying sprawled on the road with Miss Lyell's bullet in his skull. It was a salutary fate for anyone who might covet the letter. On the other hand, it would not be so very different if my own duplicity were discovered. The choice was hardly enviable.

I sat on the edge of my bed for almost an hour, trembling with my thoughts and listening to the household gradually put itself to bed. When I had counted ten minutes without any sound of movement, I stood and edged open the door. The room next to mine, the library, was dark, and I could see no light from the drawing room beyond. With my heart heaving like a bilge-pump, I slipped out of the bed-chamber. The house was quiet, save for the last embers crumbling in the hall fireplace, and my stockinged feet made little noise on the steps. I carried no candle, though I kept one of Lyell's Manton pistols tucked in my belt. How I would escape from this lonely island if I had to use it I did not consider. Almost certainly, I would not.

I paused at the foot of the stairs, then made my way through the east parlour and out into the portico. The icy stone was like cut glass under my feet; I almost yelped to feel it through my stocking, and flailed down the passage with ungainly hops to reach the study. I prayed the sentries were too busy warming their hands to see my floundering progress between the white columns. The handle to the study door was as cold as the ground, but it was not locked; I slipped through and pulled it shut behind me. Even inside, the frozen air turned my rapid breaths to vapour.

For all the effort I had lavished on bringing Tyler his letter, he had shown it a remarkable indifference once he had it. It still lay where he had left it on a workbench against the wall, beside a pickled frog in a jar and an astronomical almanac. I lifted the two sheets of paper tenderly, as if they might rip apart in my fingers, and crouched by the hearth where the fire's last glow gave just enough light to read.

As quickly as my hopes had risen, disappointment knifed through them. Tyler's correspondents had trussed up their package with secret twines and multiple seals; I should have foreseen that the message within would be equally bound up in secrecy. The symbols on the paper danced and flickered before me in the firelight, but no amount of light could have illuminated their meaning. They were like some cabalistic incantation or ancient runes: some looked like letters, though from an eclectic alphabet; others were like numbers or mathematical symbols; still others bore no resemblance to any-thing, but were scrawled across the page in fathomless combinations of squares and lines, circles and hatch-marks. Had I been told it was the hand of the devil himself I might well have believed it.

I turned to the second sheet and my hopes rekindled. This was not some opaque cipher; it was English, hastily written with many crossings-out and revisions, but perfectly legible. The ink was fresh, and sand still clung to the paper. Crouching behind the table, I held it up to the fire and squinted close.

Mr Tyler,

I received Colonel Burr's most recent communication on the 18th inst. Having satisfied myself of his true intentions and good faith, and the high chance of a profitable conclusion to his venture, I have this day despatched two frigates, the Cambrian *and the* Duke of Gloucester, *in aid of your army. They will take station about the line of twenty-eight degrees north latitude, due south of the mouth of the river Mississippi, for the stated purpose of monitoring neutral commerce, and there await word of your success. Their captains, fully cognisant of their duty, answer only to me, and will support your operations to their ultimate conclusion.*

The mails being unsafe, I am sending this by the hand of a junior officer. He is a resourceful man well known to me, and sympathetic to our designs, though ignorant of their true extent at present; you may confide freely in him. He will see this business to its end, howsoever that may be.

You will remember that the current ministry, in its pusillanimity, would condemn our ambitions if it knew them. I trust that you will recollect this fact as you conduct your operations, and shroud them in the utmost secrecy. You must not fail; to do so would be the ruin of us all.

I remain, &c

As my eyes took in the name at the end, faithfully transcribed by whoever had deciphered the letter, I almost dropped it in the fire. I snatched it back; then, slowly, held it up again to the light. I had not been mistaken.

I fumbled with the papers, bringing the cipher sheet back to the fore. With all the esoteric symbols and meaningless characters, I had not troubled to look past the first few lines. Now, I followed the cryptic message to its end. In the bottom right corner, exactly where I had expected, there was one final scribble. To the unprepared eye it would have looked little different to any of the other marks – a little longer and more expansive, perhaps, but not overly so. Yet I knew, without question, it was not a part of the code. It was a signature. A signature I knew almost as well as my own, one which had impressed itself on me at the bottom of endless letters enumerating my faults, bemoaning my failings, condemning my errors and threatening my ruin.

It was my uncle's.

14

AMID THE CONFUSION WHICH FOLLOWED, WHILE THE GREATER PART of my mind succumbed to the upheaval of all I had known, a small corner still clung to rational order. *An illegitimate alliance between war and commerce*, Nevell had said – had he known my uncle represented war's side of the bargain? I would not think him incapable of it. Certainly, it explained why Lyell had been so interested to hear of my connections, why the conspirators had trusted me so readily. Nor should it have surprised me to find my uncle implicated in this scheme: he despised the current ministry, the First Lord most of all. If he saw a chance to humiliate his political enemies, then striking at the Spanish as well would be an almost unsought dividend.

One thing was unarguable: my uncle's reputation, his career, perhaps even his life, if the government deemed it treason, were hostage to this letter. As a dutiful, affectionate nephew, I should doubtless have thrown it on the fire and forgotten forever the fact of its existence. As a nephew who had suffered more threats, tantrums and obloquy from my uncle than ever he had directed at the French, I did not hesitate. I folded both sheets of the letter, the original and the decipherment, and thrust them inside my coat. It was hard to keep from smiling. Those two papers could be the ruination of my uncle's career; they could equally be the salvation of my own. With them in my hands, what could he deny me? A rapid promotion, then a pension and a stipend in some Navy Office sinecure. After weeks of submission I felt a rare glow of purpose kindle within me. Perhaps Nevell had done me a favour. Now all that mattered was that I survive the ordeal, escape this wilderness and return to London to claim my prize.

The fire flared in the grate as a gust of air fanned it. 'What the Jesus are you doing here?'

I turned, banging my knee on the table leg in my haste. I winced as I stood, and winced again as I saw the gleam of blue metal, the twin barrels of a shotgun pointed straight towards me. Harman Blennerhassett was standing by the open door, an incongruous sight in his nightshirt, slippers and cap. He was not wearing his spectacles, though at that range even he might have hit me without them.

'It's Lieutenant Jerrold,' I said.

The gun angled down a little, though not nearly so much as I would have liked. 'And what do you mean by prying around my study so late, Mr Jerrold, when good Christian men should be abed?'

I stared around the room, trying desperately to think of some innocent excuse. All I could fix on was the pickled frog on the workbench where my uncle's letter had lain. Dear God, what if Blennerhassett noticed its absence? Even if he did not, Tyler surely would next morning.

The thought of having to surrender my prize, my hard-won card to trump my uncle, spurred my mind to invention. 'It was the letter,' I said. 'The letter I brought for Mr Tyler from England.'

Blennerhassett jerked his head. 'What of it?'

'I burned it,' I said baldly. 'I did not wish it to fall into the wrong hands.'

The gun's muzzle dropped towards the floor. A loose piece of shot trickled out of the barrel and rolled away.

'It was a good thought, Lieutenant. Your superiors in London were wise to send you.'

I almost laughed at the thought of what my superior in London would say if he knew where I was. *He is a resourceful man well known to me*, he had said. Half of it was true.

'Your caution does you credit – though it was not necessary, you know.' Blennerhassett smiled. 'You have no enemies on this island tonight.'

I returned to my room shivering with more than cold. I knew how near my escape had been. Blennerhassett might be able to peer deep into nature with his microscopes and spyglasses, but when it came to his fellow men even his spectacles could not help. Had Tyler confronted me, the outcome might have been altogether more violent. Still, I had the letter safe in my pocket and for that I was thankful. I was also inordinately tired. Back in the safety of my bed-room, I stripped off my clothes and sank gratefully onto the mattress, too weary even to pull on my nightshirt. After weeks of ignorance, I had learned so much in a single evening that the only way I could master it was to close my eyes and hope the morning would be a long time coming.

There was a knock at the door. My eyes snapped open, and I lay still as stone under my blankets. Had Blennerhassett reconsidered my excuse and found it wanting, or summoned Tyler and Lyell to interrogate me further? They would not even have to search hard for the letter: it was still inside my coat draped over a chair opposite the bed.

'Lieutenant Jerrold?'

My fears abated, and in their stead was only fuddled confusion. Was I dreaming? The handle turned, the door edged in a little and the voice came again.

'Lieutenant Jerrold?'

'Miss Lyell?'

She stepped into the room. Her hair was loose, tumbling down with unbrushed abandon. A shawl was pulled around her shoulders, but as the door closed she let it drop away. Beneath, she still wore the gown I had seen at dinner. In the darkness, it blended with her skin so absolutely that I could imagine she wore nothing at all.

Clutching the bedsheet around my waist, I stood. As she moved towards me, I could smell woodsmoke in her hair, and sweet wine on her breath. We faced each other, inches away.

'Has your father sent you?' I asked, shy of repeating my mistake at the Princeton inn.

She laughed softly. 'Not this time.'

I leaned towards her, and she came forward to meet me. Our lips touched, and so forceful was her kiss that I lost my footing and swayed back a little. I threw out my arms for balance, and the sheet which covered my modesty dropped away. With a small moan of delight, she took my hands and guided them to the thin straps on her arms. I tugged on them, and felt a thrill of joy as the silk pulled taut over her breasts, then fell to the floor with a whisper of illicit promise. Underneath, she wore neither stays nor petticoats. Her skin was pale, bare and flawless.

With a brazen confidence which surely bespoke experience, she thrust me backwards onto the bed and sprang after me, lithe as a cat. Her hair brushed over my skin, while her mouth and hands teased me with hungry urgency.

Suddenly, unbidden and thoroughly unwanted, an image of Isobel leaped into my thoughts. I shook my head to dislodge her and squeezed my eyes shut; when I opened them again, there was only Miss Lyell rising above me like a vision of Venus. I drew her down towards me, past understanding but alive to a hundred pleasures I had not known in months. There, in the little paradise which the Blennerhassetts had built themselves, I met temptation and embraced it greedily.

15

I AWOKE COLD AND ALONE. AN UGLY GREY LIGHT FILTERED THROUGH the curtains, and the clock on the mantel showed a few minutes before ten. Were it not for the strands of golden hair on my pillow, I would have sworn I had dreamed the night's encounter. Though even then, memory of the dream alone would have been enough to dispel the morning gloom.

As thoughts of the previous evening crowded in on one another, I dismounted my bed and rummaged in my coat pocket. The letters were still there and, to my relief, my uncle's signature had been no more a dream than Miss Lyell's attentions. There it was at the foot of the cipher sheet, stark and ordinary in the daylight. Using my penknife, I unpicked the threads of my coat and thrust the sheets deep in the lining. Spaniards and Americans had proved willing to kill to obtain the letter; to their number I might sensibly add Lyell and Tyler if they guessed it was not destroyed.

Breakfast was long since cleared from the dining room, but Mrs Blennerhassett was still there instructing one of the servants in some task. With her ringed hair and imperious carriage, she had the air of a latter-day Agrippina, all unbending purpose and virtue. She smiled generously as I entered.

'Good morning, Lieutenant. I am glad to find you risen at last.

Did you sleep poorly? I felt quite sure I heard you cry out in the night.'

'I slept delightfully,' I assured her. 'If there were bad dreams about last night, they did not trouble me.'

'I am so pleased to hear it. You will need all your strength for the days ahead, you know. Mr Tyler is convinced that we cannot wait here any longer. He insists that we must make ready to leave tomorrow.'

'We?' I echoed. 'Are you to accompany us, Mrs Blennerhassett?'

She frowned. 'Of course. Harman and I are quite inseparable. He led me from Ireland to London, and from London to Philadelphia, and thence to this island; now I will follow him into the west. Harman is quite brilliant, you know, but he needs a companion to ensure that others do not take advantage of his generous nature. And of course, it will be a thrilling adventure. The colonel is a man of extraordinary vision.'

I would have liked to ask her more about this Colonel Burr, whom everybody spoke of in such awe, but she was a great deal shrewder than her husband. I had already sailed too close to the wind the night before; I did not wish to find myself in irons. Instead, I excused myself and continued in search of breakfast.

I found the kitchen in one of the outbuildings, the pair of Blennerhassett's study at the end of the other colonnade. Thick smoke rose from the chimney, and my stomach began to warm at the thought of bacon and eggs, or perhaps a slice of gammon. Far from sating me, the feast the night before had only spurred my appetite. In happy anticipation, I opened the door.

Like every other room in the Blennerhassett mansion, the kitchen was clean, spacious and well ordered. Black pots and ladles hung from the ceiling, while dried herbs and jars of preserves lined its walls. Yet the wholesome industry had been disturbed: there was no haunch of venison or side of pork turning on the spit, and no white-aproned cook with her arms elbow-deep in flour. Instead, two young men in fringed shirts and tricorn hats knelt by the fire. One held a small pan in which a lead ingot was quickly melting over the flames;

153

the other an iron mould, laid open on its hinge. As I watched, the one with the pan pulled it clear of the flames and tipped it over, so that the molten lead trickled through the spout into the mould. His companion snapped it shut, then plunged it into the open water-butt beside him. A gout of steam hissed into the air.

The motion brought me into their sight, and they paused in their work. Far from the veteran desperadoes I had expected, they looked not dissimilar to the students we had encountered at Princeton, smooth-cheeked and disarmingly guileless.

I touched my hat. 'I beg your pardon. I was seeking breakfast.'

The elder of the two, the one who held the mould, gestured to a shelf in the corner. 'There's a loaf there.' Without further conversation he turned back to running his bullets.

I took the bread and departed. Looking around the grounds, I could see there were in fact few corners where martial preparations were not afoot. On the front lawn, men were stowing tents and dragging them down to the boats, while hammers knocked iron hoops around staves to assemble new casks for provisions. Near the water, half a dozen men appeared to be exercising their muskets, though by the way they flailed their ramrods and dropped their ammunition pouches they would have made any sergeant weep.

Yet what struck me most was not their inefficiency, but their numbers. Tyler had spoken of a thousand and a half men, which had seemed paltry enough to invade a colony the size of France, but here I could see not even half so many. I leaned against a pillar of the colonnade, chewing my bread, and counted them. Even making allowance for the two in the kitchen, I could only make them forty-nine. Unless Tyler had a reserve battalion secreted somewhere deep on the island, the Spanish would be able to halt the invasion with half a company of militia.

I threw the bread away, and watched a flock of blackbirds swoop down from the trees to peck at it. Were these men lunatics? I did not think so. Blennerhassett was a trifle odd, granted, but Tyler seemed sharp enough. As for Lyell, I doubted there was a more calculating, ruthless investor in all London. Surely he would not put his funds behind fifty men and an eccentric Irishman? There must be something more I had not comprehended.

For the moment, I gave up the struggle. Thoughts of Lyell had taken my mind in altogether happier directions. I did not fully understand what had brought his daughter to my bed, but I was desperate to believe she did not regret it. Certainly the passion she had shown, the fervour with which she had embraced me, suggested a more lasting attachment. I shivered with the memory and longed for the evening to hasten on.

'Would you care to take a turn, Lieutenant?'

Miss Lyell's face was peering around the pillar, almost swallowed up by the fur stole wrapped around her neck. Her lips were red as berries in the cold, and parted slightly in a mischievous smile.

'That would be delightful.'

'Mrs Blennerhassett insists that her pleasure-garden has no equal on this continent.'

'I would be happy to see it.' Though in truth I was more interested in pleasure than gardens.

Miss Lyell allowed me to take her arm, then led me around the back of the house to a second lawn bordered by neat white fences. On one side lay the kitchen garden, and a long hothouse whose clammy panes admitted views of exotic foliage; opposite lay the meandering gravel walks and well-tended beds of the flower garden. For all Mrs Blennerhassett's enthusiasm, in this season it displayed little more than bare earth and grey branches.

We slipped through a low gate and walked companionably between rows of dormant roses. In the distance I could see a rounded summerhouse standing solitary at the end of the path.

'What a curious place this is,' said Miss Lyell. 'I wonder that the Blennerhassetts can bear it, so very far from civilization.'

'They must have a great fondness for solitude.'

'Or a need of it.' Miss Lyell's eyes were sharp as icicles. 'I had it from one of the servants that they were driven here by scandal. Mrs Blennerhassett was Harman's niece and ward; he seduced her while she was in his care.'

155

It was hard to imagine the genial, ineffectual Harman seducing anyone. 'Perhaps he mistook her for someone else.'

Miss Lyell laughed. 'Very like. And now they intend to abandon this island altogether, and start anew in an even deeper wilderness.' She looked up at me with narrowed eyes. 'I hear they are bound for Mexico.'

Evidently, I had misspent my efforts. Instead of risking discovery and death with Lyell and Tyler, I should merely have enquired of the servants to learn the Blennerhassetts' scheme.

Miss Lyell still waited on me expectantly. Wary of admitting too much to Lyell's daughter, however willing she might be in bed, I judged my answer carefully. 'I believe that may be true.'

She pulled away, and slapped a reproving hand against my arm. 'You are too cruel, Lieutenant. You know very well that Mexico belongs to Spain.'

'At present.'

'You have seen all those men camped on the front lawn. What do you suppose they purpose?'

'What do the servants say?'

She pouted. 'They say that Mr Blennerhassett is to lead an army down the river to invade Mexico, that he will found a new empire and that Mrs Blennerhassett will be his queen. Can you imagine anything half so fanciful? These negroes are too, too imaginative.'

We had reached the summerhouse. Behind us, the lines and curves of the flowerbeds stretched back towards the main mansion; ahead, a hawthorn hedge ran across the garden.

'The maze,' said Miss Lyell. 'Shall we go in?'

We passed through a gap in the hedge. High walls, green even in winter, rose around us, broken only by a gravel walk too narrow for two to walk abreast. I followed Miss Lyell further in and around two turns, until we had lost sight of the entrance, when suddenly she turned on her heel and threw her arms around me. Her lips were cold and firm, but her mouth was warm and her embrace unyielding.

'I hope you do not think less of me for last night,' she whispered in my ear.

156

'I hold you in the highest esteem,' I assured her. I slipped a hand beneath her stole, feeling the tightness of her dress, and gave a little pinch. She shivered.

'My life is so dreary, Lieutenant. Papa insists I accompany him everywhere, that I pack his chest when he travels and act his hostess when he entertains his boring associates. Yet he does not admit me to his confidence. Even when he brings me so far on this adventure, you might think he had only come to admire the landscape for all he tells me.' She kissed me again. 'Are you bound for Mexico with the Blennerhassetts?'

'I believe so.' Though not if I could find any way to avert it. For once, Nevell's concern with thwarting the conspiracy, and my own need to escape as quickly as possible, were in perfect accord.

'You are so brave – and fortunate. Papa has no intention of travelling any further. We will trudge back to London through this horrid country, and you will earn fame and glory.'

I started. 'You cannot leave us here!' Catherine's attentions had been my one solace on this misguided ordeal. To lose her now, just as I had won her, seemed miserable even by my usual lot. I had hoped the previous night's encounter would augur a new, lasting attachment; instead, it must have been her farewell.

She moved closer. 'What I would not give to accompany you. But Papa insists . . .'

'Come with me,' I pleaded. 'Come with me, Miss Lyell—'

'Call me Catherine. We have been intimate enough, I think.'

Her fingers traced a line down the back of my breeches, then squeezed me in towards her. I responded with zeal – too much so, for my thrust unbalanced her and she fell back against the hedge with a great snapping of twigs. As she extracted herself, I heard footsteps on the gravel walk on the far side of the hawthorn, and voices.

She put a finger to her lips. 'Papa. He will not be pleased if he discovers us together. He thinks you are something of a rogue.'

She stuck out her tongue, but I was suddenly in no mood for her flirting. The footsteps had left the gravel, thudded up the summerhouse's wooden stairs, and halted a few feet from where we stood.

157

One voice was Lyell's, as Catherine had recognized; the other Tyler's. Neither sounded amiable.

'We've a further three dozen men coming from Pittsburgh tomorrow,' Tyler was saying. 'Maybe more. And the colonel's been recruiting down in Tennessee and Kentucky – he's another five boats in Nashville, enough for three hundred men at least.'

'If he can find them. I do not doubt your ability to come by boats and muskets. I am more disturbed that you do not have the men to man them.'

'With the volunteers from Pittsburgh—'

'You will still have fewer than a hundred men on the island. I could raise a bigger army by handing out shillings at Vauxhall. Have you dragged me four thousand miles into this forsaken place for this? Do you truly think my associates and I will risk our lives, our reputations and our fortunes on your rabble?' There was something dangerous in his voice now, and I imagined him leaning over Tyler in fury.

The American, for his part, sounded suitably cowed. 'Come down river with us,' he pleaded. 'The colonel will figure it out, you'll see. He'll find the men. And as word gets about what we're planning, others'll join us down in the territories. Then there's Wilkinson's men – half the United States army with us. You can't argue that.'

A lethal condescension overtook Lyell's tone. 'Mr Tyler, I am a man of business. If an indebted man comes to me seeking a loan, I may well consider his case, but not if he has defaulted on what he already owes no matter how much he may promise in future. If you cannot raise the thousand men you assured me would be here, am I to believe you will subsequently raise twice their number? I think not.'

'At least come far enough to meet the colonel,' Tyler insisted. 'He'll know how to mend it. This war's going to happen whatever you say.'

'Unless you can conjure another thousand men, it will happen without my fifty thousand dollars. I will not sit here waiting for some bumpkin magistrate to arrest me, and I most assuredly will not travel any further on this fool's errand on Colonel Burr's promise. If he wishes to find me, he may follow me across the mountains to New York, where I shall await the next packet to London.'

'What about the Lieutenant? Will you take him with you?'

I strained closer to hear, almost overbalancing again into the hedge. Miss Lyell's hand held me back.

'Lieutenant Jerrold will doubtless do as his duty and his orders dictate. Seeing that his superiors stand to lose as much as I do, I cannot think he will look favourably on the project as it currently stands.'

For once, Lyell had guessed my sentiments exactly.

There was a pause, and a few flat footsteps as someone paced the deck of the summerhouse. Then I heard Tyler's voice. 'At least stay with us until we find the colonel.'

'He will need a strong case to persuade me.'

Tyler sounded brighter, though his voice was fading as they left the summerhouse. 'He will, Mr Lyell, you can be assured of that. The colonel's never without a strong case.'

Catherine and I did not linger in the maze. One could not be outside on that day and keep still for long, and a hawthorn hedge was no place for the exertions I had in mind. She left as soon as Tyler and her father were gone; I waited a few moments by the kitchen garden, admiring the glasshouse in a vacant way. I had many secrets to keep from Lyell, and my courtship of his daughter was not least dangerous among them.

'Are you a horticultural man, Mr Jerrold?'

I turned, quicker than a guiltless man should have. Harman Blennerhassett was beside me staring proudly at the hothouse. It seemed no small miracle he had recognized me.

'There's little opportunity to plant at sea,' I answered, trying to fend off his question.

He chuckled. 'True enough, true enough. Then allow me to show you what I have accomplished in more fertile soil.'

He took me by the arm and steered me through the kitchen garden to the glasshouse door. Winter fell away as we stepped inside, as though we had walked into an Italian garden in summer. Fruit trees stood in regimented lines along the length of the room, budding even in December, and the air was thick with damp soil and foliage. Harman led me past each tree in turn, introducing them almost like children. 'This here's the fig, you see the leaves? And this is the citron – hasn't flowered yet, but I have hopes, you know. Last summer we were almost drowning in juice from the orange trees; Mrs B. declared she would pour it in the river and turn it orange all the way to New Orleans. The olive trees are particularly fine.'

'Most impressive,' I said. 'A true garden in the wilderness.'

Blennerhassett nodded intently. 'Of course, this is merely a humble beginning. Once we are in Mexico, the climate will be more agreeable, and I will have quite an orchard.' A rare shaft of sunlight reflected off a waxy leaf onto his face, giving him a beatific glow of contentment. 'Though of course I will miss them until we are settled.'

'Do you think that will be long?'

He shrugged, and began polishing his glasses on his neck-cloth. 'I cannot say, of course. Colonel Burr is our military expert; I put myself in his hands absolutely. A Crassus to his Caesar, or Harpalus to his Alexander, so to speak.'

I picked up a trowel which lay on the bench, hefting it idly in my hand. 'I have heard so much of Colonel Burr, yet I feel I know so little of him.'

'You will meet him presently – he will insist on it, I know. I had hoped he would be here to greet you, but . . .' Blennerhassett's voice drifted off.

I looked around. We were four thousand miles from anywhere I would have chosen to live, even with a scandal to escape, but for Blennerhassett it seemed a self-made Eden. 'I marvel that you would choose to leave this idyll.'

'But here I am only a squire. In Colonel Burr's new empire I will be a duke, or somesuch. The details are a little vague.'

'You would risk all you have achieved here against Colonel Burr's promises?'

160

Blennerhassett gave the resigned smile of a man who recognized the absurdity of his decision but was powerless to change it. 'It is the colonel, you know. He can be a very persuasive man.'

Wary of over-playing my ignorance, I almost let this comment pass. But the knowledge of my uncle's intimate involvement in the scheme had spurred my need to know more, and I trusted Blennerhassett's innocent nature to overlook my suspicious curiosity.

'You know that I was late coming to this venture,' I began carefully. 'In all our haste, no-one has told me anything of Colonel Burr. Who is he?'

'Colonel Burr? But surely you have heard of him, no?' In the heat of the glasshouse, a fine mist had condensed on Blennerhassett's spectacles. He removed them, rubbing the lenses on the corner of his waistcoat. 'I should have thought his fame – some would say notoriety, mark, but I do not – would have reached England's shores by now.'

'You forget that I have too rarely set foot on England's shores,' I said, every inch the honest sailor.

'Even so . . .' Blennerhassett replaced the spectacles on his nose. Instantly, the mist was blossoming on them again. 'Colonel Burr, Aaron Burr, is one of the most eminent men in the nation. Until two years since, he was Vice-President of the United States.'

He smiled at me, pleased at the visible impact of his news. For my part, I did not know what to say. First my uncle, now the recently second-most-powerful man in America. Lyell's riches had evidently attracted conspirators of the first rank.

'But why should he . . .' I paused, trying to frame my question with sufficient delicacy. Fortunately, Blennerhassett anticipated me.

'Why is he now embarked on this hazardous enterprise?'

I nodded.

Blennerhassett sighed. 'Colonel Burr was unfortunate. There was something of a scandal, and President Jefferson did not choose him for re-election to a second term.'

I remembered a fragment of gossip from a midnight churchyard.

'He shot a man in a duel. The Treasury Secretary, Mr Hamilton.' *The STATESMAN of consummate WISDOM*, as I recalled.

Blennerhassett stiffened. 'He was sorely provoked, I'm sure. But Colonel Burr is a visionary, and not easily cowed by reverse. He determined that if this nation would not have him, why, then he would establish his own.'

With Lyell's money and my uncle's ships behind him, I presumed.

'How did you come to meet him?'

Blennerhassett stroked a finger over a leaf which had drawn too much dust. 'It was eighteen months ago. He was making down the river, drawing up his plans, and landed on our island quite by chance. Naturally, we were honoured to receive him.'

'Naturally,' I murmured.

'And when he vouchsafed us his intentions, we offered him unstinting aid. He recognized us as kindred spirits, I think.'

Even Blennerhassett sounded a little doubtful at this. From what I had seen of the colonel's plan, it seemed more likely he had recognized the potential of Blennerhassett's wealth. Unless he planned to invade Mexico with an orchard.

Blennerhassett straightened. 'Of course, the plan is fraught with dangers. But Margaret and I are hardy souls. And if we succeed, why, I will have a garden that will make Versailles seem a mere allotment.'

Whereas if he failed, I thought, he would have a rather smaller plot of earth to inhabit.

We dined early that afternoon. After the sumptuous feast the night before this was a drab and humble meal: the candles seemed incapable of dispelling the wintry gloom which seeped through the windows, and the food was cold. Perhaps the kitchens were still given over to running bullets. Lyell stayed in his room, pleading fatigue, and Tyler was forever wandering out to oversee the preparations at the landing, so we were a reduced company. Conversation was scarce, and the scrape of cutlery on china was too often the only accompaniment.

After dinner we retired to the parlour. I doubt any of us much wanted it, but with a ragged army making ready for war on the front lawn and an unsettled expectancy hanging over the house, there seemed a greater need to assert the rule of habit. Mrs Blennerhassett played her pianoforte, and Harman his violin, while Catherine and I sat beside each other on the couch and twined our ankles when no-one was watching.

Outside, the sky was darkening and the wind rising, yet in that parlour with its rose wallpaper and French furnishings, we remained a sealed world of polite order. Servants came to light the lamps and draw the curtains, isolating us still further from the winter beyond, and the Blennerhassetts played on. Each time they finished a song, Catherine and I would applaud and compliment their playing, and each time I would pray for release. Every creak and bang and muffled voice outside offered promises of motion, of action and excitement from which I was excluded, yet manners and protocol rooted me stiff to my seat. My applause grew cooler, then positively desultory, yet it only seemed to inspire the Blennerhassetts to redouble their efforts.

Just when I thought I could bear it no more, that I would tear the violin from Harman's hands and snap its neck off, I heard running feet in the hall. They neared the door; without a knock, it flew open. The shroud which had been smothering the room was blown away; the fire flared up, and suddenly we were all standing. Tyler was in the doorway, white-faced and breathing heavily.

'We've just had news from up river. The governor's issued orders for our arrest, and for the seizing of our boats and stores. General Tupper and the militia are expected any hour to serve the warrants. Our plans are betrayed, and we are all dead men.'

To my surprise, it was Mrs Blennerhassett who kept her composure best. Turning on her bench, poised in mind and carriage, she addressed her husband, Tyler and me.

'There is nothing else to be done. You must take the boats at once and find Colonel Burr. He is your only hope now.'

Blennerhassett avoided her gaze. He looked to be entirely stricken with panic. Tyler, by contrast, had recovered some of his wits.

'You are right, of course, Mrs Blennerhassett. We are too far gone to turn back now. Victory and the river are our only escape.'

'There are six boats here, enough for all your men, and a dozen more waiting upstream at Marietta. The colonel will likely need them for his recruits: do you have time to fetch them?'

'I fear the militia will already have them impounded, but I will send some of the men to see what can be done.' Tyler was already calmed into a state of purpose by Mrs Blennerhassett's resolve. 'Will you lead the expedition, Lieutenant? What do you say?'

Much of what I had to say could barely be expressed, save in meaningless syllables of gibbering terror. The invasion of Mexico had seemed an unlikely hope in the best of circumstances; now that the weight of the American law had swung against us, a prison seemed the least we could expect. I did not know precisely what crime we had committed, but I was certain we were guilty. And if the American authorities found a foreign naval officer in this den of conspiracy, armed with coded assurances of a British fleet to aid the illicit design, they would take little time in hanging me from the nearest tree. My only choice, it seemed, was whether I would be hanged there in Virginia or in some other state down river. Or perhaps they would return me to Pennsylvania to swing for Harris's murder.

'I will oversee the loading of the boats,' I said. It would afford me some time to consider my predicament, perhaps an opportunity to slip across to the shore in the dark, now that the conspiracy seemed on the brink of ruin. Though how I could escape from the wintry depths of the American wilderness with half an army hunting me, I did not know.

'Good enough.' Tyler snatched a glass of wine from the salver and drained it. 'We must be away by midnight. I hope the taste of cannon fire does not disagree with you, Lieutenant.'

*

If there was one mercy, it was that my fears were concealed in the commotion which ensued. As I stepped out of the front door it seemed that the feeble army must have multiplied itself tenfold, so many were the men running in every direction. An enormous bonfire had been lit down by the shore, and by its angry light I could see orange figures scurrying about with their burdens of sacks, casks and muskets. Anxious to avoid company, I retreated to my room to pack my chest.

It did not take long. A clean shirt and pair of breeches, two pairs of stockings, a pair of shoes which I abandoned in favour of my boots, my razor and a comb were the bulk of my possessions. I squeezed the hem of my coat, and wondered whether I ought to destroy the incriminating papers sewn inside, but there still lingered a hope that I might survive to confront my uncle.

'Lieutenant?'

I crossed to the door and flung it open. Miss Lyell was standing there, her cheeks flushed and her eyes bright.

'Is it not exciting?' she said, advancing into the room. 'The enemy almost upon us, and our gallant heroes ready to sail forth on their quest.'

Exciting was not the word I would have preferred, but I did not contradict her. She stretched her arms around me and kissed me hard on the lips.

'You will have all the adventure, and I will have to mope back to England with Papa,' she complained, when I allowed her to draw breath.

'Your father is adamant he will not go down river with the men?'

She scowled. 'He dismisses it as a futile misadventure. He has no valour, no romance. He would rather be safe in his counting house than in the front line of battle. You will go, of course.'

It came so naturally, so smoothly, that words of agreement were falling out of my mouth before I heard what she had said. Which might not have mattered – I've acquiesced to all manner of lunacy for the sake of appearance, and never made good on it – if at that moment the door had not opened again to admit Tyler.

'All's stowed and ready. Are you with us, Mr Jerrold?'

Well, with Catherine standing there, her adoring eyes held rapt by the hero at her side, what else could I say? Nor did I think Nevell would forgive me if I abandoned my mission here and waved the conspirators on their way. I picked up Lyell's pistol in a vague attempt at bravado, then leaned over and kissed Catherine on the forehead.

'Pray for us, my dear.'

Scarcely more than twenty-four hours had passed since I landed on the island. Then, it had seemed a fantastical place of music and light. Now I found myself striding across the lawn with Tyler, past the ashes of hastily doused fires and square impressions where tents had squatted in the grass. A pair of negroes hurried behind us carrying my chest – even in the face of prison and disgrace, there was never an American to do something for himself if there was a blackie to do it instead.

The bonfire still blazed into the night, with the lamps on the boats like sparks beyond. A small knot of men were gathered beside it, and the rifles in their hands jerked anxiously at each darting shadow or ripple in the water. I could see the Blennerhassetts with them, and Lyell's black bulk, and another man I did not recognize. He seemed to be remonstrating with Blennerhassett.

'For God's sake, Harman, give up this madness. If you're innocent, you've nothing to fear, and if you're guilty you'll make nothing better by flying. Where will you go? The governor's posted militia all along the river, some with cannon. They'll shoot you down like a pirate, and not find your corpse until it washes up in New Orleans.'

You may imagine the effect his speech had on me. As for Blennerhassett, he began to squirm and look longingly back towards his house. Once again, it was his wife who showed her mettle.

'That's lies and nonsense, as well you should know, General Tupper. This is the United States, is it not? We are not in France here – we do not turn cannon on our own citizens, gentle souls who have been charged with no crime or wrong. If any man has a complaint against us, let him bring the magistrate down and charge us honestly.'

If the new arrival was a general, then I feared the time for magistrates and the law was long past. I looked about, but could see no evidence of any soldiers save our own.

'If you are as innocent as you maintain, then stay and let justice take its course,' said the general. 'I have come here as a friend, Harman. Tomorrow, I shall come at the head of the militia and it will look a bad business if you are not here. I urge you, for your family's sake, desist from this course.'

Mrs Blennerhassett stiffened. 'Harman's family are with him utterly. Now, you've said your piece, General, and we've heard you out, so you'll oblige by leaving our island.'

Whether from concern for his friend or fear for the mischief they would work, the general ignored her. He lunged forward and clasped a stout hand around Harman's arm, which hung limp as a dead rabbit. 'If you are deaf to reason, so be it. You are in my hands now. I arrest you in the name of the Commonwealth of Ohio.'

It was a brave attempt, but foolhardy. Even as he spoke, a dozen loaded rifles were lifted and trained towards his breast. Carefully letting Harman go, he stepped away and raised his hands.

'I hope you will not act rashly, gentlemen.'

'I'd as soon shoot you as not,' one of the men answered coolly.

'I'd sooner you did not.' The general bowed his head in surrender. 'This is lunacy, Harman, perhaps even suicide, but I see you will not be swayed from it. Good luck.'

He set his back to us – bravely, for the rifles were still on him – and walked across the lawn to the far landing stage.

Tyler turned to Lyell. 'So, what is it to be? Are you with us?'

Lyell snorted. Behind him, the fire seemed to flare up. 'With whom? A disorderly rabble fleeing into the night? You have deceived me, Mr Tyler. You have made a fool of me, and, worse, wasted my time. I shall not play your dupe any longer.'

'The colonel will be mighty upset.'

'Colonel Burr is a fantasist. If he even lasts a hundred miles from here I will be surprised. If he reaches New Orleans I will be astounded. But he will not get one penny more of my credit, saving he finds himself atop the walls of Vera Cruz wearing the gold crown of Mexico.'

Tyler looked as though he might like to argue further, but there was no time. Briefly, he said, 'Be sure they do not catch you here. If the militia learn that there were Englishmen with us there'll be hell to pay.'

'My daughter and I will be away by morning,' Lyell assured him.

Leaving Lyell by the fire, we ran down the sandy embankment and across the boarding planks. Even then I hesitated, but Tyler's firm hand on my back pushed me forwards and onto the boat. As my feet touched the deck, the men aboard were already casting off the mooring ropes and leaning on their poles to push us out into the stream. On the boat beside me, Blennerhassett called miserable farewells to his wife, who had chosen to stay behind with their children.

I looked back. Lyell was still standing by the fire, a great black silhouette against the leaping flames. They burned so high that their reflection licked far out onto the water, slowly fading behind us as the current took us and propelled us downstream.

In all the confusion, Nevell's words in the tavern in Falmouth again came back to me. *Learn what you can of Mr Tyler and his scheme, then stop it.* I had accomplished the first part of my charge. But as to thwarting the conspiracy, I could no more see how I might stop it than I could stem the inexorable flow of the river which carried us.

We passed around a bend and the fire on Blennerhassett Island vanished from our sight. Then we were in darkness.

16

WE FLOATED ON THROUGH THE NIGHT, FOREVER PEERING OVER THE bows for the telltale ripples of sandbars and logs. At dawn we poled the boats together and lashed them into one to hold an impromptu council of war. We had four flatboats, all little more than boxes crudely constructed for the one-way journey. It was hard to believe they would even make it that far down river. Tyler pulled out a flagon of whiskey and passed it around. Like the boats, it was crude but sufficient.

'Our situation doesn't look so good,' said Tyler. 'But I figure it's not all that bad.'

Blennerhassett and I offered equally disbelieving stares.

'We've near to fifty men, and enough arms and powder to see off anything that comes at us. We've also several hours' start on them. You can't outrun the river: they could chase us all the way to New Orleans and never catch sight of us.'

'They can ride overland,' I pointed out. I did not need a *Navigator* or a pilot to see that the river's sinuous course doubled back over itself so many times that a horseman could save many dozens of miles and emerge far below us. 'What if they bring up cannon? These flatboats can barely stay afloat as it is. One broadside would see us all drowned.'

'We will trust to luck and travel by night where we may. The Ohio is not the Thames, Lieutenant: they will not be able to meet us at every turn. We'll outpace them eventually.'

I would have argued the point further, though the river offered little choice, but Blennerhassett spoke up.

'What of Colonel Burr?' he asked.

'What of him?' said Tyler.

Blennerhassett waved an arm at our makeshift raft, and the unprepossessing crew perched around its sides with their poles. 'We'll not conquer Mexico without reinforcements. I'll be a deal happier when we have the colonel and his men to aid us.'

'Colonel Burr keeps his ears open. He'll hear we're moving, and get word to us, I don't doubt. If he's still in Kentucky, he'll come down to the mouth of the Cumberland or the Wabash. Once he's with us, then we can start in earnest.'

If, I thought, we survived that long.

With all the hazards of the river we could not keep our boats lashed together long. Tyler apportioned their command, taking one for himself and dividing the rest between Blennerhassett, me, and a subordinate named Smith. We untied the ropes and let the swirling current slowly carry us apart.

In two nights I had slept little and badly. With ten men aboard my command, there were more than enough to navigate and watch for obstacles; I appointed the least unlikely of them my deputy, then retired to the shelter of the cabin. I did not expect agreeable dreams.

As on my journey to Blennerhassett Island, the cabin managed to be both close and cold. A chill rain had started to fall, seeping through the cracks in the ceiling. Steam and smoke mingled in the air by the hissing stove, but they made better companions than the cold at the mouth of the cabin. I dragged a straw mattress as near to the fire as I dared, lay down, and pulled a lice-ridden blanket over myself.

My eyes had not been closed five minutes when I felt a small hand shaking my shoulder. With some reluctance, I forced my eyes open. With so many dangers to contend with, I doubted it could be happy news.

'Martin. *Martin*.'

My eyes were suddenly fully open. The blanket slipped off my chest as I sat up in confusion. Beside me, her skin grey and pallid in the half light, and her body almost invisible under a dark cloak, knelt Miss Lyell.

'Catherine. What in the devil's name . . . ?' I wished I had not drunk so liberally of Tyler's whiskey. 'You stayed on the island with your father.'

She grinned. 'You see I did not.'

'But this is madness. Ten to one we will all be sunk within a week – if we are not hanged first. You should not have come.'

'Do not be angry with me,' she chided. 'The dangers would be no less had I stayed with my father. The authorities will seek him, and it will be a terrible effort to cross those mountains again in December.' She squeezed my arm. 'At least now we are together.'

Together only in ruin, I feared, though I could not reward her love by saying so. I reached my arms around her and cradled her close to my chest, then tipped her head back so I could kiss her on the lips. She rose against me, her passion spurred perhaps by our peril.

'What will your father say?' I asked, spoiling the moment somewhat.

She shrugged. 'He will not come paddling after us in a canoe if that is what you fear. He will be too sensible of his own safety for that. No doubt his greatest concern will be that my capture might betray his own part in this affair. But you will protect me from that, will you not, my darling?'

A thud sounded from the foredeck. One of the crew had jumped down from the roof and was peering back into the gloom.

'Mr Jerrold? Mr Tyler's called over from the other boat. There's a comp'ny of militia down at the next point.'

It seemed Miss Lyell's odyssey might end before it had rightly begun. I scrambled to my feet, crouching to avoid the low cabin roof, and hurried into the open.

The valley had begun to narrow, its shoulders slowly squeezing in on us, but there was still a fair expanse of bottomland beside the river. It was thick with timber, uncleared by any farmer or settler, and the bare trees were threaded by a fine mist. I wiped a finger across my brow and felt it come away wet with the cold rain which had soaked me. It was hardly a propitious circumstance for a battle, though with luck it would damp the enemy's guns as much as our own.

I turned to the steersman. 'Where are they?'

He lifted the long pole in his hand so that it pointed to the starboard shore, about quarter of a mile distant, where the river had bent itself around a long promontory. The point cut off a goodly part of the channel, so that we could not but float within fifty yards of it. At its tip, where the trees thinned, I could see an American flag hanging sodden from a sapling.

'Keep four men on the corners, bow and stern,' I ordered, for the crew had given up their duties to stare at the coming threat. 'Get the rest under the lip of the cabin with their weapons – rifles if they have them, muskets if they do not. They may enjoy some hope of keeping their powder dry.'

The steersman nodded.

'One more thing. You may find a lady in the cabin.' I was not convinced I had not dreamed it. 'She is my companion, and is to be treated with the greatest respect.' I could imagine what a dozen Ohio boatmen might make of her otherwise.

Even aboard the *Adventure*, watching the Spanish ship bear down on us, I had not felt so helpless. To be on a boat with neither mast nor oars, barely even a rudder, drifting slowly past a well-ensconced troop of militia, was an impossible task. I felt a familiar knot begin to tighten in my stomach, and wondered if I could keep it from squeezing my innards out.

'Is there a telescope aboard?' I asked. There would be little profit in seeing the men who were to kill me, but it would be better than the unseen, unknown menace lingering in the trees.

One of the men ducked into the cabin and returned presently

with a spyglass. It was a ludicrous instrument, so out of place in those rude and miserable surrounds that I almost laughed. It must have been taken from Blennerhassett's study, for the brass casing was polished to a mirror, and the inscription of *Mr Dollond, London* was freshly engraved. It was more suited to staring at the heavens than battle, and damnably heavy, but I managed to steady it on the edge of the cabin roof and stare out at the promontory. Rain drizzled over its lens, while a thick fog began to condense on the eyepiece, and it took several applications of my shirtsleeve to clear a passable view. Through the streaks and swirls on the glass, I scanned the enemy position.

At first I could see only tangled scrub and tree-trunks. Then, as I looked lower, I saw flashes of blue uniform, and the thin skein of smoke where a fire still smouldered. They must have been there much of the night, and it kindled a rare spark of pleasure to think they must feel more wretched even than I. And their powder must be turned to porridge.

I squinted closer. Strangely, none of the soldiers was moving. Nor, so far as I could see, were they in position to unleash a volley of musketry. If fear had not dismissed it as a desperate hope, I would have sworn them to be sleeping – or dead. Had a party of savage Indians swooped down in the night and scalped them all? I could see no blood. It was too much to conceive that they had fallen asleep just as we arrived.

I swept the telescope back and forth, searching for a sign of their intentions. From the cabin below I heard a clatter as someone dropped a musket, and I hissed at the men to keep quiet.

A movement by the campfire caught my eye. I swung my gaze towards it. We were so close now that I barely needed the glass; with its aid, I could plainly see a blue-uniformed militiaman staggering to his feet. Rotting leaves clung to his coat from where he had lain, and he swayed slightly like a corpse in the breeze. I saw him rub his eyes, then reach down and lift a cup to his lips. We were far too far for the smell to carry, yet by the flash of sour disgust which crossed his face, followed by a mellowing smile, I reckoned I could guess the cup's contents. That would certainly explain why the man and his company were so heedless of their duty.

He was moving again, and my heart tensed. Brushing past the brambles and bracken which obscured him almost to his chest, he staggered out of the woods and down to the shore. There was now nothing between us, nothing to hide our presence from him, yet he did not look up. Instead, he fumbled at the crutch of his trousers and unbuttoned them. A fountain of steam rose into the air as he disgorged the night's indulgence into the river.

I lowered the glass. Tyler's boat, in the lead, had already passed him; now we were directly opposite. Surely he must see us.

He did. His bladder emptied, he tucked himself in and looked up. I lowered the glass, and our eyes met across the few yards of water which separated us. His unshaven features were heavy with the lassitude of alcohol, but they creased with bewildered disbelief as he took in the sight of the four flatboats. Too addled for anything else, he raised an arm in greeting, and I found myself involuntarily reciprocating.

Belatedly, he remembered his duty. Struggling with the strap, he lifted the musket which had been slung over his back and raised it to his shoulder. Our eyes met, and a strange moment of futile sympathy passed between us. Then he pulled the trigger.

Whether a night in the damp and rain had neutered the charge, or whether the gun had never been loaded to begin with, I neither knew nor cared. We were close enough that I could hear the snap of the flint as he released it, could see it spark in the pan, but there was nothing further. No explosion to shake the birds from their trees, and no lead ball to fly across the water and kill an English lieutenant far from home.

The militiaman stared pensively at his rifle, then gave a rueful smile. I could still see him watching as, one by one, our boats vanished around the bend and were lost to the drizzle and the mist.

We saw no-one else that day, nor the next, nor even the next. Indeed, we could barely keep sight of our own forlorn flotilla amid

174

the swirling rains and cloud which obscured our course. One afternoon we lost the other boats altogether, and I spent several hours in a simmering panic before we at last caught them up again. Sometimes we would pass low-lying farms, crude shingled houses which one good flood would have swept away, but never was there any evidence of life beyond a thin plume of smoke rising from the chimney. We were fugitives in plain view, had anyone been there to see us; we put ashore only to scavenge firewood, and then only when we were far from habitation. The damp logs smoked terribly, so that by the end of a week we must all have been thoroughly cured, but it was better the choking cabin than the chill and wet outside. We took our turns on watch, and otherwise huddled by the stove.

I had only two consolations in those bleak days: whiskey and Catherine. The former I took in liberal doses from the jug in the cabin, its level sinking with alarming speed; the latter I indulged as often as privacy and fatigue allowed. Sometimes, if all the crew were on deck to navigate a sandbar, Catherine and I would retreat to the rear of the cabin and grapple in hasty silence, rolling around fully clothed on the filthy straw. They were sweet moments of relief, but all too quickly the pleasure was sullied by the need to scramble apart and return to our duties.

I think Catherine had begun to regret her impulsive stowing-away. For the first few days she wandered about the boat all smiles and purpose, even taking her turn on the steering oar when no immediate hazards threatened. Thereafter, as the brim of her bonnet softened and folded in the rain, and her dress became streaked with grime, her spirits cooled. Her lip hardened into a perpetual pout, save if one of the men enquired after her welfare when she would flash the man a weary smile and declare herself perfectly content. For the most part, she confined herself to the cabin, and our rushed encounters became ever less frequent.

On the fifth night out from the island, we passed the town of Cincinnati on the Ohio shore. It was a hair-raising business, for we had heard there would be a shore battery keeping watch for us, but after lying up on a sandbank for most of the day we managed to slip past the town in darkness. The town lights flickered on the water, and I could hear fiddles and singing from the taverns. I felt more isolated at that moment than ever I had in the wilderness, and I was seized by an almost irresistible need to fall down blubbering. A stout grip on the boat's side and a tot of whiskey kept me upright, as the lights faded behind us.

After Cincinnati, our fortunes improved. The late Mr Harris had described the river well: it was the only high-road across the country, and for all its circuitousness there was no other way for news to outpace us. Whatever charges had been laid against us upstream, whatever foes massed against us, those down river remained ignorant. We were like a bullet in a rifle barrel, propelled forward by an explosive force we could feel but which could not overtake us. Where, I wondered, would we strike?

Two days beyond Cincinnati, I saw the first proof that Tyler and Blennerhassett might not, after all, be fantasists. As we made fast at a small village called Jeffersonville, a short major named Floyd came bounding down the landing stage. A bright orange moustache bristled above his lip, and his buckskin shirt dripped with tassels. Two pistols sat in holsters on his hips.

'We've been expecting you this past week,' he said, in the drawl characteristic of the Ohio country. 'Wondered if you'd settled on staying home for Christmas.'

'Do you have news of the colonel?' asked Tyler.

'More news than's good for us. Did you hear he got himself indicted?'

Tyler went white as a ghost. 'Indicted?'

Major Floyd gave a crooked smile. 'Down in Frankfort. Charged him with breaking the Neutrality Act, said he was planning to invade Mexico.'

'What happened?'

'You know the colonel.' Floyd laughed. 'He slung those government liars from one side of the courtroom to the other, and by the end of it the jury was mighty satisfied there was nothing in it. They sent him on his way with three cheers and a grand ball in his honour.'

Tyler began to recover his colour. 'He's a remarkable man, all right. When was that?'

'Ten days back. We had the news a week ago.'

'And where is he now?'

'Went down to Tennessee to raise a few more volunteers. Sent word that we're to make for Shawneetown, and lay up there until he calls us down.' Floyd gestured at our ragged flotilla. 'Is this all you got?'

'We left in a hurry,' Tyler admitted. 'There should be more coming down from Pittsburgh, if they can get past the militia. How about yourself?'

Floyd pointed down the landing, where four keelboats bobbed in the river. They were in every way superior to our own craft: longer and slimmer, with rounded hulls and solid cabins. I could smell the caulking still fresh in their timbers.

'How many men?' asked Tyler.

Floyd crossed his arms over his chest. 'Forty. But there's more waiting down river. Word of the colonel's trial in Frankfort got about, and I guess it cooled some of 'em off. They'll come when they see we mean to go through with it.'

With our fleet doubled we continued down river. Directly below Jeffersonville we spent a churning forty-five minutes in a narrow channel they called a shute, frantically poling past a mass of islets, reefs, rocks and shoals. The water foamed white all around us, and the constricted river bore us along faster than any wind. It was a great relief to be beyond it.

Three days later, at midday, we reached the appointed rendezvous at Shawneetown. It was more a village than a town, being only about thirty houses, but they were well built and prosperous on account of the salt licks which, so I was informed, supplied half the Ohio valley. We made fast at the landing – long enough to accommodate all the salt-traders, though deserted at this time of year – and waited.

The solstice came and went: Blennerhassett made some hopeful joke about the days getting brighter again, but I saw no sign of it. We could not exercise our arms for fear of being seen by the local residents, who already regarded us with open suspicion. Rumours of Colonel Burr and his projects seemed to have swept through the country, and we were unwelcome guests. We stayed on our boats for the most part, drinking and gambling and cleaning our guns until the rifling must have been quite rubbed away. And all the time, I tried to ignore the ever more disdainful looks with which Miss Lyell reproached me.

On Christmas Eve, we ventured ashore and gathered in a field behind the church. Tyler had managed to shoot a clutch of turkeys, which we roasted on spits over open fires, and the local landlord broached two casks of beer for us. Blennerhassett, as the best educated, spoke a few words of the service, and Tyler offered prayers for the continued benevolence of the Divinity towards our ambitions. The night was clear and bitterly cold, with a howling wind which seemed to tear through our very flesh itself. Some of the men sang carols, and others accompanied them on flutes and fiddles; there was much back-slapping and many high-spirited toasts, but the strain told on all our faces. One question above all was in our thoughts, though no-one asked it: what had become of Colonel Burr? For my own part, all curiosity towards him had vanished. I barely believed him to exist any longer.

It was past eleven o'clock, and I had decided to return to the boats and the dubious comforts of a leaky cabin, when the messenger arrived. I was seeking Miss Lyell among the throng, hoping I might snatch a few minutes' intimacy, when I heard the men about me fall silent. Hoof beats were echoing from along the southerly track, and in the steel moonlight we could see a dark rider emerge from the trees beyond. He was galloping his mount at full speed, lashing it with his crop, and it was only as he came into the circle of our fire that he reined in the beast.

Steam rose from horse and rider alike as he swung himself out of the saddle and approached Tyler.

'I have a message for you,' he announced, his voice clear and young. 'You're to make for the mouth of the Cumberland the day after tomorrow.'

He paused, looking around at his audience.

'Colonel Burr will meet you there.'

17

WE BEACHED OUR BOATS ON A THIN ISLAND AT THE JUNCTION OF THE two rivers, where the blue waters of the Cumberland met the grey-brown torrent of the Ohio. For a few hundred yards the two currents flowed side by side, the divide obvious on the surface of the water. Then, abruptly, the Cumberland disappeared.

There was no grand estate on this island – no sign of habitation at all, save an abandoned fisherman's shack built on exposed tree roots by the water's edge – but it was not entirely deserted. Two flatboats had been drawn up on the sandy embankment, and a freshly trampled path led into the interior. We followed it, pushing past low-hanging branches and foliage until it opened into a broad clearing in the middle of the island. A dozen men slouched around its margins, whittling at pieces of wood or carving their initials on the tree-trunks, but I barely looked at them. Directly opposite where the path emerged, seated on a grey mare which he must have brought ashore for that express purpose, was Colonel Burr.

He had been a shadowy presence for so long in my thoughts, my fears and even my dreams that the reality was, inevitably, an anticlimax. Far from being the hulking warrior of my imagination, he was in fact about five and a half feet small with a delicate complexion and dainty hands. Instead of bestriding his horse he perched atop it, and in place of a colonel's uniform he was dressed, almost to the point of fastidiousness, in a neatly tailored black suit. He held his head with a classical poise: a broad nose, a proud chin, and long sideburns, with a touch of severity in the high-domed forehead rising above. The receding, greying hair was pulled straight back behind his collar, dropping almost to the shoulder. He watched as our men entered the clearing one by one and assembled in a rough circle. As the last man filed in, and it became apparent there would be no more, I saw him bend down and whisper something to Tyler.

Tyler blushed, and murmured something I did not catch.

'No matter.' The colonel straightened in the saddle and turned to face his army. 'Gentlemen, I welcome you to our expedition. Many of you, of course, know me personally, or by sight; others among you may know me better by reputation. I hope you do not hold that against me.'

An appreciative chuckle went around the assembly.

'For you others, I am Colonel Aaron Burr, the notorious outlaw – wanted for duelling in New York, for murder in New Jersey, and now for treason in Ohio. I was also, until last year, Vice-President of the United States. God willing, I will be known by better titles before this war is done.'

If the rest of the men found this statement as absurd as I did, they did not show it. Instead, they thumped the butts of their muskets on the frozen ground and murmured approval.

Burr spread his arms wide. 'I know that you have risked hardship, reputation, even violence to stand here. Be assured, your courage and sacrifices have not gone unnoticed. Down the Mississippi, a thousand acres of prime land awaits every one of you. When all this is done, you will live as kings, your wives and children like queens and princes. What do you say to that?'

A voice from the back spoke up. 'Is it true we're going to Mexico?'

Burr smiled. 'You'll understand, I'm sure, that I cannot tell you our *precise* destination at the present. That'll have to wait for a more convenient moment. It's enough to say that I've got my eye on a silver mine down south.'

The same voice came back again. 'Is it true we'll all be hanged?'
Burr did not blink. 'Funnily enough, I've just argued that very question with a Kentucky jury. They didn't see fit to convict me. You may take it from me that you've nothing to fear. There's a war coming, everyone knows it, and once it starts there's no state in the Union that won't appreciate a well-armed band of filibusters ready to teach our enemies a lesson. Until then, we're just harmless settlers heading down river to take up some lands I happen to own in Louisiana.'

'How's a hundred men s'posed to whop anyone?' asked another man, voicing the question uppermost in my own thoughts.

Colonel Burr smiled again. 'From what I heard of your exploits, you could do it more or less single-handed.' That drew laughter, and some good-natured cheers for the man who had spoken. 'Even so, I'm figuring we'll have some help. I can't say too much, mind, but I've some friends in the garrison at New Orleans who'll see that if it comes to battle, we won't go in alone. There's five hundred more men coming down from Pittsburgh even as we speak, and more gathering in Tennessee and the territories. We're just the vanguard of this expedition. It don't take but a spark to start a fire, and once we've got it lit it'll burn like a haystack. I've supporters waiting in every capital west of the Alleghenies. Soon as they hear word of our success, they'll cause such an agitation we'll have regiments from every state marching to join us. But they'll have to wait their turn when it comes to sharing out the spoils. You men who stand with me today will have the choicest picks.'

That cheered the men no end, though I was struck again that the colonel's army seemed forever just off the horizon, its numbers swelling more in fantasy than in likelihood. I did not voice the thought. His speech over, he had dismounted his horse and was making his way around the circle, shaking hands with each of the men in turn. Tyler followed behind, making introductions where he could, though Burr seemed to possess a prodigious memory for names and faces. When they reached me, Tyler tapped Burr's shoulder.

'Lieutenant Jerrold,' he said, investing my name with a significance I did not entirely like. 'From England.'

Burr's gaze fastened onto me. Watching him from across the clearing I had not noticed his eyes particularly, but now he was so close it was hard to imagine any other part of him. All the rest of his features seemed to recede, to be nothing more than a setting for eyes which possessed a life and character all their own. They were brown as polished walnut, with a brightness which almost compelled one to look at them. Even more than that, there was something in their gaze which prompted confidence and intimacy, which made me feel they somehow saw more of me than others did.

'I am delighted to meet you,' said Burr, pumping my hand up and down. 'Without you, this adventure of ours could never have succeeded.' He leaned closer and murmured in my ear. 'We must speak more of it presently.'

I nodded, but before I could open my mouth to answer he had moved on and was listening as Tyler announced, 'Miss Catherine Lyell, Mr Jerrold's companion.'

Burr bowed low as an Ottoman courtier, then lifted her hand and pressed his lips against it. As he straightened himself, a curl at the edge of his mouth acknowledged the over-theatricality, even as his eyes invited her complicity.

'Enchanted,' he said. 'With such beauty in our ranks, who will dare stand against us? You will be our talisman, Miss Lyell, our goddess of victory.'

Catherine's cheeks flushed, and she curtsied. In four months of travel, even when she faced abduction by Harris, I do not think I had ever seen her so much at a loss for words.

Burr turned back to face the rest of the men. ' "True hope is swift, and flies with swallows' wings", as Mr Shakespeare says. We'll not make kings of ourselves by standing around this island until the meltwater comes. Get back to the boats. Mr Tyler will divide you into crews and we'll be away presently. We should make Fort Massac in two days and the Mississippi by the New Year. After that . . .' He grinned. 'Who knows where we'll get to.'

The men filed out of the clearing, and a negro boy led away the redundant horse. I was set to follow, when I heard Burr's voice in my ear murmuring, 'A word, if you please, Lieutenant Jerrold.'

He led me out of the clearing, away from the boats. A trickle of fear began to run down my spine – had he guessed my duplicity and resolved to end it? He walked briskly, pushing through the undergrowth with ease, until we came out overlooking the river. Gnarled tree-roots thrust forth from the muddy embankment like the arms of buried corpses, and a crust of ice had begun to form at the water's edge.

'I know what you must think,' said Burr.

There was an uneasy, restless energy about him, like a small animal caught on open ground. He seated himself on a fallen tree-trunk, immediately sprang to his feet and paced across to the shore, then spun about as if he had heard a noise. Merely to watch him was exhausting.

'You have come all this way from England. You have been sold promises of a great expedition, an army of conquest to sweep the Spanish out of the North Americas as Popham is sweeping them out of the South. Your friends have invested many ten thousands of pounds.' His head flicked about. 'Miss Lyell – she is Mr Lyell's daughter? The banker?'

I nodded.

'Is she married?' He shook his head. 'No, of course, not *Miss* Lyell. No matter. You are here, and you wish to know how a lapsed vice-president and a hundred territorial hayseeds will conquer the greatest empire on the continent. I confess, Mr Jerrold, I ask myself the same question. How many ships have you brought?'

I tried to remember the ciphered letter, still snug against my chest in my coat lining. 'Two frigates, I believe.'

Burr frowned. 'Is that all? I told them six. No matter. It is still twice America's strength, after Jefferson's cheese-paring.'

'I thought our enemies were the Spanish,' I ventured.

The brown eyes fixed on me. 'So they are. But it pays to be vigilant. One does not know . . .' The eyes darted away to some imagined movement in the forest. 'What do you say, Lieutenant? Will our little wager repay itself?'

His movements ceased, and for a moment the entire sum of his energy seemed fixed on me, willing the answer from my lips. My mouth went dry and I struggled to compose any answer at all. Of course I knew what I ought to do, what Nevell would have had me say: that the scheme was unworkable and should be abandoned immediately. Yet staring into those deep brown eyes, it was somehow impossible.

'It will be a difficult task,' I mumbled.

He almost snatched the words out of the air. 'But possible, you think? You are right, I am sure of it. After all, how many men did Cortés have with him? A hundred, a hundred and fifty? They made themselves lords of Mexico. Why should we not do the same?'

I fear my dismay was all too evident. Fortunately, he misunderstood it.

'Don't worry, Mr Jerrold. We won't be burning your ships when we get there. You will be admiral of the fleet. Wilkinson will be Generalissimo, and we will all be rich as kings. Surely such rewards are worth the gamble?'

'What of more local dangers?' I asked, thinking back to our desperate flight from Blennerhassett Island, the troops we had slipped past in the fog. 'We have had militia chasing us all the way down the river. What if they catch us?'

Burr waved away my objection. 'Nothing but a misunderstanding, credulous magistrates paying too much heed to rumour. I hope you will not let a few nervous provincials unseat this enterprise.'

In my mind I scrabbled for some other ploy, some reason that would persuade him to let the conspiracy die quietly. I could think of nothing.

He slapped me on the back. 'You will not regret this, Lieutenant, I promise you. Indeed, I venture, it will be the making of you. Now, let us be back to the boats. We still have many miles to travel to Vera Cruz.'

18

I SAT UP ON THE FLATBOAT'S ROOF, WATCHING THE RIVER SLUICE past. 'Was he really your country's vice-president?'

McMeekin, still steering the flatboat, nodded. 'Oh yes. Could have gone higher, too. He actually won the election – tied with Jefferson for the electoral votes, and tied him thirty-five times more when it went to the Congress. Then on the thirty-sixth ballot, one of the Congressmen changed his mind and Jefferson got the job. Burr came second, so he was Vice-President.'

It seemed an unnaturally cruel system, to yoke a man to his closest rival as leader and deputy. I thought back to conversations on the road from New York. 'But Mr Jefferson is still the President?'

'He is. That election was six years ago. We had another one two years back, and this time Jefferson fixed the constitution so he could hand pick his vice-president. Wouldn't let Burr stand – not after the duel.'

'He killed the Treasury Secretary,' I said. 'Mr Hamilton.'

'That's right.'

There was a shout from for'ard, and McMeekin heaved on the long steering oar. Slowly, the square bow turned starboard.

'What was the cause of the duel?'

'You'd have to ask the colonel. There was talk Mr Hamilton

insulted him, but I never rightly heard what it was. Must have been bad, though. After that, Jefferson couldn't have chosen Burr as his vice-president even if he had liked him. Which he didn't, they say.'

It did not speak much for Burr's wisdom that he had thrown away his career on a point of honour. Nor did I like to know that my fortunes were tied to this desperate failure, whose lost stature must have blinded him to the perils of his task. I did not want to end my life in a Spanish gaol, or an American one, trying to salvage Burr's dignity.

I left McMeekin in command on deck and went below. Four of the men were gathered around the stove playing cards, hunched over like dwarves in a cave; in the far corner, preferring the absence of fire to the presence of the crew, Catherine had buried herself under a heap of blankets and was trying to brush her hair. I crawled over, lifted the edge of the covers and huddled against her.

'Where are we?' she asked, craning her head so that her mirror caught daylight from one of the cracks in the planking.

I shrugged. 'Somewhere on the river. McMeekin believes we will make the Mississippi tomorrow. I do not suppose it will seem much different.'

'And then down to Mexico.' She pulled a golden hair from the bristles of her brush. 'Mr Burr is so brave to attempt its conquest, with so few to aid him. Is it true he is wanted for murder?'

There was a distance in her voice when she mentioned Burr which I did not like. 'He killed a man in a duel,' I said.

'So he is a man of honour, as well as daring.'

'The man he killed may disagree.'

'Is he married, do you know?'

I did not.

Catherine sighed. 'I do not suppose any one woman could compass so great a personality. The way he looked at me on the island – it was as though my skirts and spencer and stays were stripped away, and he could see me quite naked. Do you think he will truly become King of Mexico?'

'He means to try.' Personally, I thought he was as likely to become King of England.

A furious wind began to blow next day, so hard we were pushed back upstream. The horses on the stern of one of the flatboats began to bray and stamp, tossing their heads and almost overturning the shallow-draughted vessel. It was all we could do to keep the flotilla together, and to bring them one by one onto an exposed sandbank in the lee of the shore. Angry clouds raced across the sky, pelting us with freezing rain if we dared venture on deck.

I had just thrown a fresh pair of logs in the stove, and was regretting the billowing smoke they exhaled, when a dark face appeared at the mouth of the cabin. It was Burr's slave, shivering with the cold and holding an oversized cape over his head. The wind pressed it around his body like a shroud, but it was only when I beckoned him in that he dared cross the threshold. In the broken dialect of his race, he explained that his master wished to entertain Catherine and me aboard his boat until the gale abated.

I did not need a second invitation. The flatboat cabin offered little protection from the elements, and the stove could muster only a feeble reply to the bitter air. Following the young slave, we vaulted over the side and trudged through the miry sand, our boots sinking deep with every step. By the time we had hauled ourselves aboard his vessel our clothes were soaked and our fingers a shivering blue.

Burr stood as we entered his cabin. 'Welcome to my flagship,' he said grandly. 'I trust you will find the accommodation satisfactory.'

After the misery of our flatboat, his quarters were a palace. Burr had hoisted his flag on one of the keelboats, and though from the outside it would have attracted little comment, its interior was enviably fitted with plush benches, teak furniture and an iron stove which did not poison the air with smoke. The doors sat snug enough to fend off the worst of the gales, while the rear of the cabin promised the greatest luxury of all: privacy. A bulkhead divided the room in two, setting aside the aft portion as a sleeping cabin.

Through the open door I could see a porcelain bowl in a nightstand, a shaving mirror, and even an upholstered bed. If Burr was to fail in his design it would not be for want of sleep.

The boy poured wine from a decanter, and retreated into silence in the corner. Burr handed one glass to Catherine, another to me, and raised his own.

'To victory.'

Catherine sneezed. Wine spilled from her glass and splashed down the front of her dress. In an instant, Burr was at her side, proffering napkins and towels and berating himself his callous indifference to her health and constitution. Catherine took the napkin and dabbed at her garments, though there remained a few spots she could not see which Burr insisted on wiping away himself. The slave fetched a blanket from the sleeping cabin which she wrapped about her shoulders, and set a kettle on the stove to warm some egg punch. Only then did we settle back on the benches.

'I wonder that your father allowed you to venture into this damnable climate,' said Burr. 'Surely you should be at home, swaddled in furs and diamonds and warmed by the attentions of every buck in London?'

Her hair was lank and tangled from the rain; her dress still bore a few remnants of the wine; her stockings were crusted with sand and the grey blanket around her shoulders belonged more to a beggar than a lady of her fortune. Yet for all that, the emerald necklace still flashed at her throat, her skin gleamed golden in the lamplight and there was a pride on her face which made her seem at once irresistible and wholly unattainable.

'My father did not allow me to come here, Colonel Burr. I came of my own volition.'

'But why—'

'I sought adventure,' she said, cool as crystal. 'I did not suppose I should find it in London.'

Burr's eyes fixed her with such frank admiration I thought he might fall to his knees in worship. 'Did you? Well, you'll find it here, by God. You are a veritable Penthesilea, Miss Lyell, and I am

Theseus. Together, what worlds shall we not conquer? I shall make you an Empress of Mexico.'

It seemed a touch presumptuous, coming from a man who had not yet managed to reach the Mississippi, but Catherine showed no sense of its absurdity. Instead, she regarded Burr with a like frankness, even awe.

'Fine words are very well,' I said, overcome by a sudden urge to be disagreeable. 'It is actions which will decide our fate.'

Burr nodded with approval I had not sought. 'Spoken like a true man of action.'

'Though you are no stranger to action yourself,' pressed Catherine. 'You will forgive me if I am indelicate, but you have defended yourself from the vain words of others, have you not?'

Burr tried to furrow his features into noble regret, though he could not hide a certain self-satisfaction. 'I have.'

'That was a brave thing to do.'

Burr's shoulders expanded slightly. 'Mr Hamilton slandered me – a grievous insult and a stain on my honour. I could not allow it to stand unanswered.'

'What did he say?' breathed Catherine.

'Nothing that may be repeated in a lady's hearing.'

'Was it true?' I asked. No-one seemed to hear.

'Yet you stood on the field of battle, man to man, and faced down your enemy. I imagine there are few men who could do the like.'

'I heard that Hamilton purposely fired wide and expected the same of you,' I said. I had had that gossip from McMeekin.

That cracked Burr's composure. He sniffed, and leaned forward across the cabin. 'Mr Hamilton was a lying scoundrel in life, and I regret to say a lying scoundrel in death. He fired first and missed; I fired second and did not. It was typical of the man that afterwards, on his death bed, he should attempt to discredit me thus.'

I had to concede the reason in his argument. And whatever the truth of the matter, one point remained undisputed: Mr Burr had stood on a field in New Jersey and shot a defenceless man in cold blood. For all the improbability of his scheme and the affable humour he evinced, it was a fact worth remembering.

We spent most of the day in that cabin, swapping wine and punch and gossip. Despite the icy storm raging outside, inside we might have been sitting in a comfortable tavern. In the mid-afternoon Burr's boy spread out a fine lunch of cold hams and jellies, which I devoured with indecorous haste. For all his army's lack of manpower, its quartermastering was impeccable. Yet my own humour remained steadfastly gloomy. I could not help notice that though the other two indulged my conversation, and affected to find my occasional jokes amusing, their fullest laughter came at each other's wit. Long stretches passed where I said nothing – indeed, where my very presence seemed forgotten – until I almost longed to be back in the cold comfort of the flatboat. I could not help but lament Catherine's capricious attachments: evidently the lustre of our adventure together had paled.

At length – after how many hours I could not tell – there came a rap on the door, and a waterlogged sentry peered in. Behind him, the sky was dark with night. 'The wind's dropped,' he announced. 'Mr Tyler figures we can be moving again.'

'Very good. Inform the rest of the fleet.' Burr turned to Catherine. She had her feet tucked up beneath her on the bench, snug as a cat. 'I can hardly conscience you to return to that flatboat, with its leaks and its draughts. Your adventure would end in a terrible fever before it had rightly begun. You must stay with us – I will happily give you the use of my bed.'

I was not so obtuse that I had not anticipated this offer would come. I had prepared my response, and was instantly all the bustling guardian. 'That is very kind of you, Colonel Burr, but I could not allow it. Even in these far-flung wilds Miss Lyell must heed the dictates of propriety.'

Burr smiled indulgently, as though he pitied me my punctiliousness. 'Is propriety to be prized above health?'

'It is in England.'

He waved his hand. 'But you have misunderstood me. I did not intend to slight Miss Lyell's virtue. Naturally, it was my hope that you both would join me aboard.'

Having seen the two of them together I distrusted even that arrangement. But there was no denying that the flatboat was a wretched vessel, and that we were more likely to survive the journey, without catching some exotic American fever, aboard Burr's keelboat. And I could surely watch them close enough to prevent any infidelity.

I did not doubt that I would needs be vigilant. Burr had already shown himself untroubled by the rightful ownership of whole nations; my tenuous, irregular relationship with Miss Lyell would give him little pause. Not for the first time, I wondered what Mr Hamilton's lethal gibe had been, and how true it had struck.

19

WE MET THE MISSISSIPPI THE FOLLOWING DAY – OR SO THEY TOLD
me. So far as I could see, it met us, for from my vantage it looked
little different to any of the other myriad tributaries which joined
and fed the Ohio. It sometimes seemed a miracle there was any
space to inhabit this nation at all, so plentiful were its rivers.
Nonetheless, the helmsman assured me that we now sailed the true
Mississippi, mightiest of the western waters and artery of an entire
continent.

For myself, I had preferred the Ohio. Though wet and freezing for
most of our journey it had contained a picturesque elegance which
seemed, somehow, as a wilderness ought to be. Though I had found
it sinister at first, the slope of the valley and the changing landscapes
had formed a pleasing prospect. The Mississippi, by contrast,
offered no such proportion or variety. Whatever hills or elevations
had once lined its course had long since been ground down and
swept away by the all-devouring river. Now, the banks stretched
away flat as a marsh, the trees so thick that they became wooden
walls hemming us in on our sunken road. Untrammelled by any
physical constraint, the river was left to spread itself as wide as it
chose. The current broadened, and slowed, so that our progress
seemed still more excruciating.

The monotony was unyielding. Even the arrival of the new year, 1807, occasioned nothing more than an additional tot of whiskey. Burr's boat might keep us drier and warmer, but it was not a comfortable place to be. At first I made sure to keep to the cabin, following Catherine like a forlorn hound lest Burr attempt any indiscretion. Yet I could not sustain the endeavour. Sitting in that cabin hour after hour, playing backgammon without stakes or enduring inane conversations in my fledgling French, proved more exhausting than any labour. After two days of it I insisted I must join the watch, and thereafter spent my time either looking out for sawyers (the barely submerged tree-trunks which could break open a boat) or seeking a restless sleep on the benches in the cabin.

The long hours which I spent perched on the roof, staring out into the muddy stream and pulling my coat close about me, at least afforded time for reflection. Since I had learned of Burr's plan on Blennerhassett Island, and been dragged down the forsaken river, one solitary question prevailed unanswered in my thoughts. How was I to stop this business? For once, Nevell's interests, Britain's and my own were all in perfect harmony. Nevell had been right. If Burr carried out his designs, if it became known that a consortium of Englishmen had conspired to forge a new empire on America's border, then whether he succeeded or failed there would surely be a ruinous war between England and America. Whose casualties, I did not doubt, would include the unfortunate Lieutenant Martin Jerrold. Whether I was killed in battle by the Spaniards, executed for my complicity by the Americans, or murdered by Burr's men when they discovered my treachery, it did not matter. Yet even if I did somehow manage to leave the conspiracy stillborn, its failure would still leave me stranded far from home and deep among enemies.

A murmur from behind me broke into my thoughts, and I turned to see who had spoken. There was no-one save the steersman, and he was ignoring me as he concentrated on maintaining our course against the swirling cross-current. Perhaps it had been a creak in the timbers.

As my gaze slipped back up the river behind us, I stiffened. Near the horizon, where the water and the trees and the sky all came together in a mottle of greys and browns, something was moving. I almost did not see it, for its wooden hull blended into the grain of the background, and the flat-roofed cabin barely rose high enough to break the line of the bank, yet something in its angularity, its artifice, stood out like a mis-stitched thread on a sampler. If I squinted to see it clearer it only faded from view, yet I could not quite convince myself I imagined it.

I took the spyglass which I kept by my side, and trained it behind me. The far stretches of the river leaped closer, and I could see what my naked eye had only guessed at: a flatboat, floating lazily in mid-stream, with only a solitary figure visible on its deck. Even in the glass he was little more than a silhouette at that distance.

I suppose it should not have been remarkable. Every month, hundreds of boats made the same journey we did, and there were few vessels in the world so uniformly characterless as the flatboats. Yet in this depth of winter the waterways were almost deserted: outside our own flotilla, I had not seen a single other boat since Shawneetown. It was probably innocent, I told myself – a trader hoping to profit by the lack of competition, or an immigrant family who had misjudged the season.

The noise which had first drawn my attention aft sounded again. It had come from the rear skylight, I realized, propped open above Burr's sleeping cabin. It might have been the creak of wood, or the groan of a cask being dragged across the deck, but I did not think so. There was a vital, carnal quality to the sound which implied a more human origin. By the leer on the helmsman's face, I guessed he thought the same.

All my suspicions and jealousies ignited as if touched by a match. Propelled forward, I ran along the roof of the cabin. In that moment I was absolutely certain that Catherine had betrayed me to Burr; even before I reached the skylight, I could picture the two of them entwined in each other's arms, naked, the blankets cast aside and the cabin echoing with the shameless voice of their coupling. So vivid was the image that I almost wanted it to be true.

I never found out. Before I could reach the skylight a vast shudder swept through the boat, flinging me forward onto my knees. The wedge which had held the skylight open fell away and it slammed shut. Yet that was forgotten, driven out by a new and more urgent question. What had happened? Looking forward again I could see the two men by the bow frantically heaving on their poles, while behind me the helmsman splashed away with the steering oar. Belatedly, I became aware of having heard a loud thud accompanying the blow.

More of the men were on deck now, rushing out of the cabin and snatching poles or paddles from where they had lain. I heard shouts and curses, calls for a carpenter and caulking. I could see that the bow had been knocked off course, almost upstream, so that we drifted beam-on to the current.

'Shoals ahead!' shouted one of the crew. 'Get those oars stuck in before she breaks her back open!'

A great commotion of running feet and knocking wood answered his call. Above it all I heard a familiar voice asking, 'What the hell is going on?'

'Sawyer,' came the terse reply. 'Didn't see it coming. But there's worse ahead if we don't turn our bow forward again.'

I crawled to the end of the roof and looked down. Burr was standing there, his shirt untucked and his grey hair matted to a thatch. He did not appear to be wearing shoes or stockings.

Before I could be suspicious, he turned and looked up at me. 'Where were you when this happened, Lieutenant? You were meant to be keeping watch for these hazards.'

Cowering under the scorching gaze of those eyes, I mumbled something about not having noticed it.

'You'll notice it presently, I'd wager.' Burr pointed to a dark ridge snaking through the water a few hundred feet downstream. 'If we strike that we'll be rolled keel-side up in no time – if the impact doesn't snap us in two.'

Helpless impotence welled inside me, mingled with the taint of Burr's scorn and a lingering jealousy. I jumped down onto the

196

foredeck and took hold of the pole which was thrust into my hands. It barely made a sound as it slid into the water, sinking deeper and deeper as I probed for the riverbed. It must have measured fifteen feet or more, yet it sank to its tip without ever touching the bottom.

'Let it go,' said Burr. 'By the time you feel anything it'll be too late to save us. Take an oar.'

I did as he said. The current, which minutes earlier had felt so sluggish, now seemed to be a raging torrent hurtling us forward onto the shoal. I snatched an oar and plunged the blade into the river, driving it backwards and carving thin whirlpools in the water. For what seemed an eternity there was nothing but the rise and fall and heave of oars, the sluice of gallons of water being dug out of the current. Slowly, I felt our bow begin to turn, though I could not look up from my work to see it.

'Ready with the pole,' shouted Burr. 'It'll shave us close.'

For the second time that afternoon, vibrations rippled through the hull. The whole boat tipped to starboard, and a rasping noise like wind through a tree sounded below. We put down our oars and hurled ourselves to the starboard side, heeling the boat over away from the shoal. Still the rasping continued; still the boat slid forward. The bow was swinging back again as we pivoted around like a compass needle, slowing every second with the drag on her hull. The river and the mud vied to grasp us; for a moment I thought we might yet slip off.

With a slithering hiss, the boat ground to a halt. Limbs and bodies tangled together as the jolt threw the crew forward on top of one another. A sharp elbow dug into my spine.

Rubbing our bruises, we got to our feet. The boat had come to rest on the very tip of the shoal, rocking gently in the current – another yard or two and we would have been clear. It listed to starboard, though that was slowly correcting itself as the larboard side oozed down into the mud. Under the hull the diverted waters were already beginning to chew away at the point, changing the shape of the ever-shifting river once more.

One by one, I felt the eyes of the crew fix on me. Burr, standing in the cabin doorway, spoke for them all. 'Next time, Mr Jerrold, I hope you will not be so easily distracted.'

We got off that shoal, though it was a damnable effort. The other boats in the flotilla had seen us, and sent men back upstream in canoes to aid us. We threw wooden boards onto the shoal and then stood on them, digging out the mud with the makeshift spades we had made of our oars. It was precarious work, particularly with the water forever undermining the ground beneath us, and several times I was pitched forward on my face; once I was almost dragged away by the current and had to snatch at the end of an outstretched pole to haul myself in. By the end of it, I had grown a second skin of mud, black as Burr's negro slave. I remembered a scufflehunter I had once encountered on the Thames at low water, a man I had thought carved from the river clay itself. Even he might now disdain to shake my hand.

At last, with a great heave of poles and a slurp of mud, we worked the boat free. Those of us still on the shoal had to leap for the side and haul ourselves inboard, for the river was in urgent mood; several oars were abandoned behind us. I took off my shirt and trawled it in the water, trying to wring the worst of the mud out of it. As I did so, I looked back.

It was almost dark. The sun, never much in evidence that day, now only touched the tips of the forest, and a thunderhead of black clouds hung low over the river behind us. Yet even in the twilight, I could have sworn I still saw the solitary flatboat I had noticed earlier.

We had spent over two hours beached on that shoal, more than enough time for the current to carry the other boat past us. Yet even now, after so much time, it still floated at exactly the same distance as before, almost out of sight but never quite beyond the horizon.

20

A FEW DAYS LATER – I COULD NO LONGER BE BOTHERED TO COUNT them – we put in at a lonely place called Fort Pickering. Steep bluffs of orange clay rose high above the river, topped with a few ramshackle log houses. At one end of the village, a long wooden wall studded with embrasures for cannon warned of the presence of the fort.

We moored the boats and went ashore. It seemed a peculiar folly to me, having risked so much to pass the garrisons on the Ohio, but Burr was in ebullient mood and would not be dissuaded.

'This should be fertile ground for our recruiting,' he explained. 'With a little fortune, I shall charm the whole garrison into accompanying us down river.'

This struck me as a fine opportunity for observing the intricacies of the conspiracy, as Nevell would no doubt have wanted, at minimal personal hazard. Perhaps I might learn something which I could put to use in upsetting the enterprise. Besides, I had barely stepped off the boat in a week and I welcomed the prospect of exercise.

When I volunteered to accompany Burr, he considered this a moment.

'You will have to keep quiet. I doubt we are in danger, but the men of Tennessee are jealous patriots. They might not approve if they knew the English were so necessary a part of my designs.'

I did not argue, for I presently needed all my breath to climb to the top of the bluffs. A log stair had been set into the slope, a hundred and twenty steps in all, and I had worked up a considerable warmth by the time I gained the top.

It had hardly merited the effort. On a thin patch of open, rocky ground, we found a dozen crude houses and a single track leading between them to the fort. About two hundred yards inland from the cliff edge the tree wall began again, hemming in the tiny settlement. Dark birds wheeled in the iron sky above, calling their harsh cries down on us, while on the steps of one of the houses a round-faced boy plucked a mournful guitar.

We walked up the track to the gate of the fort. It was an ungainly structure, a stoccado of logs surrounding a pair of low cabins and a row of muddy tents, with a sad air of impermanence hanging over it. A single sentinel in the red-faced coat of the American army was walking back and forth before it, his musket on his shoulder and his bayonet fixed. He challenged us as we approached.

'Vice-President Aaron Burr,' said Burr cheerfully. 'Here to call on your commander.'

The soldier's eyes narrowed doubtfully, though not so much that he did not snap to attention and thump the butt of his musket onto the frozen ground. However improbable Burr's introduction might be, his manner and bearing showed complete confidence.

'What's your name, Private?' Burr enquired.

'Bynner, sir.'

'Are you a Tennessee man?'

'No, sir. North Carolina.'

'How do you like it here?'

The man shifted on his feet. 'Well enough.'

'A little cold for you?'

He gave a shy smile. 'I guess so.'

'Not much happening here, I guess.'

'No, sir.' The soldier nodded to the cluster of huts before him, then added, somewhat impulsively, 'It's deader'n a skinned 'coon around here. And colder.'

Burr laughed heartily. 'I admire a man who speaks as he thinks, Mr Bynner. Tell me, how much does Mr Jefferson pay you to keep watch on the eagles out here?'

'Six dollars a month. Less 'ductions.'

Burr put his arm around the man's shoulders and leaned close to his ear. 'Then how would you like twelve and a half dollars a month, and a hundred acres of prime Louisiana to yourself if you came with me?'

'Come with you?' The soldier shook his head, bewildered by this unexpected proposition. 'But that'd be deserting.'

'I'm sure your commander could be persuaded to give you furlough. What's his name?'

'Lieutenant Jackson.'

'A good man?'

The soldier shrugged. 'I guess so.'

Burr disentangled himself from the sentinel and stepped towards the gate. 'Think about my offer, Mr Bynner. If a dozen dollars a month and a chance of land and action aren't enough for you, I can promise you one thing. The climate'll be a whole lot warmer.'

We left the sentry to ponder Burr's offer and stepped inside the stoccado. Two low cabins faced each other across the frozen mud of a parade ground, and woodsmoke rose from their chimneys. Beyond, I could see small cannon pointing out over the bluffs, and piles of shot stacked in neat pyramids beside them. In a tower at the far corner of the wall, a pair of unhappy-looking soldiers kept watch over the river; otherwise, the men seemed to keep to their barracks.

An American flag flew from a pole over the smaller of the two buildings, and two chestnut mares were tethered to the bar outside. Burr strode over to the door, knocked, and entered.

The interior was dim and spartan, the only light coming from a pair of grimy, square-paned windows. The walls were unpainted, and the floorboards still bore the toothmarks of the saws which had cut them. At the back of the room a young man sat behind a crude desk writing some report: he wore a silver epaulette on his left shoulder, and a green cockade in his hat. The beard on his face looked to be a recent, tentative addition, for I could still see pale skin beneath the thin hairs.

'Lieutenant Jackson?' said Burr.

The man nodded, and stood to take the outstretched hand.

'Jacob Jackson?'

'Indeed.'

Burr flashed a smile which seemed to illuminate the gloomy room. 'I know your brother John, in Washington. A most able man. He spoke highly of you.'

'I am gratified to hear it. But I confess, sir, I do not know your name.'

'Of course. I am Colonel Aaron Burr, lately Vice-President of the United States and now an independent adventurer.' He arched his eyebrows. 'I am engaged on a project which will bring considerable glory to the United States, and confusion to tyrants everywhere.'

He broke off, fixing his gleaming eyes on Lieutenant Jackson. Jackson said nothing, though I noticed his spine seemed to stiffen.

'I will speak frankly. I need men for this enterprise, and I hope to find some in your outpost. You are an artillery officer, are you not? You could be especially helpful to my cause.'

Jackson sat back on his chair. 'I don't know that I understand you. What is your enterprise?'

'One which will be honourable to you; which, I dare say, will be the making of all who follow me – should they survive.' Burr adopted a stern, stoic tone. 'I won't deny there's danger involved. But a young, ambitious officer like yourself should not fear that. No doubt your greater fear is that you sit out your career in this forgotten hole, lost to glory and honour.'

There was a frown on Jackson's face. 'Again I must ask you, Colonel Burr, what exactly you intend. I am an officer of the United States army; I cannot forfeit my duty, however noble your cause.'

'My cause is bound to secrecy. However, I may say that the subjects of Spain, in Mexico and Florida, are in a very distressed situation. Relief from the tyranny of their government would be a mighty blessing to them.'

'You intend to invade Spanish lands?' Stated so baldly, I could see why Jackson looked sceptical. He could hardly have expected an erstwhile vice-president to arrive at his door with an invitation to a private war.

Burr did not answer directly. Instead, he said carefully, 'If there were to be an invasion of Mexico, what would be your opinion of it?'

'If there were to be a war with Spain I should gladly serve my country. In this, as in all things, I would be guided by my government.'

Burr pressed his palms on the edge of the desk and leaned forward, like a bird of prey launching forth over the unfortunate lieutenant. 'The leading characters of the United States favour my views,' he said, glancing over his shoulder with a conspiratorial flourish. 'They do not say so in public, lest they be taken for warmongers, but they know it to be inevitable. You know the rank I held in the administration. Will you not allow that I must know Mr Jefferson's mind, and he mine?'

Jackson allowed that this might be so. 'Nonetheless, my duty is to my superiors. Whatever intentions the President may harbour in private, they cannot justify me disobeying orders.'

'Your duty is to mankind,' said Burr grandly. 'If your commission in the United States army does not permit that you follow me, resign it. I will gazette you captain in my army and double your pay.

The lieutenant squirmed in his seat. 'What about the Neutrality Act?'

'What of it?'

'It's not legal to attack foreign countries when we're at peace with them. You were Vice-President, for God's sake – you'd not go against the laws of your own country?'

It was a curious thing to say to a man wanted for duelling and murder. Fortunately, Burr took no offence.

'I would sooner cut off my own hand than offend against the laws of this country,' he declared. 'You have heard of my trial in

Kentucky?' Jackson had not. 'They prosecuted me under an apprehension that I was about to invade the Spanish dominions, but they could make nothing out against me. Why? Because, as the jury kindly affirmed, I am entirely innocent. There is a war coming, and when it breaks I will be in the front rank with all who love freedom and honour. Even now, General Wilkinson is camped on the Sabine River, muzzle to muzzle with the thieving Spaniards who are trying to extend their tyranny. For all we know the war may already have started.'

Jackson sat up straighter in his chair. 'There, Colonel Burr, I can correct you. The last intelligence I had was that General Wilkinson has concluded a peace treaty with Spain, designated the disputed lands neutral ground and retired to New Orleans. War is avoided.'

I was standing behind Burr and so could not see his face. What I did see were his shoulders, which jerked forward as if he had been punched in the belly before reasserting their habitual poise. Even so, they still seemed to twitch sporadically under his coat.

'Of course Wilkinson has retreated to New Orleans,' said Burr, off-hand. 'He must gather his forces. Replenish his supplies. This neutral ground business is all a ploy, a feint. Surely you can see as much?'

Jackson looked puzzled. 'A ploy?'

All Burr ever sought in conversation was a chink, a crack in his opponent's reserve he could lever open with his eloquence and rhetoric. Still leaning over the desk, he almost physically pounced on the hapless lieutenant.

'You know of General Wilkinson, I take it?'

'Of course.'

'And do you believe, *Lieutenant*' – Burr invested the title with particular emphasis – 'that the ranking *general* of the United States army would conduct himself against the nation's interests?'

'No.'

Burr tapped a finger to his lips. 'Naturally, there are certain facts which I cannot yet reveal. But, if you will permit me the confidence, I may tell you, in the utmost privacy, that Wilkinson is with us. He is party to all my plans – no, that does not do him justice. He is the co-author of this great project, and when we charge home against our enemies you may be assured that General Wilkinson will be in the van. Now, from whom do you suppose General Wilkinson takes his orders?'

'The Secretary for War.'

'And above him?' Burr answered for himself. 'Only the President. Can you any longer doubt the legitimacy of this enterprise?'

At that precise moment, Jackson looked as though he might doubt his own name. 'My commission,' he mumbled, invoking it like a charm against Burr's argument. 'My commission requires me to serve at Fort Pickering.'

'Resign it. I have already promised to promote you captain. How many of your men do you think you can bring with you?'

Jackson scratched an anxious hand through his beard. Beneath it, he was coming to look vaguely ill. 'I cannot seduce the soldiery from their duty, not while I hold a commission.' He raised a tired hand to stem Burr's inevitable argument. 'I . . . I will write to the Secretary for War and resign my commission, but until he confirms it I am honour bound to serve my country.'

'I am sure you need not wait for Secretary Dearborn to reply. That will take weeks, and then you will have to come down river. You will miss all the action and glory.'

'Nonetheless, that is as much as I can do in good conscience.' A great deal more, his face suggested.

Perhaps Burr sensed he had pushed the lieutenant as far as he might. He stepped back a little, and thrust out a hand. Jackson took it cautiously.

'You will not regret this, *Captain* Jackson,' said Burr. 'But you will need a company to command. I authorize you to engage, in my name, as many men as you may and bring them down the river.' He took a wad of money from his pocket and counted out the bills. 'One hundred and fifty dollars. Let that be an advance on your pay, and a subsidy for whatever expenses you incur in travel. I will also leave a draft on Mr Ogden of New York for another five hundred dollars, which you may use to pay your men until you join with my army. The rate is twelve and a half dollars per month. I rely on your honour to account for it honestly.'

'You need not doubt my honour.'

'You will also need a boat. Obtain one as you may, and follow me as soon as your company is assembled.' He chuckled. 'I dare say you will have little trouble finding me.'

Leaving the money untouched on his desk, Jackson stood and ushered us to the door. Outside, the wind had risen again, and an armada of grey clouds was racing in from the west. With much jovial hand-shaking from Burr, and strained smiles from Jackson, we took our leave. As we passed through the gate we found the sentry, Bynner, still pacing up and down his well-worn tract of mud.

'What is it to be, Mr Bynner?' called Burr. 'Will you follow me down the river to glory and fortune?'

Bynner looked up at the worsening sky, then grinned bashfully at his boots. 'Reckon I'll stay.'

Burr did not try to dissuade him, but walked on to the head of the stair. At its foot, I could see our flotilla bobbing on the choppy waters.

'That was a wasted visit,' I observed.

Burr turned to face me. 'Not at all. The intelligence we had about General Wilkinson was invaluable, albeit perplexing.'

'I was thinking rather of Lieutenant Jackson and his men.'

'Do you think so? I think you are a little harsh. Lieutenant Jackson may have been unwilling to show his hand, but I do not doubt he will be an admirable asset to our campaign.'

I stared at him in surprise, though he did not notice. Was this how he counted his army, in evasive promises and vague assurances? I had seen Jackson's face, his manner, and I did not think him poised to resign his commission and throw in his lot with this itinerant adventurer. If he had any sense he would keep the money and go back to counting his cannonballs. I could not escape the conclusion that even here, marooned in the midst of a bleak and frozen wilderness, his situation was preferable to mine.

*

We did not talk as we made our descent, but I could see Burr's spirits darkening. He halted at the foot of the stairs.

'Fetch Tyler and Blennerhassett,' he ordered. 'We will meet in my cabin.'

I found the others and brought them to the keelboat. Burr had laid out his maps on the table, and his boy was waiting with four glasses of warmed wine. I took mine gratefully.

Briefly, Burr repeated what Jackson had told him. 'This business of Wilkinson's knocks my utopia to the devil,' he admitted. 'I cannot fathom it. Wilkinson advanced to the Sabine and the Spaniards came to meet him; it wanted only a single shot to start our war and give us all the cover we needed. That was our agreement. I cannot think why he would have changed it.'

'He may have needed to resupply himself at New Orleans,' said Tyler. 'Or perhaps he was concerned we'd not arrived. We should have been in Natchez three weeks since.'

Burr had rested his chin on his fist, and was rocking back and forth. 'Yes, of course you are right. Yet he could have withdrawn without concluding a treaty. If he truly has declared the border neutral ground, our cause for war is kicked from under us. We might as well turn our bayonets to cane-knives and make our fortunes in sugar.'

I saw my chance. 'I fear you are right. Without the cover of a justified war we would be little more than pirates.' Unsure whether this would trouble Burr unduly, I added, 'Without General Wilkinson's troops we could not hope to defeat the Spaniards. I cannot commit my ships to a doomed venture, Colonel.'

'Then what am I to do?'

'Disband your army and go home.' My blood was running high; I could feel Tyler and Blennerhassett staring at me in disbelief. Tyler seemed outraged by my cowardice, but I fancied Blennerhassett did not find it so uncongenial. 'Save your strength for another day,' I urged him. A day by which I would be long gone from his presence.

'Perhaps you are right.' Burr slumped forward. The life seemed to have ebbed from his body, and the light in his eyes was dim.

Tyler reached to touch his arm in comfort, stricken by the melancholy which had overwhelmed his captain. 'Perhaps he means to secure West Florida first.'

Burr looked up, hope stirring in his eyes. 'What?'

'West Florida.' Tyler pointed to the map, to a strip of land along the coast east of the Mississippi. *West Florida (to Spain)* read the legend. 'At New Orleans, General Wilkinson's well placed to strike into Florida, and there's no shortage of Americans settled down there who'd be quick to join a revolt against the Spaniards. We'd secure our rear before we turned west, and rouse half the country to our cause. Hell, we'd be heroes before we even crossed the Red River. There's your war, Colonel.'

Burr slapped his hand on the table. 'By God, you may be right. Drive the Spaniards out of Florida, then double back and take Mexico. Every man west of the Alleghenies would march to our banner.' He turned to me. 'Your ships could supply us at Mobile Bay, could they not?'

It was as though his spirits burned like a wick, to be snuffed or kindled in an instant. For my part, I had preferred his despond and believed that Wilkinson's change of heart might prove the end of the scheme. Instead, it seemed to have expanded its scope. The hope which had possessed me now curdled in my veins.

'Where is Mobile Bay?' I asked, delaying my answer.

Tyler indicated a place halfway across the Spanish territory, a deep wedge which almost bisected the province. 'There's a chain of coastal islands guarding the mouth – as safe a harbour as you could imagine.'

'And a safe harbour for our ambitions also.' Burr stretched out his arms, hugging me and Tyler to him. 'Wilkinson has seen it clearly. To think that I doubted him – you must promise you will not tell him so when we meet. What do you think, Lieutenant? I know you spoke in despond when you threatened to withdraw your fleet. You cannot insist on it now, when such golden opportunity beckons.'

I felt sick, dizzied by the edifice of hopes, deceptions, dreams and lies Burr had constructed. Nothing seemed real – not General Wilkinson, not Mexico, not Burr's army, and certainly not the supposed fleet I commanded. I was standing on an island in the air, soaring above reality like a cloud. How could I resist Burr? Especially with Tyler's violent gaze concentrated upon me.

'My ships will not fail you,' I mumbled.

'Your trust will not be forgotten.' Burr stood. 'Return to the boats and let us be under way. Wilkinson was right to be impatient – we have wasted too much time already. There will be no stopping now until Natchez.'

He grinned, a cocksure, infectious smile which had Blenner-hassett and Tyler beaming like simpletons.

'This adventure has barely begun.'

21

WHETHER BURR'S OVERCONFIDENCE HAD OFFENDED SOME GOD, OR whether he was simply a lodestone for ill fortune, the next few days were more a feat of endurance than an adventure. High winds blasted the river; the men on the steering oars had to lie flat against the roof lest they be carried away, while those at the sides paddled in vain against the whims of the storm. When we lashed the boats together for stability, the wind tore them apart, and several barrels of provisions were lost overboard. Often we could not move at all, but had to lie in the lee of the shore and huddle in the cabins. I had thought the keelboat tolerably well built compared to the rudimentary flatboats, yet the wind managed to find gaps even in the flagship's timbers. My only consoling thought was that the flatboat which had followed us so diligently seemed to have disappeared in the turbulence. Though I had had no signal that it meant us harm, or even that it was concerned in our business at all, I was glad to be rid of it.

Through all this, Burr retained an exemplary calm. On occasion, when he thought himself unobserved, I might see him gazing at the black skies with a pensive concern, but otherwise he evinced good humour and implacable optimism. The greater the storm's onslaught, the greater the energy he devoted to his project. It seemed he was forever poring over the large maps spread over every surface in his cabin, or ordering inventories of our powder and shot, or discussing tactics with Tyler. Often, he would consult me on naval matters.

'Remind me, how are you to make contact with your ships?'

'They will wait near the mouth of the Mississippi, at the line of twenty-eight degrees north latitude,' I said, remembering my uncle's letter. 'If we can obtain a boat in New Orleans, we should be able to meet them at sea.'

'They will have marines on board? And cannon?'

'I believe so.'

'So you could land a force of, say, two hundred men with artillery in Mobile Bay to open a new front. A touch of Nelson, perhaps. We could reinforce you overland with companies from New Orleans.'

I made some noncommittal answer. Privately, I reckoned that if I could only find a boat in New Orleans I could sail it east and be on a packet from Charleston or Norfolk before Burr was any the wiser. The thought of wading ashore under Spanish guns with a paltry force, relying on Burr's conjectured army for support, filled me with horror. Nor could I believe that the promised frigates were any more substantial than Lieutenant Jackson's company. My uncle had written of them, true, but that had been many months previous. By now anything could have happened: a change of heart or government, impatience with Burr's delay, the discovery of how feeble his scheme actually was. A pair of frigates could not keep their illegitimate station indefinitely. Burr, however, placed great store by them.

'It is your frigates which are the key to this venture,' he was fond of telling me. 'All the Mississippi is ripe for revolt, but each man fears to show his hand before his neighbour. Once they see your ships sail into Mobile Bay, their broadsides blasting apart the rule of Spanish tyranny, then their doubts will fall away. Why, I sometimes think that without your ships to rely on I would give up this whole enterprise.'

How many times did I wish I could look him in the eye and

convince him his quest was futile, that my ships were fantasies? Yet each time I tried, I did not have the courage.

One afternoon, five days after leaving Fort Pickering, we put ashore for firewood. Burr disliked the delay – we were within two hundred miles of New Orleans now, and he was forever consulting his *Navigator* to measure our progress – but we were cold and miserable, and would not continue. Grudgingly, he allowed us to beach our boat at the mouth of a shallow creek on the eastern shore. There was no thought of trying to keep the flotilla together: gales and eddies and sawyers had divided us far apart, and there was no order save to rendezvous down the river at a place called Bayou Pierre.

For once, the weather had abated a little. An icy wind still blew, but the lashing rain had passed on and there were even cracks of blue opening in the sky. Leaving only a solitary picket to guard the boat, we mustered on the foredeck, eager to touch land and stretch our legs. When Catherine emerged from the cabin I noticed she had a bundle of clothes in her hands.

'My dresses,' she said, when I enquired. There was a distance in her manner towards me now, and I smarted each time I felt it, though I had no cause to suspect any further indiscretions with Burr. The past week had been too numbing for any of us to think of indulgence. 'They are quite bedraggled with all we have endured on board this boat, and I could sooner wash them in a sewer than in this filthy river. I hope to find a stream inland.'

'You won't go alone, will you, miss?' asked one of the crew. All the men worshipped her as a goddess in their midst. 'This is Chactaw country.'

'Jackdaws?' said Miss Lyell, puzzled.

The man, little more than a youth, giggled, then broke off as he saw that Catherine was in no mood for sport. 'The Chactaws is Injuns, miss. Fearsome cruel. You don't want to come across one of their bone pickers.'

'What is a bone picker?' I felt a strong premonition I would rather not know.

The youth leaned close. 'When one of the Chactaws dies, they leave the corpse in the woods to soften up some. When it's nice and ripe, the bone pickers come.' He raised his arms before him, curling over the fingers like talons. 'They tear that flesh clear off the bones, clean as carrion. Some say it's to burn it, but I heard tell they eat it.' He lowered his voice. 'I also heard that sometimes, if they catch a white man, they don't even wait for him to die.'

I was beginning to suffer grave reservations about going ashore. Catherine, however, briskly dismissed the warning. 'Well, they cannot practise such abominations in this climate. It would be April before the bodies thawed.'

That seemed a poor premise on which to hazard her life. I began to edge back towards the cabin, suddenly far less keen on exploring the shore.

'I hope you are not abandoning me, Lieutenant. I am sure you would never forgive yourself if I were torn apart by savage Indians.' Catherine stood poised on the bow, ready to leap down onto the riverbank; most of the others had already landed.

'I was merely going to get my pistol.' And plenty of ammunition.

'If it comes to that, make sure you save the last ball for yourself,' advised the youth. 'You don't want them taking you alive.'

I could quite happily have turned the pistol on him, but I refrained. A few minutes later, my pockets bulging with powder and shot, I emerged from the cabin and reluctantly dropped over the side onto the shore. Catherine followed, disdaining the hand I offered.

'I am told there may be a stream further up the creek,' she said. 'You need not accompany me; I am quite able to protect myself.'

I did not disagree. I remembered too well the fatal shock on Mr Harris's face when he discovered what she kept in her reticule. She wandered away up the creek, stepping carefully over the exposed roots and fissures in the bank. I was left alone.

For a moment, I felt a powerful temptation to follow her, to press my affections and see if her coolness towards me would not melt. Reluctantly, I dismissed the notion. I would more likely earn scorn than pity. Instead, I chose a path which led away from both the river and the creek, through the silent forest. The rest of the crew had dispersed, and though they could not have gone far I had neither sight nor sound of them. The grey palings of leafless trees were my only companions.

I trudged along the path, up a shallow hill heading inland. The ground was thick with fallen leaves, frozen together in clusters which crackled and broke apart beneath my feet. With a part of myself I lazily scanned the ground for firewood, though I did not take any. I could collect it on my return, I reasoned. Sometimes I would pick up a stick or a twig, but only to snap it into pieces and discard it. Then I remembered the unpleasant habits of the Chactaws, and decided it would be best not to signal my presence.

I suppose I ought to have enjoyed my walk. Away from the cheek-by-jowl of the boat it was a rare moment of solitude, a chance to breathe without constriction and to consider my predicament in private. Yet the fears and pressures which bound me could not be left behind in the cabin. If anything, they were more present there in the woods, for aboard the boat I could at least take solace in my helplessness. Now I had no such excuses. But nor did I have any conception of what I might do to extricate myself. I was still hundreds of miles from civilization, in the company of a lunatic whose delusions would most likely see us all massacred by the Spaniards. Had it not been for the menace of the Chactaws, I might have run there and then, right across the Mississippi valley until I found the sea. But that was an idle hope, and an almost certain death.

The rustles and murmurs of the forest seemed to tighten around me as I progressed. Still I could see no sign of Burr's men. Belatedly, I began to wonder what creature had made the path I trod; might it be a Chactaw trail which would lead me straight into their encampment and the lacerating attentions of the dread bone pickers?

I turned, and paused. What had seemed an obvious path on the way up had now vanished completely; all I could see was a mottled carpet of leaves and debris. I had not even left footprints in the frozen earth. With mounting desperation, I searched the surrounding woods for any hint of the way I had come, but that only disoriented me further.

Where were the others? I had not come so very far from the boat – I should surely have seen some of them by now. What if they had left without me, abandoned me to a lingering death in the desolate wilderness? Had that been Burr's plan? Had he known of my treachery and resolved to be rid of me where my fate would remain forever unknown? Had he even, perhaps, contracted with the Chactaws to be sure that even my bones could never be found? In my mind's eye, a pair of talons reached forward to claw me apart and I cried out in horror.

The noise of my own cry returned me to my senses. Listening to the sound echoing in the dead woods, I became aware of another noise, the trickle of water. I hurried towards it, and in a few moments found a stream running along the bottom of a low gully. The surface was frozen, but the water still flowed beneath the ice, breaking into the air every so often where a steeper drop or a cluster of rocks speeded its course.

Relief flooded my spirits. The stream must empty into the creek or the river; I could follow it to its mouth, and then make my way along the shore back to the boat. I scrambled down the embankment. The going was treacherous, for the damp ground had frozen solid, but I could cling to the overhanging branches to steady myself. In this manner, I lunged and slithered my way forward, looking up occasionally to find the next purchase or hazard, but otherwise keeping my gaze rooted to the sloping ground.

I must have gone about two hundred yards when, as I glanced up, a movement ahead caught my eye, flitting through the trees on the far side of the gully. Thinking it must be one of the crew I was about to hail him, when the image of the bone picker's hands once more invaded my thoughts. I did not wish to betray my presence to an enemy. Trying to be as silent as possible, I carried on, peering forward with every step. Occasionally the figure would come into view, though even then I could not see much of him; more often he melted into the depths of the woods.

After another hundred yards the gully opened out into a bowl, a shallow impression in the forest floor strewn with boulders and fallen trees. The stream flowed across it, spreading into a succession of gentle pools before resuming its course. Kneeling beside one of them, with Burr's greatcoat wrapped tightly about her, was Catherine. She had chopped a hole in the ice and was dunking a green dress into the water beneath; two more dresses and a pair of petticoats were arranged carefully on the adjacent rocks, though they were more likely to freeze there than to dry.

'Catherine,' I called.

She looked around, startled.

'Martin? What are you doing here?'

I put my fingers to my lips and crept over. Catherine watched with mounting alarm, perhaps fearful of what dishonour I might intend. I tried a smile of reassurance, always keeping a wary eye for the figure in the woods beyond.

'What is wrong with you, Martin? You seem quite distracted.'

'There is a man over there,' I whispered. 'Hiding among the trees.'

To my consternation, she laughed. 'Do not be so silly. Do you think it is a jackdaw come to eat your flesh? It is probably one of the crew, or Colonel Burr. He promised to help me carry my laundry back to the boat.'

'I do not think it was Colonel Burr.'

Catherine wrung out one of her petticoats. 'Really, Martin, you may be a lion at sea but you are a veritable lamb ashore. You—'

She broke off in a scream as a shot exploded from the forest opposite. A cobweb of smoke hung between the trees, and as I dropped to the ground I smelled the black tang of powder. I rolled down the last few feet of the slope almost landing on top of Catherine, and dragged her behind the shelter of a boulder. Only then did I realize I was bleeding.

'My cheek.' I touched it. My hand came away smeared with blood. Had I been hit?

Catherine pointed back to the slope where I had stood. The bullet must have struck a rock, carving a white scar in the surface and throwing up a shower of splinters. One of them had cut my cheek.

As the shock of the blood began to recede, I pulled out my pistol and rammed home the ball. My hands still shook, and black powder spilled over the ground as I tried to prime the pan. Beside me, Catherine's pistol was in her hand, her laundry forgotten.

'Pass me that dress.'

Catherine looked mystified, but did as I asked. The damp cloth was heavy as a corpse and I struggled under the burden. Passing my pistol to Catherine, I cast around among the leaves for a stout branch. When I had found one, I prodded its end through the sleeves of the dress and edged my makeshift scarecrow around the edge of the boulder.

The reply was instantaneous. Another shot rang out from the far side of the stream, closer than before; the dress twitched off its stick and flopped to the ground as a bullet ripped through, ploughing into the earth with a flutter of fallen leaves.

I tugged on the hem of the dress and dragged it back behind the boulder. A neat, round hole had been punched two inches below the collar, with a corresponding mark between the shoulders where the ball had come out.

Catherine gave a chill smile. 'I shall have to darn that when we get back to the boat.'

I barely heard her. I was counting the seconds since the shot, wondering whether I had time to risk one of my own. By the time I had made up my mind the opportunity was past.

I looked around. The boulder was large enough to shield us for the moment, but we were at the bottom of the dell with open ground all about. We could not reach the woods behind without exposing ourselves to our opponent. But if we stayed, we would be trapped in a lethal game of hide-and-seek, trying to guess which side of the boulder the enemy would come around. His last shot had come from our right – would he stay there, or double back to our left? And what of Burr and his men? Surely they had heard the shots and would even now be coming to our aid.

Remounting the dress on my stick, I handed it to Catherine. 'Wave this to your right. And give me your gun.'

She held out the decoy while I edged around to the left. Every sinew in my body was drawn tight, clenched with fear. Catherine now had the dress extended well past the rim of the boulder, but still the shot did not come. Had our enemy guessed the deception?

Too late, I realized that if he had seen through the ruse, he would also have guessed which way I was coming. Even as the thought occurred to me I saw a flash of movement from around the corner. A shudder of terror convulsed through me – too much for the delicate trigger of the duelling pistol. It jerked back, and a spray of sparks and smoke erupted in my face as the shot went harmlessly wide. I was dimly aware of another shot, the noise overlapping my own like two stones cast into a pond, and had just the wit to recognize that I had provoked my opponent to fire. Instantly, I saw my opportunity. Dropping the Manton, I switched Miss Lyell's gun to my right hand and stepped smartly out around the boulder.

My enemy stood before me. He was a slight man, little taller than Burr, and dark-skinned, though no savage Indian. He was dressed in a brown suit. His black hair was ruffled where he had lost his hat, and there was something inexplicably familiar in his moustachioed face which I did not dwell on. I raised my gun and fired.

He was only yards away; even I should have been able to put a bullet clean through his heart at that distance. Yet whether by my haste, the shock in my veins or the icy numbness of my hands, I did not kill him, did not even touch him. The ball bored harmlessly into the frozen earth, a danger only to rabbits.

I looked down at my gun in disbelief, then raised my gaze to my enemy. Only then did I notice what I had not seen before. He too had pistols in both hands: one smoking gently at the muzzle; the other trained on me with the hammer still cocked. His features loomed large in my vision; inconsequentially, I suddenly remembered his name. Vidal. The Spaniard who had tried to take my package on the road to Princeton. He must have followed me all the way down the river. Now, I presumed, he meant to kill me.

With nothing left to me but instinct, I dived to my right. Sheer luck timed the move almost perfectly: had I moved a moment earlier, he would have allowed for it and adjusted his aim; a second afterwards and I would never have moved again. Even so, I was too slow. Vidal dissolved behind a cloud of smoke, and I felt a bite on my arm as if it had been snapped in two, though curiously no pain.

Vidal stepped through the smoke and stood over me. One of the spent pistols still dangled from his left hand; the other he had discarded. In its place he held a long hunting knife. He said nothing, but lifted the knife like some terrible priest of the ancients bent on sacrifice. Lying flat on the frozen earth, with pain rushing into my arm even as the blood seeped out, I did not have the strength to move.

Without warning, another shot exploded in the clearing. From the corner of my eye I saw a telltale puff of smoke at the edge of the treeline, but my attention was seized by the blurred hiss of a bullet rending the space which divided me from Vidal.

For a moment we looked at each other – or rather, at the air between us – each wondering which had been the marksman's target. Then Vidal turned and ran. At any other time that would have sufficed me, but now it served only to unleash a new wave of dangerous euphoria. Swept forward by a wave of dizzy courage – madness, I later decided – I lifted myself off the ground and followed. We sprinted up an incline, darting between trees and vaulting over the rocks and gullies which littered the forest floor. He was faster than I – long, sedentary weeks on the flatboats had seen to that – but I managed to keep him in sight. I needed to keep close enough that he did not have time to turn and reload. That thought, and the energy still pouring through my veins, sustained me in pursuit.

A voice called something from behind me and I ignored it. Again it came; through the madness and confusion it almost sounded English instead of American.

'*Get down!*'

An ingrained habit of obedience penetrated my thoughts. I flung

219

myself forward into the frozen leaves. Behind me, I heard the crack of a rifle; the bullet whizzed overhead and thumped into a tree-trunk. Ahead, Vidal checked over his shoulder and changed direction, weaving this way and that between the trees. I crawled after him; then, when no more shots came, I pulled myself to my feet and kept running.

The forest was thicker now, the going slower. Vidal was barely visible, though it was easy enough to follow the erratic course he had torn through the undergrowth. Without warning, the trees gave way to open space. Caught unprepared, I stumbled forward down an earthy embankment and almost fell on my face. I had come out on a sunken track, stretching away on both sides, and I felt a convulsion of fear at being so suddenly exposed. I looked to my right. A chestnut stallion with a white blaze on its nose was standing quietly by the roadside, its reins looped around a stump. Vidal was running towards it, either oblivious or careless to my presence; once more the beating need to prevent him reloading drew me after him. He arrived at the horse and snatched its reins off the stump, lifted his foot into the stirrup and swung himself up. The whole manoeuvre was accomplished with the ease of habit, yet it gave me enough time to cover the scant distance between us. I pointed Catherine's pistol at him but he merely laughed, knowing as well as I did that it was empty.

'*Adios*, Señor Jerrold. Maybe we meet again down the river.'

I flung myself at him and tried to grab his leg, but he kicked himself free. Thankfully, he was not wearing spurs or he might have slit my throat. I recoiled, then made one final lunge to stop him. My hands fastened around his saddlebag and I tugged it back with all my might. I heard a terse '*Hah*' as he urged the horse forward, and I tightened my grip; then there came the crack of snapping leather and a stinging blow to my cheek. With a cry of despair I felt Vidal break free. Suddenly I was pulling against air. I stumbled backwards and fell on my backside.

Dazed, I opened my eyes. Vidal was riding away, his horse's hooves kicking up great clods of mud as it accelerated. I did not even try to reload my pistol, for he had galloped around the first corner before I could have pulled out my powder horn. My only consolation was that he seemed more bent on escape than on prolonging the battle.

All at once, the fervour which had driven me drained away. The chill air clenched tight about me and I began to tremble uncontrollably. There was an ache in my arm, I realized, and when I looked down it was to see my sleeve dyed red with blood. I pulled off my jacket and tore open the gash in my shirt. A deep cut had been gouged in my upper arm, and when I tried to move my elbow it sparked a searing pain which had my screams echoing through the woods.

I crawled across to the edge of the track, slumping back against the earthen embankment. Burr's men had been following me; they would be here soon, I promised myself. I tried to wrap my coat around my shoulders to stem the shivering. Something cold and damp touched the end of my nose; then the back of my hand; then my cheek. Looking up, I saw a flurry of fine snowflakes drifting down between the trees, dappling the grey trunks with a white haze. Those which landed on me quickly melted to water and dribbled off, but those which touched the frozen ground settled instantly. Where were Burr and his men?

Between the snow, the cold and the pain of my wound, I could barely see a thing. I closed my eyes. In a short while I heard footsteps crunching towards me but I could not be troubled to look. Even when I felt firm hands tugging on my arm and binding a cloth around the wound, I barely opened my eyes. In the gathering darkness, through the haze of snow and half-shut eyelids, I could see a stooped figure in a dark coat kneeling beside me. His hair was very white, though perhaps that was just the snow settling on it. Something about him seemed familiar. In my delirium, I could almost imagine I was back aboard the *Adventure*, and that Fothergill the steward was at my side helping me to a glass of claret.

He stepped away from me, allowing himself a brief approving murmur at the results of his work. He might have bound the wound – I could not see – but the pain was as unbearable as ever.

Some way down the track, I heard cracking branches and shouts of consternation as the rest of Burr's men finally found the road. I opened my eyes further. There were men running towards me down the road, but of the man who had tended me I could see nothing. Had my delirious mind conjured him from nothing? No – if I reached my good arm across my body I could feel his bandage still wrapped tight.

Whatever had become of him, the rest of my pursuers had now reached me. I looked up, and saw Burr's eyes blazing down on me in concern.

'Thank God we found you,' he said. 'There is no time to lose.'

22

THEY HALF CARRIED, HALF DRAGGED ME BACK TO THE BOAT AND laid me on the bench in the cabin. At least, I suppose that is what they did – I fainted not long after we had left the road, and presently came to flat on my back, staring up at the ceiling. Burr and Blennerhassett were conferring beside me.

'How bad is the wound?' Burr asked.

I rolled my head to my left and saw Blennerhassett crouching low over my arm. I shuddered, and Blennerhassett leaped back. The weeks since we departed his island had not proved agreeable to him: his eyes had retreated into his skull, so that the great, hooked nose became yet more pronounced, and his pale skin seemed veritably moribund. It did not make for a comforting bedside presence.

'How is your wound?' This time, Burr addressed me directly.

I tried to lift my left arm and instantly abandoned the attempt, giving full voice to the pain which knifed through my shoulder into my chest.

'I fear there is still some pain,' said Blennerhassett, superfluously. 'I am not a surgeon, you know, Colonel Burr. I may patch the hole, but I cannot mend it.'

Burr thrust his hands into his pockets and turned this way and that. 'You must forgive me, Lieutenant: it is my own foolishness that has brought us to this pass.' He shook his head in emphasis of his shame. 'I have been so assiduous recruiting my army, yet I have forgotten our need for a surgeon. Even against the Spanish, we cannot trust that *all* their shots will go astray.' He tapped me playfully on the shoulder, seeming not to notice the fresh hurt which made me grimace. 'Your sacrifice is not in vain. Imagine if this had happened in the deserts of Mexico. We will retain a surgeon before we reach Baton Rouge, you may depend on it.'

I feared we would have more call for an undertaker, though I did not want to be the man to prove the need. I groaned, and reached my right arm across to paw at the wound.

'We'll need a surgeon,' Blennerhassett insisted. 'I've cleaned the wound as well as I can, but I can't say it won't fester if it's left. We must find a doctor to see to it, or risk having to amputate.'

I had not warmed to Blennerhassett, with his distant manner and unusual preoccupations, but now I felt a surge of good-feeling towards him. Burr, by contrast, showed no such humanity.

'Come, Harman, amputation would not be so bad. If Jerrold is to be my Admiral Nelson he can certainly manage single-handed.' He bobbed his head, delighted with his joke and oblivious to its effect. At last, seeing the anger on my face, he relented. 'I will take my boat ahead to Bayou Pierre and call on my old friend Judge Bruin. I had intended to consult him anyway, and he is as likely as any man to rouse a doctor in these parts. You will stay here, Harman, and wait for the rest of the fleet to arrive, then follow us down.'

He spoke briskly, though even then it seemed that he was animated more by a desire to finish the discussion than to assure my health, for he kept shooting covetous glances towards the door of the sleeping cabin. Before he could depart I flapped my good arm to stay him.

'Are you not curious as to who inflicted my wound?'

He shrugged. 'I had assumed you met with a Chactaw. It was as well he did you no worse injury. They have in their tribe the most terrible savages, you know, bone pickers who—'

224

'It was not a Chactaw.'

'Then who—'

'It was a Spaniard.'

I slumped back on the bench, pleased to have pinned his attention at last. Briefly, I explained my encounter with Vidal on the stage from New York, and my subsequent battle with him in the forest. All the while, Burr paced the cabin with increasing agitation.

'You are sure it was him?'

'I stood as close to him as I am to you now.'

'That is troubling.' Burr put his hand to his chin, squeezing the jaw between finger and thumb. 'That the Spanish suspected our designs, we knew. That their agent has followed us so assiduously, and dares attack us on American soil, is cause for the greatest concern. What other traps may they have awaiting us down river? And how much of our scheme do they know?'

Not enough to have identified the English officer caught up in it, I hoped.

'No matter.' It was not in Burr's nature to be cast down for more than a few moments. 'They can hardly have marched an army through the Mississippi Territory, and we are well enough equipped to repulse whichever spies and agents they send against us. No, there is nowhere they can attack us until Baton Rouge, and by then we will have shown our true colours in any case. We have nothing to fear.'

He nodded to himself. 'I leave it to you, Harman, to gather our forces and proceed down the river. For now, you will forgive me if I retire to my bed.'

He hurried down the cabin and pushed through the bedroom door, shutting it tight behind him. The bolt within snapped closed. With a doubtful glance after him, Blennerhassett made to leave.

'Wait,' I mumbled. 'What became of Miss Lyell?'

Blennerhassett's long nose seemed to droop further in discomfort. 'They found her in the woods, where you had left her. She was quite unharmed, so I hear.'

'Where is she now?'

His gaze shied away from me. At once, he seemed to take an unusual interest in the planking of the wall. 'She went to bed. Colonel Burr was afraid she might take a little melancholy for her ordeal.' He offered a weak smile. 'But she'll be well, I'm sure.'

With that, he scuttled out of the cabin. Through the skylight, I heard him relaying Burr's instructions to the crew on deck.

I lay back on the bench, feeling the hull twitch in the current as we cast off and rejoined the river. My arm still throbbed, but the pain went unheeded as thoughts of Catherine and Burr consumed me. Twisting my head around to see the door, I could almost glimpse Burr crouching over her pale, flawless body, running his hands over places I had believed my own. With every creak of timber or howl of the wind, I imagined I heard Catherine's moans as she gave herself to him, or Burr's frenzied, porcine grunting. I wanted to leap to my feet and tear the door from its hinges, run Burr through with a bayonet and implore Catherine to remember that I had saved her life in the forest; or else stagger on deck and drown myself in the river. I had suspected their connection for some time now, but to have it confirmed, and compounded by Blennerhassett's embarrassed pity, was almost more than I could bear. Burr had called me his Nelson. Instead, I had become his William Hamilton.

I must have fallen asleep, though my preoccupations were the same both awake and in dreams. In both, enticing visions mingled with mute rage. Sometimes I saw Catherine, and sometimes Isobel; sometimes it was I who caressed them, at other times I stumbled upon them in lascivious embrace with Burr. Periodically, I would roll over in my makeshift bed and awake with a yelp, but the void within always sucked me back into sleep. Perhaps it was one of these cries which summoned Catherine, for when I opened my eyes she was standing over me, luminous in her white night-dress.

'My poor, gallant hero,' she cooed, stroking a hand over my forehead.

'I saved your life.' There was a sour dryness in my mouth which parched the strength from my words, though she seemed to understand them.

'I cannot tell you my gratitude.' There was an honesty in her words, but it only worsened my melancholy. If she truly felt grateful, how could she betray me to Burr?

'Burr,' I mumbled. 'Burr.'

She touched a cold finger to my lips. 'Hush. He is not your concern.'

I wanted to leap up, to cry out that he was my concern: that he had dragged me down this cursed river, that he had more than once nearly seen me killed and that, to crown it all, he had stolen Catherine's affections from me. But I did not. Instead, I nursed my hurt in silence.

I was woken by a flat, iron-grey light pressing against my eyes. The boat no longer seemed to be moving, and the doors at the far end of the cabin had been thrown open to admit daylight. I shivered, trying to pull the blanket further over my neck, but the motion sparked a stab of pain. At least the attendant yelp attracted some attention. Burr's slave boy hurried to my side and, with many beggings of my pardon and deferential 'Massas', tied a handkerchief into a rudimentary sling for my arm. Then he indicated that I should get out of bed. I was little more than a spectator as he lifted me up, pushed on my boots and hung a greatcoat over my shoulders before leading me outside.

Even with the greatcoat on I felt the bite of the hoary air, its sting in my nose and its grind in my throat. At some point during the night we had passed into a different world: the greys and browns which had surrounded us for weeks had vanished under a crystalline blanket of snow, shimmering and glittering in the pale winter morning. Even through the cold it offered a hopeful purity which could not fail to lift my spirits.

The river too was different. The broad expanse and rapid current of the Mississippi had gone; we were now in a narrow, stagnant piece of dark water, hemmed in by willows and poplars. The boat was moored to a short wooden landing, which led on to a broad path cut through the trees. From somewhere not so far away I could smell woodsmoke.

Footsteps sounded on the deck behind me, and Burr came around the corner of the cabin. He had wrapped himself in a military cloak which evidenced many years' active service, and had a tricorn hat jammed over his ears. As ever, his bumptious energy was unflagging.

'How do you do this morning, Lieutenant?' he greeted me.

I tapped my right hand against the sling. 'Painfully.'

'You'll not feel the hurt of that wound for long in this cold – better than brandy for dulling pain, as General Washington used to say when we were at Valley Forge. And we will have a doctor to see to you soon enough, though you may need more than the cold if he calls for his saw.'

He winked, as though the prospect of amputation were a tremendous joke between us. I did not even pretend amusement.

'Where are we?'

'Bayou Pierre.' Burr pointed away through the trees. 'Judge Bruin has his house over there. He is an ally in this venture. A warm hearth and a stout meal will doubtless mend your spirits – and I fancy we may find he has gathered more men to our cause.'

Taking great care to keep from slipping, I followed Burr over the side of the boat onto the icy landing. It was hard to keep balanced with one arm bound across my chest, especially trudging through snow four inches deep, but Burr's boy took my elbow to steady me while his master hurried on in front. There was something childish in his character which was forever driving forward, always chafing to be over the horizon.

The line of trees along the shore was not deep: after fifty yards or so the path opened on to a snowy meadow, running up a slope to a low ridge where a handsome brick house stood. Railed fences rose out of the snow, dividing the fields and marking out a track which led straight up the hill before us. Even between the railings the snow was untouched by man or beast; it crunched and creaked under the weight of our boots as we ploughed through it.

We had gone about halfway up the slope, and were in the centre of that pristine white meadow, when the door to the house opened. The light on the snowfield dazzled us, reflecting the sun onto our squinted eyes like a mirror. I cupped my free hand around my face and stared, but I could make out nothing save a dark, round figure hurrying down the hill so fast I feared he would lose his footing entirely. He slid to a stop in front of Burr just as the boy and I came level with them.

'Colonel Burr,' he said, breathing hard. 'I thought it must be you.'

Even though he lived in the depths of the wilderness, the frontier life had not appreciably hardened him. A rotund belly pressed out between the folds of his fur-trimmed cloak, and his face seemed to have been steeped in red wine. Two tufts of white hair trimmed the side of his head; otherwise, beneath a fox-fur cap, he was entirely bald.

Burr took his hand and shook it with his customary enthusiasm. 'Judge Bruin. May I present Lieutenant Jerrold? The rest of my company will join us tomorrow, but for the moment we are the vanguard. What news of the territory? You must tell us everything, for I have heard conflicting reports up the river. Has Wilkinson announced the war yet? How many volunteers have you gathered? Do you know the state of the defences at Baton Rouge?'

The questions rattled off his lips like drumbeats, each so hard on the last that the judge could barely open his mouth to reply. Bound up in the flow of his own rhetoric, Burr did not notice the fearful alarm which spread across Bruin's face, nor the agitation with which he wrapped and folded his fingers together. At last he could bear it no more, and blurted out, 'You are too late, Colonel Burr. Have you heard nothing?'

Burr paused, cocking his head like a robin. 'Too late for what? We have been alone on the river this past week, and have met no-one. Has the war started without us?'

229

Bruin pulled a flask from his coat and gulped down its contents. 'By God, Colonel, but you have chosen a poor time to sequester yourself. The war has started, yes indeed, but not the war you wanted. Your designs are known and the country is in uproar. Jefferson himself has issued a proclamation for your arrest on charges of treason. You are finished.'

23

THE SPARKLING SNOW RENDERED BURR'S FACE ALABASTER WHITE.

'What? How do you mean my designs are known? How widely?'

Bruin reached inside his cloak and extracted a folded newspaper. Burr took it and gazed on it, his head jerking about as if he did not know where on the page to look. Peering over his shoulder, I could not make out the full story, but the bold headline told the tale well enough: VILE CONSPIRACY TO DISAGGREGATE THE UNION. MILITIA MUSTERED. LEGISLATURE PROROGUED. GOVERNOR ORDERS ARREST OF BURR CONSPIRATORS.

'They have even printed my correspondence,' Burr murmured. 'How . . . ?'

'Read on,' said Bruin.

' ". . . all of which information the patriot General Wilkinson has supplied to the President of the United States, and to the governors of the various States and Territories threatened by the Arch Conspirator".' Burr looked up. 'Wilkinson? But he is our ally, second only to me in this scheme. I had expected to meet him within days to plan the course of our war. Why should he have done this?'

'He has betrayed you,' said Bruin. 'A Brutus to your Caesar.'

I was still staring at the paper. VILE CONSPIRACY TO DISAGGREGATE THE UNION. What could that mean? Burr had intended to wrest

Mexico from the Spanish, not conquer territory already held by America. Yet he had not denied the headline, nor even remarked upon it.

I suppose I ought to have felt elation. This must surely be the end of Burr's conspiracy: the primary object of my unlikely mission had been achieved. Yet my orders had been to see that it died silently, unnoticed. I doubted Nevell would welcome it being emblazoned on the front pages of the newspapers. Who could tell what other aspects of the conspiracy might yet become public?

'Anyway, there is no gain in freezing to death for it,' said Bruin, commendably practical. 'Your thoughts will come clearer indoors, with a good fire and a warm glass.'

Burr seemed not to have heard him. 'That duplicitous, perfidious traitor. Wilkinson could have been Generalissimo of half a continent. Now he will be nothing – I will break him as surely as he has ruined me, until his name echoes in history with Benedict Arnold, Cataline and Judas.' He seemed to have forgotten, temporarily, that it was in fact he who had conspired to provoke a war. 'I have friends, power-ful friends, who will aid me. Go back to the boat' – this to the slave boy – 'and order them to attend me in the house. We may be reversed, but Aaron Burr is not finished yet.'

Leaning on Bruin's arm for balance, I struggled up to the house at the top of the ridge. Despite its size it was a sober, lean building, square-cut and simple; within, dark floorboards and heavy wains-coting lent it a mournful countenance. Even with all the curtains pulled open and the dazzling snow outside, little light seemed to disturb the gloom. With the smell of liquor thick in the air, it was not unlike being on the inside of a rum barrel.

In all the shock of Burr's betrayal, my own predicament had gone unnoticed. 'I beg your pardon,' I said to Bruin as we stood in his hall, 'but I have need of a doctor. I was shot in the arm yesterday.'

Bruin's face creased with concern. 'You did not encounter the militia, I hope?'

'A Spanish spy.'

'That is a great relief. I shall send for Doctor Cummins immediately.'

Why the provenance of my injury should matter so much I did not know, but I was satisfied enough when Bruin despatched a slave to fetch the doctor. With a mumbled excuse, he and Burr disappeared into an anteroom for a private consultation, leaving me in a sparsely furnished drawing room. I seated myself in a comfortable chair, glad of the rest, for the pain in my arm still throbbed fiercely.

A copy of the newspaper lay on the occasional table beside me. I picked it up one-handed and dangled it before my face, trying to catch as much wan light as strained through the windows. There were three pieces on the subject: a proclamation from the governor of the Mississippi Territory ordering Burr's arrest; an article describing in breathless detail the extent of Burr's supposed transgressions, including his intention to disunite the American states; and, most curiously, a copy of a letter purporting to be from Burr to General Wilkinson in New Orleans, which (the accompanying text revealed) 'the patriotic General, famous to all America for his recent negotiations on the Sabine frontier, rendering that happy state of peace and amity between the American and Spanish nations, felt obliged to forthwith supply to the President of the United States'. Why the patriotic general should have been party to such correspondence, why Burr should have written to him on terms of such confidence and intimacy, the paper did not question.

I skimmed the letter. Much of it was unremarkable, though typical of Burr: pompous invocations of honour, requests for men and supplies, details of expenses. The disunion of the United States was mentioned not at all, and the invasion of Spain only in the briefest, most oblique terms which would have been wholly incomprehensible without the newspaper's assurance that it referred to damnable schemes of treason and conquest. But among all the rhetorical vagaries, one brief sentence leaped out with unmistakable clarity, transfixing me utterly: *'Naval protection of England is secured.'* In the smudged, thick-set type of a provincial American newspaper, all the world could see that England had conspired with Burr. And here was I sitting in a magistrate's drawing room, the human proof of that same connection.

A harsh squeak like the call of a crow sounded from the door, and I dropped the paper. To my relief it was only Burr, his eyes as bright and vigorous as ever.

'So you have read it.' He pointed to the paper on the floor. 'It is all nonsense, of course. They have not a shred of evidence.'

'But the letter . . .'

'It says nothing. Show me where I declare my intention to divide the states, or to wage an illegal war with Spain. I tell you truthfully, Jerrold, that I did not even write half those words. Much of this supposed letter of mine is an invention – Wilkinson's, I presume.'

'Why should he have done that?'

'Because evidently, despite his reputation, he is a knave and a coward.' Or possibly, I thought, a realist. 'He has worried at our delay, or suffered some unlikely moral fit, and panicked. He will pay for it eventually, even if I must suffer a charge of murder in a second state.'

This much I will say for Burr: for all his delusions, there was never any doubting his sincerity. Whether that spoke better or worse of him, I cannot say, though at that moment I did not incline to indulgence. All along, my position had been perilous; now that Burr's English co-conspirators were a matter of public knowledge, there would be a great many men all too eager for a frank interview with the naval officer who accompanied him.

'I know what you must think,' said Burr, though I doubted it very much. 'You and your confederates were persuaded to my cause by promises of the riches of Mexico and the wealth of the Mississippi, and now I cannot even guarantee my own liberty. Our predicament seems bleak. But I have been in worse scrapes. If they take me to court, then I am as confident as a man can be that I will walk out of it vindicated and free. Why, this is barely the beginning . . .'

He continued with his bluster, but I did not hear it. I was too much preoccupied by what he had said, words which had slipped out almost unthought. *The wealth of the Mississippi.* So it was true, what the *Mississippi Messenger* had reported: Burr *had* planned to combine his Mexican empire with the western states. To have invaded neutral Mexico and claimed it for his own would have been provocative, illegal even. But to then annex half the existing United States to his empire would have been plain, outright treason. No wonder Jefferson and his government were in such uproar now that they knew the full audacity of Burr's scheme. Doubtless they would visit a terrible vengeance on him – and even more on the Englishmen who had conspired to steal back half their former colony. I squeezed myself deeper into the chair, feeling my hopes diminish with every turn.

'At any rate,' concluded Burr, 'the Mississippi Territory never played large in my plans. Tyler and the rest of the men should be here tomorrow, and once they are assembled we can chart our course. It may be we can escape and carry out our plans before the governor is any the wiser that I have passed through his territory.'

'*Carry out our plans?*' I echoed. 'But General Wilkinson has betrayed you. Without his men you will not stand a chance against the Spanish.'

Burr waved away the objection. 'Cortés managed without Wilkinson. And we have what he did not – your frigates, poised to strike in our cause. While they sit in the Gulf of Mexico our wagers are still on the table. We need not throw in our hand just yet.'

He had restored his spirits, if not my own, and he bounded out of the room like a dog in search of a bone. I was left to wonder how, with my promise of those damnable frigates, I had become the guarantor of my own destruction.

My solitary piece of cheer that day came from the doctor, who called in the afternoon and spent half an hour unpicking the bandage from my wound, swabbing it out and applying a fresh dressing. 'If it stays clean, there's no lasting harm,' he assured me. 'The bullet took a bite out of your flesh, but the bone and muscle are untouched. Rest easy, and you'll be set fair in a couple of weeks. Though you'll maybe not see so much rest while Colonel Burr's about. I guess he's got the whole territory jumping like catfish.'

We spent a dark and draughty night in Bruin's house, and midway through the following morning the rest of the flotilla pushed up into the creek, or bayou as the Americans called it. Burr summoned the men to parade on the field at the bottom of the hill, and soon the virgin snow was churned grey and brown under their boots. Burr sat on a horse he had borrowed from Bruin, stern as the Duke of York, while his meagre army marched back and forth in ragged lines. After a few minutes he called them to a halt and surveyed them from his saddle. There cannot have been more than sixty of them, but Burr had divided them into six companies, each with a lieutenant, a sergeant and two corporals he had appointed. The ranks owed little to ability or experience. 'These officers will form the backbone of our army,' he had once confided to me. It had always seemed an unlikely hope; now, as they stood in single files with their officers at their heads, it seemed the most outlandish notion. Behind them, a crowd of women and children – perhaps half as many as the men – watched like spectators at a hanging.

Burr looked down on them from his horse. 'Well, gentlemen, I guess you know how it stands.'

It was remarkable, I thought, how Burr's manner and even his voice could adjust themselves to circumstance. In polite company he could be genteel as a squire, with conversation that would have passed in any drawing room in England. In speaking with the men, his vowels grew harsher and his consonants dropped away, so that he adopted the rougher manner of an unschooled frontiersman.

'You've followed me more than a thousand miles down the river, and I'm grateful for it. But now we've hit a snag, so to speak. The governor's put out a proclamation that I'm to be arrested, on grounds of conspiracy against the United States.' He raised a hand to quell the muttering. 'It's nonsense, of course – cheap slanders that ain't worth a continental. We're all patriots here. Lord knows I've told you plain enough and often enough: if there's a war, we'll fight it; if there's not, we'll settle my lands in Louisiana and turn our hands to farming. But this governor, he's got it in his head that we mean mischief, and if the militia find us here they'll oppose us. Now none of us wants to turn his guns on the state militia . . .'

Three-score cold faces nodded earnestly, while my spirits strained with the hope that this would prove the end of the matter.

'. . . but I'm not for surrendering myself to their hospitality just because the governor's taken a dislike to me. Seems to me that's behaviour that belongs more in King George's England than in our proud republic.'

That did not draw nearly so much agreement. He hurried on.

'I guess all I can do is put it to you clean. Will you stand together with me, or does it end here?'

Sixty shivering, wretched faces, and their women and children behind, spoke plainly that they would far rather be at home in New York or Pennsylvania or Ohio than waiting to be drummed into a Mississippi gaol as traitors. But Burr was a hard man to resist outright, and it was hard to forget that for all his improbabilities he had once held the penultimate power in the land. One by one, their features strained with cold and misgivings, the men mumbled that they would stand by Burr until the governor had seen sense.

Burr beamed, visibly swelled to have kept their confidence. Like so many politicians his own spirits were an empty balance, rising and falling with the weight of popular approval.

Hardly had the decision been taken than a grey mare came cantering around the side of the hill. With the snow still thick on the ground, neither horse nor rider could have seen their footing, and I feared lest they both find their limbs snapped apart by some buried rabbit hole or hidden rock. Happily, no disaster befell them. The rider – one of Burr's men, whom he had posted as a picket at the judge's gate – reined in his horse and looked across at Burr.

'The militia's here.' There was an awestruck terror in his voice. 'A company at least, coming up the road. I seen their bayonets.'

A collective groan shuddered through Burr's army, who doubtless now regretted their haste in committing to his cause. For a moment I feared we all might die in it, that Burr would insist on making a stand on this meadow until the snow froze red with our blood. But however often he let his optimism seduce him, his instinct for his own preservation remained master.

'Back to the boats,' he called, waving his sword like a charging dragoon. 'We'll cross the river to the Louisiana shore. We'll be safe from the governor there, for the time being.'

My hopes had been in vain. Burr would not relinquish his conspiracy quietly – not in the face of public exposure, not even in the teeth of an oncoming army. What chance did I have, had I ever had, of dissuading him? As we tramped back to the boats, my feet numb in the snow, I wondered how many other disasters he would inflict on us before the inevitable defeat.

24

I CLAIM LITTLE KNOWLEDGE OF AMERICAN LAW, BUT FROM WHAT little I had seen it seemed a curious business – and more curious still, as I later discovered. They put great store in their states, which I had always supposed to be no more than shires or counties, and paid little heed to the nation at large. So it was that Burr could be wanted for duelling in New Jersey (where he had shot his opponent), and for murder in New York (where the man had actually died), but could roam free across the other fifteen states and assorted territories. It was as if a man condemned in Kent could claim his innocence merely by strolling into Surrey. Hence the reason that on that wintry morning, with the shouts of the militia sounding ever louder from over the hill, we hurried back to our boats and repaired to the far side of the river. On the east bank was the Mississippi Territory, whose governor had taken so much against Burr; on the west was the Louisiana Territory (neither place having yet attained that height of civilization or population expected of a state). There, so we supposed, not only the broad river but the entire edifice of American law protected us. 'The governor has not the least sanction over us here,' boasted Burr – though I noticed that he posted pickets around the perimeter of our camp nonetheless.

As if to prove Burr's wisdom, an hour after we had crossed the river a quartet of dragoons came to the water's edge opposite. They waited there some time, staring at us and conferring together before riding away. That evening, a small watch-fire glowed on the far shore while Burr, Tyler, Blennerhassett and I held a council in his cabin. As ever, Burr's spirits were high.

'They cannot touch me, of course. I fancy if they even tried, half the country would rise up in arms and we would endure the horrors of a civil war.'

He rather over-estimated the strength of his fellow citizens' good-feeling, I thought.

'I say we fight our way out,' declared Tyler, who had evidently spent too many hours imbibing Burr's madness. 'If we stormed Baton Rouge and took it, all Mississippi would rally to our cause.'

Blennerhassett did not like that plan at all, and said so. It occurred to me that ours must be a desperate plight indeed if a half-mad, half-blind Irishman was the only man among us who could see sense. This time, though, Burr concurred.

'That would be an act of war contrary to the Neutrality Act.'

'What does that signify?' retorted Tyler. 'Once a fire's blazing no-one looks for the match.'

'It signifies everything. Shoot a man one day and you are a murderer; shoot him the next and you may be a patriot. Every pair of eyes west of the mountains is trained on us, and we cannot afford a single mis-step. They can march a hundred regiments of militia to meet us, but as long as we're on the right side of the law we're untouchable. There isn't a court in the land that would convict me for what we've done so far.'

Blennerhassett stirred. 'They might if they found five hundred stands of arms on our boats.'

'But they will not. We will hide them away until the danger is past.'

'And what about this business of splitting the Union?' Blennerhassett persisted. 'That's treason. If they convict us—'

'That is enough,' hissed Burr, in an aggrieved whisper. 'It does not do to speak of such things. It will only give succour to rumour-mongers and villains, and we do not know what ears may be pressed against our keyhole. As you all know,' he said loudly, 'my plan has always been to confront Spain only if the country was at war. Even Mr Jefferson cannot have objected to that.

'Though I concede,' he added in a quieter tone, 'that if he did discover my full ambition, and the allies I had enlisted, perhaps he might have taken it amiss.'

Or perhaps, I thought, he had guessed it all along. He cannot have harboured much love for Burr, who had almost snatched the presidency from him and then tainted it with his duelling. Perhaps he had merely bided his time, waiting for Burr to show his hand and condemn himself outright.

If such was the case, an English lieutenant caught with Burr would be worth several feet of the hangman's rope. Clearly, the sooner I was away from this lunacy the better. From what I had gleaned, we were now not more than a few days from New Orleans, whence I could surely find a packet to start me home. I touched my hand to the lapel of my coat where I had hidden my uncle's letter, cheering myself with the thought of the benefits to come when I confronted him.

I cleared my throat. 'Perhaps it would be best if I made contact with my ships, informed them of these developments. That way, they could be on hand if we needed reinforcements.'

I had long since dismissed any notion that these ships might actually exist, that they might be any more substantial than the rest of Burr's conjectured army, but I knew he placed great store in them. This time, unfortunately, the argument did not sway him.

'I would prefer it if you did not. It would not do, at the present time, to call attention to our English connections, valuable as they undoubtedly are.' He fixed me with a beaming smile. 'If you were to be captured by the militia, it would be quite disastrous for our cause.'

For all Burr's confident humour, it was evident to all that his dreams were fast receding. We clung on at our encampment on the

Louisiana shore for almost a week, while a succession of officers rowed across to present their exhortations, blandishments and threats. One day we had a Colonel Wooldridge, who was treated to tea in the day cabin while Catherine and I hid in the sleeping cabin and listened through a crack in the door. With a great show of reluctance and delicacy, he enquired after Burr's intentions, and was delighted to hear Burr's solemn undertaking that he had never intended more than the settlement of some lands he happened to own in Louisiana. When the visiting colonel alluded to the arsenal Burr was commonly supposed to have brought, Tyler assured him that they had nothing more than rifles for hunting and shooting Indians. This was true enough: I had seen to it myself using a smuggler's trick learned in Dover, dropping the guns over the side where a well-swung grapple might easily draw them up again.

Colonel Wooldridge departed well satisfied, and for a time Burr seemed to think that that might prove the end of the business. Regrettably, the Mississippi governor did not share this apprehension, and the following day sent a second colonel who intimated that if Burr did not surrender himself peaceably, he might well forfeit the protection of the law.

'That is nonsense,' said Burr, who revered the law on a plane with the divine. 'This is the United States. No man may be deprived of the protection of the law.'

Nonetheless, he cast anxious glances at the three-score dragoons who had chosen to exercise on the far bank. And when the governor sent a letter the next day remarking that he had assembled a great quantity of militia, 'to guard this Territory against any designs inimical to this Government', Burr sank still deeper into thought.

On the fourth day, a major came, together with a sharp-looking attorney named Poindexter. Whether this signified a diminution of the governor's regard, or whether he had exhausted his supply of colonels, Burr passed several hours in conversation with them. When they had left, with many solemn handshakes and mutual declarations of honour, Burr summoned Tyler, Blennerhassett and me.

242

'I have agreed that tomorrow I will cross the river and meet with Governor Mead. He has promised me safe conduct and an honest parley – I will see what he has to say.'

'A dozen to one he will say, "You are my prisoner," ' said Tyler angrily. 'Can't you see what he's doing? He'll cut off the army's head, and as soon as you're gone he'll send his men to round up the rest of us. He's already landed a company of militia on our shore – how's that for your safe conduct?'

'Has he?' I craned my neck around and peered out of the cabin window, though of course it was dark outside. 'I thought you said they could not touch us here.'

'Well, if that's so then Governor Mead forgot it.' Tyler pulled a pistol from his belt and thumped its butt on the table. 'I say we hoist up the muskets we stashed, gather the men and march down tonight. Mead's men have no tents – I spied out their camp myself – so come the dawn they'll be frozen, stiff and weary. We'll sweep them into the Mississippi like so much sawdust.'

Burr shook his head. 'And then what? We will not rally the local population to our side by massacring their sons and brothers. All Mississippi and Louisiana would turn against us. Wilkinson would come north with his army, and we would either die in battle or be hanged from the highest tree in the territory.'

Having just begun to wonder how I might escape Tyler's lunatic expedition, I was glad to hear Burr forbid it with such force. Yet even that was little consolation. If Burr had at last been driven to acknowledge the reality of our predicament, it must truly be desperate.

Burr left the following afternoon, a stiff, solitary figure in the stern of a little bateau dwarfed by the magnitude of the river. Soon he was lost to view. Grey clouds hung low in the sky, threatening deeper snow to come, and a melancholy stillness seized our camp. For a time we tried to continue with the normal business of the expedition – chopping firewood, cleaning rifles, caulking leaks in the boats – but after a couple of hours, by spontaneous accord, we drifted away from our tasks and sat silent by the fires, like a parliament of widows gaunt-eyed with grief. I even saw a tear on Catherine's cheek – the first I had seen in all our perils and adventures.

As dusk was falling, a small light was seen working up the river, and presently we saw the skiff making its way towards us. We all of us leaped up and ran down to the water's edge, straining to see whether our captain had returned. I confess that even I felt a strange tug of hope, though I owed Burr nothing but hardship and danger.

It was not Burr. It was the colonel of dragoons who had visited us three days earlier.

'Burr is under arrest,' he called, as the boatmen worked their oars to keep the skiff stationary in mid stream, a few yards off the bank. 'He has submitted to the governor and will be taken to Washington and placed under recognizance. A fortnight from now, he will stand trial for treason.'

25

A FORTNIGHT – HOW MANY OF THOSE HAD I SPENT ON THIS wretched adventure, wishing the hours gone in vain hope of some future consolation? True, I had spent many fortnights at sea in my time, but then the rhythms of the ship and the work of maintaining it had absorbed me. Now, whether on packet-ships, mail coaches, horses or flatboats, it seemed all I did was idle away my time without any benefit of leisure or repose. And, of course, with the threat of capture or murder always hanging over me. With the ice and snow thick on the ground, it was little wonder some of it seemed to have entered my soul.

Which is not to say it was an uneventful fortnight. On the contrary, few days passed without activity. It emerged that in surrendering himself Burr had also surrendered his army, so we were all under a sort of arrest, though permitted for the most part to remain in our camp. As the camp was certainly as miserable as any prison, that was scant concession. A succession of militia officers came to inspect us, searching for muskets (which they did not find) and occasionally moving us to some more convenient location down the river. Even though they could see our feeble strength, and readily agreed we posed an unlikely threat, they could not shake off the terror which had convulsed the country. They wandered through our camp wide-eyed and anxious, peering under every cask and blanket as though it might conceal a troop of charging hussars or a company of artillery. It was as if Buonaparte had landed on Dover beach with only a ragged platoon of *voltigeurs* for his army – no-one could quite believe it.

Nor could their fears have been eased by the rumours which still swept down the river. Burr might be captive, but the general opinion held that this would only enrage his partisans further and drive them to violent rebellion. Nobody could believe that the men with Burr were anything more than a vanguard, or perhaps a suitably cunning ploy to deflect attention from his main force. How could it be otherwise, they asked? The sheer weight of rumour alone confirmed it. So the tales multiplied: if everything we heard was to be believed, the upper reaches of the Mississippi were as busy as the Thames at Westminster. First it was reported that two thousand men were descending in a fleet of flatboats, armed to the teeth and ready to die for Burr's cause; then came the counter-rumour that ten gunboats were bound for our camp by the personal command of the Secretary of the Navy, to seize Burr and drag him in chains back to Jefferson. Needless to say, all these rumoured reinforcements proved as chimerical as the rest of Burr's army.

One week after he had left us, Burr returned to the camp for an afternoon. In the intervening days I had consoled myself that however forlorn my predicament, his must be worse, but even this transpired to be false. He bounded out of his boat with great good humour, shaking our hands and joking with the men as though we were at a country fair. He had obtained a smart new suit and a snug cloak, and showed no distress at all at having been taken from us.

'We have nothing to fear,' he declared offhand. 'Wilkinson and Jefferson have emptied their broadside half-cock – they have nothing against me save malice. I will make fools of them in court, and we will be on with our business within the week. Have our reinforcements arrived? I have had word that there are two thousand men a few days up river.'

Tyler answered that we had not yet heard from them.

'They had best hurry, or they will miss the glory.'

'But what of yourself?' Blennerhassett asked. 'Are they treating you well?'

Burr shrugged. 'It is not altogether drab. I have many friends in these parts, so I do not want for company. My friend Colonel Osmun has been kind enough to host me at his manor. Is Miss Lyell present? The citizens of Natchez are to hold a ball in my honour tomorrow night and I fancy I will need an escort.'

Natchez was a town of some prosperity thirty miles down the river, not far from the territorial capital of Washington where Burr was to be tried (not, as I had originally supposed, the eponymous national capital). It seemed odd that its citizens should throw a ball for a man accused of treason, though I suppose it was not so very different to the adulation shown the highwaymen of old as they marched to the gallows. There are few spectacles so seductive as a caged and unrepentant villain. Far more aggrieving was the prospect of Catherine and Burr dancing their gay nights away – with who knew what other intimate exertions? – while I froze and fretted in the wilderness.

Naturally, that was not her principal concern. 'What shall I wear?' she asked, when the invitation was put to her. 'All the clothes I brought from Pittsburgh are quite worn out, and none of them is suited to a ball in any event.'

'Do not fret yourself over that,' said the ever-gallant Burr. 'The dressmakers in Natchez are the finest in the territory. They will run you something up in no time, and every buck at the ball will vie to have his name on your card.'

Her fears thus allayed, Catherine consented to accompany Burr.

'As for the rest of you,' he said, 'I will join you as soon as I have cleared my name of these slanders. For now, stay here and stand fast.'

I believe Burr had intended his visit to cheer our morale, but in this, as in so much else, he was to be disappointed. Indeed, it seemed to have the contrary effect. Men who had previously sworn they would stick by their colonel come death or damnation now muttered that it was all very well him living like a lord with his rich friends, but they were left cold, hungry and forgotten. Some remembered that they had been promised twelve and a half dollars a month yet had seen not a cent of it; others wondered openly whether he had been entirely honest with them as to his intentions. Of course, Burr himself was not present to answer the criticism, so they turned with increasing frequency to the casks of whiskey we carried. Blennerhassett tried to soothe them as best he could, but his scholarly manner was not the thing to calm a gang of drunken, failed revolutionaries. In the end he retreated to his boat, while the men discussed how they might sell our provisions to buy more whiskey.

The trial began a week later in the town of Washington. Sensible of the ammunition my presence would afford his enemies, Burr had ordered me to lie low and keep quiet, but in this I defied him. Though reluctant to admit it, I had fallen sufficiently under his spell that I wanted to discover what would become of him. Mostly, I hoped he would be found guilty, which would bring an end to my unfortunate association with him, but there was a perverse part of me which, against all reason, still hoped he might escape.

The night before the trial, I took a room at King's Tavern in the town of Natchez, some six miles down the road from Washington. Both town and inn were busy with spectators for the trial, but I managed to find a seat in a dim corner and order some food. I ate alone: Burr was at his friend's manor, with Catherine most likely accompanying him, and I thought it best to avoid being seen in public with his known accomplices. I could not entirely escape company, though, for the boy who brought my food had an enquiring spirit.

'I guess you're from England,' he said, apparently having deduced this from the few words I used to request the food.

I produced the lie I had prepared for such enquiries. 'A long time ago. I came over on a ship to New York and gradually worked my way down the rivers.'

'You been to London?'

'On occasion.' I picked up my knife and fork and began sawing at the meat, keen not to discuss my English provenance.

Ignoring the signal, the boy leaned back against the wood column and started expounding on all the facts he had heard about London. 'Some day, I'll go down to N'Awlins and make me a sailor, get on one of them ships and see the world. I'll—'

To my great relief, the gentlemen next to me had finished their dinner and made to withdraw, forcing the boy out of their path and away to the demands of his other patrons. The empty seats beside me were quickly filled, but I ignored the new arrivals and kept my attention resolute on my meal.

'Loo-tenant Jerrold, is it?'

I glanced up, a piece of beef suspended halfway between my plate and my mouth. Three men had seated themselves beside me, hemming me into my corner – three of the most dangerous, villainous-seeming men I had ever seen. All were dressed in the manner of trappers or Indian traders, with fringed, coarsely dyed shirts and low hats which hid their eyes. All had pushed back their chairs just enough that I could see a fearsome array of bone-handled knives and long pistols jammed in their belts. All were looking at me with venomous intent.

'It is Loo-tenant Jerrold, ain't it? Or Leff-tenant, perhaps I should say.'

'Who are you?'

'Moses Hook,' answered the nearest of the three. He smiled, exposing a maw of black and crooked teeth. 'I reckon I've a few questions you could answer for me.'

'I would rather eat my dinner,' I told him.

He reached down and tugged out a pistol. It made a menacing thud as he laid it on the table, the muzzle aiming at my ribs. 'I'd rather you told me what I want to know.'

My eyes flickered past him to the crowded room behind. None of the other patrons seemed to have noticed my predicament, or perhaps the sight of guns on the tables was not uncommon here. Hook's two companions leaned in closer. For all their wicked appearance, none of them seemed quite comfortable with it: there was something stiff in their bearing and professional in their manner which reminded me more of soldiers than banditti.

Hook shrugged. 'Well, if you won't answer here perhaps you'll come down to N'Awlins with me. There's a gentleman there mighty keen to speak with you.'

I shied away, pressing myself against the brick wall at my back. 'I will do no such thing. Is this the liberty for which America is famed? I—'

I broke off as Hook's bony hand reached out and closed around my wrist. 'You'll come down to N'Awlins with us, you and Colonel Burr both. General Wilkinson's got a whole lot to ask of you.'

He stood, dragging me to my feet. Without his steely grasp on my arm I would probably have fainted under the table; as it was, I could do nothing but follow him through the busy room, his two companions close on my heels. Panic consumed me. What would the Americans do to an Englishman who had conspired to overthrow the Union and take command of the continent – if I even made it so far as the American authorities? I doubted that these desperadoes brazenly kidnapping me from a public house would bother with even summary justice.

We were halfway to the door, pushing between the crowded benches, when I looked down and spied a half-eaten plate of stew on the table beside me. In desperation, I reached out my free hand and swept the plate away from its owner, over the edge of the table and onto the stone floor. The tin dish resounded like a gong, while hot gravy sprayed over the ankles of nearby customers.

There are certain sounds which will halt conversation and draw attention in any setting, even a tavern on the American frontier, and the sound of a plate dropped on the floor is one. The company fell silent, as if all air had suddenly been sucked from their lungs, and every eye settled upon me. The only noise was the scrape of a bench, as the gentleman whose dinner I had spoiled rose to his feet.

'What the damn hell do you think you're doing?'

In any other circumstances, a confrontation with an irate, ox-like

American would have terrified me. Now, the prospect of a fight served only to increase the attention we had drawn.

'You must help me,' I gasped. 'These ruffians are kidnapping me.' My antagonist looked uncertainly at the trio surrounding me.

'That's horse shit,' said Hook. ' I am Captain Moses Hook of the United States army; these are my lieutenants. We are arresting this man on account he's conspired with a certain gentleman – you may've heard of him – who's put this territory to a great deal of trouble.'

'You don't look like officers to me,' said a voice from the back of the room.

'And even if you are, I never heard the federal army had a right to detain a free man against his will.'

'Not without a warrant. You got a warrant?'

'And Colonel Burr's an innocent man, leastways until the court says different.'

I could hardly believe this – it was as if I had stumbled upon a convocation of lawyers. By the black look on Hook's face he could scarce credit it himself. I saw him glance to the door, but a stout ostler had placed himself before it and seemed disinclined to step aside.

Hook paused, testing the hostility in the room. Soldier that he was, he could see when surrender had become inescapable.

'I guess we may've made a mistake,' he said. 'Best be leaving before Mr Jerrold spoils someone else's dinner.'

He jerked his hand off my wrist and pushed through the crowd, his lieutenants hurrying behind. He turned by the door and looked back at me.

'I'll be seeing you around.'

I passed the night with the door barred and a knife at my bedside. At first light, I went downstairs and found a group of men setting out for the spectacle in Washington, who readily agreed to let me accompany them. All along the snowbound road I kept fearful watch lest Hook and his men be lurking in the trees, but I arrived at my destination unmolested. Even at that hour the courtroom was almost full, but I managed to squeeze in on a wooden stool at the back.

A black-cloaked beadle announced that the Supreme Court of the Mississippi Territory was in session, and the officials processed in. I stared in astonishment. There were two judges and two lawyers, and three of the four were known to me. Putting the case for the prosecution was Mr Poindexter, the sharp young attorney who had come to our camp to arrange Burr's surrender. Opposing him, defending Burr, was none other than Major Shields, the officer who had accompanied Poindexter on his errand and who had been quite determined to prise Burr out of his Louisiana redoubt. It seemed Burr was unlikely to obtain a full-blooded defence from him, unless his views had markedly altered in the past fortnight; but perhaps that did not matter when one considered the men who would sit in judgement on him. One was a man named Rodney, a stoop-backed, owlish man with a high forehead and cheeks like a sow's ears. The other, to my utter amazement, was Judge Bruin, at whose house we had first had word of our betrayal. I had not spent long in his company, and most of that in a delirium of pain, but surely Burr had counted him a loyal supporter and partner? Perhaps Burr had good reason to confide in the protection of the law. He was there now, sitting at the front with his lawyers, and though I could see only the back of his head he seemed in a bullish humour.

Judge Rodney announced that the court recognized the Attorney General for the Mississippi Territory, Mr Poindexter.

Poindexter rose to his feet. 'May it please the court, Your Honour, I move that the proposed bill of indictment against Colonel Burr be dismissed.'

There was a moment's silence, then uproar throughout the chamber. Rodney had to bang his gavel several times before order was restored. He fixed Poindexter with a piercing, angry stare.

'Am I correct in apprehending that the counsel for the *prosecution* wishes to dismiss the case?'

Mr Poindexter agreed that he did.

'On what grounds?'

'On two grounds, Your Honour. First, that the territorial Supreme Court, being an appellate court only, enjoys no jurisdiction over a case *de novo*. Second, that none of the crimes imputed to the defendant have been committed within the territory of Mississippi.'

Another wave of consternation surged through the audience, some voices decrying Poindexter's arguments and others defending them. Once again, Rodney had need of his gavel.

'This is extraordinary,' he declared. 'It sounds as if it has been prepared for you by Colonel Burr himself.'

Judge Bruin leaned forward over the table. 'I must say I find much merit in the prosecutor's motion. I am minded to grant it.'

'Well I am not,' snapped Rodney. For a moment, I feared he might use the gavel in his hand to assault his colleague. 'Colonel Burr has been summoned here for trial, and try him we will.'

'I concur, Your Honour,' said Shields smoothly, leaving me utterly befuddled.

Had I misunderstood the whole enterprise? Was American justice such a topsy-turvy affair? Here was the prosecutor pleading to dismiss the charges before they had even been laid, and the defendant's attorney countering equally vigorously that his client *would* be prosecuted come what may. It was an extraordinary impasse, and the judges seemed to have little notion how to manage it. They conferred in whispers together for some minutes before Rodney announced to the court, 'As the bench has divided on the merits of Mr Poindexter's motion, it is considered denied. The trial will commence.'

'If the bench divides over the question of my guilt, will that also be considered denied?' enquired Burr. For a man on trial for his life he exhibited not the least concern. He sat comfortably on his chair, leaning back and examining his cuffs, occasionally waving to some familiar face in the audience.

'If the defendant has anything to impart, he may say so either in the witness stand or through his attorney,' said Judge Rodney. 'He may have been the flashest lawyer in New York city, but he is not recognized in this courtroom.'

He turned to the jury and extracted solemn oaths that they would discharge their duties honourably and with due reverence for the laws of the United States. I counted twenty-three of them: it seemed that an American needed twice as many judges and jurors to try him as an Englishman, though I did not know why that should be.

Next, Rodney set out the jurors' duties. It was a long speech, chiefly notable for its irrelevance. Beginning with Cain, he offered a comprehensive treatise on treachery through the ages, touching on Absalom, Judas Iscariot, Cataline, Macbeth, the Old and Young Pretenders and Benedict Arnold. Burr, he implied, would find himself among kindred spirits in their company – though it took Rodney the greater part of an hour to actually mention him. When he did, it was with the severest of reprimands.

'This once illustrious citizen has been lately accused of a nefarious design to separate the western country of the United States from the Union, and to combine it with a part of the whole of Mexico, and to erect them into a new and independent empire for himself, or for some rich patron under whom he acts.'

I shrank into my seat. Had he accompanied us all the way from Pittsburgh, he could hardly have produced a more accurate summary of Burr's ambitions. Was he equally well aware who Burr's rich patrons had been?

'This accusation,' Rodney continued, 'has agitated the people and alarmed the government in such a manner as to put them to a great deal of trouble and expense. It will be with you, gentlemen' – he indicated the jury – 'to enquire into the truth of this accusation.'

A great sigh rippled through the courtroom, either satisfaction that the malefactor had been brought to the seat of justice, or relief that Rodney's interminable address was finished. It soon turned to dismay, though, when it transpired that the public entertainment had concluded, and that the jury would now retire to read through a bundle of depositions taken from all the principals in the affair. I think the audience had hoped to see Burr on the stand blazing righteous anger and innocence, shooting down Rodney's charges as coolly as he had shot down Mr Hamilton, but in that they were disappointed. The courtroom emptied. Burr and Shields hung back until the end, and I waited for them to pass.

'What did Rodney mean by the rich patron under whom you acted?' I called, tugging Burr towards me. 'Is every facet of your scheme known?'

Burr frowned. 'Not so loud. As for Rodney, pay him no heed. He is merely casting his net as wide as he can, hoping to dredge up some charge which will damn me. He knows nothing. I had thought I could rely on him, for he was a friend of mine, but I fear a higher power has exerted itself on him. His son, Caesar Augustus, is the Attorney General of the United States, and no doubt he has communicated Jefferson's desires plain enough.'

'Then what will you do?'

'I will put my faith in American justice.'

'But if the judge—'

'Judge Rodney holds no sway over my fate. That will be decided by the men of the jury, twenty-three men good and true. All the better and truer for the fact that Bruin has packed them with Federalists, who hate Jefferson almost as much as they hate the Spanish.' He clapped me on the back. 'The court will find in my favour, and we will be free to continue our enterprise. Regarding which, I had meant to ask you something. One of my drafts on Mr Ogden has come back protested, and it is greatly inconvenient that we should be without funds at present. Can you think why Ogden should have done this? You were with Lyell in New York – he deposited his investment without difficulty, did he not?'

I confirmed to Burr that I thought he had.

'Then it is most peculiar. But no matter: it is probably an error on the part of a bank clerk.'

I murmured an agreement, though privately I doubted it. Even if news of our current difficulties had not yet reached Lyell, he had seen the paucity of Burr's army on Blennerhassett Island, the long odds against him. Knowing the old miser as I did, I would not have been at all surprised if he had returned to New York and reclaimed his investment. One by one, Burr's friends were falling away as the

255

noose around him tightened, however many of the jurors he may have befriended.

'I was at King's Tavern in Natchez last night,' I said. 'Three men cornered me there, and would have abducted me had I not escaped. They dressed as ruffians, but in fact they admitted to being officers in the army.'

We had progressed out of the courthouse into the narrow corridor which led to the street. With this last intelligence, Burr turned suddenly and stared up at me. 'Wilkinson's men?'

I nodded. 'They meant to capture both of us and prove you had conspired with England to betray your country.'

Burr slammed a fist against the wainscoting, one of the few times I had ever seen his temper. 'I knew it. Wilkinson will stop at nothing. He knows that I can ruin him – that I *will* ruin him, by God – for his treachery. He means to murder me, I am sure of it, so that his part in this scheme sinks with my coffin. How did these villains appear?'

I described them briefly. 'Their leader named himself Captain Moses Hook; the others, he said, were his lieutenants. They were armed to the teeth.'

Burr peered along the corridor, as if Hook and his men might even now be advancing on him. 'This is most alarming news. I will retire to Colonel Osmun's house and lie low. We will depart this place as soon as the jury deliver their verdict.'

The jury duly delivered it the following afternoon. Burr was not in court, but his attorney was there looking pleased with himself. We rose for Judges Rodney and Bruin, then watched all twenty-three of the jurors shuffle into the room. Their foreman stood. In his hand he held several pages of notes, which seemed extravagant when only one or two words were required of him.

Judge Rodney rapped his gavel, bringing the courtroom to order.

The foreman cleared his throat.

'The grand jury of the Mississippi Territory, on due investigation of the evidence brought before them, are of the opinion . . .'

He looked up to ensure that he held the audience's attention.

'. . . that Aaron Burr has not been guilty of any crime or misdemeanour against the laws of the United States, or of this Territory.'

Whatever else he had to say was lost as the courtroom erupted in cheers, whooping and applause. Shields turned around and began shaking hands with Burr's supporters, while Poindexter sat stoically in his chair and watched the proceedings with indifference. He gave no sign of being surprised by the verdict.

At the judges' bench, Bruin was smiling and exchanging pleasantries with his friends in the crowd, mimicking the happy motion of a raised glass. Beside him, Judge Rodney glared angrily. He banged his gavel with sepulchral monotony, so often that I thought the handle might snap off, but it must have been five minutes before anyone heeded him. At last, the hubbub subsided enough that he could address the court.

'This is a most irregular verdict,' he began.

Almost immediately, he was interrupted by the jury foreman. 'Excuse me, Your Honour, but I've not finished.'

Rodney fixed him with a glare like a bayonet. 'What else do you have to say?'

The foreman consulted his notes. 'We've some more findings to announce.'

Rodney clearly wished to hear nothing more from this lamentably uncooperative jury, but Bruin waved the foreman to continue. Whereupon the entire assembly was treated to a ten-minute harangue on the iniquities of first the governor, then General Wilkinson, and finally President Jefferson himself. In the jury's eyes, it seemed these men were a gang of despots who had usurped their powers and abominated justice to a degree not seen in history since the tyrants of ancient Rome. Governor Mead had declared a private war on an innocent citizen; Wilkinson had destroyed personal liberty; while Jefferson had ravished every principle of their cherished constitution. It was as well the gentlemen concerned were not present, or by the end of the speech they might have found themselves standing trial in the dock.

Through all the speech, Bruin had been nodding sympathetically, while Rodney's face contorted into ever more outlandish scowls and shades of crimson. When the foreman had finished, Rodney needed almost a minute to bring his fury into abeyance.

'Thank you, gentlemen. You are dismissed.'

Shields rose. 'If it please, your Honour, I would like to move that my client be released from his recognizance, and the bail he has paid returned to his bondsmen.'

Rodney cracked down his gavel. 'Denied,' he barked. 'Colonel Burr is still under the supervision of this court and will be required to report here again. Do not think this is the end of the matter.'

'But he has been found innocent,' Shields objected. For the first time, the quiet confidence he wore had slipped. 'You have no authority to hold him.'

Rodney leaned forward over his desk, like a preacher blasting forth fire and damnation. 'Do not presume to tell me my authority, Mr Shields. In this courtroom and this jurisdiction, my word is law. Where is Burr now?'

'Awaiting delivery of the verdict at Colonel Osmun's, I should think,' said Shields.

Rodney turned to the sheriff. 'Fetch him here.'

The sheriff departed, and the two judges withdrew to their chamber. I cannot imagine what they said to each other there. The rest of us sat in the cold courtroom and waited, talking in subdued voices. From those around me, I gathered that holding a man who had been declared innocent was an unheard-of innovation, a travesty of American justice.

After half an hour the sheriff returned. Judge Rodney and Judge Bruin took their places. Burr was nowhere to be seen.

'Well, Sheriff, where is Colonel Burr?' asked Rodney.

A bashful sheriff doffed his hat and held it before him, as though warding off an impending blow. 'He hasn't come, Your Honour.'

'What do you mean he has not come? You were ordered to bring him here by any means necessary. Did you find him?'

The sheriff shifted in discomfort. 'I did, Your Honour, and then I didn't. Burr was there when I got to Colonel Osmun's house, but begged me five minutes to compose himself. I waited five minutes on the porch, knocked on the door, and waited another five minutes. When he still didn't come out, I started pounding on that door fit to break it in, until one of Colonel Osmun's negroes opened it. He played dumb, pretended he'd never heard of Colonel Burr, but I got past him and searched the house, top to bottom. Burr ain't there. He's run.'

Once again the room erupted in pandemonium. It did not subside until Rodney had beaten it back, swinging his gavel like an undertaker hammering nails into a coffin.

'The said Aaron Burr is a fugitive and an outlaw,' he announced with malicious pleasure. 'His bail is forfeit. A reward of two thousand dollars is hereby offered to any man who brings him before this court.'

His pronouncement was almost drowned out by the tumult in the room, though he no longer made any effort to quell it. Through the din, I heard his final words.

'Alive or dead.'

26

THE COURTROOM EMPTIED IN AN INSTANT. MEN POURED OUT OF IT, some claiming that they would defend Burr against any who came to arrest him; others that they would find him and drag him back on the end of a noose. Each boast was as idle as the other, of course, for no-one knew where Burr might be.

A strong arm grasped my collar. Tyler was standing behind me looking grim.

'Back to the camp,' he hissed. 'If Burr has gone, it'll not be long before they come for us.'

I did not doubt he was right, though I wondered whether returning to our camp would be the best way to evade capture. There was no time to argue, though, for Tyler was already drawing me towards a pair of horses tethered to a nearby rail. Even then I might have broken away – I would far rather have taken my chances alone than with Burr's known accomplice – but as I looked around for a break in the crowd I saw three high-crowned hats pushing a purposeful path towards us. They were still some distance away, yet there was something in their rigid formation which spoke of military discipline. I fancied I had seen the hats before at King's Tavern.

Without further complaint, I untied the horse's bridle, swung myself into its saddle, and kicked hard against its flanks. Glancing back, I saw the three men in the hats redouble their efforts to reach us, but the throng of spectators was too thick, and we were cantering away down the road to Natchez before they were free of it. Even so, I did not relax until we had put a full league between ourselves and Washington.

We returned our mounts to the stable in Natchez, and descended by a steep path to the landing. I suppose it was a mark of the town's development that its docks were already as rough and dissolute as any seaport's: gentle folk built their houses on the heights above the river, while a ramshackle village of taverns, whiskey-shops, gaming halls and brothels clustered under the bluffs below. Even in February, with the river trade much reduced by winter, these houses thrived with every sort of licentious activity. Songs of raucous merriment drifted out of their ill-fitting doors, and I felt a longing pang to be in a warm place with laughter and a willing lady squeezed against me.

Sadly, Tyler allowed no time for such indulgence. He hailed a boatman and engaged him to carry us up to the creek where our flotilla was moored. The wharf was busy, for a boatload of ironware from Pittsburgh was being unloaded, and we had to weave our way between the stevedores to reach our skiff. Intent on keeping my head from being staved in by the packing crates, I was not looking down, so the blow to my stomach seemed to come from nowhere. A small, dark figure had collided with me head-on, slamming the wind out of me. By the time I could draw breath to berate him for his negligence, he had slipped past me and vanished without trace.

No, I noticed – not entirely without trace. As I tucked in my shirt and straightened my neck-cloth, I saw that a small piece of paper had been pressed into my hand. I unfolded it.

If you are together, keep together, and I will join you two nights hence. In the meantime put all your arms in perfect order.

There was neither signature nor date. I showed it to Tyler, who read it quickly then immediately thrust it into his pocket, glancing about to see if we had been noticed.

'That's the colonel's writing.'

'He might find better ways to deliver his correspondence,' I muttered, rubbing the bruise on my stomach.

'Never mind that.' Tyler stepped into the waiting skiff and took his place on the stern thwart. 'We'll tell no-one of this message, but keep the men together in the camp and wait for his return.'

'Then what will we do?'

Tyler shrugged. 'Burr will have some scheme or other.'

No doubt he would. And almost as certain, I would want no part in it.

For two days, our camp was turned upside down as every militiaman in the territory combed it for the fugitive. They searched our boats, our tents and even our supplies, as though Burr might have been secreted in a cask of salt beef. They did not find him. On the second day, a frustrated militia captain concluded his visit by nailing a piece of paper to a willow tree which grew beside our boats. In bold, hysterical print it proclaimed that Burr was a fugitive from justice, and that two thousand dollars would await any man who apprehended him. Which might have tempted me, if I'd known where Burr was to be found – and if Tyler had not kept a close eye on me.

The only other person who might have known Burr's whereabouts was Catherine. She returned to our camp the morning after the trial, having apparently bade him goodbye on his flight, but would not speak of it: she retired to the sleeping cabin on Burr's boat and bolted the door. Even under the shadow of mortal danger, her rebuff cut me, and though I damned myself for a fool I spent long hours pondering how I might seduce her affections back.

In truth, there was little else to consider. Attorney that he was, Burr had taken elaborate precautions to keep within the letter of the American law, but once he had fled he was beyond its protection (though naturally he would have protested otherwise). That left me at the foot of a two-thousand-mile river, in the depths of a foreign wilderness, without friends, without freedom, and without any thought of how I might escape. My mission to stop Burr's invasion might have succeeded, though little thanks to my own efforts, yet in the broader spirit of my instructions I had conspicuously failed. I had no doubt that I would soon be arrested and held as evidence of a monstrous British conspiracy to disunite the states, a crime whose only fitting punishment must be war. If Hook and his men had not yet called at our camp, it could only be because they were preoccupied with finding Burr. Once he was caught, I had little doubt they would come for me, yet even that spectre failed to raise me to action. After all, where could I go?

Burr arrived, as he had promised, two nights after the trial. No-one saw him come. He came alone, slipping out of the surrounding forest at twilight, and was in our midst before any of the pickets had seen him. In an instant, every man and woman in the camp had surrounded him and was plying him with questions. Where had he been? What would he do? What would become of them? They were like disciples who had found their messiah returned to them, but Burr waved aside their concerns and scrambled up onto a boulder to address them for the last time. The last rays of sunset gilded his face with a serene countenance.

'I guess you'll all know by now that the court acquitted me, but I guess you'll also know that it doesn't signify a cent in this territory. Governor Mead and President Jefferson have gotten it into their minds to ruin me, and it seems there's no court in the land where the law'll stand up to them.'

'We'll stand up to them!' shouted a man in the crowd. To my relief, no-one echoed the sentiment.

Burr shook his head. 'We'll give them no cause to condemn us. It's me who they want; there's no use you all being martyred in my cause. I'm releasing you from my service.'

A chorus of desultory lamentation sounded among his assembled followers. A few implored him to reconsider, to stand with them and teach the governor a lesson, but their pleas soon died out.

'You've been loyal comrades, and you deserve better than you've had from me.' With that at least I could agree. 'I wish I could give you what you deserve, but my bills have been protested and my credit's not so good right now.'

The sounds of regret in the crowd grew markedly less.

'But I'll give you what I've got.' He gestured towards the little flotilla drawn up impotent on the sandbank. 'Sell the boats, and as much of the stores as you don't need, and divide the profits among yourselves. The muskets too, if you can find where they're hid. I won't be needing those where I'm going.'

'Where's that?' asked one of the men.

'It's best you don't know. Far from here. They'll take me again if I stay around, so I guess I'll flee from oppression.'

He looked around once more, an air of finality in his gaze. When he spoke again, his voice quavered with emotion.

'You've been the finest army a soldier could wish to command. In another time, we might have done deeds to rank with Cortés and Pizarro, maybe even Caesar himself. All I can say is I hope it comes out for you as you deserve. God bless you.'

He jumped down from the boulder, out of the sunlight and into the hazy dusk gathering on the ground. The moment he did so his followers were all around him, besieging him with good wishes and pressing to shake his hand. Many looked grief-stricken – particularly the women, I noticed – and Blennerhassett's cheeks glistened with tears. Was he mourning the ruin of the man who had captivated him, I wondered, or was he contemplating his own destruction? He had invested his reputation and a large part of his fortune in Burr's scheme; now both were lost, and it would not be long before he himself was dragged into a courtroom for his part in the matter. If he'd had any sense, he'd have run there and then. If he was feeble enough still to adhere to the man who had led him to this disaster, that was his affair.

I had had enough. The lethargy and indecision which had gripped me were gone, as if Burr's farewell had loosed me from his spell. Suddenly my way was clear: Burr had abandoned his scheme, and I need only escape unnoticed to bring my mission to an entirely favourable conclusion. I would go to New Orleans and take ship for England, and not trouble Nevell too much with the details of my ineffectual role in events. Between his gratitude and the damning letter I could hold over my uncle, I might even come out of the affair at considerable advantage.

I was in the day cabin of Burr's erstwhile flagship, packing my few belongings into my chest, when I heard a footfall at the door. Burr was standing there, having somehow escaped the fawning throng, and if he felt dismay that I had acted so promptly on his dismissal he did not show it. Indeed, he seemed to approve.

'You are putting your house in order, I see. That is very good. We must not leave any trace when we are gone.'

Something in his words roused my suspicion. 'When *we* are gone?'

'Of course,' said Burr briskly. All trace of his valedictory melancholy had vanished. 'We are not finished yet.'

It was not what I wished to hear. 'But the men – the boats – the arms. You dismissed them.'

'They are superfluous. Where we are going, we will have no need of boats.'

'Where is that?'

Burr waved a proprietorial arm towards the south-east. 'West Florida. Hundreds of Americans have settled there, but they live under the tyranny of the Spanish king.' As so often, he had slipped effortlessly into his orator's garb. 'They are a powder keg, wanting only a spark to blast the Spaniards to Glory.'

Or more likely blow up in our face. 'But what of your army?' I asked again.

'They have served their purpose. In truth, Jerrold, I do not believe they were well fitted to the task. We will recruit a new army among the settlers on the Tombigbee. They are stout souls who will not scruple from a fight. And of course, we will have your ships and sailors to reinforce our position. You will be able to summon them, I presume?'

Still dazed from the onslaught of this new madness, I suddenly saw my opportunity. 'If I am to summon them, it would be best if I went through New Orleans. I could hire a boat, rendezvous with my fleet, and join you at the designated place.' And be halfway across the Atlantic before Burr realized the betrayal – if his plan had not already ended in disaster.

But Burr would not be persuaded. 'You cannot do that. Wilkinson is in New Orleans, and his fist is clenched tight around the city. He has declared martial law, terrorized the populace and arrested several of my allies. He knows that his complicity in my schemes is widely suspected, and he will not rest until every ounce of evidence is destroyed. If you passed through there he would surely hear of it; he would imprison you and turn you over to Jefferson, or worse. I need not tell you what that would mean for our respective countries.'

I no longer cared much what happened to my country, or his, but I cared a great deal what happened to Martin Jerrold. The force of Burr's argument unnerved me. There did not seem to be any advantageous path, though I was certain that following him would be the worse option.

Before I could order my thoughts, Burr continued, 'It will be much better if you are with me. Your presence will assure the Florida settlers that we are in earnest, and you will be able to communicate my exact position to your frigates. Will you be able to find them?'

'They are keeping station at the line of twenty-eight degrees north latitude,' I murmured. 'I can find them there. But—'

'Then it is agreed. Our time is short. It is a hundred and fifty miles as the crow flies to the Tombigbee, and we will needs be quick with our enemies close behind. We will move by night, and travel by Indian paths. I will disappear for a few hours now – I dare not stay too long in this camp, and there are arrangements I must make – but I will return for you at midnight. Meet me by the boulder where I gave my address. Until then, *au revoir.*'

He vanished out of the door. It was the last time I saw him on that doomed venture, though sadly not the last time our paths met, and it remains my abiding memory of him: a jaunty figure, striding away to hopeless dreams of conquest with a smile on his

266

face. I later heard it said of him that he was as far from a fool as could be, yet as easily fooled as any man. Most of all, I think, he fooled himself.

None of which was in my thoughts as I stood in that cabin, watching the light fade outside. Burr would return at midnight; I would have to be away by then or I would surely find myself dragged still deeper into the mire of his conspiracy. I threw the last of my clothes into the chest, then rummaged in the boat's cupboards until I found a case of Burr's pistols. I had not forgotten his warning that Wilkinson awaited me in New Orleans, that I might well anticipate Captain Hook's work by delivering myself to my enemies on their own doorstep.

'What are you doing, Martin?'

I turned. The door to the sleeping cabin had been opened, and Catherine was standing just behind me dressed in coat, cap and boots. Her face, always pale, now seemed more fragile, and there were dark smudges below her eyes which no amount of powder could hide.

'I am going to New Orleans,' I said, uncertain how much I could trust her. 'I, ah, have an errand for Colonel Burr.'

'That is a lie.' She said it without emotion, as though it were perfectly natural. 'He wishes you to accompany him to West Florida – I heard him say so.'

So I was a liar and she a spy. 'What of it?'

'He has asked me to go to Florida too.'

'Then go.' I spoke harshly, from a keen sense of the injustice she had done me.

'I do not want to.' She took a step towards me and laid a tentative hand on my arm. 'Martin, I have been a foolish little creature, I confess it. Colonel Burr was all compliments and kindnesses to me, and I felt so alone in this wilderness that I succumbed to him when I ought not have. I regret it, Martin, truly I do. Ascribe it to my age, or my sex, or my ingenuousness, but forgive me, I beg you.'

I stared at her in astonishment. For weeks I had dreamed of hearing these words, had imagined myself putting a consoling arm

267

around her, before slipping into her skirts to prove I bore no grudge. But now that the apology had actually come I did not know what to make of it.

'Colonel Burr is a devious, deceitful little man who will promise anything to have his way.' She could no longer restrain herself; she flung herself into my arms and rested her head against me, sobbing into my shirt. 'I have wronged you, Martin; pray do not punish me more than I deserve. If you are leaving, take me with you.'

Somewhere in the back of my thoughts I remembered her words on Blennerhassett Island, the ardour she had professed for adventure. There was a certain satisfaction in seeing the scales fall from her eyes. But that was of no moment. I still did not know whether to forgive her, to trust her or even to believe her, but when a beautiful woman has her arms clasped around your waist and is thrusting her bosoms against your ribs, measured judgements are impossible.

'Come with me, then,' I said. 'I am going to New Orleans, and thence by ship to England.'

She stretched up and kissed me on the lips. 'How I long to see it, my love.'

In that at least I did not doubt her sincerity. She threw her few effects into my box, and then together we hauled it out of the boat. I did not want to arrive in New Orleans in Burr's flagship. Instead, I cast around the camp and quickly found half a dozen men only too keen to leave Burr's army before the militia returned. They needed little persuasion that New Orleans would prove the perfect place to forget their associations with Burr, and readily enlisted as crew for my flatboat. Only one showed any qualms.

'But it ain't your boat to take,' he objected.

'Of course it is. Colonel Burr owes us for our service and our loyalty; he has already told us to sell the boats in lieu of that debt. Taking it to New Orleans only ensures we'll get a higher price.'

'And we'll all take equal shares?'

'Naturally.'

There was no attempt to keep us from leaving. We hauled the boat off the sandbank into the creek, and soon felt the tug of the Mississippi speeding us forward. On we went – away from Burr, away from Natchez, away from the heart of that wild continent – down the final stages of the river towards the sea.

27

IT WON'T SURPRISE YOU TO LEARN, AS I LATER DID, THAT AARON
Burr never did conquer the Floridas, or march on Mexico and found
his great empire. Thomas Jefferson saw to that. His soldiers caught
Burr down near Mobile Bay, alone, and rode him all the way back to
Virginia to stand trial for his life. Which was a mistake: if Jefferson
wanted to be rid of Burr, he should have put a bullet in his back out
in the pine barrens of the Tombigbee and had done, for there was
never a courtroom built that Burr couldn't sway. I sometimes think
he would have had Vera Cruz and all the treasures of Mexico if he'd
only issued a writ against the Spaniards, instead of prancing around
like George Washington playing at rebellion. As to what became of
his sorry army, Harman Blennerhassett and Comfort Tyler and the
few dozen simpletons who thought they'd make their fortunes in
Mexico, I never did discover. Doubtless theirs was an unhappy fate.

All of which was far in the future and far from my thoughts as we
poled our way down the Mississippi on a sunny February morning.
The snow had melted, and we had emerged from the wilderness at
last. Below Natchez, the riverbanks had been entirely cleared of
timber to produce a belt of open farmland punctuated every mile or
so by grand plantation houses. It was as though the river had taken
us out of America altogether and swept us off to the West Indies, for

the fields now grew tall with shivering walls of sugar cane, which armies of negro slaves besieged with billhooks, hoes and knives. After so long in a wretched, lifeless land, we had been borne into a garden of delights. Even the river eased its hostility, for the current was now so strong that all snags and sawyers were swept before it. Each day, the towns and villages we passed grew more numerous, and the traffic on the river increased until, five days after leaving Burr, we rounded a bend in the river and came in sight of New Orleans.

I may say 'in sight', but in fact there was precious little to see. The front of the city had been embanked with a vast earthwork, a levee to stem the depredations of the river, and that in turn was obscured by the horde of ships, flatboats, wherries and barges moored three-deep in front of it. We had to float past almost the entire mile-long waterfront before we at last found a spot to put ashore.

'Wait here,' I told the men. 'Miss Lyell and I must make enquiries. We will return presently.'

'Where're you going?' demanded one of the crew – the same who had questioned my right to take the boat at Cole's Creek. He pointed to the top of the levee, where a file of soldiers was parading along with fixed bayonets. 'I figure there's a price on our heads, an' I'd not want you stealin' away to claim it.'

'Don't be absurd. If any of us merits a reward it is me. Even if I wanted to betray you – which, I assure you, I do not – I could not, for they would clap me in gaol straight away.' I regretted saying this as soon as it was out, for my companions had spoken volubly of the money they were owed during our five-day voyage, and I did not wish to sow further thoughts of profit among them. 'Allow me one hour, and then we will settle our debts and have done,' I promised the men.

Catherine and I stepped ashore, though we were off it again almost immediately, for the boats were so numerous and so closely moored that it was easier to move between them than around them. Race-boards and gangways had been laid between the vessels, becoming the streets and avenues of a thriving, floating city whose

271

colonnades were rows of masts, its roofs the sheets of canvas drying in the sun, its citizens the sailors of a hundred nations. Ships recently arrived from the West Indies made markets of their wares – tobacco, calicoes, sugar and rum – while on the open decks seamen danced jigs and hornpipes. Every stratum of society was present: white-gloved, dark-eyed ladies with parasols who watched the sailors with discreet admiration; merchants in handsome suits bartering for the latest cargoes; jet-black negroes, some dressed in the full livery of footmen, others in humbler attire. And all about me gabbled the sounds of a dozen different languages – Spanish, French, English, Portuguese, African, and some which appeared to have borrowed equally from all the others. The ever-present murmur of the Mississippi, lapping between the shackled hulls, seemed the only common tongue.

I fear we spent more than an hour in that company, breathing in the exotic smells and gaping at the sights. Eventually, after some investigation, we learned of a brig bound for Philadelphia the next morning, and by and by found ourselves on her deck. Her captain was a gruff man, a New Englander from Nantucket he told us, but proved willing to give us passage on his vessel.

'I guess that'll be forty dollars for each of you,' he said.

Out of habit, I had dropped my hand into my pocket and was searching for my purse before I realized how little money I had. Having travelled first with Lyell and then with Burr, I had neither gathered nor needed funds of my own. I had a few coins, but they only amounted to four dollars.

'Of course, I will be able to obtain a draft on my bank when we reach Philadelphia,' I said.

The captain scowled. 'I'm sure you can, sir. But if your bank doesn't oblige, I can't very well sail back here just to make it square between us. So I'll thank you to settle with me now, or else find another voyage.'

He set his hands on his hips and stared at us impassively. A knot of seamen gathered behind him, ready to unload unwanted cargo.

'I can obtain the money here in New Orleans,' I muttered, thinking of the flatboat. 'When do you sail?'

'Noon tomorrow.'

'We will be here.'

'And you'll need to call at the Customs House first,' the captain added. He pointed back along the levee, towards where our flatboat was moored. 'Get your boxes examined.'

'Surely that will be unnecessary? Perhaps for an extra consideration you would overlook it if we lacked the time . . .' With Burr's nemesis General Wilkinson in command of New Orleans, presenting myself at the Customs House seemed the height of folly.

The captain would have none of it. 'Perhaps you've misunderstood me. I'm no Havana smuggler or Baratarian pirate. I'm an honest man with an honest ship, and I'll carry honest passengers who pay up before we sail. Now, if you've a dislike to my terms you can find another berth, before I get to wondering why I shouldn't report you to the governor. There's strange doings been happening here of late, much talk of rebels and traitors, and I'm sure General Wilkinson'd be curious to hear of a couple of foreigners trying to sneak out of the city. What did you say your names were?'

'Beauchamp.' I stepped back towards the rail. 'Mr and Mrs Beauchamp. We meant no insult, Captain – we are merely in a hurry to be home. We will see you tomorrow morning, and I assure you all our affairs will be in order.'

For a moment I feared we had lost our chance, that the captain would succumb to his obvious misgivings and refuse us altogether. But his business was commerce, and he would not lightly surrender the prospect of eighty dollars. He gave an ill-tempered nod.

'And make sure you bring your passports,' he called as we departed. 'There's a Spanish garrison at Plaquemines who'll want to see them before they let us pass.'

We abandoned the archipelago of ships and hurried back on the road which ran along the crest of the levee. I had already broken my promise to return within the hour, and I did not want to try the

273

crew's patience too far. Citrus trees studded the wayside, and our height afforded a fine vantage over the city. We could see the streets laid out in a regular grid, the handsome brick houses which lined the nearer streets and the cruder wooden buildings beyond. It was easily the largest and most substantial city I had seen since New York, yet it did not sit easily on its situation: by comparison with the water on the opposite side of the dyke, it seemed to lie at some depth below the river level. It would be typical of my luck, I thought, if the levee broke and washed it away during my brief sojourn there.

'This is impossible,' I declared. 'Even if we sell the flatboat we will barely have the money for our passage; we cannot visit the Customs House for fear of discovery; and should the captain overlook those facts and take us aboard, we will promptly have to present ourselves to a Spanish garrison. I do not see how we can escape.'

'Oh! Do not carp and cavil so.' There was more heat than warmth in Catherine's words, and her narrow eyes glistened with tears. 'You were at Trafalgar – surely you can surmise some means of escape?'

'We could hide in the hold until we were past the Spanish garrison. If it were only a matter of escaping their attentions, perhaps the captain would indulge us. And if we abandoned our baggage, we could avoid the Customs House quite honestly.'

'*Abandoned our baggage*? But how long is the voyage to Philadelphia?'

'A fortnight,' I hazarded.

'We cannot pass a fortnight on that ship with nothing but the clothes we wear. Why, even the lowest Jack tar takes his sea-chest with him.'

'The lowest Jack tar probably has a passport, and is not usually chased after by the armies of two nations.' I spoke brusquely, for I was beginning to find her objections tedious. 'What other choice do we have? You sought adventures; now you see that they do not always allow dressing for dinner, or a train of porters to carry your boxes. You have been living on riverboats these past two months – surely you are used to it?'

She stopped walking, snatched her arm away from my own and

stamped her foot down hard on the levee. 'Yes I am, Martin, and I have grown tired of it. Besides, the adventure was perfectly agreeable when I was with Colonel Burr. He gave me his cabin, attended my wardrobe, and invited me to balls and dinners. It is only when I am with you that I must suffer these hardships. I think you are a very mean sort of adventurer indeed!'

Well, I couldn't care a sixpence about my adventuring prowess – drinking and fleeing have always been my chief accomplishments – but I rebelled at the comparison with Burr. Liars, libertines, frauds and fantasists we both might be, but at least *I* did not casually ruin others in pursuit of my folly.

'If you prefer Colonel Burr's company, then I am sure you can find a horse to take you to West Florida, and discover whether it was the Spanish or the Americans who hanged him first. I will happily surrender you your share of the flatboat's price. For my part, I am going back to England even if I must stow myself in a sugar box to get there.'

Instantly, Catherine was all contrition. 'Forgive me, Martin. I spoke rashly. Of course you are right.' She hugged me close, her thin body trembling with emotion. 'But you are so brave and resourceful, and I so weak, that sometimes you must make allowances for my foolishness.'

The tears flowed down her cheeks. I pulled out my handkerchief and wiped them away. Being with Catherine in such inconstant humour was not unlike standing on deck in a roaring gale: the sensations produced in my stomach were near identical.

'There, there,' I murmured. 'I know you meant no injury. Perhaps I am too bold in setting our course.' That did not seem likely. 'I have over-stepped myself. We will sell the boat, see how much we profit, and then choose our best line of escape.'

We had started walking again, and were now at the edge of the city where the houses gave way to forests and cane fields. We were also alarmingly close to the pentagonal fort which guarded the river. I turned my back on it, and looked down the embankment to the water.

275

Our flatboat was gone.

My first thought, as ever, was panic. General Wilkinson must have heard of our arrival: the boat was captured, the crew imprisoned, and it would be only a matter of minutes before we joined them. I stared around, looking for the soldiers who were surely behind me ready to plunge a bayonet in my back. To my surprise, there was no-one save a girl with a basket of oranges.

Reason asserted itself. 'They have probably moved the boat downstream a little. Perhaps they took fright when we did not reappear promptly and sought a less conspicuous mooring.'

Catherine looked doubtful – as well she might, for in truth the only moorings downstream were the plantation landings. Before she could voice her thoughts, I spied a negro boatman swabbing the deck on a neighbouring scow and hailed him.

'The boat which was here this morning – did you see it depart?'

He leaned on his mop and looked up at me, though contriving to keep his eyes fixed somewhere about my feet. 'Yes, suh.'

'Where did she go?'

He pointed a sleeveless arm across the river, to the far bank almost a mile distant. 'Tha'way.'

'And was there anything irregular in her departure?'

He did not seem to understand the question. 'Irreg'lar, suh?'

'Unusual.'

'No, suh. They paid up an' jes' took her off to the yard.'

Perhaps it was his accent, but it seemed there was something I had misunderstood. 'Whom did they pay? The harbourmaster?'

'No, suh. The men from the yard.'

'Which men? Which yard? What were they paid for?'

We gazed on each other, each of our faces plainly speaking the belief that we conversed with a halfwit. It was one of the strictures of his race that he could not say so openly.

'The men from the yard – they came fo' the boat an' bought it, an' took it over the river.'

A horrible suspicion began to build in my mind. 'These men came and bought the boat from the crew?'

The negro rewarded my comprehension with a benevolent smile, his teeth as white as pipe-clay. 'Sho'ly did. Paid eighty dollahs.'

I sank my head in my hands, cursing the crew for a gang of thieving, dishonest, mercenary villains. All our plans were in vain, our hopes lost. We might as well present ourselves to Wilkinson and be done.

Catherine, though, remained composed. 'That is not so bad. We will cross the river and inform these men that they have been deceived. If they are honest men, they will return the boat to us at once.'

The negro chuckled, then remembered himself and bowed his head. 'I don' think they will, ma'am.'

'Why not?'

'Unless you wants some sawdust an' half a side of a house.'

'What?'

Again that brilliant smile. 'They was from the breaker's yard, ma'am. They bought your boat for timber. Right now, she nothin' but a heap o' planks.'

I would have sat down on the levee and wept, careless of what Catherine might think, but at that moment I saw another file of soldiers marching towards us along the road. We climbed over the embankment and hastened into the city, moderating our pace just enough that we did not look to be fleeing. We added to the disguise by linking arms, trying to pass ourselves as a respectable couple, though there was no affection in Catherine's taut grip.

I did not care for New Orleans. For one, there was the constant fear of discovery by Wilkinson's men, the sidled glances checking for his soldiers and the stabbing fear when I saw them. There seemed to be a great many on duty. For another, there was an abiding awareness of our low situation – geographically, I mean – that we were one earthwork away from inundation by the Mississippi. But even beyond those fears, New Orleans was an unsettling, mysterious place. Some of the houses had no front doors, only looming carriage arches leading into shaded courtyards; others, by contrast, seemed to be all doors, yet these were often closed by painted shutters. Behind the houses, gardens overflowed with fruit trees – oranges, citrons, pomegranates, figs – casting dappled shade, while balconies and galleries looked down on us, trailing vines from their latticed railings. Every so often I would hear a peal of laughter, or snatches of a melody from a pianoforte, or the soft groan of a creaking bed, but all these sounds were muted and distant, as though perceived through the wrong end of a telescope. Everywhere I felt the sense of imminent activity, of dealings being done and amusements taken, yet all concealed from me behind high walls and shuttered windows. It was the middle of the afternoon, yet the streets were almost empty save for a few slaves and servants on errands. It was far from the drunkards' paradise I had heard extolled so often by the boatmen on the Mississippi, yet there was something undeniably permissive in the air, implicit pleasures ripe for the picking.

Destitute and homeless though we were, we could not stay on the street. We were already beginning to draw searching looks from the soldiers, and with so few people abroad we were all too conspicuous. Hailing a passing servant, we quickly established that there were no good inns to be had, but that the custom among visitors was to stay in boarding houses. There were many nearby, he informed us, but the most convenient was kept by Madam Shaboo.

'And who is Madam Shaboo?' I asked. 'She sounds like the offspring of a gypsy and a Mahometan.'

On the contrary, the servant assured us, she was a most respectable lady. And so she proved, after some knocking on her front door. Despite her outlandish name she was no more than an Irishwoman – her hair a little too red, her cheeks a little too powdered, her bosoms a little too pronounced, but otherwise quite ordinary. We introduced ourselves as Mr and Mrs Beauchamp.

'You're from England, are you?'

'Once upon a time,' I said, noncommittally. It seemed an impossible age since I had left Falmouth on the *Adventure*.

'I had a gentleman here just yesterday asking me if I'd any Englishmen here. "None at the moment," I told him. And now here you are on my doorstep. What name did you give again?'

'Beauchamp.'

'Ah, that's not it then. He was wanting a Mr Jerrold.'

'Was he an American, this gentleman?' I asked, my most artificial smile stitched across my face. Had Wilkinson had word that I was in the city? If so, a pseudonym and an Irish landlady would hardly suffice to protect me.

'Oh no – an Englishman, like yourself. I suppose he wanted some company of his own sort. Perhaps you would like to call on him? I'm sure he would be very grateful. One can become quite melancholy so far from home and kin, as I'm sure you know, though I manage happily enough.'

I did not know who this man might be, but I was determined to avoid him at any cost. 'Did he say where he might be found?'

'At Madam Reillard's house on Rue Royale.'

'And did he give his name?'

Madam Shaboo frowned. 'He said that if his friend Mr Jerrold arrived, I was to be sure to tell him at once, as he so very much hoped to see him. They'd met on their travels somewhere in the north, you see, and agreed that if they reached New Orleans they would seek each other out. But, do you know, I don't remember that he left his name.'

There were any number of men I had met in the north of the country – Mr Ogden the banker, Mr Vidal the spy, Mr Merry the ambassador – and none I wished to meet again.

'Still, there's no call to worry,' added Madam Shaboo with a smile. 'It was Mr Jerrold he wanted, not you.'

We repaired to our bedroom. Madam Shaboo took four dollars for it – the entire sum of our remaining coins – but at that moment I would have paid almost any price for solitude. I pulled the wooden shutters over the window and peered through the slats for any sign of watchers on the streets below.

'Who could it have been, I wonder?' said Catherine.

'No-one who means us well.' I had been chasing the same

question myself, though to no gain. As every possible answer spoke danger, I preferred to ignore it. 'Whoever he may be, our best course is undoubtedly to board the ship to Philadelphia and flee.'

Catherine sat on the edge of the bed, swinging her stockinged feet back and forth. She scowled at me. 'But how will we get aboard the ship? We have no money.'

'I am a sailor. I could work my passage home.' A fairly dismal sailor, admittedly, but with luck we would be far out to sea before they discovered it.

'What of me?'

'I'm sure we could find you a berth in the fo'c'sle. Perhaps in lieu of my pay.'

I could see by Catherine's face that the suggestion did not suit her. She leaned forward. 'Do you love me, Martin?'

I started in surprise. That seemed quite beside the point. 'Of course.'

'Then do not ask me to spend three months confined in seamen's quarters with neither comfort nor society.'

'Would you rather spend the time in gaol?'

'I do not see there would be much difference.'

'You would see the difference soon enough. I have been in gaols, Catherine, and I would rather a year as a fo'c'sle hand than a day in captivity.'

'I would rather neither!' Her voice had risen, and she stood up from the bed. 'Ever since I followed you I have suffered every manner of indignity and discomfort. Now we are sunk to penury as well – a disgrace I never in my life expected. If you cannot bring me home as befits a lady, if all you offer are the humble circumstances of a sailor's woman, then I will arrange matters for myself.'

'How?' I asked. 'Whore yourself on the docks until you have saved forty dollars?'

'You insolent . . .' She slapped me hard against the cheek. Her white gloves did nothing to cushion the sting of the blow. 'How dare you?' She strode to the door clutching her reticule. I watched it carefully, remembering the fate Mr Harris had suffered from its contents.

280

'I will find a gentleman who requires a companion for the long voyage and attach myself to him. Or perhaps I will obtain the money some other way. Evidently you do not care what becomes of me. Goodbye.' She stepped out of the door and slammed it shut. By the time I had opened it and peered into the corridor, the echo of feet stamping down the stairs was all that remained.

I did not pursue her. I doubted further conversation could improve matters, and I feared to be abroad in New Orleans. If she relented her anger she would find me. If she did not, then, as my bruised cheek attested, I was safer alone.

I stayed in that room for the rest of the afternoon, and all through the evening. They were dismal hours, perhaps the worst of the whole venture. My fears had populated New Orleans with such a cast of enemies that I dared not even sit in the parlour; a brief expedition downstairs to borrow one of Madam Shaboo's books was enough to set my heart racing, and I quickly retired. I lay on the bed, staring at the book without reading, and tensing at every sound which penetrated the room. Outside, the city was beginning to rouse itself from its afternoon slumber: I could hear the music of fifes and fiddles, hawkers calling out their wares and friends greeting each other. It sounded very gay. Worse, though, were the noises within the house. Every tread on the stair or creak in the corridor had me sitting bolt upright, mangled between the fear of capture and the hope that Catherine had returned. Madam Shaboo's guests were both numerous and active. After an hour listening to their comings and goings my nerves were ruined; after three hours, even the click of billiard balls from the tavern across the road had me quailing on my bed. When the maid knocked to bring my supper, my heart almost failed, and as soon as I had eaten the food I only wanted to be rid of it.

At length, when I was wrung so dry I had no more hopes to fear for, I fell asleep.

Some time later, I woke. I had not undressed, had not even pulled off my boots, and I felt the soiled feeling which attends sleeping in

281

one's clothes. Even in February the room had become stuffy and airless. I crossed to the window and pulled it open, then unlatched the shutters and stepped out onto the balcony. The cool night was a tonic to my cares; I breathed it in, savouring the rare tranquillity. I must have slept some hours, for the street below was deserted, though I could still hear faint sounds of merriment from within the neighbouring houses. Perhaps the Mississippi boatmen had been right: it seemed that pleasure never slept in New Orleans.

A movement in the gloom under the opposite balcony caught my eye, and in an instant all thoughts of peace and pleasure were forgotten. It was difficult to be sure – life in New Orleans was forever half obscured behind shutters and wrought-iron railings – but I thought I had seen a shadow move. Was I being watched? It was probably nothing, but I pressed myself back against the wall and stared hard at the darkness. Nothing stirred.

I had almost persuaded myself to forget it when a new danger threatened – the thud of heavy footsteps on the stairs. Holding my breath, I waited for them to die away or turn into one of the adjacent rooms. They did not. They drew ever nearer, marching down the corridor with a measured, inexorable tread until it seemed they must be outside my very door. Even then I tried to reason away their presence, until a booming knock dispelled all doubt. Fear seized my tongue, and I did not answer.

'Martin? It is Catherine. You must let me in. I know I have been a wanton, horrid companion, but I have learned something you must know.'

It was the voice I had ached to hear every minute of that long evening. Forsaking caution, I crossed to the door and unbolted it. She must have been as eager as I, for at the sound of the lifting latch she pushed open the door so hastily I was forced back into the room.

An enormous figure filled the doorway, all but blocking out the flickering light in the hall. He was nothing more than a silhouette, yet his menacing shape was unmistakable.

It was not Catherine; it was her father.

*

He stepped through the doorway, bearing down on me so hard that I was forced to retreat. Over his shoulder, I saw Catherine follow him in with a candle. She wore a grey pelisse, and her face was cold and pale as marble.

'Mr Lyell,' I stammered. 'I confess you are the last man I expected to see.' Or wanted to see – though I might overlook that in hope of affording the passage home. 'Did you follow us down the river?'

Lyell grunted. 'I preferred a more comfortable route. From Blennerhassett Island I returned to Pittsburgh, thence to Philadelphia, and at length by sea to New Orleans. I have been waiting here this past week.'

'But how did you know where to find us?'

'Catherine and I arranged our rendezvous before we parted on Blennerhassett Island. I presumed the Mississippi would eventually flush you out.'

'Arranged it?' I glanced at Catherine. 'But you told me you had come in defiance of your father, alone.'

Her face was unmoving, fixed with the same intensity I had seen when she shot Harris. 'Can you be so blind, Martin? How could I have come with you if not by my father's instruction?'

'Burr's plan was doomed to fail,' said Lyell. 'So much was clear the moment we stepped ashore at Blennerhassett Island. From then on, my only imperative was to see that its demise did not redound against us and drag us all into a disastrous war. I sent my daughter with you to see that did not happen. To ensure that no Englishman would be taken alive with Burr.'

His every word seemed spiked with malice, and I noticed his right hand had delved into his coat pocket. I tried to ignore it – and the implication of what enormity Catherine might have perpetrated on me had the need arisen.

'But all that is now moot,' I said. 'Burr's tilt at treason is finished, and Catherine and I have escaped. There is nothing now to prove an English connection, though the sooner we are gone from America the better.'

Lyell ignored me. 'Burr's catastrophic exploits were not all the news I had on my travels. Another packet had arrived from England when I reached Philadelphia, bringing a letter from my associates in London. Can you imagine what it contained?'

He spat those last words at me like bullets. A feeble shake of my head was all the reply I could manage.

'It brought a most alarming report – that Lieutenant Beauchamp, our original envoy from the Admiralty, had been maliciously waylaid in Falmouth and robbed. That his papers had been stolen, and entrusted to a government spy who was to mimic Beauchamp's purpose and insinuate himself into our confidence, with the express aim of thwarting our schemes and exposing us to justice. Can you guess who this traitor might have been?'

I could, though at that moment my mouth was too dry to name him.

'You followed me to worm your way into my secrets. You stole my papers. Do you deny it?'

He had begun advancing towards me again, pushing me back almost to the threshold of the open window. I could see the burnished walnut grip of his pistol emerging from his pocket. I looked to Catherine, still standing behind her father and watching me without expression.

'Will you let him murder me? All the attachment you showed me, is that forgotten?'

She did not reply.

'I love you,' I said.

'That cannot be helped.'

Everything thereafter happened in an instant. Lyell had the pistol out of his pocket and was raising it towards me. I did not have time to turn, let alone to run, but my body could not stay still in the face of danger. With no other choice I lunged towards Lyell, conscious even as I sprang that I was too slow and too far away. Lyell's Manton could kill a man at a hundred paces, and its hair-trigger needed only the breath of a touch to fire. Perversely, that was my salvation. The master gunsmith had not made his graceful weapon for a man of

Lyell's lumbering bulk: he twitched with surprise in the face of my unlikely attack, and the movement in his clumsy hand was enough. The pistol erupted in a shower of sparks, deafening me, and the ball ploughed harmlessly into the floorboards. A hail of splinters scratched and tore at my legs but I did not feel them. Still moving, I cannoned into Lyell, and though his weight kept him upright the momentum drove him back a few steps. He collided with his daughter; the candle was knocked from her hand, fell to the floor and went out. The room was in darkness.

The gunshot still rang in my ears and my eyes wept from the smoke; I had neither wit nor time to think. Mercifully, my instincts were enough. With Lyell still blocking the door, I turned and ran onto the balcony, vaulted over the wrought-iron balustrade and dropped down to the street below. My knees gave way under the jarring impact and I rolled sideways, stirring up a cloud of dust. As I picked myself up, bruised but unbroken, I saw three men standing at Madam Shaboo's front door, watching me in surprise. Doubtless they did not expect to see a gentleman falling from the skies in the middle of the night, still less one who peered anxiously up at the balcony for signs of pursuit, and stepped quickly into its shadow. Forgetting their business with Madam Shaboo, the three men moved towards me. White crossbelts and steel gleamed in the moonlight.

'Leff-tenant Jerrold. I was about to come up and fetch you, but it seems you've saved me the bother.'

The coarse shirt and high-crowned hat were gone, replaced by an army captain's uniform, but the threat in his voice was unchanged from our encounter at King's Tavern in Natchez. The evil-looking pistol in his hand seemed equally familiar.

'I figured you'd be meeting Moses Hook again.'

28

THEY TOOK MY ARMS AND DRAGGED ME THROUGH THE EMPTY
streets. I did not resist them or attempt to run, for what would have
been the use? I had fled from Lyell only to fall quite literally into
Hook's hands; who knew what other enemies I would meet if I
escaped again. Besides, though they treated me roughly they did not
seem to want to kill me.

I had thought they would take me to the fortress by the levee, but
instead we kept away from the river and quickly came to a tall town-
house. I could see little of it save that the lamps were still lit behind
the first-floor shutters; then I passed under the looming arch of the
carriageway into a dark tunnel. There seemed to be a courtyard
beyond, but just before we reached it we turned again up an open
stair, climbed it, and came through a hallway into a warm, brightly lit
room.

It was the most elegant, opulent home I had set foot in since
Blennerhassett's mansion. Candles and crystal sparkled in a lofty
chandelier, while two opposing gilt-framed mirrors reflected back
the shimmering light. The walls were papered a deep, warm yellow,
and a good fire burned in the grate. Yet none of that could keep the
chill from my heart as I saw the two men who awaited me. One I did
not recognize – a portly, red-faced man of about fifty who sat behind

a mahogany desk strewn with papers and an empty decanter. He appeared to be in an advanced state of dissipation: numerous chins sagged down over his throat where the stiff, upright collar of his coat could not contain them, and his wine-stained lips were pursed with the lascivious satisfaction of a man peeping into a lady's dressing room. His eyes were dark and feminine, his white hair pulled back in a severe widow's peak. Yet he had clearly found time to make something of his life, for the blue uniform coat he wore was festooned with gold: gold epaulettes dripping golden tassels over his fat shoulders; gold braid blazed across his lapels; gold buttons; and a great gold buckle stamped with a golden eagle on the sword-belt across his chest. He could not have ranked less than a general, though even a field marshal might have felt shabby beside him. Unless there were two generals in New Orleans so eager for my acquaintance that they would abduct me in the middle of the night, it could only be one man. General Wilkinson.

But the general was not alone. Standing in the corner, leaning against the wall and rolling a cigarillo, was a man I knew immediately. I had sat opposite him on the coach to Princeton, chased him through the frozen forest above Bayou Pierre, and felt the touch of his lead. Now Vidal's path had crossed my own once again, and I was helpless before him. He smiled, baring a familiar row of bone-white teeth.

'Good evening, Señor Jerrold.' He waved to the two soldiers who held me. 'Wait outside the door.'

They loosened their grip and retreated out of the room.

'What do you want of me?' I asked Vidal.

He ignored my question and bowed towards the general. 'Do you know General Wilkinson, Señor Jerrold?'

'Only by reputation.'

Vidal chuckled. 'And what is this reputation you have heard?'

'That he conspired with Burr to betray his country and invade your own. That he then suffered a change of heart and betrayed Burr's scheme to President Jefferson.'

'You think the general has betrayed everyone.' There was a wry amusement in Vidal's voice. 'You are mistaken. The general is a true patriot. In fact, he is more patriotic than most men, for he is a patriot of two countries: Spain and the United States both. Is that not so, General?'

Wilkinson stirred, his cascading chins wobbling between the wings of his collar. 'For two thousand dollars a year, I'd be a patriot to anyone.'

His words were slurred and bloated, in marked contrast to Vidal's precise humour.

'The general gains no profit from a war between his paymasters,' said Vidal.

'But Burr said—'

Vidal sighed. 'Colonel Burr – such a mistaken man. He thinks General Wilkinson will start a war and take him to Vera Cruz and all the gold of Mexico. He thinks the English will control Orleans and the Mississippi. Instead, he has nothing.'

I looked around me. 'Has Burr been captured?'

'Not yet,' grunted Wilkinson. 'But he will be. All the country knows his crimes. It will only be a matter of days before we snare him.'

'Burr thinks he has many friends, but he is wrong,' said Vidal. 'He has instead many enemies. Spain is his enemy. Jefferson is his enemy. Wilkinson is his enemy. All of these, they know what he is doing and they permit him to continue. They see him crawling down the cannon's mouth and they do nothing. They wait until he comes to the end and is trapped. Then they give the spark, and . . .' He balled his fingers into fists, then flicked them apart. 'Boom.'

'What will you do to him?'

'General Wilkinson will send him to Washington to be tried for treason. He will be found guilty, and he will hang.'

'Colonel Burr has been tried for treason twice already, and acquitted both times,' I pointed out. 'I was in court myself. Even the prosecutor admitted there was no evidence to convict.'

I had hoped to dent their confidence. Instead, to my consternation, I only seemed to have added lustre to their polished assurance. Wilkinson leaned across his desk and licked his crimson lips.

'One fact seems to have escaped you, Lieutenant. When it comes to the courtroom in Washington, the jury will find that a material witness has come forth, one who was not present at the last two trials. Someone who'll put more rope around Burr's neck than the hangman himself. Someone who'll testify that Burr not only planned treason against the United States, but conspired with a foreign power, our oldest enemy, to overthrow the republic.'

By the way he and Vidal were staring at me, I did not struggle to guess the identity of this damning witness. A familiar nausea started to rise in my stomach.

'But what if I testify that Burr was not the only man in league with a foreign power – that you were a partisan of the Spanish all along?'

Vidal gave an elegant shrug. 'It does not matter. You are a prisoner and a foreign spy: of course you will say anything against your enemies.'

'Besides,' added Wilkinson, 'by then my co-operation with Mr Vidal will simply seem foresighted. Spain and America will be allies, at war against our common foe.' A cruel smile etched itself across Wilkinson's face.

'If you think Britain will go to war on my account—'

Vidal cut me short. 'Of course not. They will go to war because President Jefferson will declare war on them. When the country hears that England joined with Burr to steal the Mississippi lands, they will demand it.'

'But there was no English plot to support Burr,' I pleaded. 'The ships were a figment, a fantasy, nothing more.' The letter in the lining of my coat suddenly weighed heavier than ever.

Vidal tutted. 'I do not think you came all this way to tell him nothing. But it does not matter. By the time you are in Washington you will know what to say.' He smiled at me with unalloyed menace. 'We will teach it to you.'

Vidal crossed to the door and opened it to call in the guards. I turned to Wilkinson.

'For God's sake, General, there is no need for you to do this. If you wanted to destroy Burr, then very well – he is lost. If you want me to swear that he is a villain, a liar and a traitor then I will happily oblige you. I myself only came here to thwart his conspiracy. But do not drag me into your courthouse, or make me the pretext for a war between our nations.'

Of course I did not care a whit for my country, but if war came on my account I guessed I would not likely survive it. That was no concern of Wilkinson's.

'Of course you disown him now, but a court will decide the truth of it. We will put you on a boat for Washington tomorrow. My duties keep me in New Orleans at present, mopping up the remnant of Burr's partisans, but I will follow shortly. I will certainly be there in time to see you on the gallows.'

Hook and his men took me back downstairs and into a small court-yard behind the house. I saw the shadows of palm fronds and ferns, and smelled the scent of jasmine in the air, together with the staler smells of horses and men. On one side of the courtyard rose a high, windowless wall; on the other, adjoining the main house, a two-storey outbuilding. I took it to be the stables or the carriage house, but when my captors led me in I found a clean, whitewashed store room piled with sacks of meal and flour. They did not bind me, but contented themselves with bolting the door. There was no furniture in the room, but by rearranging the sacks I made myself a tolerable bed. Outside, the monotone tread of the sentry in the gallery above was the only sound.

However I considered it, it had been a ghastly night. Every one of my enemies, and a few I had not known before, had descended on me in concert, and the best that could be said was that I had exchanged Lyell, who would have killed me immediately, for Wilkinson, who would kill me presently. Catherine, who had pro-fessed to love me, had betrayed me, and now it seemed that I was destined to start a war which would surely be the ruin of England. Even by my lamentable standards, that was poor work.

A rare anger possessed me. I flailed about the room kicking at the sacks and pounding on the walls. A white floury cloud filled the air – it was like being back in the forest on the Mississippi, battling Vidal as the snow fell. Outside, I could hear the sentries laughing at my blundering madness, and that spurred me to a greater rage. I had to escape. The wooden door shivered under my blows, and I could hear the clang of the bolt knocking against its shank, but it did not give. I even tried scrabbling at the earthen floor, and soon my hands were stained with a grey paste of mud and flour.

At last, exhausted, I lay back on my bed of sacks. Ever wilder schemes of escape raced through my thoughts, each ending inevitably with visions of Hook and Vidal shooting me down with pistols, or running me through with their swords. I broke into a torrent of uncontrolled sobbing, then fitful convulsions, and eventually settled into blessed sleep. Astonishingly, given what I had endured, I had no nightmares.

I suppose a noise from outside must have woken me, though I was not aware of it. The air was clammy, and though it was not cold I found myself shivering in my damp clothes. A bar of grey light seeped under the door, heralding the dawn; the foreign songs of unknown birds had replaced the tramp of the sentry's boots. I stood, rubbing my stiff neck.

Iron rasped on the far side of the door as someone drew back the bolt. Even the thought of meeting my enemies again was too much, and I sat back down. I would not resist them, but neither would I oblige them.

The door opened. Outside, the dawn was not so far progressed as I had thought – the night still had a little time to run – and I struggled to recognize the silhouette on the threshold. He seemed too tall for Hook, too thin for Wilkinson and too stooped for Vidal. Whether by a trick of the light or the fashion of his dress, I could see not a patch of white on him, not even his shirt. A low hat covered his eyes, and for a moment I wondered if he might not be the devil himself, come to claim me.

He beckoned me forward. 'Hurry.'

I was too fuddled to obey. With an anxious glance back into the courtyard, the figure crossed the room and hauled me to my feet. The wide-open door behind him admitted enough of the pre-dawn light that his features became apparent. The ghostly-white skin of his face, the eyes sunk deep in their sockets, the slight stoop brought on by too many weeks serving passengers in the mess room below decks.

It was Mr Fothergill.

Had he not been holding me by my collar, I would have collapsed back onto my sackcloth bed. In some distant region of eternity I could almost hear the gleeful laughter of the malevolent fates who mastered me. First Lyell, then Vidal, now Fothergill: truly all my enemies had conspired to visit me this night. It would not have surprised me to see my uncle loitering in the doorway.

'Which party sent you?' I asked wearily. 'Are you a friend of Lyell's, an ally of Spain, or some newly manifested enemy?'

Fothergill had already started dragging me towards the door. 'I am a friend,' he declared.

I gave a short laugh of disbelief.

'Or perhaps I should say, the friend of a friend.'

'I was not aware that I had any left.'

He chuckled. 'Don't say that, sir. He'd be sorely affronted to hear it.'

'Who would be?'

Fothergill poked his head into the courtyard, peered around, then tugged me forward.

'Why, Mr Nevell, of course.'

29

I HAD NO TIME TO DIGEST HIS EXTRAORDINARY ANSWER, FOR ALL AT once I was out in the courtyard and being hurried towards the carriageway. I looked up over my shoulder, expecting to see the soldier in the gallery, but all I could see was an indistinct lump lying behind the railing. The front gate was similarly unguarded, not even locked.

'Where have all the sentries gone?'

Fothergill edged open the iron gate and slipped around it. 'Asleep, perhaps.'

'How did you—'

'Hush, sir.'

As calmly as if he were serving port after dinner, Fothergill walked into the street. I followed. With each step I felt certain that Wilkinson must peer out of his window and see me escaping, or that Vidal would come out on the balcony above and shoot me down, but neither appeared. It was as if Fothergill had worked some magic spell that allowed us to move through locked doors and solid walls unnoticed.

Around us, the city was rousing itself. Butchers' boys hauled dray-carts full of meat; bakers stoked their fires and pulled out the morning's first loaves; slaves hurried to the markets to find their masters' breakfasts, or trudged home with wicker baskets piled high on their heads. The high buildings still blocked any sign of the sunrise, but a fragile blue had begun to infuse the sky.

It was all I could do to keep from running as fast as possible, but Fothergill maintained a measured, deliberate pace as he navigated us away from Wilkinson's house, only lengthening his stride when it was well behind us. None of the passers-by paid us the least notice; the alarm was not raised, and no-one raced through the streets crying that a dangerous villain was at large. In my mind, a hundred questions demanded answers from Fothergill, but as he always contrived to keep two paces ahead of me I could never quite gain his attention. Only when we had crossed several streets and turned inland did he allow me to draw level with him.

'I do not suppose a friend of Nevell's is much inclined to offer explanations, but how did you come to be here?'

'The same as you – down the Mississippi.'

'I never saw you.'

'I was instructed not to be seen.'

I paused, allowing a woman with a basket full of chickens to pass before us. 'Do you mean to say that you followed me all the way from New York?'

Professional modesty prevented Fothergill from claiming so much. 'Your midnight flight from Princeton confused matters a few days. And in my haste, I actually overtook you on the road to Pittsburgh. Otherwise, I was generally no more than a few hours behind you.'

I wondered how many other spies I had trailed behind me as I blundered across the continent. 'I am surprised you did not encounter Mr Vidal on your travels.'

'We met several times. Once, we even stayed in the same inn. But he was intent on his quarry, and did not notice me.'

'Do you know who he is?'

'An agent of Spain. He has been watching Burr for some time, ever since the Spaniards heard of his plans to appropriate their empire.'

'He was in league with General Wilkinson – were you aware of that?'

Fothergill nodded. 'In addition to his duties with the army of the United States, Wilkinson has been employed by the Spanish authorities for almost twenty years. I dare say they know every secret and stratagem that America has ever pursued against them.'

'How unfortunate, then, that Burr should have enlisted Wilkinson in his plan to attack both Spain and America.' It was, I thought, entirely typical of Burr's luck and judgement. 'Wilkinson and Vidal planned to use me as a pretext to bring America into the war against Britain.'

'That is why we must get you away from New Orleans with all despatch.'

As he said this, we came to a halt outside a grand stone building. I glanced around nervously, for we were in the heart of the city here: I could see the twin spires of the cathedral at the end of the street, with the main square and the levee beyond. It seemed a curious place to come to escape. Fothergill, though, had already stepped between the square columns and through the high wooden doors. I followed anxiously.

If I had wondered at Fothergill's direction before, the interior of the building left me entirely mystified. It appeared to be some kind of assembly room: the floor was paved with chequered squares of black and white marble, and in the niches in the oak-panelled walls I glimpsed graceful figures talking and laughing. A broad staircase rose from the middle of the room to the upper floor, from where I could hear the improbable strains of a minuet. Stale perfume and tobacco filled the air.

A negro footman dressed in immaculate scarlet livery sidled up to us.

'Are you come for the ball, suhs?'

'We're seeking Mr Lafitte,' said Fothergill.

The footman bowed. 'M'sieur Lafitte, he'll be in the ballroom upstairs.'

Fothergill made to move forward, but a slight cough from the footman and an almost imperceptible tug on his arm paused him.

'Admission is two dollars each for gen'lmen.'

Fothergill pressed some coins into the man's palm. With another bow, he melted into the shadows by the wall.

The music grew louder as we climbed the stairs, mingling with the sound of chattering voices and chiming crystal. Another footman in the same scarlet livery bustled past us bearing a tray of wine; as if in a dream, I reached out and took a glass. I had emptied it before I reached the head of the stairs, yet I hardly noticed, for a pair of double doors opened on to a high ballroom admitting the most fantastical vision. Outside, dawn might be stirring the city, but in here all was midnight. Vast swags of cloth covered the windows against the morning, and teams of servants criss-crossed the room replacing burned-out candle-stubs with fresh tapers. The musicians at the far end of the hall still played with fervour, their bows flying over their strings, and though the dance was the same as in England, the whirling abandon of the dancers made it seem a different thing entirely. Glossy boots twined with satin slippers on the dance floor; damask skirts swirled around shapely ankles, and ruffled shirts brushed demurely covered bosoms. Along the walls, half hidden in shadow, exotic ladies in turbans and feathers fanned themselves and watched.

'What is this . . . ?' My question tailed off as I noticed Fothergill had left me and was deep in conversation with another footman.

Looking back to the centre of the room, I watched the dancers whirling and spinning as the music gathered pace. Many of the women were strikingly beautiful, I observed – far more so than the assortment of whey-faced squires' daughters and maids you would have found in England. I could see one girl – she could not have been more than eighteen – with skin the colour of gold; another so dark she might have been mistaken for a negress. No two appeared the same, yet gradually I began to discern certain features that all had in common: dark hair, full lips, and skins every imaginable shade of brown.

I looked around, my eyes darting from woman to woman. Not a

single one, neither the nubile creatures on the dance floor nor the stately matriarchs around the walls, was white. In confusion, I turned my gaze on the men: all looked to be as white as I. Yet they danced with the negro women as easily and promiscuously as if they had been their own wives.

'What is this place?' I wondered aloud.

'A quadroon ball,' came the answer from my side. Fothergill had returned unnoticed and was steering me around the room to an open doorway. 'The gentlemen of New Orleans come here to choose their half-blood mistresses.'

'What do their wives say to that?'

Fothergill shrugged. 'Whatever they say in London, I suppose. Less, perhaps – I understand that the quadroon girls are rather more virtuous.'

Had New Orleans not been populated with men seeking to kill me, I might have chosen to get better acquainted with it. As it was, I followed Fothergill through the doorway into an adjoining room where several green baize tables were laid out for cards. The quadroon girls were evidently unwelcome here, or not interested, for it was filled exclusively with men. Many had removed their jackets and undone their cravats; they slouched around the tables casting jealous glances at their rivals.

Fothergill approached a table at the back of the room, set between two enormous window arches. The game seemed more urgent here: all the seats were filled, and a great many observers hovered behind the players. Coins danced and spun on the table as the gamblers hurled them carelessly into the middle; cigarillos wilted into long fingers of ash. The sound of the orchestra in the ballroom was still audible, but the predominant rhythm here was the slap of cards being dealt.

Fothergill manoeuvred his way through the audience to a small man standing by the table. He was watching the game with rapt concentration, though rather than watching the cards or the players' faces his gaze seemed fixed on the ever-changing sums of money in the centre. He turned as Fothergill touched him on the shoulder, and if he was bothered to be disturbed in his observance he hid it well behind an enormous smile as broad as his face.

'I would greatly value a private word with Monsieur Lafitte,' Fothergill murmured.

The smile never dimmed. 'I am afraid, monsieur, it is impossible. Monsieur Lafitte cannot be disturbed in his game.'

'Tell him that he will win far more by what I propose than from his game.'

The small man nodded, still smiling, and began edging his way around the table.

'Who is he?' I asked Fothergill.

'Monsieur Laporte. He is an associate of Jean Lafitte.'

There was a great deal I could easily forget in that room – that it was morning outside, that the commander of the United States army would presently be scouring New Orleans for me – but one thing struck me immediately. 'Laporte, Lafitte – they all sound French.'

Fothergill nodded.

'Is it prudent to entrust my life to a Frenchman?'

'Jean Lafitte is no friend of the Americans. He is a *contrebandier*, the finest in New Orleans.' Fothergill's lips pursed in distaste. 'He is particularly adept at moving human cargoes.'

I was about to ask Fothergill to identify this smuggling prodigy, but a glance across the table made it evident enough. Directly opposite, where the diminutive Laporte had halted, a man sat with his back to the wall and a great pile of silver at his right hand. He was far from the swarthy, barrel-chested pirate I had expected: tall but not broad, with pale skin and a silk shirt which shone with a soft sheen in the candlelight. His cheeks were clean-shaven, his eyes dark and wide, and his thick black hair hung in curls over his collar. Despite the languid air about him, I noticed he did not miss a moment of the game while Laporte whispered in his ear.

Laporte made his way back. Across the table, Lafitte attended to the constant flow of cards and coins without ever so much as glancing at us. As Laporte returned, I saw that the smile had contracted ever so slightly.

'Monsieur Lafitte is too busy with his game. He cannot give you a private audience. *Désolé.*'

'But we must speak with him,' protested Fothergill.

The smile stretched out to its full, beaming width. 'I did not say he will not speak to you. I said he will not speak in private.'

'But our business—'

Fothergill broke off as he realized that the room had fallen silent. The crowd around us had withdrawn so that we stood in our own pocket of space, and every man around the table was staring at us – none more so than Lafitte himself, who had put down his cards and fixed us with a curious stare.

'There is something you wish to ask me?' he enquired.

'I would prefer to ask it in private,' said Fothergill.

Lafitte spread his arms wide. 'We are all friends here. Jean Lafitte keeps no secrets from his friends.'

'Very well.' Fothergill paused, clearing his throat. 'My colleague and I need to leave New Orleans in some haste, and in the greatest secrecy. I have heard that you are the man who can effect this. For a suitable fee, naturally.'

'Your colleague? Who is he? Can he speak?'

Lafitte's eyes settled on me. I looked to Fothergill for guidance, but his face was expressionless.

'My name is Martin Jerrold.'

'You are English?'

'Yes.'

'What are you doing in New Orleans, Englishman?'

'*J'essaie m'échapper.*'

It was no more than the truth, and spoken in fairly rudimentary French, but it drew a chuckle from Lafitte. The rest of the audience followed him, and I felt a rare spark of hope. Perhaps Miss Lyell had not served me entirely ill.

'I know your name, Englishman.' The opening in Lafitte's humour had snapped shut again. 'You want to escape, but there are men in this city who would much like to keep you here.'

'We will pay you one thousand dollars if Mr Jerrold escapes successfully,' said Fothergill.

Lafitte shrugged. '*Ça n'importe rien.* General Wilkinson offers one thousand dollars to any man who brings M'sieur Jerrold to him. How do I choose?'

'General Wilkinson is no friend of yours. If he found you he would hang you.'

'Maybe so, but he has still been a very dear friend to me. Each time that he stops trade on the river or declares martial law, the price of my goods, it doubles. And the English do not like my trade either. They stop my ships, they seize my cargoes. *C'est malheureux.*'

'They might view you with a kinder eye if you gave them reason to be grateful,' said Fothergill.

'So might General Wilkinson. You are in England's navy, M'sieur Jerrold?'

'Yes.'

Lafitte took a sip from the glass he kept beside him. 'How many Frenchmen have you killed?'

My throat suddenly felt very dry, and I looked with longing at Lafitte's drink. 'Not many.'

'You are not a good sailor?'

'No.' I cringed, feeling the contempt in the crowd.

Lafitte turned to Fothergill. 'But he is worth one thousand dollars, you say.'

'He is worth one thousand dollars to you, sir. What he is worth to us . . .' Fothergill diplomatically left it unsaid.

Lafitte leaned back in his chair. 'So, Mr Jerrold, you are worth one thousand dollars to your friends, and one thousand dollars also to your enemies. But Jean Lafitte is not your friend or your enemy. How shall he decide?' He spread his hands and moved them up and down like scales, weighing his choices. I could not keep from staring at them, watching my life rise and fall in their balance. At length he clapped them together. '*Eh bien.* We play for it. *Deux cartes, s'il vous plaît.*' He grinned at me. 'It is a very easy game. Two men, two cards.

If my card is higher, I give you to General Wilkinson. If your card wins, I bring you to the sea. *C'est bon?*'

Fothergill's funereal demeanour, normally so impassive, was exercised by a rare burst of emotion. 'That is hardly fair, sir. If it is a question of payment I am sure that more—'

Lafitte cut him short with a wave of his hand. 'I do not do this for the money.' He considered this a moment. 'For the money, yes, but also *pour le plaisir.*'

Excitement buzzed through the room – this was more to their liking. From the corner of my eye I saw several onlookers arranging their side-wagers. The men at the table before me moved aside, and I found myself thrust into an empty seat opposite Lafitte. The din of the crowd, the bodies pressing all around me, Fothergill's consoling hand on my shoulder – all fell away. I saw only Lafitte's wide, dark eyes fixed on me with toying amusement, and the green baize square between us.

Two cards dropped onto the table. Mine stared up at me, bespeaking doom, and I gazed back with dread. I could not take it, could not even lift my hand to slide it towards me. It lay where it had fallen.

Lafitte had no patience for such delays. With a dismissive toss of his head, he pulled his card to the edge of the table, put his fingernail beneath it and flicked it onto its back. A murmur ran through the crowd as they saw the jack of spades winking up at them, innocent and evil.

Lafitte laid his hands flat on the table and looked at me. '*À vous.*'

30

I DON'T BELIEVE I FAINTED – FOTHERGILL TOLD ME LATER THAT I
never lost the power of my own legs – but the next thing I knew
I was being bundled into a carriage waiting outside the door. The
sun was high enough that its rays now touched the street, and the
azure blue of an immaculate late-winter sky drifted overhead, but I
barely saw them before I was in the carriage with the curtains drawn
and the door slammed shut. Someone shouted instructions to the
driver; then we jolted forward.

Fothergill and I were alone. Neither of us spoke. I was too
exhausted even to feel relief, and still shadowed by the fear that
Wilkinson must surely be hunting us. When the driver reined in the
horses beside the levee and led us over to a small wherry, I pulled
my coat up high to mask my face, and as we were rowed across the
mile-wide expanse of the river I sat stiff in the terror of a bullet
ripping through my shoulders. None came, nor did anyone challenge
us when we moored on the far bank at an imposing plantation house.
We passed the house, and soon we were walking down a lane
between cotton fields. With the sun on my face I felt a blissful peace
warming through me, something I had not felt since . . . it was too
much effort to remember.

Gradually the fields gave way to copses, then to forest. Though I had seen no rain since I reached New Orleans, the ground grew steadily damper, and my boots started to slide and squelch. In some places the path was so bad that wooden boards had been thrown down over the mud, though even these were already rotting into the mire. Flies swarmed around us, and strange animals cackled and called in the ever-thickening undergrowth. Matted curls of grey-green moss hung like beards from the overhanging branches, brushing my shoulder. Even the sun disappeared, dappled into dim fragments by the leaves and foliage above.

Just as the path was in danger of foundering entirely, it stopped at the edge of a narrow strip of stagnant water. It did not look deep – I could see the fibrous bottom through the tea-brown water – but three wooden canoes, little more than hollowed-out logs, were drawn up on the bank. They looked to be perfectly abandoned. Lafitte's coachman, who had accompanied us all the way, knelt beside one and rapped three times on its hull.

I almost yelped with surprise as two negroes stepped out from behind broad tree-trunks. They were barefoot, wearing ragged canvas trousers, short-sleeved shirts and broad-brimmed straw hats. Knives and pistols were crammed into their rope belts.

The coachman addressed the nearest of them, a dark-skinned man whose forearms were creased and puckered with an almost solid mass of grey scar tissue. He had said barely a word to us since we left the ballroom; now he spoke in an incomprehensible patois that was by turns French, Spanish, English, and something else foreign to all of them. I thought I heard my name, and Fothergill's, and several repetitions of Lafitte's; otherwise I could understand nothing of it.

The coachman turned back to me. 'You go with Dubois,' he said, pointing to the scarred negro.

Dumbly, I obeyed. I crawled into the bow of one of the canoes, taking great care not to upset it. The draught was so shallow, and the sides so low, that it hardly seemed I was in a boat at all. Instead I felt like one of the spiders I could see scuttling across the stagnant surface, bending the water but never breaking through.

The canoe slithered down the silvery mud, rocking gently as someone clambered into the back. Even that small movement was almost enough to tip the gunwale underwater. Craning my head back, carefully, I saw the negro Dubois sitting cross-legged on the stern thwart, a paddle in his hand. Fothergill and the other boatman were in the neighbouring canoe, also on the water, while the coachman looked on from the bank. I raised my hand in farewell; then we started moving through the water, and he was quickly lost among the moss and branches.

Most of that journey passed in a trance. Lacking sleep, drained by the misadventures I had suffered since reaching New Orleans, I lay back in the canoe and watched the swampy forest glide by. We were in a labyrinth of water: channels met and diverged with dizzying frequency, some almost wide enough to be rivers, some little more than muddy puddles. Our watery road wound around itself so many times that I soon lost all sense of my bearings. In places the overgrowth hung so low that the branches scratched my face even when I lay supine; in other places tall trees arched over the watercourse in high cathedral splendour. Everywhere about us was darkness and mystery. Knobs of wood rose out of the water like the tentacles of unseen beasts; trees picked up the skirts of their trunks and tottered on exposed roots. Sometimes I could see broad, verdant meadows, flat as bowling lawns and green as serpents, inviting me to come and lie down on them. Only the faintest ripples in the surface betrayed them to be carpets of scum, waiting to suck in any who trod on them.

All through this dream, the only human sounds were the splash and push of the paddle behind me, and the whispering of the hull. My companion, Dubois, spoke to me only once, when I absentmindedly let my hand drift into the water.

'No do that,' he said, reaching forward and tapping me between the shoulder blades with the paddle. 'Gators.'

'What is a gator?'

'It's the local term for crocodiles,' answered Fothergill from the boat behind. 'They'll take off a man's hand, or his arm or his leg, as easy as you'd take a bite of cheese.'

'Do they inhabit these waters?' I asked, snatching back my hand and staring out at the still bayou.

'Many,' came the guttural voice behind me. 'Many many.'

After that, I kept my hands knotted firmly in my lap.

We must have paddled all day, gliding through the waterlogged forest. At one point, which may have been midday, the boatman handed me a piece of salt fish and a few crumbs of cheese. Once, we had to disembark to lift the canoe over a place where silt had completely blocked the channel. The mud rose almost to the rim of my boots, and it was only by much swaying and fidgeting that I managed to pull them free. After that we were confined to the canoe again.

I marvelled that the boatman never hesitated in his course, never showed the least concern when confronted by the diverging streams. Of course he might have been taking us in circles for all I knew – there was little to distinguish one part of the swamp from another – but I gradually came to think that he must be following some pre-ordained path. The more I looked at the forest, the more I noticed certain curiosities whenever a choice was to be made: three bunches of the hanging moss set all in a row; a forked branch thrusting out of the water; a squirrel's tail tied around a stump. Some of these signs seemed almost calculated to deceive – a branch which appeared to block a channel, for example, which swung away like a well-oiled gate when we touched it.

It was nigh impossible to measure time, but at length the light on the leaves began to glow orange, then to fade. Mist rose off the water, and new sounds began to intrude on the dusk. I turned back to the boatman, still paddling as serenely as ever.

'Will we continue through the night?' I asked, uncertain whether he understood me and less certain still whether I would like his answer. General Wilkinson's threat, so urgent this morning, now seemed impossibly remote, while fear of the crocodiles loomed ever larger in my thoughts.

In reply, Dubois lifted his paddle and gestured forward. 'We sleep here.'

I looked forward again. In the time that I had been turned around we had come round a corner, and the channel now opened out on to a round pool perhaps fifty yards across. It was the biggest expanse of clear water I had seen since we crossed the Mississippi that morning. If creeks and bayous were the byways of this strange world, then this pool was a crossroads fed by at least half a dozen channels, though I could see none of the clandestine signs I had noticed earlier.

'Where will we sleep?' I doubted there were six feet of dry land to be had in that place. Nor did I wish to rest where a crocodile might come upon me and tear me apart as I slept.

Once again, Dubois answered by pointing his paddle, this time to the far side of the pool. Perhaps it was the eastern side – certainly it seemed the darkest – and for a moment I could see nothing save the usual tangle of tree-trunks, leaves, and vines. Only as we paddled nearer did the picture begin to fragment: trees which had no leaves; foliage which seemed to hang in the air without recourse to branches; straight lines and perpendicular angles quite distinct from the twisting natural order.

We crossed the golden circle of light in the centre of the pool and passed into the shadow beyond. I looked up. Now I could see plainly that the trees were in fact high stilts rising proud out of the water, their branches the beams on which platforms had been built, their leaves the palm-fronds which thatched the makeshift rooms. It was a house, of sorts – or rather a village, for there were several of these strange stilt-huts all built together around the edge of the pool. They loomed over us like giants, their unframed windows dark, vacant eyes.

The canoe butted gently against the pilings and came to a stop. Everything about this fabulous construction seemed moulded from the fabric of the forest: some of the stilts were in fact live tree-trunks, while the ropes which bound the edifice were woven from swamp creepers. While the boatman held the canoe steady, I scrambled out onto a makeshift landing stage at the foot of the pilings. Hardly had I stepped out than a challenge rang out from above. Apart from the few words I had exchanged with the boatman it was the first voice I had heard since entering the swamp, and I almost fell in the water in my fright.

The boatman answered with words I could not understand. A rope ladder dropped down to us and I climbed up, swaying precariously. As I hauled myself over the lip of the platform three pairs of eyes fixed on me, luminous in the near-darkness within. Had the rungs of the ladder not been quite so rotted, and had I not heard Dubois climbing up behind me, I might have excused myself and clambered down immediately; instead, I crawled onto the grimy floor, out of the way of the doorway. The eyes followed me in silence. I mumbled an introduction but got no response – the eyes did not even blink. Only when the boatman arrived did they suddenly burst into life, jabbering and chattering in the same unnatural dialect.

As my eyes resolved the darkness I saw that there were three of them, two men and a woman, all dressed in patchwork rags, with untamed hair and dark skins. Though they spoke no English they were hospitable enough – by which I mean that they offered us bowls of shrimp, gave us mouldering blankets, and otherwise ignored us. There was only one room in the high hut; after supper Fothergill and I made our beds in a corner while our hosts and the boatmen sat around the fire laughing and talking in their wild language, and drinking rum.

I lay down on the rush mats which covered the floor, but I could not sleep. Within myself I was all contradictions. My limbs ached with exhaustion though I had done nothing that day save sit in the canoe, yet now I was in bed I felt wide awake. I rolled over to face Fothergill.

'Where are we?' I whispered, anxious not to disturb our hosts.

'They call it Barataria,' said Fothergill. 'Do you know Cervantes?'

'Is he an ally of Vidal?'

Fothergill gave a dry laugh. 'Perhaps. I was rather thinking of the author of *Don Quixote*.'

Even in the darkness, I blushed.

'Barataria was the kingdom given to Sancho Panza to punish him for his sins. This place is well named. If ever there was somewhere for sinning, we are here. It is all a wilderness of swamps and marshes, uncharted rivers and hidden creeks which run to the sea. This is Jean Lafitte's kingdom, a haven for pirates and a turnpike for smugglers.'

And this was the man Fothergill had chosen to aid our escape.

'Do you trust him?' I asked.

'We have no choice. The river is controlled by the Spaniards, and Lake Ponchartrain, the other passage to the coast, by the Americans. This is the only way we could have hoped to escape once Wilkinson discovered your flight, and Lafitte is the only man who knows its ways and commands its inhabitants.'

'He might yet betray us.'

'He might.' Fothergill sounded resigned to the fact. 'But I doubt it.'

'Because of the money you promised?'

'That's nothing to him. What matters more is that our ships in the West Indies keep from searching his vessels. He has lost a great deal of cargo to us; by helping you, he understands that we will turn a blinder eye to his smuggling. That is why he agreed to our bargain.'

'But he did not agree – I beat him in his game of cards. It was purely a matter of chance.'

Fothergill laughed again. 'Is that what you believe? Do you think that Jean Lafitte ever loses a hand of cards at his own table unless it suits him? He had made up his mind before he ever proposed the wager, and he knew your card before it was dealt.'

'Then why—'

'For his own amusement. Or to impress his followers. He cannot be seen surrendering to every itinerant petitioner who crosses his threshold.' Fothergill turned over and set his back to me. 'Now go to sleep. We will need all our wits in the morning.'

Fothergill slept; I did not. The hardness of the floor, the terrors which haunted me, and the mysterious sounds drifting over from the fire fed a frenzy of half-formed thoughts which would not abate. Every cracking twig or splash from the water below convinced me that Hook's men had come for me, or that a crocodile must be crawling up the pilings. I tossed and turned; I cocooned myself in my blanket, then threw it off; I tried to make a pillow of my coat and felt the rustle of my uncle's letter still sewn safely inside it.

Perhaps I did sleep eventually, though if I did my dreams were no kinder than my waking thoughts. At least it meant that when I saw a dark face with staring eyes looming over me, shaking my shoulder and hissing in my ear, I convinced myself that I was dreaming and did not scream. Only with the greatest reluctance did I at length acknowledge that it was Dubois, and recognize his urgent words.

'We go. They comin'.'

I sat up. 'Who's coming?'

'The gen'ral's men. Come, we go.'

Dawn was breaking over the swamp as we paddled away from that curious village, spreading soft-hued pinks and oranges across the furrowed clouds. Soon we seemed to reach the edge of the forest: the lofty trees gave way to saplings and scrub, then vanished altogether. As the sun rose and the clouds melted from the firmament, I saw we had entered an entirely new landscape, a never-ending field of golden reeds which rustled and whispered in the breeze that fanned them. After the tangled murk of the forest there was something bright and honest in the reeds, though they were no less impenetrable. Sitting in the canoe so close to the water I could not see over their stalks; I was like a mouse scurrying through a field of August wheat, hemmed in on all sides.

Dubois had said that General Wilkinson's men pursued us, and though I saw no evidence of it I did not doubt him. A shipload of American soldiers could have sailed past twenty yards away and we would not have known it. I presumed that Lafitte's men knew who trespassed the borders of his kingdom, and when Dubois thrust a paddle into my hands I took it obediently.

After that I had little opportunity to examine the scenery. All my strength and spirit was centred on the paddle: digging it in, driving it back, lifting it out and repositioning it. My arm was quickly soaked with swamp-water, then with sweat, for the low-lying reeds offered no shade from the ascendant sun. Its rays scalded my face; I could almost feel the colour rising in my cheeks and on the back of my neck. It must have been evident to Dubois, too, for he took pity on me and offered me his broad-brimmed straw hat, which I gratefully accepted. My shoulder began to ache.

We paddled on. Once, I almost capsized the canoe craning around at a sudden noise. A flock of brown birds had risen out of the marsh behind us, squawking their indignation with short, yapping calls and wheeling in the sky. Dubois nodded, though I had not said anything.

'Somethin' 'sturbed 'em.'

'General Wilkinson's men, do you think?'

Somehow, never breaking his paddle-stroke, he contrived to shrug his broad shoulders. He looked more like a pirate than ever now, for he had removed his shirt and tied it over his shaven head. I could see the muscles rippling beneath his ebony skin as he dug the paddle into the water again and again. Beside his strength, my own efforts must have been pitiful indeed.

We forged on under the noon sun. The endless banks of reeds might make for an austere landscape, but the channels between them were as baroque as ever. Gradually, though, they began to widen. The shores drifted away. Fothergill's canoe came alongside us so that we moved like two horses in the traces, yet the expanse of water on our quarter never narrowed. The tang of salt, which had teased my senses all morning, became inescapable: when a clumsy stroke of my paddle splashed water in my mouth, it tasted like the sea. The breeze stiffened, until at last we came around a turn and saw open water on every horizon, sparkling like a field of mirrors in the sun. I never thought I could feel such delight in seeing the sea. I put down my paddle and gazed in stupefied wonder.

A gust of wind caught us on the beam, rocking the canoe and threatening to tip us both in the water. When it had calmed, I turned back to Dubois.

'What do we do now?'

With nothing to hinder it, the breeze was whipping up white-flecked waves which would swamp our shallow craft. Even in the mouth of the channel we risked capsizing. Ignoring my concern, Dubois paddled across to the reedy shore and then, to my astonishment, slipped over the side of the boat into the water. It rose to his chest, slopping over his shoulders and drenching his shirt-tails where they hung down over his neck.

'What about the crocodiles?' I asked, stabbing at the water with my paddle in an effort to keep the canoe from drifting out to sea.

Dubois's reply was all but lost to the wind, though I thought I heard something concerning salt water. Breasting through the water like the bow of a ship, he moved up to the reeds and vanished among them. My attempts to maintain the canoe's position grew more frantic, and I might well have pitched myself overboard if Fothergill's craft had not come alongside to steady me. Between us, we just about managed to keep ourselves still.

'Is this the Gulf of Mexico?' I asked Fothergill, concentrating hard on my paddling.

'Not yet. This is a lagoon which leads into the gulf. It is still ten miles to the coast.'

'How will we get there?' I glanced back up the channel we had come by, half expecting to see Captain Hook standing by a cannon in the prow of a gunboat. Nothing moved.

A rustling in the reeds answered me. Dubois had reappeared with a slimy, weed-caked rope held over his shoulder. As he hauled it forward I saw a wooden bow, then a scarred hull, and finally the whole length of a small yawl. She would have looked small enough against a ship's longboat, or even a cutter, but she dwarfed our canoes.

Dubois drew up the boat alongside and gestured that we should climb aboard. As soon as we were in he dragged the two canoes out of sight into the reeds, while the other boatman unwrapped the large canvas bundle which lay in the bilge. It yielded a mast, a brown sail furled around its yard, a brace of rifles, a tin of powder and shot, and

311

three pairs of oars. With Fothergill and me assisting him he stepped the mast and settled the yard in its parrels, though with the breeze coming straight up the lagoon he did not raise the sail. Instead he fitted the oars between the thole pins and then busied himself loading the muskets.

Dubois emerged from the reeds and hauled himself inboard. With a quick glance at the scrap of ribbon tied to our masthead, which still blew obstinately inland, he seated himself on one of the thwarts and took a pair of oars in his hands. Fothergill and the other man did likewise, while I sat by the tiller in the stern. The oars bit the water and we were away into the lagoon.

Even with three men on the oars it was hard work. Our southerly heading put the wind dead against us, and every wave seemed to buffet us back. I kept a constant eye on the shore, not so much to guide me as to watch for the mouth of the lagoon. Each time I saw a cove or inlet in the reed banks, my hopes rose that it would give way to open sea; each time the shore swept back in to dash those hopes.

Perhaps because I was so intent on looking forward, I was the last to see our pursuers. We had rowed about a mile and a half down the lagoon – though it was impossible to judge any distance in that unchanging landscape – when I saw Dubois frown and call something back to his colleague. Fothergill, sitting on the forward bench, had noticed it too – something behind us.

I turned around and squinted through the glare. In that sea of infinite horizons, where the world was reduced to water, reeds and sky, the two boats were easy to see, dark against the golden background. I could not tell their size from that distance, but there seemed to be a great number of oars sprouting from their sides, rising and falling in unison like giant wings. Amidships, sheaves of bayonets glittered in the sun.

I looked at Dubois opposite me.

'The general's men?' I asked hoarsely.

He did not reply. All the answer I needed was in those scarred arms, heaving on the oars with new and desperate power. I shifted myself around on the thwart so that I could glance both ahead and astern. Even in that short time, the general's boats seemed to loom larger.

It was a desperate race, and one we were bound to lose. Though their boats were larger and heavier than ours, weighed down by the soldiers they carried, their oarsmen outnumbered us six-fold. We were too few, and too wearied from a day and a half in the canoes. On Dubois's orders I abandoned the tiller and crawled forward to sit beside Fothergill, so that we could double-bank our oars. It made little difference – our pursuers still ate away our advantage. Now I could see the American ensigns fluttering from their sterns; I almost fancied I could see Hook himself crouched in the bow.

'Can we escape into the marshes?' I shouted to Dubois. I could not tell whether he heard me, for my only answer was another heave of his almighty shoulders as he pulled on his oar. Indeed, without any hand on the tiller our course seemed to be turning westwards, further out into the middle of the lagoon.

Rarely can I have suffered such perfect torment. With my back to the bow, unable to turn around, I could not even look forward and hope. All I could see were the boats behind us, steadily closing. My hands were virtually chained to the oar: when salt spray splashed in my eyes I could not wipe it away but had to endure the stinging pain; when blisters rose and burst and rose again in the scars I could not even tend them. The wound in my shoulder throbbed so hard I feared it would reopen in a gush of blood. Always, I had to row.

The man in the bow of our leading pursuer stood. It must be Hook, I was sure of it – I recognized the squat frame, the high-crowned hat he wore against the sun. A rifle was handed to him, and it must have been loaded for he did not even check the priming, but lifted it to his shoulder, peered down the barrel and fired. The flat report echoed across the lagoon, rolling on for an eternity. A small splash, like a gull diving for fish, told where the ball fell: behind us, but not nearly far enough. Hook threw the musket back into the boat, and almost immediately another was passed forward to him.

I could row no further. My hands had started to bleed, my head was almost split in two with pain, and my back felt as though it had tasted a dozen strokes of the cat. I slumped over my oar. The yawl slewed around; Dubois shouted imprecations at me. I did not care. I tipped back my head and stared at the sky in defeat.

Above me, the small scrap of ribbon tied to the masthead streamed out to larboard. I watched it dance in the breeze, wishing I could melt away and float off in the air.

I rubbed my eyes and looked around. All three of my companions were still pulling desperately on their oars, though we were losing ever more ground. A cloud of smoke in our pursuer's bow suggested Hook had fired again, though I had not heard it. I tugged on Fothergill's arm, flinching to see the wild gaze he fixed me with. All the time I had known him he had been a prodigy of serene confidence; now his eyes were sunken in, his cheeks gaunt, his hands as raw as my own. I pointed to the masthead.

'The wind,' I croaked. My salt-crusted lips cracked with the effort. 'The wind has changed.'

Fothergill was no sailor but he took my meaning immediately. He shouted something in French to Lafitte's men, pointing furiously at the sail. The words were barely necessary. Forgetting my bleeding palms, the agony in my shoulders and all else, I had seized hold of the halyard and was hoisting the yard towards the masthead. The sail followed behind it, flapping and snapping in the breeze. Even spurred by hope it was more than I could manage; I almost let it go completely, but Fothergill was at hand and together we hauled it snug against its block. Dubois took the sheet and pulled it taut, then paid it out as his companion reached for the tiller and put us about. The canvas stiffened and bent; the seams strained. For a moment I thought it might split apart, but then it bellied out and the yawl began to gather speed.

I heard shouts behind us, and a ragged volley of musketry. They were close enough that one ball actually struck our hull, biting a deep wedge out of the gunwale, but mercifully none hit the sail. Looking back, I could see our enemies in a great state of confusion. They were trying to step their mast, but with so many soldiers in the way they fouled their lines and had to lower it again. In the bow, wreathed in smoke, Hook was waving his arms and screaming like a madman.

We boated our oars and stowed them in the bilge, then lay on the benches in utter exhaustion while Dubois took over the tiller and steered us south-east. I could hear water hissing under the hull, and our bow slapping against the wavelets. I felt I had spent half a lifetime on river craft – flatboats, keelboats, canoes and bateaux; now I lazed back and let the wind speed me to the sea.

A hand on my arm roused me. Fothergill was peering forward, examining something on the horizon. Reluctantly, and with a slice of pain cutting through my shoulders, I pushed myself up.

The landscape had changed. Ahead of us the lagoon seemed to taper to a narrow channel, blocked by a low island. A spine of thick trees ran along its ridge, while pearly sand fringed the water. As our course took us nearer I saw huts and houses clustered beneath the trees. Some were little more than shacks of matted palm leaves; others had stone walls and shingled roofs. I could see gulls pecking at the fishing nets which were draped out over posts to dry, and a flotilla of small boats drawn up on the beach.

'Is this the coast?' I asked.

Fothergill nodded. 'That is the island of Grand Terre. The Gulf of Mexico is on the far side. But we are not out of danger yet.'

He turned and pointed behind us, and my hopes sank. Hook's two boats still chased us, and though we had increased the interval to about half a mile they had at last managed to raise their masts and bend on the canvas. Their heavy-laden hulls wallowed in the water: they were not gaining, but nor were they falling back.

The green island slid past. I could see more of it now: the slanted trees stretching towards us; the late-afternoon sun reflecting off the waxy leaves like glass. Dark-skinned children played at the water's edge, pointing as we passed. There was great consternation when they saw the soldiers in the boats behind: they raced along the beach to keep pace with us, their numbers swelled ever greater by a growing throng of men and women.

'Baratarians,' said Fothergill. 'Grand Terre is a pirate colony. They will not take kindly to having Wilkinson's army sailing past their island.'

Indeed they did not. As I watched, I saw a group of men run down to the boats and start dragging them into the lagoon. When the men were waist-deep in the water they heaved themselves over the sides with practised ease, and in seconds had their oars sweeping through the waves. In the bow of each boat was mounted a small swivel cannon.

At first Hook's men tried to ignore the threat, but though the Baratarians lacked sails they were fearsome oarsmen and rapidly closed the distance. I could see their gunners priming the cannon, and the flash of steel as men drew cutlasses. Belatedly, Hook recognized the threat. His sails came down as he tried to clear space for his soldiers to fire, so quick that he must have cut the halyards, but that only compounded his disadvantage. Some of his men were buried under the sheets of canvas, while others became tangled in the ropes. Without sail, and with the oars trapped where they had been stowed, the boats lost steerage; they bobbed on the water almost as if sitting at anchor, while turmoil engulfed their crews.

The Baratarian flotilla closed around them. I heard shouts exchanged, then shots – the crack of muskets and the louder blast of cannon – and screams. The Baratarians rowed in, and very quickly all was lost in a shroud of white smoke, rising off the water like steam. Even so, I could not keep from staring back until we passed a sandy promontory and the cloud vanished. Then I looked around.

We had come into a crooked bay, beyond which I could see the foam of surf and hear the crashing of breakers. The beach was deserted, and no houses squatted in the shade of the trees, but it was not empty. Riding at anchor a few hundred yards away, the white band along her gunwale turned gold by the setting sun, lay a solitary schooner. Everything about her was immaculate, from her gleaming topmasts down the stiff rigging to the black paint at her waterline, yet I could not see a single man aboard.

'Whose is this?' I murmured.

The wind had dropped and the evening air was still. None of the others spoke, or questioned what we were about; they seemed to understand it perfectly. Furling the sail, we fetched out the oars and rowed the last quarter-mile to the ship, without urgency this time. The only sound was the creak of the oars in their pins, and the gentle ripple as the blades teased through the water.

I had my back to the schooner, so did not see its approach. Far sooner than I expected, Dubois put the tiller over and nestled the yawl up against the schooner's hull. I looked up, but still no-one appeared to challenge us. Fothergill gestured at me to climb the ladder.

Squeezing every last ounce of strength from my limbs, I hauled myself inboard. Immediately, I saw that the ship was not deserted. Her crew, most of them in striped shirts and short trousers, had been on deck all the time, sitting out of sight in the lee of the gunwales. One of them scrambled to his feet as I arrived. He was not dressed as a sailor, nor as an officer either, but in a plum-red coat and sparkling black shoes. With an awkward smile he offered me his hand; then, seeing the raw state of my own hands, he reached his arms around me and clasped me to him in a firm embrace.

'Jerrold,' he said. 'Thank God you are here.'

It was Nevell.

31

THE WIND ROSE AS THE SUN SET; AT LAST LIGHT, THE SCHOONER
weighed anchor and slipped out into the Gulf of Mexico. The two
boatmen who had brought us safe through swamp and bayou accompanied us to the mouth of the lagoon; then, when they had piloted
the ship past the last hazards of the channel, they clambered down
into the yawl and sailed back to the island. Nevell had invited them
to stay and take up honest service in the navy, but they wisely preferred Lafitte's employ, though they did accept the bag of golden
guineas and the large cask of rum he pressed on them.

I saw none of it. The moment Nevell freed me from his embrace
I had collapsed to the deck and been taken below to the stern cabin.
There, aided by a draught from the surgeon, I slept, all through the
night as we beat our way south, and well into the morning. When I
woke, I found my boots clean, a new shirt and breeches laid out for
me, and a cold breakfast awaiting me on the table. Only when I had
devoured it, and twice summoned the steward to replenish my
coffee, did I venture out into the mid-morning sun.

We were alone on the ocean. An archipelago of vast white clouds
floated in the blue sky above, and a modest swell surged around our
hull. The ship was close-hauled against the wind, which had backed
around to the south, and making good speed. Nevell was deep in

conversation with the master at the starboard rail, but he broke off as soon as he saw me and hurried across.

'You are awake at last. For a time we feared that your exertions might have overwhelmed you.'

'You would have had only yourself to blame.' I spoke testily, for I did not yet feel well enough recovered to forgive Nevell the hardships he had inflicted on me. 'I have come rather further than Pittsburgh since you gave me that letter to deliver.'

The smile vanished from Nevell's eyes and he looked downcast. I relented a little. 'Even so, it is good to see you. Is it worth my asking how you came here?'

Nevell laughed. 'Not particularly. Suffice to say that a great many pieces of evidence suggested that the conspiracy might come to fruition in New Orleans, and I decided to witness it for myself. Then I received a message from Fothergill that you were in the city, that your enemies had captured you, and that he would attempt to bring you out through the swamps. Needless to say, I am delighted to find he succeeded.'

There at least I was in heartfelt agreement. 'But where now?' I asked. 'And what is this vessel you have conjured out of the Orleans marshes? Is it a navy ship?'

A devious smile flashed across Nevell's face, a look that intimated he was saying less than he might, and wished you to know it. 'Not precisely. We did not feel that the navy were entirely . . . *reliable* in this matter. I have the ship under contract. Her crew are not navy men, but you will find them useful enough in battle.'

I looked down the length of the deck and almost laughed. Nevell's schooner might be suited to lurking in swampy coves and navigating shallow waters, but she was no more built for battle than the yawl. Though pierced for ten guns she carried only four twelve-pound carronades. With a deck measuring little more than fifty feet, a single hostile broadside would reduce her to her waterline before she had fired a shot.

'As to where we are going,' Nevell was saying, 'you will be relieved to hear it is London. I think our business in the New World is concluded – thanks in no small part to your own efforts, naturally. Whether Burr is captured or no his plans are ruined, and with your escape we have removed all evidence implicating Britain. But you must tell me everything that has happened.'

We went below, and for the better part of two hours I recounted all I had done since I sailed out of Falmouth on the *Adventure*. Nevell sat at the table and scrawled details in a notebook, halting me only to sand the pages or to press me on some detail. He showed particular interest in Lyell, and also in the letter I had carried.

'It was from within the Admiralty itself, you say. Did it name any of the conspirators?'

'It was vague on that point,' I lied. 'Certainly they must have been men of substantial influence.' It was not that I wished to withhold the information from Nevell – though God knew he had done it to me often enough – nor that I had any sentimental loyalty to my family, but there were my own interests to consider. If I was to use the letter, still safely sewn in my coat, to gain concessions from my uncle, it would not do to have him stripped of his rank and pleading for his life in the Old Bailey.

'And what of the naval aid the letter promised? Did you ever see any sign of it?'

There I could be more honest. 'None whatsoever. In truth, I believe it must have been either a lie to encourage Burr, or a pledge they hastily repented.' Every other ally had failed to provide Burr his army; why should the Admiralty have proved any different?

I continued to recount the story from Blennerhassett Island – the flight, the absurd trial in Washington, and Wilkinson's treachery in New Orleans. The events were raw in my memory, and several times I had to reach for the bottle to steady my nerve. When I had finished, I was gratified to see Nevell watching me with frank admiration.

'An extraordinary tale,' he murmured. 'Tragedy and farce, treason and honour all knotted together. One almost feels sorry for Mr Burr.'

'I do not,' I said harshly. 'He might easily have started a war, but he would never have won it. If we were in London I would have him consigned to Bedlam. He was a fantasist.'

'Nonetheless, it was as well you escaped him – and more urgent than you know. While you were away, Buonaparte issued a decree from Berlin. Having failed to subdue us with his army, he now means to strangle our finance. The entire continent has been closed to our trade. Had the Americans turned against us, all would have been lost.'

'And what of South America?' I asked, suddenly reminded of it. 'Burr's operations in Mexico were only half of Lyell's plan. The other half, as I understood it, was that a co-opted army would invade Spain's southern empire and take it for themselves. I heard they had already captured Buenos Aires some months ago.'

Nevell nodded. 'They enjoyed some success there for a time, but that has now soured. The Spanish have retaken Buenos Aires and inflicted a heavy defeat on General Beresford, Lyell's ally. They have gambled recklessly with men's lives and with the fate of nations, and lost both wagers. It is thanks to you that the damage is not greater.'

We pondered this a moment, I sipping my wine and Nevell reading back through his notes. A knock at the door interrupted the silence.

'Come in,' said Nevell, snapping his book shut. A small trail of sand trickled onto the floor.

The master peered in. 'Begging your pardon, Mr Nevell, but I've just taken the noon sightings and I'll be needing to write them in the log.'

'Of course.'

The master crossed to a shelf in the bulkhead and reached down a furled map, a pair of dividers and a weatherbeaten brown book. Nevell and I obliged him by holding down the edges of the chart while he plotted our position, then copied it into the logbook. I was gratified to see we were well away from the American mainland, though to our north the three-mouthed neck of the Mississippi estuary still stretched down into the gulf, as if even now it hoped to suck me back in.

'What is our position?' asked Nevell.

The master peered in his book. 'Eighty-nine degrees and thirty-eight minutes west longitude by twenty-eight degrees north latitude, sir.'

Nevell murmured an acknowledgement and began some subsidiary question as to the time it would take us to reach Florida, but I did not hear him. Something in the master's matter-of-fact reading had tugged an unpleasant cord in my memory. *Twenty-eight degrees north latitude.* That was where—

A cry from on deck echoed down the companionway and through the open door.

'Sail in sight!'

32

NEVELL, THE MASTER AND I STOOD BY THE TAFFRAIL, OUR SPY-
glasses trained on the ship to our south. She was a frigate, of thirty-
six guns, and near enough that she already filled the telescope's
compass.

'Can we run?' Nevell asked.

The master shook his head. 'Doubtful, sir, not while she's got the
weather gage. If we ran upwind we'd not get past her; downwind,
and we'd find ourselves on a lee shore.'

'She's run up her colours,' called one of the seamen.

Looking through my glass, I saw a red ensign flapping from her
stern. She was evidently sailing under Admiralty orders; I could
guess the man who had written them.

'Hoist the Union flag,' said the master.

The frigate's response was swift. 'She's signalling us to heave to.'

The master and I both looked at Nevell, but the sea was not his
element and he could offer no more than a shrug.

'You say we cannot run.'

The muted roar of a distant cannon was like a drumbeat under-
scoring his word. The frigate had fired her bow-chaser. It was only a
warning, but the threat was unmistakable.

'I suppose we had better heave to and wait,' said Nevell at last. 'If she is an English ship, we should have nothing to fear. She probably thinks we are a merchantman and merely wants to inspect us for deserters.'

I cleared my throat. 'Actually . . ' Briefly, I explained my fearful suspicion.

'But you said you thought these ships a fantasy, as ephemeral as the rest of Burr's army.' Nevell frowned. 'Can they actually have been real?'

For any man who had accompanied Burr on his deluded crusade down the Mississippi, who had seen the sad figment of his army, it was hard to credit. Yet in another way it was all too easy to believe. It would, after all, be entirely consistent with my own dismal luck.

'Though even if it is one of Burr's ships, there is no cause to fret,' said Nevell hopefully. 'They cannot know your involvement in the scheme, and they certainly cannot expect to find you here.'

Whether they did or not, we would have little say in the matter. We furled our sails and waited for the frigate to come.

When she was about four hundred yards off our beam, she backed her sails and lowered her pinnace. We stood on the schooner's deck and watched her crew row across. I had wanted to go below and hide, but Nevell discouraged it. 'The best hiding place is always in plain view. If they searched the ship and found you lurking in the bilge they would certainly take you for a deserter.'

The pinnace had almost reached us. Looking down, I was astonished to see a pair of stiff golden epaulettes on the shoulders of the man sitting in the sternsheets. Why would the frigate's captain come to visit us in person? In addition to the sailors on the oars, I noticed four marines perched in the bow. It seemed the captain did not trust our hospitality.

The pinnace rapped against our hull. All the schooner's crew were on deck, gathered in a knot by the foremast. They watched in silence as a pair of gold-cuffed sleeves reached over the gunwale, then as the white cockade of a cocked hat rose into view, and finally as the captain clambered over the side. He looked to be somewhere

324

in his forties, with a rigidly old-fashioned bearing and a grey, sour face that betold ill health. Despite that, I noted a brusque vigilance in his eyes which I guessed would miss little. As his marines mounted the ladder, he brushed the dust off his lapels and turned to the master.

'Captain Chatfield of His Majesty's frigate *Duke of Gloucester*,' he announced.

'Ezekiel Strong, master of the *Gannet*.'

'Where from?'

'We hail from Bristol, sir, but sailed from New Orleans two days ago.'

'Your cargo?'

His words were stony, but the master retained his humour. 'Molasses, sir.'

Captain Chatfield surveyed the schooner's deck, his eyes flitting over every line and belaying pin. The crew stared back.

'As you will know, our navy is sorely depleted by traitors and deserters who enlist aboard American merchantmen,' he said at last. 'Our duty is to apprehend them and restore them to their rightful station, or to see them punished. You will oblige me by mustering your men, and any supernumeraries or passengers, with whatever passports or papers they possess. I will also require your log and muster books.'

Though he issued the orders sharply enough, I fancied I heard a bored indifference in his tone. Perhaps he had boarded too many vessels of late and was tired of it, although if that were the case he could easily have sent a subordinate. To my thinking it was more as if he already knew what he would find, that the search was merely a formality. His grey eyes scanned the deck, and I became convinced they fixed on me more than any other.

The master emerged from the cabin with a pair of books in his arm. He handed them to Captain Chatfield, then took his place among the men by the foremast. Chatfield turned a few pages of the log without interest, then opened the muster book. He tapped the page with a bony finger and stared at the assembled crew.

'I will now read the muster,' he said crisply. 'When you hear your name you will kindly step forward and present your papers to the corporal. If they are found to be in order you will then stand by the mainmast.'

The marine corporal took up his position beside the main hatch, while his three subordinates stood by the starboard rail, their muskets in their hands. The master and his mate, who were anyway exempt from impressment, waited at the mainmast.

It did not last long, for there were only eighteen men in the crew. As Chatfield called each name the man in question handed his papers to the corporal, who scrutinized them carefully before waving him aft. Once or twice he questioned the men as to their home towns, or the ships they had served on, but their responses satisfied him. Soon Nevell, Fothergill and I were the only men left in the bow.

Chatfield nodded towards us. 'Who are these?'

'Passengers,' said Strong.

'Is there a manifest?'

Strong produced it, and Chatfield stared at it for some moments. Did I see a flicker of recognition cross his face? I could not be sure, but I felt a familiar sense of inevitable doom crawling through my guts.

He called Fothergill forward and directed him to the knot of men by the mainmast. Now only Nevell and I remained under his gaze.

'Which of you is Nevell?'

Nevell stepped forward to give his papers to the corporal, but Chatfield intervened and took them for himself.

'You are in the employ of the Post Office?'

'I have that honour.'

'What was your business in New Orleans?'

'I was delivering a letter,' said Nevell, the merest hint of insolence tinting his voice.

Chatfield grunted. 'And you,' he said, turning towards me, 'I take it you are Martin Jerrold.' There was a horrible familiarity in the way he said my name.

'I am.'

'Your passports?'

'I have none,' I whispered. 'They were in my trunk. It was stolen from me in New Orleans.'

'That is inconvenient.'

'On the contrary, it is of no consequence whatsoever.' Nevell moved forward from the mainmast. 'I can vouch for Mr Jerrold.'

Chatfield did not seem to have heard him. 'In the absence of your papers, I must assume that you are a fugitive from His Majesty's navy. You will accompany me to my ship, Mr Jerrold, and remain there until I bring you before a court martial.' He looked aft to the master. 'As for you, Mr Strong, I have found a great many irregularities with your vessel. You claim that you sailed out of New Orleans two days ago, yet your logbook makes no mention of it. You harbour deserters. You may well have carried on trade with enemy nations in violation of the Rule of 1756. I am seizing your ship. I will send one of my officers and a prize crew to take command and sail her to Jamaica.'

'But that is monstrous,' protested Strong. 'You have no evidence, sir, that we—'

'If you wish to protest it you may do so in the Admiralty Courts.' Chatfield permitted himself a thin smile. 'In London.'

Two of his marines took me by my arms and dragged me to the side. Sick with fear and futile rage I glanced back at Nevell, imploring him for help. His fingers were straying towards his coat pocket, but his eyes were on the *Duke of Gloucester* and the irresistible broadside she had trained on us.

It was the first time I had seen him defeated, and the sight crushed what little hope remained in my soul.

Captain Chatfield said nothing as the pinnace rowed the short distance between the ships, but stared at his command with a curious discontent. Keeping well clear of the bayonet which the marine corporal had angled towards my chest, I followed his gaze. A great deal of activity was happening aboard the *Duke of Gloucester.*

topmen swarming up the rigging, sailors scurrying around the guns, and officers on the quarterdeck peering north through telescopes. They were not watching the schooner; instead, it seemed they looked to the opposite horizon, though I could not tell what they saw. Only two people on the frigate's deck seemed to pay us any heed: a stout, dark-suited man and a slender white figure at his side. Before I could examine them closer, we came into the lee of the hull and they vanished from my sight.

Chatfield was first up the side; I followed, painfully conscious of the bayonet that awaited me if I slipped and fell back. The frigate heeled over in the rising swell, and the slapping waves threw spray up on the ladder, but I kept my grip and hauled myself onto the deck. Chatfield had his back to me, already busy in urgent consultation with his subordinates, but the two figures whom I had seen from the boat were still there, waiting. The man in black leered at me in triumph, while the woman at his side met my gaze with pitiless dispassion. Truly it seemed that there was no distance I could travel, no path so circuitous, but that I would eventually end up face to face again with Lyell.

Chatfield paused his conversation as he noticed my arrival. 'Is this the man you sought?'

Lyell bared his teeth. 'Indeed it is, Captain. Well done. He escaped me in New Orleans, but I doubt he will find it so easy to go leaping out of windows this time. Had he lived to reach London he could have been the ruin of us all.'

'So you have told me,' said Chatfield curtly. There seemed little natural sympathy between my two captors, though I doubted I would gain anything by it.

'He has already proved trouble enough. It would be best if we dropped him over the side immediately.'

Chatfield stiffened. 'That would not do at all, sir. We are not pirates, and whatever his faults Mr Jerrold is a gentleman.'

'Would a duel on the main deck suit your honour better?' sneered Lyell.

Chatfield did not welcome the sarcasm. 'Have a care, Mr Lyell. I do not know what passes for manners among London merchants, but aboard my ship you will be pleased to render me the courtesy I am due. Now, if you will permit me, there are rather graver matters to consider. The lookouts have reported a sail to the north.'

'Is it not one of your own?' Lyell remained uncowed by Chatfield's outburst. 'I thought there were to be two ships on this station.'

'The *Cambrian* frigate sailed for Jamaica two weeks ago. I am not aware of any other British ships in the vicinity.'

Hardly had Chatfield spoken than a sailor came sliding down the backstays, dropping onto the deck just in front of us and staring at the group of officers and civilians gathered around him. Uncertainly, he tapped a tarry fist to his brow.

'Yes?' snapped Chatfield.

'Beggin' your pardon, sir, but we've got the enemy in sight.'

'Enemy?'

'Spanish, sir. Fifth rate, forty-four guns.'

'God damn them.' Chatfield strode to the rail and stared out, then turned back abruptly. 'Set the tops'ls, then beat to quarters. Signal the schooner to keep away from the battle, but to maintain her station until it is decided.' His gaze swept over the ship and settled on me. 'As for Mr Jerrold, take him to the orlop and lock him in the store room. We will decide his fate after the battle – if we survive it.'

The marines took my arms and led me below.

33

ANOTHER DARK HOLE IN THE DEPTHS OF ANOTHER SHIP, WITH another battle about to be joined: it was like Trafalgar, only worse. For one thing, I had had some hope of surviving Trafalgar; here, win or lose, I would die. Even more usefully, during Trafalgar I had been blind drunk. What I would not have given for a glass or a bottle at that moment. I fumbled around the dark hutch, wondering if by some divine grace they might have locked me in the purser's stores, but there was not even the sniff of brandy. With that last hope denied, I lay down on the floor and rested my head on my knees.

Had I had the daring of a Nevell, perhaps I would have prised a splinter from the floor and used it as a picklock; or found a piece of hardtack and gnawed it into a chisel to cut through the hull. Instead, all I possessed was the cowardice of a Jerrold – in which light, surprisingly, my situation seemed rather less dismal. What would escape have achieved? I could hardly skulk around the ship unseen, and there was certainly no way of leaving it. If I dressed myself in slops and pretended to be one of the crew, I would likely put myself in the way of Spanish iron. Far better to cower on the orlop, well out of harm, and survive the battle intact; only once that was assured would it repay me to worry about Lyell's threat. With luck, the Spanish might even despatch him for me.

It has ever been a fact of my life that no sooner do I resign myself to some present catastrophe then the predicament changes – generally for the worse. Sitting there in safety, however illusory, I could almost forget the dangers ranged against me. But the sound of a key turning in the door banished all respite, and immediately I was drawn back to the horrible, hopeless present. Had Lyell come to put a bullet in my skull while the ship was distracted?

A small figure in a large midshipman's hat stepped through the door. 'Mr Jerrold, sir?' The voice was high and too obviously trying to master its own fears. 'Captain Chatfield...' He swallowed. 'Captain Chatfield requests you join him on deck, sir.'

I found Chatfield still on the quarterdeck, though he now had his sword buckled on and a telescope in his hand. Lyell was nowhere to be seen. The *Duke of Gloucester* was beating to windward under tops'ls; while I had been below, sand had been scattered over her planking, rolled hammocks stuffed into her breastworks, and netting hung above the decks. Gun crews crouched by their guns with swabs and rammers in hand, while the sail trimmers worked the sheets. Off the larboard quarter, I could see the billowing sails of the Spanish frigate now barely a league distant. Through my aching terror, I felt a strange nudge of nostalgia. I had spent the past year sailing on cutters, brigs, packets and schooners; now at last I was back on a proper man-of-war with long guns and stout bulwarks. It was small comfort.

Chatfield excused himself from the officers and midshipmen around him and ushered me to the side. He showed no apprehension at the prospect of battle, only dogged purpose, but I sensed a tinge of embarrassment in his drawn face as he spoke.

'I am sorry I was forced to lock you below earlier. It seemed the most convenient course under the circumstances.'

An apology was the last thing I had expected of him. I gaped in confusion.

'There is much about this business which I do not understand,' he continued. 'And this is no time to question it. However, it sits ill with me to imprison a fellow officer when battle threatens, particularly at the urging of a fellow like Mr Lyell. I do not trust him. He is not a gentleman.'

'He is extremely wealthy,' I murmured. In some circles, in our modern age, that would have excused any magnitude of faults, but I guessed a man like Chatfield might think otherwise. Indeed, it only seemed to indispose him further to Lyell.

'Mr Lyell came aboard my ship yesterday afternoon and has made a damned nuisance of himself ever since. He professes to support the plot against Spain yet has done precious little to aid it, and now that we face a Spanish ship in battle he has absented himself to the lower deck.' He squinted at me, uncertain how much he could say. 'I volunteered for this business because I wished to strike at Spain, not so that a confederacy of bankers and merchants could profit by it. All I have done is linger in these waters this past month awaiting a message that did not come.'

He fixed his grey eyes on mine. 'Did you deliberately work to thwart our scheme, as Mr Lyell alleges?'

'Nothing I did contributed to its failure in any way,' I said honestly.

'You give me your word of honour?'

'Of course.'

I would not have valued my word of honour a farthing, but it sufficed for Chatfield. 'I have heard that you were at Trafalgar.' He glanced over at the Spanish frigate steering ever closer. 'I would value your experience on the quarterdeck this afternoon.'

No doubt he meant well, but the prospect appalled me. I could almost have fallen to my knees and implored him to confine me on the orlop again. 'There is really no need,' I murmured.

'As to the uniform, your own blue coat will suffice, and one of my lieutenants will lend you a hat. I can provide a brace of pistols and a hanger, if you require them.'

'Thank you.'

'I fear you may have need of them. There will be hot work to do before the day is out.'

*

A quarter of an hour later I stood by the bulwark in a borrowed hat, fingering the gold wire on the hilt of Chatfield's sword. I had not served in a frigate action before, and had never troubled to read the breathless accounts in adoring newspapers. Perhaps I would have gleaned some wisdom. For the moment the two ships manoeuvred for advantage like prize-fighters circling in the ring, but it would come to blows soon enough. Chatfield was trying to sail upwind of the Spaniard, though it was a dangerous game: each time we came about he had to choose between showing the enemy our stern or risking being caught in irons. The question became more vital as every change of tack took us nearer the enemy.

A tongue of flame lashed out from the Spaniard's side, and a second later I heard the cannon's low report rumble across the water. A fountain of water rose where the ball had dropped a few score yards distant.

'Hold your fire!' called Chatfield. 'Wait until we close and throw no shot away.'

I put my telescope to my eye, preferring to view the world through its narrow confines. We were almost level with our enemy now, and I could see her bow coming round towards us. 'She's bearing off.'

Chatfield turned to the first lieutenant. 'Bring the ship about, if you please, and lay her as close to the wind as you can. We will try to cross her stern and rake her.'

Behind me I heard the lieutenant giving the orders, preparing to tack. I kept my gaze on the Spaniard. Her mizzen gaff and mainsail were brailed up to the yards, while all her hands were working to brace the foresails around. 'She's wearing ship.'

'Fore-sheet, fore top bowline and jib sheets let go!' shouted the lieutenant.

The helm went down and the *Gloucester* began to turn towards the wind. Her masts and spars creaked with the effort, like rusted hinges pushed against their will.

'Off tacks and sheets!'

'She's passed us to leeward,' I said. 'We've taken the weather gage.' A half-hearted cheer rose from the maindeck.

'Let go and haul!'

As the afterguard ran past to trim the mizzen topsails, I found my sight of the enemy obscured. I put down the telescope and stepped away from the rail. A midshipman had come running aft from the bow and skidded to a halt before the captain. His face was flushed red, though whether by fear, excitement or exertion I could not tell.

'Beg your pardon, sir, but Mr Timmins got sight of her stern as we came round. She's the *Hernando*, sir.'

Chatfield nodded. 'Very good. Return to your station.'

Never one to lose sight of my enemy if I could help it, I threaded my way through the knot of men at the side and looked out. I put my glass to my eye, then lowered it in surprise. The *Hernando* was not where I expected her to be off our larboard beam. I turned my gaze to the left, peering through the mizzen shrouds. Further and further round . . .

'Captain Chatfield!'

Disrespecting all the conventions of rank, I almost seized him by the shoulder. He had seen it too – indeed the whole ship now seemed to be pointing at her. The Spaniard had followed us right through the wind and now lay on the same tack fine on the larboard quarter, only three hundred yards away.

Chatfield's jaw tightened. He looked to the sailing master. 'What do you say? Can we wear ship again and rake her bow?'

The master shook his head. 'Too close, sir. As like as not she'd ram us.'

'Very well.' Chatfield raised his voice. 'Heave to, then get to your guns.'

All our manoeuvring had been to no advantage. Glancing back, I saw that the Spanish captain had acknowledged Chatfield's challenge. He was backing his own sails, and sending his men to the guns. There would be no subtlety or stratagems in our encounter. Instead, in the best tradition of the navy, we would pound each other broadside to broadside.

The *Gloucester* slowed until it seemed only the current moved us.

With her steerage way gone, the bow began to drift towards the wind. The *Hernando* was overhauling us, though losing momentum, and as she came into our lee her progress halted. The two ships faced each other little more than a hundred yards apart, like duellists drawing breath and waiting for the handkerchief to drop.

Chatfield drew his sword and raised it in the air. 'Run out the guns!'

Men hauled on the tackles. Ports squeaked, and eighteen cannon rumbled to the gunwale. Across the water the *Hernando* did the same. It was like looking in a mirror: we were so close that I could see every one of the officers clustered near her wheel, the marines in her tops and even the glow of the slow matches on her maindeck.

'Fire!'

Forty guns – eighteen of ours, twenty-two of theirs – exploded almost as one. For a split second I saw the line of flames erupt from the *Hernando*'s hull like a giant scar opening along her side. Then her broadside struck. Her iron screamed above our heads and ripped into the cordage; several lines broke loose and snaked down through the smoke. Some of the shot had gone lower: I could see at least one man clutching the shoulder where his arm had been, and one of the stern lanterns had been cut clean away. Beside the gunwale the black-faced crews worked feverishly with swabs and irons to ready their guns. A hundred yards away our enemy's deck had disappeared in a teeming cloud of white smoke, and all I could see were her masts rising from the fog like gibbets.

'Fire!'

Though the terror of battle was a familiar companion, I had forgotten the sheer overwhelming noise that accompanied it: the thundering discharge of the guns, the whip-crack of the breeching ropes and the thud of the recoil; the shouts of the officers and the screams of the men; the crack of musketry from the tops and the grate of cannonballs which had fallen loose and rolled across the deck. Even the smoke itself seemed to roar like a torrent in my ears.

Another broadside bellowed out from the *Hernando*. The flames were little more than smudges of orange behind the fog, but the impact was sharp as ever. Spars shattered, blocks and tackles fell on the netting above, and men died. Enemy musket balls ricocheted off the deck – I could have sworn I heard one striking the ship's bell.

'That's the way, Mr Jerrold. Show them no fear.'

I turned and saw Chatfield striding across the deck. Apart from the sword in his hand and the graze above his eye, he might have been exercising his dog, so calm did he appear. I stared at him, wondering at his compliment, until I realized that in my awestruck shock I had stayed rooted to my spot.

'That's the way you did it at Trafalgar, I suppose. And Nelson.' He paused beside one of the gun crews. 'Do you hear that? You're firing twice as often as those shiftless Diegos. A few more broadsides and you'll have her timbers for—'

He broke off, spun around and fell to the deck. Blood bubbled from the small hole just below his collarbone. For a moment, our small corner of the quarterdeck was an island of silence amid the cacophony as the gun crew, the attendant midshipmen and I all gaped at his body.

I looked to one of the midshipmen. 'Help me take his arms.' We knelt beside Chatfield and raised him from his waist. 'No, wait. Hold him there.' The midshipman held Chatfield upright, pressing a handkerchief to his wound, while I pulled away his uniform coat and hat. Taking them in my arms, I ran forward to the capstan and draped the coat over it, putting the hat on top of the drum. As I returned to Chatfield's body I noticed the midshipman gazing on me with suspicion. 'That will give the Spanish sharpshooters something to aim at,' I explained.

'Is it honourable, sir?' the boy asked doubtfully.

'Nelson himself did it,' I lied.

We took Chatfield to the lower deck. He still breathed, though barely, and the surgeon grimaced at the sight of him. Everything in the room was doused in blood – the surgeon's arms and face, his apron, the floor and even the ceiling timbers – all mingled with piteous cries of despair. I might otherwise have lingered to stay out of the battle, but even the quarterdeck seemed a more appealing hell than that shambles. As I left, I saw the surgeon put down his saw and take a bloodied pair of forceps from his assistant.

Just as I came to the top of the ladder on the gundeck, the cannon fired again. The bellow rang in my ears, and I squeezed my head between my hands to try and damp it out. Deafened, I looked around. I was in the waist of the ship, behind solid walls but with the sky open above me, though I could not see it for all the smoke and tangled cordage. I moved along the deck so that I stood under the overhang of the quarterdeck. At last I felt some small crumb of safety. I might even make myself useful, or at least hide my cowardice, for I could see no officer commanding the guns. Drawing my sword, I stepped towards the nearest cannon, waited until the crew had sponged, reloaded and run out, then shouted, 'Point your gun!'

The gun captain looked at me as though I were mad. His shirtless back shone black with sweat and grime, and he had a red cloth tied around his ears; without speaking, he gestured with his powder horn towards the gunport. Crouching down and squinting through, I saw his reason. Between the smoke from her own guns, and the smoke from ours being blown down on her, the *Hernando* had entirely disappeared in a white haze. We might even have disabled her: it had been some moments since I heard her broadside.

'Fire!' I ordered, undaunted.

The gunner took hold of his lanyard and stepped aside; the rest of his men turned their backs and covered their ears. And then, just as he was about to fire, a new, alien sound tolled through the din. It was a hollow echo, like a ladle knocking against a bowl, only far deeper. The cannon rocked on its trucks.

I leaned down and peered out through the gunport again. The white fog had vanished, but in its place a black wall had appeared, filling the horizon entirely. Our cannon must have struck it, for as I watched I saw the muzzle pressed back with such force that the gun rolled inboard.

An instant before we collided I recognized the black wall for what it was: the hull of the *Hernando*. A profound shiver rippled through the *Gloucester*'s timbers, from her keel to her topmast, as the ships collided. The impact threw me gasping to the floor, and I heard frantic shouts from the deck above.

'*Boarders*! *All hands to repel boarders*!'

We had no time to prepare ourselves; they were on us in an instant. Those of us in the waist of the ship were trapped like cocks in a pit: men poured over the *Hernando*'s side onto the gangways above, then leaped down to the attack. Some were thrown back by the marines' musket-fire, but many more gained the deck. One foolhardy soul swung across on a rope which dangled from the main yard; he fell from the sky but landed badly, and lay on the planking screaming until one of the gun crews stove his head in with a worm-iron.

Men were all around me; I did not know where to look. I saw one Spanish seaman with an enormous boarding axe moving towards me, and in an instant I had discharged one of Chatfield's pistols at him. In the tumult and the choking smoke I did not see if I had hit him. The crew around me fought ferociously with whatever tools were at hand. One man drove a marlinspike into his opponent's chest; another whirled a rope-rammer above his head like a mace, cracking any forehead which came within his compass. Some even picked up weapons from the Spanish dead and turned their enemies' weapons against them.

Even so, we were outnumbered and outgunned. Gradually, we were pushed back towards the side. I stepped in some blood and slipped; looking down, I saw one of the *Duke of Gloucester*'s marines lying dead by my foot, still clutching his musket. I bent down and tugged it free – just in time, for as I did a Spaniard came looming out of the surrounding fray. I pointed the musket at him and pulled the trigger, though of course it was not loaded; I lunged with the bayonet; he sidestepped the thrust and seized hold of the barrel, pulling it and me towards him. For a moment I could not even think to let go, but clung on like a fish on a hook. Then I released my grip. The Spaniard lost his balance, and as he stumbled back another bayonet plunged into his chest. A marine had come up beside me, though he barely seemed to notice me. With a snarl, he pulled the bayonet free and plunged forward.

A shout from the quarterdeck cut through the battle. '*She's struck her colours!*'

I looked up in despair. Had the *Duke of Gloucester* struck? Down in the waist we still opposed the Spanish, but perhaps they had taken the quarterdeck and cut down our ensign. I looked to the mizzen. The broadsides were long since finished, and the battle was too close for muskets and pistols to be reloaded, so the pall of smoke had begun to clear. To my surprise, the shout seemed to have been a lie: the red ensign still flew proudly above the ship, and the fierce struggle on the quarterdeck showed no hint of defeat. Had I misheard? Or . . .

I turned my gaze to the *Hernando*. Her masts and rigging were far more intact than our own, for our guns had aimed lower than hers, but I had a clear view of her stern. Her flag was gone, and with most of her crew aboard the *Gloucester* her decks were almost deserted.

I did not pause to consider that curiosity. '*She's struck!*' I shouted. '*The Spaniard's struck her colours!*'

The sight sparked new hope among the *Gloucester*'s crew. Men who moments earlier had been on the brink of surrender now lifted their weapons and redoubled their onslaught. The Spaniards, by contrast, were failing, staring back at their ship in incomprehension. Some threw down their weapons and capitulated immediately; others fought on but without conviction. On the gangway above, I could see our enemies clambering over the bulwarks and retreating to their own ship, our own seamen and marines pursuing them.

Not all the Spaniards had fled though, and not all would admit defeat. Distracted by our changing fortunes I almost failed to see a Spanish officer coming at me. He had lost his hat, and bled from a wound in his arm, yet his eyes were wild with bitter hate: perhaps, I thought, in a moment of inconsequence, he had expected to command the *Duke of Gloucester* as a prize. He drove towards me; I had just time enough to draw my second, unused pistol and fire it at him. In my panic I pulled the trigger too soon and the ball went wide. He slashed at me with his sword, missed, and as his arm went past me I hurled myself into him, knocking him backwards. It gave me space to draw Chatfield's hanger, then he was on me again, and I was frantically parrying his swingeing attacks. There was no refuge, for the crowded battle around us seemed to have moved on and we were in open space. I had no thought of attack: Chatfield's unfamiliar blade was heavy in my exhausted arms, and it was all I could manage to lift it to fend off my opponent. I gave ground easily, blocking and retreating, edging towards the bow and wondering when someone would recognize my plight and rescue me. If they could only have tripped him with a mop-handle it would have sufficed.

The Spanish officer came at me again, and this time my clumsy defence was too weak. The blade came past my guard and hummed before my eyes, so close it almost took off my nose. With a squeak of fear, sparking contempt in my adversary's eyes, I leaped back. As my foot touched the deck it slithered in blood; I stumbled backwards and flung out my arms for balance. It was tantamount to suicide: my blade slipped from my hand, and my wide-open arms almost seemed to embrace the killing blow as the Spaniard lunged for my chest.

He did not strike. Already reeling, I felt my heel knock against some obstruction at my feet and pitch me backwards. Yet I did not land on the deck as I had expected. In a floundering jumble of limbs and rungs and blows and darkness, I fell through the hatchway and crashed to the bottom of the ladder. I lay there a moment, bruised and winded, wondering if I could possibly have survived such a fall without breaking my neck. Miraculously, I seemed undamaged.

The Spanish officer stood on the deck above me framed by the open hatch. His sword was still in his hand, and he seemed minded to leap down and finish me; then some other danger must have threatened, for his head snapped around and he vanished from my sight. I was left lying in a heap at the foot of the ladder, battered and defenceless but alive.

'Jerrold?'

I turned. Through the ache in my skull where I had knocked it on the ladder, and the bleariness in my senses, I heard something familiar in the voice which had spoken my name. I knew the sneer, the haughty superiority and the chill absence of any emotion, all present even in the two meagre syllables of my name.

Whether I recognized the voice, or the overweening figure standing in the shadows of the lower deck, or even the blue sheen of the pistol's barrel, I do not know; thankfully, I had just wit and strength enough to roll away from the ladder as the pistol exploded towards me. By the flash of its muzzle I saw Lyell crouching near the bow, a cruel leer of triumph on his face, and the pale figure of his daughter a little to my left. The leer soured as the ball buried itself in the ladder; then he was lost to sight again. Through the darkness and the smoke I heard the clang of steel as he fumbled with the pistol, trying to reload it. My own guns were spent and my sword lay where it had fallen on the upper deck; with no alternative, I picked myself up and flung myself towards Lyell. I collided with him and tore the gun from his hand. With an oath he reached his fat hands to my neck, trying to throttle me, and suddenly I was fighting for my life again. I kicked against his shins and pulled on his wrists, but my efforts merely rebounded off his vast bulk. I could feel his thumbs squeezing against my throat, his fingers lifting me by my neck so that my head was crushed against the low ceiling. I could not even draw breath to scream.

But Lyell's time was too short. His shot had echoed along to the surgeon's table, and the men there, perhaps fearing that the enemy had penetrated to their deck, were running forward. Even through my agony I heard their shouts and footsteps, though I barely knew what they signified. Lyell heard it too, and turned to Catherine while never relenting his hold.

'Quick,' he hissed, 'your gun.'

Twisting my eyes around, I saw Catherine's dim outline standing to my left. Without pause, her arm came up and I heard the harsh click of the lock being dragged into place.

'No,' I pleaded, though nothing emerged save a gurgle.

The cramped deck exploded in a cloud of smoke, flame, blood and bone. I fell to the floor.

The sweet smell of brandy opened my eyes. I was lying propped up against the side, with the blood-soaked surgeon kneeling beside me holding a tin cup under my nose. I snatched it from his hand and put it to my lips. I could taste blood in my mouth as well as the spirit, but that did not deter me from draining the cup and looking about for more.

A little to my right, Lyell lay sprawled on the floor in a pool of blood. The puddle was still spreading, draining out of a hole in the back of his skull. One of the loblolly boys was trying to plug it with a rag, though more for the sake of order than healing, I thought. Lyell was dead. On the far side of the deck, I could see Catherine sitting with her head in her hands while one of the *Gloucester*'s officers offered comfort. Her small pistol lay smoking on the deck beside her: I supposed I owed her my life, though I was not inclined to gratitude.

'I thought the brandy would wake you.'

Slowly, so as not to stir the pain in my head, I turned my gaze to my left. Nevell stood at the foot of the ladder, a double-barrelled pistol in one hand and a cutlass in the other. His plum-red coat was torn, his shirt spattered with soot and blood, his face black with powder. Half of his queue had broken free of its binding and flopped down over his cheek. He looked bowed and weary, yet he could not entirely keep the satisfaction from his eyes.

'Am I hurt?' I asked, reaching for the fresh cup which the surgeon, who knew his trade, had fetched.

Nevell shook his head. 'No – or at least, no worse than before.'

'What happened?'

'We defeated the Spaniards.'

'How . . . ?'

'The *Hernando*'s crew were so intent on taking the *Gloucester* that they did not guard their larboard side. Once Mr Strong had put the

342

schooner alongside her we had little difficulty climbing aboard and taking her.' Nevell offered a tired smile. 'My first naval action. I think in future I will leave such affairs to you.'

'Now that I have seen how the Post Office conducts its business, I would rather a sea-battle any day.'

'Be careful what you wish for,' Nevell chided me. 'We still have many miles of hostile ocean to travel before we reach harbour.'

With considerable effort, I raised an eyebrow. 'Harbour?'

'Falmouth.' Nevell crouched beside me and lightly clapped my shoulder. 'We are going home.'

34

I RETURNED TO FALMOUTH UNDER LATE-SPRING SKIES. THE AIR WAS mild, and the quayside seemed more than usually busy. Perhaps it was because of the two carriages which blocked the thoroughfare. One was painted scarlet and black, with bright red wheels and a brass horn to speed it through the turnpike gates. It was the Post Office coach, and if any observers thought it strange that our schooner had brought no portmanteaus of mail, they did not remark on it. The second carriage was a far grander affair, with gold trim around the doors and thick curtains behind the windows. As I looked at it, the postilion leaped down and flung open the door, almost grovelling in obsequy. Miss Lyell, immaculate in her mourning black, climbed past him and arranged herself within. The door slammed shut.

'I suppose she will not be wishing us goodbye,' Nevell said.

'Certainly not *au revoir.*'

Despite our close confines on the voyage home, we had spoken only once. One evening, somewhere past the Bahamas, I had found her on deck staring out over the rail. She had not heard me approach, but at the touch of my hand on her arm she shuddered as if scalded.

'Stay away,' she hissed. 'Have you come to gloat on the ruin of my family?'

'I came to thank you for saving my life.'

I knew it was a delicate thing to say – how, after all, do you thank someone for shooting her own father on your behalf? – and I had prepared myself to expect tears, or fury, or even a faint. Instead, the gaze she turned on me was void of any emotion. The steel moonlight left her face unfathomably cold, her pale hair like a shroud of cobwebs.

'Saving your life?' she echoed. Had it not been such a monstrous notion, I could have sworn I saw a chill smile flicker across her face. 'You know very well I did no such thing, Lieutenant. The pitch of the deck knocked my aim awry. Had my bullet gone true it would be your body now laid in the hold steeping in brandy.'

She said it without malice and I took no offence, though I kept a wary eye on her reticule nonetheless. 'Come, Miss Lyell, you were barely two yards away from me. I have seen your facility with that pistol. I cannot believe you missed accidentally.'

'Do not be so vain,' she snapped. 'Do you think that girlish affection swayed my hand? That some lingering, sapheaded sentiment drove me to spare you?'

'Not at all.' I had come to know enough of Catherine's mettle not to presume anything so foolish.

'What, then?'

Her flashing eyes invited me to go further, challenging me, but I demurred. I had nothing to say that she would hear, and she would never give me the satisfaction of confirming my suspicions. Once, I would have thrilled to spend all night parrying words with her and trying to earn her favour; now, I went to bed.

Just before I ducked my head under the companionway, I looked back. Catherine's black dress melded almost completely with the night so that only her pale face and hands were visible. She had not turned to watch me go, but leaned out over the rail, staring down on the water below. What was she thinking? And what thoughts had crossed her mind in those confused seconds on the *Duke of Gloucester*'s lower deck? Had panic skewed her aim? It seemed unlikely. Or had she seen, in that instant, that her father was undone and his plans laid bare; that shooting me would do nothing but brand her a murderer; that by killing him she could save herself and win her inheritance? Looking at the dark, grim figure behind me, I could not tell.

'Though I do not see how she will profit from it,' I had mused to Nevell the following day. 'Surely a hanging awaits her when we return home, or at least transportation. She and her father were each as deep in this scheme as the other.'

Nevell had laughed. 'I'll wager you a guinea to a farthing she never sets foot in a courtroom, much less a gaol.'

'But—'

'Who do you think would bring a prosecution against one of the most beautiful and eligible young orphans in England? Any man who took the stand against her would be branded a knave and a brute. The Post Office will watch her, and those with whom she associates, but we cannot touch her. Before she reaches London she will have had three proposals of marriage; within two days of her return, every bachelor in London will be calling at her door.'

'Not every bachelor,' I corrected him. 'I will be quite content never to see anything of her again.'

'Then there will be two of us immune to her charms.'

I hoped so. I could not be sure that some corner of Nevell's devious heart might not find something to admire in Miss Lyell's ruthlessness.

'But whatever we think, others will not be so sensible of her faults, or will overlook them in consideration of her wealth. Society will wrap its mantle around her, and powerful guardians will see that no injury befalls her.'

'I doubt she will need them. I never met a woman with such a talent for self-preservation.' I had encountered more than my share of murderous lunatics on my voyage – Burr, Lyell, Wilkinson and Vidal not least – but put me on a dawn field with a gun in my hand and I'd choose to face any of them over Miss Lyell.

*

346

We arrived in London in the middle of May. Each day of our journey, from the wilds of Cornwall and Devon, through the placid farmland of Dorset and Hampshire and into the closely built towns and villages around the metropolis, I had seen the sun slowly prising the clouds apart and dispelling them as summer flexed its hold. It did little to affect my humour; indeed, my spirits took the opposite course. Before we left Falmouth, I had found a letter awaiting me at the inn.

Jerrold—
Call on me at the Admiralty the instant you return to England.

There was no signature. It did not need one.

With a familiar quake of fear, I wondered what it portended. Of course I had no cause for concern – my uncle's secret letter was still safe inside my coat, and no quantity of his threats could blunt its damning contents – but it worried me nonetheless. My ill temper must have shown, for several times in the coach I saw Nevell fixing me with keen, probing glances, but he did not press me on it.

A little after four o'clock on the fifth day, we drew up outside the Admiralty. It was a perquisite of travelling with Nevell that we were not bound by the usual stages but could travel where we pleased. As I alighted from the coach, Nevell peered down after me.

'Come and find me at the Secret Office in a few days' time, when you are feeling more yourself,' he said.

'As long as you have no more letters for me to deliver to distant parts.'

Nevell pulled the door closed and I waved him goodbye, then walked under the shadow of the Admiralty's arch. I was evidently expected, for no sooner had I given my name to the porter than I was led upstairs, along a broad corridor and into a familiar anteroom. The budding summer had not yet penetrated here: a small fire still burned in the grate, and the clerk at the desk kept his woollen coat buttoned tight.

'Lieutenant Jerrold,' murmured the porter, disappearing as quickly as he dared.

The clerk put down his quill and scowled at me, then resumed his writing. Only when he had reached the end of the document, folded it, dribbled wax over it and stamped it with the Admiralty seal did he rise and knock on the inner door. A gruff voice called him in. When he returned, after some moments, he shut the door carefully, returned to his chair, and only then looked up to announce: 'He will receive you.'

I stepped into my uncle's office. I had not seen it often, but it seemed unchanged from my last visit. His broad desk still commanded the room and was still littered with books, ledgers and papers. A map of the Mediterranean covered one wall; opposite hung a painting of the *Minotaur* in action at the Nile, and a portrait of an officer who might, with some charity on the part of the viewer, have resembled a younger and more dashing incarnation of the man behind the desk.

He did not rise, but waved me to sit before him.

A strange and unwonted calm descended on me as my uncle shuffled through some papers, then lifted his gaze and bored it into me. For perhaps the first time in my life, I held it unwavering.

'I understand you have been in America,' he said at last.

I murmured that I had.

'A damnable country. Nothing but rogues, traitors, lunatics and republicans. I am surprised they have not yet all murdered one another. Did you enjoy yourself?'

'Not particularly.'

'Hah.' My uncle leaned forward across his desk. 'It might have suited you better to have stayed there. Your meddlesome villainy has caused a great deal of inconvenience which neither I nor my associates are persuaded to forgive.'

Once, the mere tone of his voice might have reduced me to tears; now I enjoyed a position of strength. Shooting him a cool stare, I reached into my coat and pulled out my two copies – the autograph and the decipherment – of his letter.

'I received Colonel Burr's most recent communication on the eighteenth inst.,' I read. 'Having satisfied myself of his true intentions and good faith, and the high chance of a profitable conclusion to his venture, I have this day despatched two frigates—'

With a howl of rage my uncle lunged across his desk and snatched at the paper. I jerked it away, and held it just out of his reach.

'Where did you get that?' he hissed, his face scarlet.

'In America. You will observe I have the autograph copy here as well.'

My uncle's eyes bulged, then narrowed; he tilted his head and watched me carefully.

'Very well, you have my letter. What of it?'

'It implicates you in a treasonous conspiracy.' The soaring joy of besting my uncle left me giddy, but I tried to maintain a measured tone.

My uncle huffed through his nose. 'Nonsense. It implicates me, if at all, in a patriotic attempt by true Englishmen to make war on our enemies. A war, I may say, that our superiors at the time were criminally negligent in prosecuting.'

'That may be, but your duty was to obey their orders.' I could hardly believe that I was sitting there in my uncle's office lecturing him on duty. 'Your well-intentioned recklessness came within a hair of turning the Americans against us, adding another ally to Buonaparte's coalition and cutting off the Atlantic trade. Britain would have been in worse straits than when you began. Indeed, she might have been bankrupt inside three months now that the continent is closed to us.'

My uncle did not dispute the charge. He leaned back, and offered me an appraising stare.

'By the fact that you have come to confront me with this here, rather than approaching my political masters, I take it you do not wish to ruin me publicly.'

'It would be a cruel blow to my mother if I shamed her brother.'

'Hah. And what price do you want for it?'

I had expected my uncle would be forthright in his negotiations, and I was suitably prepared. 'Promotion to post captain. A sinecure ashore, perhaps at the Navy Board. And the promise that I need not fear retribution from your disappointed conspirators.' Lyell might be dead, but I guessed there would be others in London who still harboured thoughts of vengeance towards me.

'Is that all?' My uncle gave a short, snorting laugh. 'A gold-plated carriage and four, perhaps? An apartment at St James's Palace and a royal princess in marriage as well?' He sniffed. 'And otherwise? What if I do not yield to your extortion?'

'Then, with the utmost regret, I will lay your letters before the First Lord and tell him all I know.'

My uncle tipped back his head and stared at the plaster mouldings on the ceiling. The starred epaulettes on his shoulders rose and fell with his laboured breathing. At length, he levelled his gaze and reached for the slim cord which hung by his side. A bell chimed in the anteroom behind me, and the clerk appeared at the door.

'Offer Lord Mulgrave my apologies for the disturbance, but inform him that I would value a brief word in my office at his soonest convenience.'

The clerk vanished, and for some minutes we sat in an uncomfortable silence. I drummed my fingers on the arm of the chair and gazed at the map on the wall; my uncle affected to read through the papers on his desk.

'Are you recently returned?' he asked suddenly.

'I arrived in London this afternoon. The Falmouth coach brought me directly to your gate.'

'What exemplary despatch.'

The rage was gone from my uncle's face, and in its place a wintry smirk had appeared. It disconcerted me, but before I could question it I heard footsteps in the anteroom and an obsequious voice saying, 'In here, my lord.'

My uncle shot me an ominous look. 'Say nothing.'

We both stood as the door opened. The man who entered did not wear a uniform, but by my uncle's deferential bow I gathered that he must be of some significance. He was a portly man, a little past fifty, whose grey hair grew in thin curls close to his scalp. He had a genial face, and his large eyes and furrowed brow gave him an air of perpetual, well-intentioned puzzlement.

'Lord Mulgrave,' said my uncle warmly. 'I must apologize again for calling you here.'

The visitor gave an affable wave of his hand. 'It is no trouble, Admiral – I was not busy this afternoon.'

'May I humbly introduce my nephew, Lieutenant Jerrold. He has called on me and was naturally anxious for the honour of your lordship's acquaintance.'

Lord Mulgrave nodded to me.

'Lieutenant Jerrold distinguished himself in Dover last year, and has just returned from a delicate embassy to America.'

'Has he?' Lord Mulgrave peered at me with new, discomfiting interest. 'I was not aware of it. How did he fare?'

'We have not yet had opportunity to talk of it,' said my uncle.

Mulgrave smiled happily. 'Then I shall leave you to your discussions.' He turned to me. 'Your uncle follows your exploits with great avuncular affection, it seems. I trust you repay his concern.'

'I endeavour to, sir.'

'I am glad to hear it. We need sound, enterprising officers. I hope I will hear more of your career in future.'

'I hope so, sir.'

Mulgrave ambled out of the room and the servant shut the door behind him. I sank back into my chair.

'That was Lord Mulgrave,' said my uncle, carelessly examining a paper.

I felt as though my belt had tightened a notch. 'And who is Lord Mulgrave?'

'Lord Mulgrave? Why, he is my superior – and yours too. He is now First Lord of the Admiralty.'

'But I thought Mr Grey—'

'Tut, Martin. You have been away too long. Mr Grey is now an earl, but he no longer holds any office of state. There has been a change of ministry. The Pittites are in power and the talented Foxites are where they belong – in opposition.'

'How . . . ?'

My uncle gave a wicked smile. 'Their ambition over-reached itself. First they abolished the slave trade, which was just about tolerable; then they tried to emancipate the Catholics. Well, a blackie may be one thing but an Irishman is quite another. They lost the King's confidence and he dismissed them.'

It was clear from my uncle's gloating face that the natural order of things, in his estimation, had been restored.

'Lord Mulgrave is a particular friend of mine.'

'He knew of your scheme to conquer Mexico,' I muttered.

'Of course. He supported it absolutely. As did many in the new ministry.' My uncle stood and stretched out his hand. 'Which is why, Jerrold, you will now do me the kindness of returning my correspondence.'

I was defeated. Yet I had carried those papers for thousands of miles, risked countless agonies and humiliations for them. Even had I willed it I could not simply have surrendered them.

Mistaking my hesitation for defiance, my uncle clicked his tongue. Yet he did not abuse me; instead, checking his irritation, he actually said, more moderately, 'Both our interests are served this way, Martin. You cannot bring about my ruin, but you could certainly embarrass me. I, on the other hand, could turn a great number of influential men against you. But why should I? It was Burr's doing, not yours, that the expedition failed; he is the villain of the piece. We were fools ever to trust him. And though you did not aid the scheme, you prevented a great deal more mischief by escaping undetected. We owe you gratitude for that, if nothing else.'

Still I resisted him. Either my uncle was overly sanguine, or he was bluffing me. Even under the new ministry, surely the papers would do more than embarrass him if I made them public. But would I survive the ensuing storm any better than he?

His face clouded with impatience. 'This is a fair bargain, Jerrold. Give me those papers and I will see that no blame attaches itself to you, either publicly or among my associates. They are men you cannot afford to displease. If you keep silent, I may even find you a commission. It will not be the indolent sinecure you craved, but it will not be disagreeable.'

I stared at the floor, then thrust the papers into my uncle's hand. He did not look at them, but pulled the bell-cord immediately. The clerk entered.

'Can it be May?' my uncle asked, passing the papers to the clerk. 'It feels as chill as January. Can you rouse that fire?'

The clerk nodded and retired. Through the open door, I saw him fold the papers carefully and then drop them onto the coals, pressing them down with the poker until every last morsel had turned to ash.

My uncle sighed. 'I suppose we will have to forgive each other eventually,' he said, with rare insight. 'Neither of us has acted entirely with distinction, but nor with malice either. The mistakes we have made were, at the least, honest mistakes.'

Perhaps they were, though as I walked out of the Admiralty and towards Charing Cross I doubted whether the same could be said of the financiers and bankers he had conspired with. Certainly there had been nothing honest about Lyell's actions. His animation had been greed – hunger for the riches to be had by opening America to our trade. Yet it was trade, ultimately, that I had fought to protect: the vital trade with the United States which brought gold to the Treasury and allowed us to fill the seas with ships and our guns with powder.

I looked about me. The vast edifices of Whitehall loomed behind me like giant mausolea, while ahead of me the crowds thronged thick as ever among the coffee houses, taverns, shops and merchants on the Strand. Who could tell what commerce was transacted there – and in every drawing room, counting-house and bedroom in the city? Doubtless there were new Lyells plotting the increase of their wealth, and future Burrs dreaming fantastic schemes of conquest. None of them would think his business unjust, and each would believe his mistakes – if he admitted them – to be honest mistakes.

353

What did I care? I was home and alive; and if I was little better off than when I had departed, I was at least no worse. To the Lyells and Burrs of the world that would seem a poor return on the adventure, but to me it seemed cause for celebration.

I went into a tavern and ordered myself a drink.

Historical Note

ONLY THE MOST UNLIKELY PARTS OF THIS STORY ARE TRUE. IN THE presidential election of 1800 Aaron Burr tied Thomas Jefferson in the electoral college, and on thirty-six tie-breaking votes in the House of Representatives. When Jefferson eventually won, by a single vote, runner-up Burr (in a quickly abandoned procedure) became Vice-President. Four years later, Burr shot former Treasury Secretary Alexander Hamilton dead in a duel, and was subsequently dropped from Jefferson's re-election ticket. By 1805 his political career was over.

A man of enormous energy and charisma, Burr responded to this reverse by deciding that if his country would not have him, he would have another country – specifically, the Spanish colony of Mexico, which at the time covered much of Central and North America. Seeking backers for his scheme among all the great powers of the day, he found a sympathetic reception with the British ambassador in Washington, Anthony Merry. Merry passed the suggestion on to his government but there is no record of any official reply; that did not stop Burr writing, in August 1806, that 'naval protection of England is secured' and that one of his associates 'is going to Jamaica to arrange with the [British] admiral there and will meet us at the Mississippi'. Historians have tended to dismiss these claims as empty bravado.

Nonetheless, there is no doubt that at this time British naval personnel were engaged in a great deal of dubious activity around Spanish possessions in the Americas. In April 1806, Commodore Sir Home Popham and General William Beresford took ships and troops from the Cape of Good Hope (which they were supposed to be defending) and launched a unilateral invasion of South America, hoping to open it to British trade. They quickly took Buenos Aires but failed to make further progress, and were eventually driven out by the Spanish with heavy losses. Neither Beresford nor Popham received more than a reprimand. Meanwhile, General Beresford's brother John, a navy captain, had been supporting the liberationist General Miranda in a Bay-of-Pigs-style attempt to spark a rebellion in Venezuela. Again, early successes quickly came to nothing. A British-backed attack in the north would have fitted with these other expeditions as the northern element of a concerted, three-pronged attack on Spanish America.

The execution of Burr's plan unfolded much as it does in this novel, and was at least as hapless as I have portrayed it. Entrusting a key part of the conspiracy to a Spanish double agent was unfortunate, but even without that disadvantage he was never in much danger of success. The army of thousands he had expected (and catered for) never materialized, but Burr pressed on with astounding tenacity. Meanwhile, his misplaced optimism, combined with reckless indiscretion, convinced the nation that he threatened the very foundations of the Republic, and the full weight of the government was mobilized against him. Being personally loathed by the President was the final nail in his coffin.

Or not. From Natchez, Burr was taken to Virginia and tried for treason, where the very ineffectuality of his conspiracy proved to be his salvation. The framers of the constitution (who had, after all, begun their careers as traitors against their sovereign government) had defined treason solely as levying war against the United States. Given Burr's total failure to levy war, whatever his intentions, and his lawyerly instinct for staying on the right side of the law, he was acquitted, much to Jefferson's fury. He went into exile in England, returning to America in 1812.

Harman Blennerhassett was taken for trial with Burr but was released after Burr's acquittal. Broken by the experience, his life afterwards was a woeful tale of ever-worse tragedy and penury, involving dissipated fortunes, crop failures, ill-timed commercial speculations, apoplexy and a rabid fox. His story has since become a popular subject for romantic novelists. His extraordinary mansion on Blennerhassett Island was first looted by militia, then burned to the ground in 1811. It remained in that condition until 1984, when the enlightened attentions of the West Virginia state government rebuilt it as a museum. It is well worth a visit.

The United States did not complete the conquest of Spain's North American territories until 1848. Then, almost as if working from Burr's blueprint, they provoked an unnecessary war with Mexico, invaded, and seized what is now California, New Mexico, Nevada, Utah, Arizona and half of Texas. Had Burr lived to see it he might well have applauded the audacity, while remembering Talleyrand's cynical formulation that treason is only a question of timing.

Acknowledgements

Martin Jerrold was not the only Englishman travelling down the Ohio and Mississippi rivers in this period. I owe a particular debt to two of his compatriots, Fortescue Cuming and Thomas Ashe, whose published descriptions of their own journeys provided me with a wealth of information and inspiration, as well as to all the other travellers and settlers whose accounts I read. Many are preserved in the Library of Congress's exemplary online American Memory archive, particularly the Early Western Travels and the First American West collections. Also online, the David Rumsey Historical Map Collection (www.davidrumsey.com) was an invaluable resource for establishing the geography of America in the early 1800s.

I am grateful, as ever, to the British Library, and to Laura MacPherson and the staff of the National Library of Scotland. At various points further west I profited from visits to the National Maritime Museum Cornwall in Falmouth, to the several sites run by the Friends of the Cabildo in New Orleans, the Mississippi River Museum in Memphis, the Ohio River Museum in Marietta, Ohio, the Senator John Heinz History Center in Pittsburgh, and especially the Blennerhassett Island Historical State Park in Parkersburg, West Virginia.

Other debts: to Emily Cullum for answering my questions about horses; to Natalia Nowak-Kerigan and Caroline Dodds for rummaging through old newspapers; to Andrew and Melanie Lerchen who gave me the chance to research sailing conditions on the Gulf of Mexico firsthand; to all the Americans whose hospitality made my research trips so much easier; to Werner and Nina Lutgering who provided much help in a lost cause; and to my wife Emma who stoically accompanied me on my adventure along the Mississippi and didn't try to shoot me at the end of it. At Transworld, Simon Thorogood and Selina Walker were generous in accommodating my delays, and as incisive as ever in straightening the flow of the text whenever it meandered too far. My agent Jane Conway-Gordon watched from her eyrie and missed nothing.

Finally, in deference to the good residents of the Buckeye State, I should clarify a deliberate inaccuracy in Chapter 12. Ohio does not mean 'bloody', though this was a common misconception at the time; it in fact means 'beautiful'.